PAUL GITSHAM started his career as a biologist, working as such exotic locales as Manchester and Toronto. After stints as the world's most over-qualified receptionist and a spell making sure that international terrorists and other ne'er do wells hadn't opened a Junior Savings Account at a major UK bank (a job even less exciting than being a receptionist) he retrained as a Science teacher. He now spends his time passing on his bad habits and sloppy lab-skills to the next generation of enquiring minds.

Paul has always wanted to be a writer and his final report on leaving primary school predicted he'd be the next Roald Dahl! For the sake of balance it should be pointed out that it also said 'he'll never get anywhere in life if his handwriting doesn't improve'. Over twenty-five years later and his handwriting is worse than ever but millions of children around the world love him.*

You can learn more about Paul's writing at www.paulgitsham. com or www.facebook.com/dcijones

*This is a lie, just ask any of the pupils he has taught.

Also by Paul Gitsham, featuring DCI Warren Jones:

Forgive Me Father

PAUL GITSHAM

ONE PLACE. MANY STORIES

HQ
An imprint of HarperCollins*Publishers* Ltd
1 London Bridge Street
London SE1 9GF

This paperback edition 2019

First published in Great Britain by
HQ, an imprint of HarperCollins*Publishers* Ltd 2019

ISBN: 9780008330934

MIX
Paper from
responsible sources
FSC™ C007454

This book is produced from independently certified FSC™ paper
to ensure responsible forest management.

For more information visit: www.harpercollins.co.uk/green

Printed and bound in Great Britain by
CPI Group (UK) Ltd, Croydon CR0 4YY

For those who weren't believed.

Prologue

Scaling the ancient stone wall wasn't difficult. The metal spikes that lined the crumbling edifice were over three hundred years old and those that hadn't been lost were rusting to nothingness. The whole wall needed major repair work, but the cost of restoring the medieval brickwork to its former glory would run into hundreds of thousands and the fundraising had barely started. Besides, who would want to break into the ruins of a deserted abbey?

Nathan Adams gallantly laid his coat over the top of the wall in the gap created by two missing spikes, then cupped his hands. The wall was about five feet tall and his companion, Rebecca Hill, easily pushed herself up. Nathan enjoyed the view as her short black skirt briefly rode up, exposing more of the snow-white flesh already tantalisingly revealed by the strategically placed rips in her black tights.

Nathan passed up the plastic carrier bag of cheap cider, before attempting to pull himself over as well. It was harder than it looked, and he wondered if he was going to have to drop back down and take a run-up, when his scrabbling feet found purchase. Rebecca grabbed the handle on the top of his backpack and with her help he finally flopped onto the wall, the rough stone scraping his stomach where his jacket had opened. The drop to the grass on the other side was slightly less, and he rolled clumsily over the wall, landing in an untidy heap.

'Are you OK?' hissed Rebecca.

'Fine.' he said, ignoring the pain in his shoulder. The weed in his pocket and the booze would take the edge off it, and if all went to plan, he might even get a shoulder rub later. He put that thought quickly to one side, lest he embarrass himself.

Raising his arms and suppressing a wince, he helped her down to the ground – for a brief instant, their faces were bare millimetres apart. He froze. Should he kiss her or should he wait until they were a bit more mellow? His indecision lasted just seconds and then the moment was gone. Was that a flash of disappointment in her eyes?

Rebecca had been here before and she took charge, taking his hand and leading him further into the abbey grounds.

An evening in the graveyard of a ruined abbey, in winter, wouldn't be Nathan's first choice for a romantic date, but he was happy to let Rebecca call the shots; he'd spent most of the previous week persuading her to give him a chance tonight and he wasn't going to ruin it with a bit of squeamishness. An afternoon spent trawling through her Facebook and Instagram posts had revealed her favourite music – death metal bands, all of which sounded the same to him when he'd streamed their albums on Spotify. The T-shirt he'd ordered online had arrived that morning – all shiny and smelling of plastic packaging. He hoped it wasn't obvious that a week ago he'd never even heard of Flesh Kitchen.

The graveyard was in the centre of the abbey's grounds. Nathan dimly remembered the layout from school visits, but it looked different in the dark with only a sliver of moon to light their way. The glow of Middlesbury town centre behind them did little to pierce the gloom. He stumbled along behind Rebecca, hoping it wasn't much further. The weather had been dry and the skies clear, but February was February and the cold was beginning to bite. Rebecca had promised that she knew a cosy spot inside one of the crypts, and that they could light a fire with no one noticing.

2

His mates were right. She was definitely weird.

But she was also cute and interested in him, and right now, that was all that mattered.

Finally, the low wall that surrounded the graveyard started to emerge out of the gloom. A few more paces and the ghost-like statues adorning the tombs of Middlesbury's most prominent citizens from centuries past also appeared. Nathan repressed a shudder. Rebecca was marching confidently onwards and he wasn't going to show any sign of weakness.

To the left, a squat building was black against the night sky. Suddenly, Rebecca stopped dead and Nathan barely avoided knocking her over.

'Can you smell that?'

He sniffed the air.

'Smoke.'

He groaned internally. Somebody else had clearly had the same idea as them. He doubted Rebecca would want to get too... cosy... if there were other people about. He started frantically thinking of a plan B, somewhere else they could go. His mum and dad were both in, vegetating in front of the TV, and her place was out of the question – she'd said her parents were really strict.

'I think the fire is in that building.'

She was right. A faint orange glow was visible through ground-level windows.

'We should go, before somebody calls the fire brigade.'

If somebody had set the building on fire, it wouldn't look good for them if they were found trespassing with a bag full of fire-making equipment. Not to mention the weed in his back pocket.

Rebecca ignored him, taking a few more paces towards the building, as if drawn to the light and warmth.

'I think that's the old chapel. There's an undercroft, that's where the glow is coming from.'

The crackling of the flames was now clearly audible, the glow becoming brighter.

'We need to go,' repeated Nathan.

The evening was ruined already. It was too cold to go and sit on the common and the youth club would be packed full of losers this time on a Friday night. Besides, they wouldn't get in if they were drunk or stoned. The best he could hope for was a slow walk home and a goodnight kiss. The last thing Nathan wanted was for the evening to end in a police cell.

'Becky?'

She let out a sigh. At least she sounded as disappointed as he did.

They turned to leave the way they had come, before she stopped again.

'Did you hear that?'

Nathan heard nothing; he shook his head.

'There it is again.'

He strained his ears.

Still nothing.

No, wait.

They both heard it now.

Louder.

Clearer.

'Oh my, God, Nathan. There's somebody in there!'

Chapter 1

The light drizzle had started within minutes of DCI Warren Jones' arrival at the scene of the fire. He'd almost welcomed the phone call at first, an hour and a half after the alarm had been raised at twenty past nine that night; he was well on his way to yet another comprehensive Scrabble defeat by his wife Susan. Now, even though the precipitation slid off his plastic-coated paper suit, he'd changed his mind.

'You're clear to enter the scene, sir.' The familiar, portly figure of Crime Scene Manager Andy Harrison was easily identifiable, even with his facemask on. 'Professor Jordan has done his preliminary examination of the body, and it's ready to be transported.'

'Tony, do you and Moray want to join us?'

DI Tony Sutton was standing a little way off, also dressed in a paper scene suit. Beside him stood DC Moray Ruskin – whose huge bulk meant he had to bring his own suits to crime scenes in case the CSIs didn't have his size in the back of their van.

The path between the outer cordon and the doors to the old chapel was shielded from the rain by a hastily erected tent, and the proscribed route to the front entrance was covered by raised plastic boarding to protect any undiscovered shoe prints or other trace evidence.

'What did the kids who phoned it in have to say for themselves?' asked Warren as the three police officers carefully picked their way along the walkway. A slip now would not only be undignified, it might also destroy evidence.

'Not much.' Ruskin had replaced his facemask. This combined with his thick beard and broad Scottish accent, meant Warren had to listen carefully to the man's report.

'They were a bit cagey about why they were here; they've admitted that the carrier bag of nasty-looking cider is theirs. They also had some matches and fire-lighters, both still sealed in their original packaging and unused. They're only fifteen and wearing death metal T-shirts, so I'm guessing tonight's plan was a bit of drinking in the local graveyard, perhaps a bonfire to keep warm, and if all went well, a bit of hanky panky.'

'Hanky panky? I'm pretty sure the last time anyone used that phrase was before you were born,' scoffed Sutton.

'I was trying to use language that you old folks would understand.'

'Cheeky sod.'

'What did they see?'

'Very little. It was dark and they were trying not to trip over, so they weren't really paying attention. Neither of them saw anyone or heard anything. The first they knew of the fire was the smell of smoke, then they spotted a glow from the undercroft windows. It wasn't until they heard the screams from the victim that they realised it was serious. They claim to have phoned the fire brigade immediately.'

The three men were now at the entrance to the chapel. The heavy, wooden door was wide open. More plastic boarding covered the ancient stone floor.

To the left of the doorway was the entrance to chapel proper; to the right, a low archway led to a flight of steep, stone steps that descended into the original, medieval undercroft. Portable lights running off a generator chased away the shadows. Nevertheless,

6

the shiver that ran through Warren wasn't only due to the late-night chill.

'Did the witnesses step into the chapel or disturb the scene?'

'The young man tried to open the chapel door, but it was locked,' said Ruskin. 'He walked around trying to find another entrance. His companion stayed back by the tree-line and called 999.'

'We'll need their fingerprints and shoeprints to exclude them,' said Warren. He looked at his watch. 'It's getting pretty late. Where are they now? Have their parents been informed?'

'They're in the back of a car. I believe there is some debate over whether we should phone their parents or just drop them off outside their homes.'

'I'll bet,' said Sutton.

'It's not a pretty sight, officers,' said the CSI that greeted them at the entrance. 'The stairs are only wide enough for one person at a time; make sure you don't trip over the hoses or the power cables. Try not to brush against the walls, or the door, in case there are any loose fibres we haven't collected yet and mind your head, the folks that built this place were tiny by modern standards.'

The instructions were easier said than followed, especially for Ruskin, who eyed the narrow stairwell dubiously.

Taking the lead, Warren stepped carefully into the space. Despite his facemask, the lingering smoke was starting to make his eyes sting. As he descended, a familiar smell joined the odour of singed wood. Petrol? A few more steps and another aroma entered the mix. The smell of burnt meat. Behind him, he heard Tony Sutton breathing through his face mask.

'I hate bloody fires,' he grumbled.

The undercroft was huge, its farthest reaches fading to invisibility beyond the few square metres illuminated by the CSIs working the area closest to the stairwell.

'Stay inside the marked area, we're going to need to do a

fingertip search of the rest of the room once we've removed the body,' instructed CSM Harrison, who'd joined them.

The figure curled in the foetal position next to the toppled chair was dead. Of that there could be no doubt. Most of the corpse's clothes had been burnt away, along with much of the skin on the torso and the legs; that which remained was charred and split. The hair on the victim's head was all but gone.

The sight of the burnt flesh seemed unreal underneath the powerful lamps, yet it wasn't that sight which Warren knew would dominate his dreams. Warren knew that fire caused the tendons and connective tissue in a body to shrink, but that knowledge failed to make the corpse's rictus grin and protruding tongue any less haunting.

'The flames were pretty much out by the time the firefighters broke in. A paramedic first responder confirmed the victim was deceased.' Warren recognised the American accent of Professor Ryan Jordan, one of Hertfordshire's registered Home Office pathologists.

'What else can you tell us, Prof?' asked Sutton, as he circled the body.

'Not much until we get him back to the morgue and I do the post-mortem. I can't tell if he died of burns, smoke inhalation or something else, although I'm told the kids that discovered the body heard screaming, so I suspect he was conscious at some point. Like I said, I'll know more later.'

'"He?" Definitely male then?' asked Ruskin.

'Almost certainly, although again I'll be more confident after the PM. The muscles have contracted, which makes it difficult to estimate build; I'd be prepared to go out on a limb and say he's not a child, but anything more will have to wait.'

Warren looked at the chair lying next to the man; a sturdy affair, the wood looked scorched but not burnt.

'One of the seats from the chapel, you can see the kneeler fixed to the back,' offered Harrison.

'Why didn't it catch fire?' asked Ruskin.

'The fire investigators will tell us for sure, but my nose suggests that the body was doused in petrol before being set alight. You can see that his clothes clearly caught, and then his skin, but the petrol probably vaporised and didn't soak into the wood sufficiently for it to catch.'

Ruskin's voice was thick when he spoke.

'Who would do such a thing?'

Before Warren could answer the young officer's rhetorical question, Harrison spoke up.

'Don't jump to conclusions, son.'

'What do you mean?' asked Sutton.

'We found a petrol canister and matches next to the body, alongside some whiskey and a pill container. The container was melted from the heat and only part of the label is visible. I reckon you'll get the prescription details but not the patient's name. They've been sent off for analysis. And I've not seen any sign that the deceased was restrained.'

'What are you suggesting?' asked Warren.

'Well, the door from the chapel to the undercroft was locked; I'm no locksmith, but the large metal key we found next to the chair looks like it matches the only entrance to this place.'

It took a few moments for the importance of the discovery to sink in.

When Ruskin finally spoke, his voice was filled with horror.

'You mean the victim did this to himself?'

Saturday 21st February

Chapter 2

Warren stifled a yawn. He'd arrived home very late the night before, the adrenaline of the night's activities soon giving way to a bone-weary exhaustion. He could have handed over the 8 a.m. briefing to DI Sutton, but his second-in-command had been up just as late as his DCI. And what would be the point? Despite his tiredness, sleep had proven elusive. The nightmares that had plagued him since the events of the summer had returned, and he'd eventually given up and driven into work, trying his best not to disturb Susan.

At the back of the room, he spied Moray Ruskin busy regaling another detective constable with a no-holds-barred description of the body from the previous night. He at least looked refreshed – a fact that had more to do with him going straight home than the resilience of youth, Warren told himself.

'Dunno where the kid gets his energy,' muttered Sutton. 'He's already been for a run and a session in the gym this morning. He's helping train Mags Richardson for her first half-marathon.'

'It's just because he had a good night's sleep.'

'Keep telling yourself that, sir.'

Warren chose not to respond, instead bringing the room to order. After briefly summarising the events of the previous night,

11

he projected a photograph of the body onto the briefing room screen.

'We have yet to identify the victim, however preliminary indications are that the fire was self-inflicted. But until that is confirmed we'll be treating the death as unexplained.'

Detective Sergeant Mags Richardson beat DS David Hutchinson to the first question.

'Have we eliminated the kids who called it in? Some folks get a kick out of these things.'

'That's underway. Forensics are analysing their clothing and belongings for traces of accelerant and have finger-printed them and taken impressions of their shoes. The locked door is supposedly the only entrance into the undercroft large enough for a person to fit through, although we will be checking the state of the bars on the windows.' Warren smiled. 'Moray, they might respond better to someone closer to their own age. Can you do a follow-up interview with them later today?'

Ruskin acknowledged the thinly veiled reference to his own cheeky comments the night before with a grin.

'Have English Heritage been contacted?' asked Hutchinson.

'We managed to get hold of them late last night, Hutch, and they referred us to St Cecil's Home for Retired Clergy, who are actually responsible for the maintenance and upkeep of the abbey,' said Sutton, referring to his notebook. 'The retirement home is actually situated within the abbey grounds, but at the far end from the chapel, and shielded by trees, so none of the residents were aware of what was happening until the fire engine turned up. A Deacon Gabriel Baines is in charge of the whole site, and he called the groundsman. The property was secured and I've arranged for a meeting with him first thing.'

'I'll take that,' said Warren. 'I want to get out there again.'

'Any indications who the victim might be?' asked DS Rachel Pymm.

'All we have so far is that it's an adult male,' said Warren. 'When

12

we have a better description, we'll contact missing persons and homeless shelters. I'm going to visit the abbey immediately after this briefing, and see if they can help. Any further questions?'

When none were forthcoming, Warren started assigning roles to the team.

'Mags take charge of collecting CCTV; I'm sure they have cameras inside the grounds for security; our victim may have driven or walked, see what's available from the surrounding area. Hutch, scope out any residential properties nearby and see if there are any witnesses. I'd also like you to arrange a team to interview any of the residents that live on site after I've visited.

'Moray, bring the kids that called it in down to the station and sweat them a bit. At the moment it's looking like a suicide, but I want us to keep an open mind. Rachel, I'd like you to set up an incident desk and get information inputted into HOLMES; if this does turn out to be something more sinister, I want us ready to react quickly.' Warren suppressed a grimace as he remembered his early morning meeting with his superior, Detective Superintendent John Grayson. 'Somebody burning to death in the crypt of Middlesbury's number one tourist attraction is likely to generate headlines for all the wrong reasons. The sooner we deal with this the better.'

Chapter 3

Deacon Gabriel Baines was a sparsely built man with a full shock of white hair and a ruddy complexion. He'd greeted Warren at the main entrance to the abbey grounds, unlocking the trades' entrance next to the imposing double doors that served the public. A printed sheet pinned to the door apologised for the abbey's unexpected closure.

'These doors date back to the eighteenth century and are pretty much impregnable – it's just a shame the same can't be said about the rest of the perimeter walls.'

'I saw that there have been a number of complaints of trespassing and criminal damage going back several years,' said Warren.

'We've given up reporting all but the most serious cases. Our groundsman chases people out of here at least once a month; mostly kids like those two last night, but occasionally we find drug paraphernalia in some of the open tombs. Every once in a while, somebody sprays graffiti or damages some of the gravestones.

'It's upsetting, but what can we do? We're raising money to repair the walls, in part to stop this sort of thing, but at the rate we're going it'll be another thirty years before we can even make a start.'

'I thought English Heritage were responsible for the abbey's upkeep?' said Warren.

'Unfortunately, we aren't, strictly speaking, owned by English Heritage. I'm assuming from your accent that you never had the obligatory primary school visit to the ruins?'

Warren admitted his ignorance; he'd been brought up in Coventry which had too much local history to justify a trip all the way to Middlesbury to see an old church. And somehow, he'd never found time in the three-and-a-half years since he'd moved to Middlesbury to take a tour.

'Then let me give you a quick tour,' suggested Baines as they walked into the grounds. 'The area inside the walls was the original site of the thirteenth-century Middlesbury Abbey. It was founded in 1220, by a group of Andalusian monks from what is now Granada in modern Spain and for three hundred odd years, it served Middlesbury and the surrounding villages. When the plague came to town in the mid-fourteenth century, the brothers expanded their priory to become an infirmary and built a new gatehouse so that sick people could receive medical care without infecting the rest of the abbey and complex – remarkably prescient given that they didn't have any understanding of germ theory at the time.' Baines paused and directed Warren to a gap in the tree line.

'You can see the new gatehouse there.' He pointed to an imposing set of double wooden gates in the far perimeter wall. 'It's on the opposite side of the grounds to the visitors' entrance we've just come from, and is still used by staff and residents. Unfortunately, the old infirmary building was knocked down and built over a couple of hundred years ago.'

Baines continued to lead the two men up a roughly tarmacked path, just wide enough for a single vehicle to drive down without brushing the trees and shrubs either side. A signpost directed visitors to turn right along a narrow pathway for the chapel or left for the education centre. The road continued straight on, but another signpost marked it as 'Private. Staff only beyond this point.' Baines continued walking straight ahead.

'Of course, daily life came to a halt in 1539 during the dissolution of the monasteries by Henry VIII. The monks abandoned the abbey and returned, we presume, to Andalusia. The abbey fell into disrepair and was basically the ruins that you see today until 1700 when Sir Howard Langton bought the grounds. He was ostensibly a respectable Anglican landowner and businessman, making his fortune from sourcing locally produced textiles to sell at the market, but we know now that he was really a Roman Catholic. At that time, Catholicism was still a crime, punishable by death, but he was careful to make donations to the right people and didn't proselytize, so if anyone suspected his true faith, they said nothing.'

Baines pointed towards the chapel where the fire had taken place the previous night. Partially visible through the trees and the lingering mid-morning mist, the building took on a moody, almost sinister appearance. Even during daylight hours, Warren could see the fascination it would hold for some; he suspected that without a major upgrade to the site's perimeter walls, they were fighting a losing battle against trespassers, with the previous night's tragedy likely to increase the attraction.

White and blue police tape demarked a cordon twenty metres beyond the chapel's perimeter. As they watched, a couple of white-suited CSIs emerged from the tent protecting the chapel entrance.

'Despite its older appearance, the chapel was actually built by Langton in the first years of the eighteenth century, over the top of what had been the original abbey's undercroft. He took care to preserve the walls that originally formed the abbey's kitchen and scullery and there is also evidence to suggest that the undercroft was used to hold illegal Catholic services. When Catholicism was no longer a crime, the chapel became Middlesbury's first public place of worship for Catholics. We still serve a small, but loyal parish.'

'How do worshippers access the chapel?'

'We open the main visitors' gate and let them through.' Baines smiled tightly. 'In anticipation of your next question, we take it on trust that they are attending the chapel, not trying to get into the site for free.'

Warren filed the fact away for future reference. Although the policy meant that potentially anyone could have been wandering around the site, it also meant that everyone that entered would be caught by the cameras on the main entrance. He'd make certain to have the CCTV checked thoroughly.

'So where does English Heritage come into this?' asked Warren. The organisation's distinctive red, crenelated square logo was prominently displayed on the signage leading into the abbey grounds.

'English Heritage, or the Ministry of Works as it was back then, first became interested in the site in the Fifties. Langton and his descendants had lived here from about 1700 to the early years of the 1900s. They built a large house overlapping the ruins of the old infirmary, expanded the graveyard, resurrected the walled vegetable gardens and planted an apple orchard. Much of this was done before the 1791 act effectively decriminalised Catholicism, and so the house has a number of hidden rooms and priest holes. All boarded-up due to health and safety concerns now, of course,' Baines said ruefully.

'By the turn of the last century however, a combination of no suitable heirs and bad financial decisions meant the family were all but bankrupt. The house was abandoned, and aside from being requisitioned during the Second World War, was left empty.'

'Which was when you took it over?'

'Pretty much. The Catholic Church had always had an interest in the site, as it is part of our heritage and one of the few monasteries and abbeys founded by the Granadians, whose influence has largely disappeared even from their own region of Andalusia. However, the land had been seized during Henry VIII's power grab and exactly who owned it was a bit of a legal quagmire.

English Heritage were interested, but didn't really want to do anything beyond preserve the ruins as they were. In the end a deal was brokered, whereby English Heritage would manage the upkeep of the actual historic ruins and run it as a visitor attraction, whilst the church would pay a symbolic one-pound annual rent and maintain the rest of the grounds, using proceeds from the gardens and other business ventures.'

'Which is why all the staff working here are priests?'

'Not all, but you are right that many of the staff are members of the church.'

He gestured towards a large building just visible in the distance behind a clutch of trees. 'That was the original family home built by Howard Langton. It was extended several times and was part of the land bought by the church. We didn't do much with it at first, most of our efforts were focused on the original medieval abbey, and we ignored the later additions. But by the Nineties the church was starting to face a retirement problem. Lots of our clergy were getting old or ill, leading to a shortage in priests, as well as increasing the numbers of our brothers needing care.

'We'd wanted a dedicated retirement home in the area for some time. Many of our priests have lived in the area for fifty years and don't want to give up their ties to the community. Renovating the house was the most cost-effective option and it was opened in 2004; the name St Cecil is an anglicised version of Caecilius of Elvira, the patron saint of Elvira, modern day Granada. Now we have up to twenty priests at any time, ranging from those who are still quite fit and healthy, and still say Mass occasionally, to the fully-retired who need some day-to-day assistance. We are also providing hospice care for a couple of our brothers who are soon to receive their eternal reward. Those that are well enough are encouraged to help in the grounds. We also have three sisters who support us.'

'Are any of the residents likely to have been outside in the grounds at the time of the fire?'

Baines pursed his lips. 'Unlikely, I'd have thought. I will ask

Bishop Fisher of course, but most of our brothers typically rise before six to take part in the breviary and so tend not to stay up late. I don't live in the house, so I knew nothing of what had happened until I was called at about a quarter to ten. The old warden's house and orchard block most of the view of the chapel and graveyard so nobody in the house had any idea what was going on.'

'Who is Bishop Fisher?'

'Bishop Emeritus Nicholas Fisher was the driving force behind the conversion of the house into a retirement home. When he reached 75 and it came time for him to slow down himself, he opted to live amongst his fellow brothers and attend to their pastoral care, rather than take up residency somewhere more in keeping with his office.' Baines smiled. 'His Grace might be elderly, but he's still very much in charge.'

'So what is your role?'

'I am, for want of a better term, our business manager.'

Warren raised an eyebrow.

'I was called to serve God later than many, after a career in business. Bishop Fisher asked me to make the community and abbey more financially self-sufficient. It's why all the food in our gift shop and most of our café dishes are made from produce grown on our own grounds. We have an apiary producing honey and we've recently resurrected Middlesbury Abbey cider. Quite a kick, if you ever get the chance.'

'Would I be able to speak to Bishop Fisher? And I'd also like to have a word with the groundsman.'

'Of course.' Baines looked at his watch. 'Bishop Fisher will probably be in his office, I can get Rodney to join us there.' He pulled out an iPhone, and gave Warren an amused glance. 'It is the twenty-first century, Chief Inspector. We even have wireless broadband.'

* * *

The house was even bigger up close than it appeared and Baines was clearly very proud of the community he had helped build.

'We have twenty-eight bedrooms spread over three floors. At present we have nineteen residents, not including Bishop Fisher. We are also fortunate to have Father Boyce, a trained medic, who helps care for our sicker brothers when the care assistants go home for the day, and Sisters Clara, Angela and Isabella who assist Father Boyce and are responsible for cooking and cleaning. The remaining rooms are guest rooms for visiting relatives. The Langton family liked to entertain and so the kitchen and dining room are big enough for us all to eat together as a community.

'Below us is the basement. The Granadians were well-educated by the standards of the day, and very keen diarists. They recorded everything that happened, no matter how inconsequential. Nobody is really sure why. Howard Langton was very keen to preserve these records and so he made the basement secure and dry. We have been working with a local historian to write a history book, and those original records have been invaluable, providing a remarkable insight into day-to-day life at the abbey.'

The inside of the building reminded Warren of many of the stately homes that he and Susan had toured with her parents, keen members of the National Trust. The ceilings of the entrance hallway were easily fifteen feet high, the walls painted bright red, with gold edging. Wide, south-facing windows filled the room with bright, early morning sunlight.

'Is this house open to the public?'

'No. We considered it, but in the end we felt it would be too disruptive for some of our residents.'

The wooden floors creaked as Baines led Warren deeper into the house, pointing out the small room used by the community for their daily worship.

'Don't you use the chapel?'

'No, we attend Mass there on a Sunday and take it in turns to lead the service on weekday mornings, but the local lay congregation is too small for us to justify the cost of opening it up at other times, especially very early in the morning or last thing at night for divine office. Besides which, it's a bit of a trek for some of our less-mobile brothers, especially in the winter.'

Warren couldn't blame them. He'd not noticed any lighting on the paths and could only imagine what it would have been like in the dark, with the trees pressing in on all sides and the rustle of unseen animals in the bushes... He pushed away the thought, repressing a shudder.

Bishop Fisher's office looked much like Warren would expect. The walls that weren't hidden by six-foot wooden bookcases filled with academic-looking volumes, were the same red as the hallway outside. The faint smell of furniture polish mingled with fresh coffee. The bishop himself sat behind a large wooden desk, opposite a picture of the current pope and a small, porcelain statue of the Virgin Mary. An elderly looking desktop computer and an even older inkjet printer took up only a small proportion of the available desk space.

Portraits of earlier popes covered a wall to his right. Warren recognised Pope Francis, Pope Benedict XVI and Pope John Paul II. The remaining images probably represented others that had also held the position of Bishop of Rome since Bishop Fisher's own ordination.

Bishop Nicholas Fisher trembled slightly as he stood, his back stooped. Nevertheless, his handshake was firm and his gaze steady. He wore the first dog collar that Warren had seen since arriving that morning; Deacon Baines' thick fleece jacket hid his.

'Welcome to St Cecil's, DCI Jones. I'm sorry that it is under such sorrowful circumstances. I understand that it is believed to have been a suicide?'

'Thank you for seeing me, Your Grace. We are keeping an open mind at the moment, however it is looking that way.'

The bishop shook his head. 'Such a terrible affair. Let us hope that he has found peace from whatever was troubling him. If there is anything we can do to help his loved ones at this time, please don't hesitate to let us know. We will of course be praying for his soul.'

'That's very kind, Your Grace. In the meantime, I wondered if it would be possible to question the residents and staff to see if anyone saw anything?'

'Of course. I spoke to about half of the residents at breakfast this morning, nobody mentioned seeing anything. I will arrange for anyone who thinks they may be of assistance to speak to you.'

'What about staff who live off-site, such as the groundsman? Do you know who was present last night, or who may have been in the grounds?'

'Gabriel can get you a full list, but I believe the volunteers who help in the abbey visitor centre typically go home about five-thirty?'

Baines nodded. 'And they use the old infirmary gatehouse exit behind the house, rather than the public entrance, so they wouldn't have gone past the chapel anyway. The same goes for the carers that tend to Fathers Kendrick and Ramsden during the day – they'd have been here until about 8 p.m. – I'll get their contact details for you.'

A quiet knock on the door signalled the arrival of the groundsman.

Rodney Shaw was a fit-looking middle-aged man, dressed in a grubby green fleece and black corduroy trousers.

'I've been planting bulbs ready for the summer,' he said, by way of an apology for not shaking Warren's hand.

He'd finished work at his normal time of 5 p.m. the day before, then headed to his small flat on the other side of Middlesbury. He'd been watching the end of the news, and planning on an early night when his mobile phone had rung.

'Deacon Baines called me as soon as he was called, and I arranged to meet him here. At first I assumed that it was just kids.' He shrugged. 'It wasn't until I got there and saw the ambulance that

I realised that it was a bit more serious. I had no idea that some poor bastard had died in there. Excuse my language, Your Grace.'

'The doors to the chapel and the undercroft had been locked. These keys were found with the deceased. Do you recognise them?' Warren showed the man a photo on his phone of the keys retrieved from the scene. Forensics hadn't finished with them yet, and it was still speculation that they fitted the doors.

'Yes, they're the ones. Those locks are over a century old; I must have taken them apart and fixed them a half-dozen times over the last twenty years.'

'Are these the only copies of the keys?'

The groundsman shook his head. 'No, those are the ones that hang in the vestry. I have a second set at my house for safekeeping.'

'Are the keys in the vestry accessible?'

'Yeah, they're hidden and you need to know the code to the door, but the brothers take it in turns to open the chapel for morning service, so everyone knows where they are.'

'What about this key? It was found in the deceased's trouser pocket.' Warren flicked to the next image.

Groundsman squinted, then pointed at the screen. 'That's the key to the padlock for the main tool shed. I recognise that red blob of emulsion.'

'Is that also in the vestry?'

'Yeah, although I use my own copy so I don't know how long it's been missing.'

'One final thing.' Warren flicked to the next image.

'Yeah, that's the petrol can for the lawnmower. It's kept in the main tool shed.'

'Dear Lord, it would seem that the victim, whoever he may be, might be one of our community.'

Fisher's tone suggested that he hadn't considered that possibility until now.

'I'm afraid that is quite possible, Your Grace – either one of your residents or a regular volunteer.'

The room fell silent for a moment.

After an appropriate pause, Warren asked if anyone had checked the whereabouts of everyone living in the house. He also requested a full list of volunteers and regular visitors who might have the necessary knowledge to find the keys to the chapel and undercroft. Identifying the victim was his first priority.

Before anyone could reply, there came a soft knock at the door.

Shaw answered it, before announcing the visitor needed to speak to Baines urgently. Warren caught a glimpse of a grey, ankle-length skirt and matching blouse before the door closed behind him.

A few seconds later Baines returned, ashen-faced. 'I think that list might not be necessary. Father Nolan didn't come down to breakfast this morning. Sister Clara says his bed hasn't been slept in.'

Chapter 4

It took less than an hour for CSIs from the Scenes of Crime team working down at the chapel to seal off Father Nolan's room and do a preliminary sweep for evidence. Tony Sutton supervised the search, whilst Warren continued interviewing Bishop Fisher and Deacon Baines. Until the body found in the chapel was positively identified as Father Nolan and the cause of death determined, it was still regarded as unexplained, and so the room was being treated as a potential crime scene.

The note was written in a spidery script, on lined paper, and had been placed folded on the dresser. A photograph of it was on Sutton's tablet computer, sitting on the bishop's antique desk.

'Forgive me Father, for I have sinned.'

The seven-word opening refrain was familiar to any Catholic who had ever partaken in the sacrament of confession. Warren felt the slightest twinge of guilt – the typical following statement, detailing how long it was since the penitent's last confession, would be measured in decades, rather than years, for him.

'Sinned in what way? In a general sense or something more specific?' asked Sutton.

Fisher shrugged wearily. 'I have no idea.'

'Did Father Nolan give any indication that anything may be troubling him?' asked Warren.

'I shall ask others if he had said anything in public, but I had not heard him say anything openly.'

'What about privately?' asked Sutton, casually.

Fisher fixed him with a stare. 'If you are referring to the holy sacrament of Penance, then you are no doubt aware that the seal of confession is sacrosanct.'

Sutton looked as though he had more to say, but a glance from Warren stopped him.

'There was an open, empty container of medication next to the body. The part of the label that we could still read indicates that it originally contained Doxepin, which according to the internet is usually given to patients to combat depression and help with sleep. Was Father Nolan suffering with any mental health issues?'

Fisher paused before answering.

'Father Nolan had struggled with depression for a number of years. I'm sure that his doctor can furnish you with more details.'

'Do you know what lay behind the depression?' asked Sutton.

Fisher shrugged again. 'As I am sure you aware, clinical depression is a medical condition, it does not necessarily have a "cause". His doctor may be able to shed more light on his condition.'

'Deacon Baines tells me that Father Nolan was 76 years old,' said Warren, 'you said that he has been a resident here for eight years. That would make him 68 years old when he retired. My understanding is that priests normally retire at 75 or later, especially if they are physically fit and able to continue in their ministry. Was the depression the reason for his moving here?'

'In part.'

Warren paused, but no more was forthcoming.

'Thank you for your time, Bishop Fisher. I don't suppose that you have a sample of Father Nolan's handwriting?'

'I am certain that we can find one.' The elderly bishop hesitated before continuing. 'Will it be necessary for somebody to identify the body?'

An image of the burnt corpse, with its rictus grin, appeared in Warren's mind's eye.

'Unlikely. We should be able to confirm his identity from his dental records and a DNA match from his toothbrush.'

With nothing more to do until Forensics had completed their search, Warren and Sutton left the bishop's office and headed outside, into the cool, winter air.

'Let's work on the assumption that the body is Father Nolan for the time being. Liaise with Deacon Baines and arrange for statements to be taken from Father Nolan's acquaintances. Also, chase down his GP and see if we can find out if he was suicidal.'

'For all the good it will do.'

'What do you mean?' asked Warren, picking up on the edge in Sutton's voice.

'They're all bloody Catholic priests. You heard what Bishop Fisher said in there. "The seal of confession is sacrosanct" – they'll use that as an excuse to tell us what they want us to know and hide behind their vows for the rest.'

'That's a bit harsh, don't you think? The seal only applies to what is said in the confessional, and I can't imagine Father Nolan confessing to suicidal thoughts. Anything said outside of that relationship is open for discussion,' countered Warren. 'It's no different to the privileged status given to clients and their solicitors.'

'I disagree. Solicitors are duty-bound to report serious crimes to the authorities – Catholic priests think they are above the law.'

Warren eyed his friend with concern.

'This really bothers you, doesn't it?'

Sutton let out a puff of air.

'I just don't like the implication that the law applies differently to some people.'

Chapter 5

Warren wasn't a big fan of autopsies. Ordinarily he would just wait for the results to be emailed or phoned to him, or rely on a summary from someone like Tony Sutton. Unfortunately, Sutton was busy and Moray Ruskin hadn't seen a burn victim up close. With all his detective sergeants otherwise occupied, Warren took it upon himself to oversee this part of the probationary constable's training. His own mentor, Bob Windermere, had done the same for Warren in the dim and distant past. On the way over he'd grilled the young officer about the interviews he'd conducted with the two teenage witnesses who'd reported the fire; from the sounds of it, Ruskin's questioning had been thorough, but hadn't uncovered anything new.

Professor Jordan greeted them at the door to the morgue, situated under the Lister Hospital in Stevenage, where the pathologist's office was located. The two officers had already slipped protective clothing over their street clothes when Warren's phone vibrated.

'Good to see you again, Constable Ruskin. Shall we begin?' said Jordan.

Warren motioned for them to carry on without him.

The text from Susan was brief and to the point.

Scan fine, everything looking good. Just waiting for blood
test. Sxx

Warren responded with a simple 'W*xx*', before going to re-join
Ruskin, who by now was peering eagerly at the body, which lay
on its left side in a similar position to how it had been found at
the scene. A discreetly placed metal wastepaper bin stood to the
left of the table, in case the sight and smell were too much. That
didn't look as if it would be a problem, at least not for Ruskin.
Warren had been breathing through his mouth since entering
the cooled room.

'Tell me what you see, Constable,' invited Jordan.

'The skin on the upper torso is badly charred, probably third-
degree burns. Skin that isn't charred is swollen and split. The
crown of the head is so badly burnt it's unclear if the victim
had hair or was bald.'

Ruskin did a complete circuit of the body, before bending over
to look more closely.

'The skin on the front of the thighs is very badly burnt, with
little evidence of the clothes that he was wearing, whereas the
clothing on the backs of the thighs is scorched but intact.'

'Suggesting what?' asked Jordan.

'That the deceased was sitting down initially – if an accelerant
was used it was probably poured over the top of his head, splashing
down to cover his torso and upper thighs.'

'Good. What about the position of the body? Describe its
position.'

'Classic pugilistic or boxer's pose, hands up as if defending
his face from attack.'

'Which implies what?'

Ruskin' eyes crinkled, betraying the smile beneath his mask.

'Nothing. The positioning is caused by the heat shortening
the ligaments and tendons.'

29

'Good.'

Lesson over for the time being, Jordan summarised his findings.

'DC Ruskin is correct; the deceased was likely sat down on the chair when the accelerant – probably petrol – was poured over his head. That could have been self-inflicted or by persons unknown. The deceased remained seated for at least some time, whilst the fire took hold; the accelerant will have burnt off fairly quickly but remained long enough to ignite his clothing. In the final stages the clothing and accelerant had gone, but the deceased's skin and tissues continued to burn until he was extinguished. At some point he toppled off the chair onto his left side.'

'Was he alive?'

Jordan nodded. 'I believe that the witnesses reported screams, which only lasted a few seconds. If accurate, then assuming that they came from the deceased, he was almost certainly alive for at least some time – presumably until the fire took hold. Pathologically, I've found traces of soot below the larynx which indicates that he was breathing in the smoke.'

'Christ,' muttered Warren. 'Do you have a cause of death?'

'Fire is the best I can do at this stage,' said Jordan flatly.

Ruskin frowned.

'It's impossible to be more precise. I measured his carbon monoxide concentration at 42 per cent. That's on the low end of fatal. Similarly, the intense temperature of the fire did serious damage to his internal organs and ultimately clotted his blood. Unfortunately, I can't tell you if that killed him, or if he died of other causes before the damage reached a fatal level.'

'What other causes?' asked Ruskin.

'He had moderate cardiovascular disease. It's possible that the stress of the situation triggered a cardiac event. It's difficult to tell what damage to the heart was pre-mortem and what was post-mortem – regardless I'd still regard that as being caused by the fire.

'I've sent off for toxicology reports. There was a significant volume of alcohol in his stomach and there was an empty container of medication near to his body. Doxepin has sedative properties, enhanced by alcohol. It's always possible that he succumbed to their combined toxicity before the fire killed him.'

Ruskin shook his head slowly. 'All the other evidence suggests that it was suicide. But how is that possible? The burns on his thighs make it look as though he remained sitting for at least some time before falling off his chair. The witnesses I spoke to are clear that they heard screaming, so he must have been conscious at some point. I've seen the videos on YouTube of those monks setting themselves on fire. They shrieked and ran around.'

'Could the alcohol and doxepin have numbed him?' asked Warren.

'Possible, and he could have passed out quickly from the initial pain,' said Jordan. 'The witnesses did claim that the screams only lasted for a few moments. Much of the burning is also third-degree, full-depth, which destroys the nerve endings. Falling out of the chair may have happened after he died, from the post-mortem muscle contraction caused by the fire.'

'I assume that asking for a time of death is pointless, Ryan.'

'I'm afraid so, Inspector. Time of death is a mug's game at the best of times, but fire messes up everything. I can't assess rigor mortis since his muscles are already contracted, and the damage to his skin makes it impossible to look for staining due to blood pooling. You'll have to settle for witness reports.'

'What about positive identification?'

'My investigations so far are consistent with a man of Father Nolan's age and build. I've sent off for dental records and taken a DNA sample if you need it.'

Warren looked closely at the man's hands, the skin was charred and split.

'I'm not even going to ask about fingerprints.'

Sunday 22nd February

Chapter 6

'Bad news on the CCTV front, sir.'

Mags Richardson screwed the lid back on her ever-present bottle of water. It was first thing Sunday morning, and most of the team were already hard at work. Richardson was Warren's first visitor that morning.

'Broken?' asked Warren.

'Worse. Almost all the cameras inside the abbey grounds are fake, just a deterrent. There are cameras above the main entrance, so we have a record of paying visitors, but once you're in the grounds, there's pretty much nothing. According to Deacon Baines, they recently installed covert cameras in the gift shop and the café, but they are focused on the tills – they don't pick up anything outside.'

'Above the tills? Do they suspect the staff of theft?'

'He was reluctant to use that word, but he reckons there is a mismatch between the takings recorded at the various till points and the money deposited in the bank. The cameras are there to help them figure out if anyone is "making a mistake". His words, not mine.'

'How much?' asked Warren.

'Not much. He reckons it's twenty quid after each daily take, as it's a hundred and forty on each weekly bank run, but that soon adds up. Deacon Baines figured it was probably some sort of systematic error, since the figure was always exactly one hundred and forty pounds, and made all the till staff undergo fresh training. When that didn't work, he installed the cameras. So far he hasn't spotted anything obvious, like people slipping their hand in the till. He still thinks it's likely to be a mistake. The money is kept in a locked safe, before delivery to the bank, so he thinks it's at the point of sale.'

'Have they reported the thefts?'

'Like I said, he didn't want to use that word.'

'Twenty quid every day could be systematic error, I suppose,' mused Warren. 'Maybe they are inputting the wrong figure for the daily float? But it sounds like he's being naïve. If there is a thief, either they're in every day and stealing from the till, or the money is going missing between cashing up and going to the bank, which is surely a much shorter list of suspects.'

'I think Baines is in denial. And if there is a thief, I suspect that they will want to deal with it themselves, rather than bring in the police.'

'What does the missing total stand at now?'

'Six hundred and eighty pounds.'

Warren let out a whistle, 'That's not insignificant. Why haven't English Heritage called in the police?'

'I get the impression that the loss is being deducted from the gift shop takings that go to the abbey, not the money deposited into English Heritage's account from the entry charges.'

'So they are keeping them in the dark?'

'Sounds like it.'

'Well, if they aren't willing to report it to the police, then there isn't a lot we can do about it. I'm not sure what the link is to our death, but keep me posted. How much footage have you secured from the wider neighbourhood?'

'I've got teams knocking on doors. There's a row of shops

nearby that looks promising, and it's a rough neighbourhood, so some of the houses have cameras outside; we'll seize what we can. There are a number of junctions with ANPR cameras in the vicinity of the abbey and a petrol station.'

'Stay on it,' instructed Warren.

He leant back in his chair, and sucked on the tip of his pen, contemplating what Richardson had just told him.

The note in Father Nolan's room had read, 'Forgive me Father, for I have sinned.'

Stealing was a sin...

* * *

'I appreciate that our Scenes of Crime teams can be unsettling, but we will try to keep the disruption to a minimum, Your Grace. Hopefully, it won't take much longer. We'll restrict our access to the side entrance, where possible.'

Two days after the fire and dental records had confirmed Father Nolan as the victim. The final cause of death would be determined by the coroner at inquest, but Warren was already under pressure to dismiss it as a suicide. The sooner Warren advised DSI Grayson that the death was non-suspicious, the sooner the priest's body could be released and arrangements made for his funeral, and the sooner St Cecil's retirement home could return to its usual, peaceful routine, and Middlesbury's main tourist attraction could reopen.

Before that happened though, Warren was still treating Father Nolan's room as a potential crime scene, and he had decided to visit the home in person again to reassure Bishop Fisher that they were progressing as quickly as possible.

Father Nolan's room had been on the ground floor, furthest from the main entrance. The room next to him was occupied by Father Carlos, a frail, stooped, octogenarian with poor eyesight and poorer hearing. The room directly above was an empty guestroom. Not only did this mean that nobody was likely to have heard anything, it also meant that anyone coming or going via the fire exit at the end of the corridor was unlikely to have been spotted. Nor, for that matter, were the CSIs dusting for prints and looking for other evidence likely to be disturbed.

Father Nolan's room had been simply furnished, but clean and tidy. He shared a bathroom with the other occupants in his wing of the house, but had his own small sink and mirrored medicine cabinet. A tall bookcase filled with a mixture of weighty academic tomes and fiction paperbacks, was one of the few furnishings that hadn't been removed by the CSIs. A quick perusal revealed that the late priest's recreational tastes ran toward classic science fiction, with well-thumbed copies of Arthur C. Clarke and Isaac Asimov vying for space with Kurt Vonnegut and Philip K. Dick.

On top of the bookcase, a number of framed pictures were neatly arranged. A faded black and white wedding photo was probably of the late priest's parents. Next to that, a less faded image contained the same couple; recognisable but significantly older, flanking a younger man dressed as a priest. Father Nolan's ordination, Warren assumed. A few other photographs, these newer and in colour, depicted Father Nolan surrounded by different groups of people. In one, he was blowing candles from a cake decorated with a '25' pattern. Judging by his age in the photograph, Warren guessed that it was the twenty-fifth anniversary of his ordination.

The single bed had been neatly made, the pillows plumped up and it had clearly been unslept in when the priest's disappearance had been discovered. However, a dent at the foot of the bed suggested that somebody may have sat there, facing the room's single wooden chair, and so the bed had been stripped and the bedding taken away for forensic analysis. A wooden chair had also been removed, after being dusted for fingerprints.

According to Deacon Baines, the rooms were cleaned once a week by one of the sisters that helped at the home and so he was assisting the forensic team in obtaining exclusionary prints.

Sister Clara who had reported that Father Nolan was missing had already been questioned by Tony Sutton, but had been unable to give any more details.

The small wooden table underneath the window had been dusted, and two glass tumblers, that appeared to have been recently rinsed out, had been sealed in plastic evidence bags and removed for processing.

Professor Jordan had suggested that the victim had taken prescription drugs and drunk whiskey before the fire. If the pills were dissolved in the drink, that potentially shone a whole different light on things. For completeness, the sink trap was in the process of being dismantled to see if anything had been discarded down there.

Hopefully the findings would come back soon, and Warren could sign the death off as a tragic suicide and everyone could move on.

Chapter 7

'I've completed those PNC checks.' Pymm drained her glass tea cup. Sutton looked at the dregs with dismay.

'Are those twigs in there? Comic Relief raises millions so that people in Africa don't have to drink water that looks like that. Would you like me to email Lenny Henry for you?'

'Piss off, it's chamomile and rosehip. Caffeine-free, organic and 50 per cent off this week. It's a hell of a lot better for you than that over-priced coffee that you and the rest of the team guzzle all day.'

'Palpitations are a small price to pay for the performance boost,' sniffed Sutton. 'Anyway, enough of the backchat, *Sergeant*, let's see what you've got.'

'I've run the names of the residents, *Inspector*, and as you'd expect, nothing's come up. I've also done the volunteers and staff. Most of them are in the clear too. Nothing more exciting than a couple of driving offences and one old caution from thirty years back for being drunk and disorderly.'

'You said "most".'

'Well spotted. Rodney Shaw, the groundsman. He was sentenced to twenty-eight months back in 1984 for possession of class A drugs, multiple counts of burglary and wounding with intent.'

Sutton let out a whistle.

'When did he start working there?'

'1996. He did casual work in the abbey grounds at first, before becoming groundsman shortly before the home opened in 2004.'

'Anything since?'

'Nothing, not so much as a speeding ticket.'

'Would his employers have known about his convictions?'

'Not necessarily, they would have been classed as "spent" under the Rehabilitation of Offenders Act, so they couldn't ask about it at interview.'

Sutton scratched his chin. 'A history of violence from decades ago, hidden from his employers – a connection or a coincidence?'

'If he hadn't voluntarily disclosed it to his employers and it looked as though it was likely to come out, he could have been worried that he was going to lose his job. Could Father Nolan have got wind of it and tried to blackmail Shaw?' The look on Pymm's face showed her own scepticism.

'Why? What would he have achieved? And how could he have found out? Blackmail's not exactly priestly behaviour, is it?'

The pair lapsed into silence, before Sutton straightened.

'Well, good work anyway, Rachel. See if you can find out any more details about his original conviction. I'll take it to the boss and see what he thinks. It's our only lead so far.'

* * *

Rodney Shaw officially became a 'person of interest' an hour later when DS Hutchinson returned to the office.

'Father Nolan was generally popular,' started Hutchinson. 'Nobody had a bad word to say about him. At least not directly.'

'Go on,' Warren blew across his mug of coffee. He'd forgotten to buy milk and was slurping the coffee black; the caffeine hit was good, but Warren had already burnt his tongue that morning.

'Apparently, Father Nolan had a loud disagreement with Rodney Shaw a couple of weeks ago.'

'About what?'

'Well, that's where we have a problem. It seems the disagreement is common knowledge amongst the staff and residents. A couple of the sisters also mentioned it, but nobody is sure what it was about, or even who overheard them. To be honest, it has the feel of a bit of gossip; I guess small communities are all the same, even those based on holy orders. So much for "thou shalt not bear false witness."'

'It depends if it's false, I suppose,' said Sutton.

Warren puffed his lips out.

'It's still pretty tenuous. It seems a bit far-fetched that Father Nolan would suddenly discover Shaw's murky past, then threaten to expose him. For what reason? Blackmail? If it was murder it wasn't a spur of the moment thing so this threat, if it existed, hung over him for at least as long as it took to plan it. Why would Father Nolan hold onto that knowledge?'

'And if it was blackmail, what did he want in return?' asked Sutton, playing Devil's Advocate against his own theory.

'What does any blackmailer want?' asked Hutchinson.

'Most obvious is monetary or material gain,' answered Sutton.

Warren shook his head slowly. 'Shaw is two steps up from a gardener. Before then, he was a homeless drug addict, stealing to maintain his habit. He's hardly going to be rolling in money.'

'He could be dealing again,' suggested Hutchinson. 'Besides, how much money does a Catholic priest need or want? You've seen Father Nolan's room, he was a man of frugal tastes. His food and board is paid for. He has no family to speak of and so far we've found no evidence of expensive mistresses.'

'What about vices? He wouldn't be the first priest who developed a taste for Communion wine outside of church,' said Sutton.

'The autopsy was inconclusive in terms of liver damage, although the fire makes the results unreliable,' said Warren. 'Do a bit more discreet poking around, Hutch. Find out if he had any expensive habits.'

'Will do.'

'Why else do people blackmail?' asked Warren.

'Control? Is there something that Shaw could do for Nolan that he couldn't do himself?' said Hutchinson.

'Again, what does a retired Catholic priest need or want?' asked Warren.

'I can't imagine Father Nolan standing around on street corners buying drugs,' said Sutton, 'although you never can tell.'

'Hopefully the toxicology screen will answer that question,' said Warren, 'but if it's not booze, drugs, money or favours, then that leaves secrets. Keep your mouth shut about my transgressions, or I'll expose yours."

'And what might Nolan's transgressions be?' asked Sutton. 'With all of these ongoing inquiries into abuse and cover-ups in the Catholic Church, you have to wonder…'

The silence stretched as they contemplated the uncomfortable implications of Sutton's statement.

'This is all speculation,' said Warren finally. 'We need a lot more before we even treat the death as suspicious let alone make Shaw a suspect. Hutch, see what you can find out about Father Nolan's finances and carry on looking into his background. Keep an eye out for any hints or allegations of inappropriate behaviour. Meanwhile, I think a discreet chat with Bishop Fisher may be in order.'

'Good luck with that,' muttered Sutton.

Chapter 8

It was past nine when Warren finally got home. A call to Bishop Fisher had revealed that Shaw's past problems with drugs were not only well-known to him, but were in fact a source of pride; Shaw was held up as an inspiring example of how someone could successfully overcome challenges within their lives through prayer. He and Deacon Baines worked together to take that message around schools, youth clubs and homeless shelters.

Tony Sutton had pointed out that if Rodney Shaw had started using drugs again, then the shame of letting everyone down might have been enough for him to commit murder, but even he hadn't sounded convinced.

But something still didn't feel quite right. In his mind's eye, Warren could picture the crime scene, the harsh lights bringing the horrifying tableau into sharp relief. What was he missing? What clue was there in front of him that he just couldn't see?

Or was he missing anything? Perhaps it just his tired, over-worked imagination seeing shadows where there were none. Warren knew that proximity to death – especially violent death – tended to make him morose; that had only worsened since the events of the summer. Was that all it was? The counsellor that he'd seen in the immediate aftermath of Gary's death had warned him to look out for the symptoms of post-traumatic stress disorder. Was this one? The dreams that had plagued him the night before were unpleasant, but understandable. Everyone had bad dreams, didn't they, especially after what he'd just seen? And the frequency of the dreams that had started in the summer had lessened in recent months. He'd mention them at his next meeting with Occupational Health, but he didn't think it was worth requesting an earlier appointment.

Regardless, a nagging feeling in his gut wasn't enough to warrant spending any more time on the death and so Warren decided that first thing in the morning, he'd follow Grayson's instruction to close the case and pass it over to the coroner as a probable suicide. Then he could complete the paperwork so that he was ready for whatever came across his desk next.

With his mind made up, he'd turned off his computer, grabbed his coat and headed into the damp, misty evening. A quick call home revealed that Susan was ploughing through a stack of marking that she wanted to finish that evening, and so Warren had offered to stop off at the local Indian takeaway.

The dining room table was covered with GCSE controlled assessments when he arrived home. As Susan cleared them some space, Warren went into the kitchen and distributed the food. He was midway through pouring a well-deserved beer when the lights went out.

'Shit,' came Susan's surprised voiced from the dining room.

The unexpected transition to pitch black also caught Warren by surprise and he froze. A few seconds later the sound of glugging beer turned into the sound of dripping liquid as the glass frothed and over-flowed.

'Shit,' echoed Warren as he tried to place the bottle back on the counter without knocking anything off.

When the lights didn't return after a few more seconds, Warren turned slowly to take stock of the situation; even the ever-present hum from the fridge-freezer was suddenly notice-able by its absence.

'It looks as though the whole street is out,' called Susan. 'Not even the street lights are on.

By now, Warren's eyes were starting to adjust to the sudden darkness. Faint, grey shadows slowly took form as the dim moonlight seeped through the slats in the still open kitchen blinds.

'I think I left my mobile in my handbag, can you use yours?' called Susan from the other room. Feeling foolish for forgetting that his phone was essentially a torch, Warren fumbled in his jacket pocket. Nothing. It must still be in his overcoat, hanging in the hallway.

The faint moonlight didn't penetrate this far into the house and Warren found himself reaching out with his hands, shuffling slowly like a mummy from a childrens' cartoon. They'd lived in the house for nearly four years, but he couldn't for the life of him recall how many steps there were to the coat pegs. The flashing red light on the alarm system did nothing to help him judge the distance.

Or see Susan's book bag at the bottom of the stairs.

After picking himself up and reassuring Susan that he was OK, Warren finally located his coat, and then his phone.

The light from its screen was dazzling, and Warren had to blink several times before he could focus enough to locate the icon that turned the phone's camera flash into a powerful torch.

'It's a good job I got takeaway or we'd be eating cold baked beans like cavemen,' joked Warren.

'Well, unless we want to eat in the dark, we'd better find some candles soon, my phone battery is only on 10 per cent.'

Warren checked his, and found it wasn't much better.

It took a couple of minutes of fumbling around before Susan located the box of candles left over from Christmas dinner at the back of a cupboard. Fortunately, she kept a box of matches in her school pencil case.

'I knew there was a reason I married a science teacher, instead of a geography teacher,' teased Warren.

'I assumed it was the leather elbow patches that put you off geographers,' replied Susan as she lit the candles. She reached around the table and gave Warren's backside a playful squeeze. 'Eat up quickly before the power comes back on, you know how candlelight makes me feel.'

Warren said nothing as he fumbled for his phone.

'How could I be so stupid,' he muttered, ignoring his wife's flirting.

No signal. The power cut must have been quite extensive to have also taken out the local cell-tower.

Ignoring Susan's questions, Warren scrolled through his contacts as he made his way to the hall phone. Fortunately, the local telephone exchange still had power and Tony Sutton picked up on the second ring.

'You OK, boss? Have you lost your mobile or something?'

'Have you got electricity?'

'Yeah, course, I live in Middlesbury not Cornwall.'

Warren ignored the man's attempt at humour.

'I need you to check your email for Andy Harrison's scene inventory and read it out for me.'

Still confused, Sutton nevertheless complied.

'That's it?'

'That's everything that's listed. Andy's pretty thorough, you know that. What's this all about, Chief?'

Warren explained his flash of inspiration. There was a silence at the end of the phone before Sutton spoke again.

'You'd better call Grayson and let him know. He needs to be the one to escalate the death to murder.'

Monday 23rd February

Chapter 9

Judging from the time displayed by the flashing clock on the oven, the electricity had been restored some hours previously, at about 1 a.m. A statement from the electricity company had been read out on the local radio as Warren drove into the office at 6 a.m., apologising to the thousand or so customers affected by a fault at the local substation.

Warren was half contemplating writing a letter of thanks.

'Sorry I didn't spot it sooner,' said Warren.

Grayson waved a hand. 'Nobody else did. So either somebody was with him when he set himself on fire, holding a light, or he was set alight by persons unknown? There's no way he could have done it himself?'

Warren shook his head firmly.

'The last reliable sighting of Father Nolan was after dark and there was hardly any moonlight. I can just about accept that he could find his way to the chapel, then let himself into the undercroft, but it would have been pitch black down there. There are electric lights, but they were turned off at the switch at the top of the stairs. I can't believe that he would have gone down there, set up the chair, then gone back up the stairs, locked himself in, switched off the lights, come back

47

downstairs, doused himself in petrol and then set himself alight in the pitch black.'

'And there were no other sources of light at the scene?'

'Nothing. No torch, his mobile phone was back in his room and there were no candles.'

'He had a box of matches, could he have used those?'

'Doubtful, the box was almost full and Forensics only found a single spent match in the whole area. Besides which, you know how volatile petrol is. It's doubtful he could have slopped petrol over himself with an open source of ignition in the room, the vapour would have ignited immediately. Forensics didn't find any burnt paper or rags at the scene to indicate that he made a fire to see by.'

Grayson pulled at his bottom lip. 'You're right. I'm not quite ready to publicly declare it a murder, but it should remain an unexplained death for now.'

'There's more,' interjected Sutton. 'I was thinking about this after last night's call. There was no sign of any restraint, and I believe that the working hypothesis was that Father Nolan drank enough whiskey and took enough sleeping pills to numb the pain sufficiently not to run around like a mad thing when he set himself alight.'

Warren agreed; he could see where Sutton was headed.

'Well, is it likely that somebody that far out of it would have the manual dexterity to light a match, apparently first time?'

The three men were silent as they thought through the implications.

'We need the results of the toxicology,' said Warren finally.

'Call the lab and get it fast-tracked, I'll authorise the cost,' ordered Grayson.

'If the bloods come back and show that he was so insensate that he could be covered in petrol and ignited without any signs of restraint or a struggle, then that raises questions about how he got in that state in the first place,' said Sutton.

48

'Go on,' said Warren.

'The way I see it, there are two possibilities. First, that he drank the whiskey and potentially took his sleeping pills *in situ*. That is more believable if it was a suicide, otherwise how would you convince him to do it otherwise? There was no sign of a restraint or struggle. And why on earth would he go down to the undercroft with somebody?'

'He could have been threatened or coerced in some way?' suggested Grayson.

'In which case it's likely a murder,' continued Sutton, 'or he took the whiskey and pills elsewhere, probably his room, as it is private, and was then led down to the undercroft by his killer, who left the bottle and pills there to mislead us.'

'Or a combination of the two scenarios,' interjected Grayson.

'Either way, it implies that he must have known his killer, at least to some degree,' said Sutton. 'Not only would they need him to have been comfortable enough to drink with him in his room or to go down to the chapel with him, they would also need to know about his medication.'

'Which means we need the results back from the forensics in his room, and the likely route he took down to the chapel,' said Warren. 'We also need to know the whereabouts of all of the other residents, staff and carers that night.'

'Then let's see what Rachel Pymm has for us,' said Grayson, getting to his feet.

Chapter 10

'Preliminary results are back in from the forensic examination of Father Nolan's room,' said Rachel Pymm as Warren, Sutton and Grayson joined Ruskin around her workspace. In deference to the fact that her job was almost entirely computer-based, her desk was adorned with three large monitors, arranged in a horseshoe.

Warren felt a pang of sadness, quickly repressed. One of his last requisition requests from Gary Hastings had been just such a set-up. He'd largely taken over from DS Pete Kent as the unit's expert user of the HOLMES2 crime management system and 'officer in the case', the person in charge of keeping track of the all the information flowing into a major inquiry, such as a murder. DS Rachel Pymm now did that job full-time.

'Give me the highlights.'

'First of all, surfaces that we'd expect to have Father Nolan's fingerprints on, as well as whoever cleaned his room last, are completely clean,' said Pymm.

'What about the glass tumblers?' asked Warren.

'Again, suspiciously clean, with no observable fingerprints. Both glasses had also been well-rinsed. Tests are ongoing of the droplets of liquid in the bottom of the glass but early indications are that it was almost entirely tap water, with traces of ethanol and complex aromatic compounds of the type typically found in a grain-based spirit.'

'Sounds like whiskey,' suggested Grayson.

'That's what they think. More detailed tests should be able to confirm that and possibly identify the brand.'

'So he shared a drink with his killer?'

'Perhaps. They are doing their best to isolate any stray DNA from around the rim of the glass, but CSM Harrison says don't hold your breath.'

'Anything else?'

'Nothing much. Just some residue in one of the glasses that may be an anti-depressant.'

Warren choked back a response; Pymm smiled sweetly.

'They also found tiny polymer fragments in the sink trap that could be from the capsule surrounding a timed-release tablet, again consistent with the anti-depressant prescribed to Father Nolan. Identification has been fast-tracked.'

'Bloody hell,' breathed Warren. 'Anything more?' His tone suggested that the time for teasing was over.

'Several different shoe prints have been isolated from the ground outside the fire exit and the corridor immediately adjacent to it. Their orientation suggests that people have walked both in and out of the exit. Some of the prints on the ground outside heading away from the house match examples in the footwear reference database for men's size ten Clarks of the type Father Nolan was wearing the night he died. Obviously there was too much damage from the fire to make a definitive match between these prints and his shoes.'

'So, Father Nolan could have exited the house via the fire exit. Is the door not alarmed?' asked Ruskin.

'The wires to the contacts that trigger the alarm if the door is opened look as though they may have been tampered with, although it isn't conclusive. The crash bar on the door is also suspiciously free of prints, but a clear hand-print on the right-hand wall as you look towards the door could be from Father Nolan. They are looking for a better source for comparison prints amongst his belongings before they declare a positive match.'

'So, Father Nolan walked out of the fire exit, without triggering the alarm. As he did so, he leant against the wall – which might be an indication that he was unsteady on his feet, from having consumed alcohol and prescription drugs,' suggested Sutton.

'I'd be interested to know how mobile Father Nolan was,' said Warren. 'Assuming these footprints are from when he left the house with his killer, then he was still on his feet at that stage – the drugs and alcohol hadn't rendered him entirely helpless. What about by the time he made it to the chapel? Was he still upright or did he need carrying? That might indicate if there was more than one killer.'

'Forensics are still examining the most likely routes between the house and the chapel, but the pathways up by the house are pretty well-trod and weren't immediately closed off,' said Pymm.

'Why aren't Father Nolan's footprints inside the hallway?' asked Ruskin.

Pymm answered, 'The footprints outside are impressions in the soft earth. The footprints inside are transfer from the dirty soles of somebody's shoes. They were only visible using electrostatic transfer.'

Ruskin paused, before blushing slightly. 'Oh, I see. Father Nolan only walked out of the fire exit. The killer entered from outside, tracking mud inside, then walked back out with Father Nolan.' He paused again. 'Do any of the unknown footprints head in as well as out?'

Sutton clapped the young constable on the shoulder. 'Exactly the right question to ask, Moray. Rachel?'

'Yes, two sets.' She smirked. 'We'll make a detective out of you yet, junior.'

'Bugger off,' the Scotsman muttered as everyone chuckled.

'Bugger off, *Sergeant*, show some respect,' responded Pymm primly.

'What next, Moray?' asked Warren.

'We should try and identify who the other shoe prints belong to and find out who has access to the fire exit. Was anyone spotted nearby in the hours before and afterwards?'

'Anything else?' prompted Sutton.

'Who would know about his medication, and who would he be comfortable enough with to let his guard down in their presence, assuming he wasn't taken against his will?'

'And what else?'

The young constable thought for a moment, 'We should also speak to a forensic pharmacologist about the likely effects of the amount of sedatives and alcohol found in his system.'

'Good,' said Warren. 'As luck would have it that's exactly who we are waiting to get back to us.' He turned to the rest of the team. 'You all heard the man, let's get going.'

Tuesday 24th February

Chapter 11

The report from the forensic pharmacologist was waiting in Warren's email inbox when he arrived at work that morning. He took one look at it and headed to the coffee urn. He'd slept poorly the night before; suddenly, the journey that he and Susan were about to embark upon seemed real. For months, the couple had undergone endless tests, spoken to numerous specialists and now the time had come. At exactly 8 p.m. the previous night, Susan had injected herself with a shot of hormones, triggering the start of the IVF process. The injection had been over in a matter of seconds, yet Warren couldn't clear his mind of what was happening inside his wife's body. All being well, her ovaries should now be gearing up to produce mature eggs, ready for the fertility specialists to harvest.

Amazingly, an hour or so after the injection, Susan had simply gone to bed, falling asleep within moments of her head hitting the pillow. Unfortunately for Warren, sleep wasn't as forthcoming. He'd lain awake for hours listening to his wife's breathing, picturing the next nine months with an alternating combination of excitement and fear. When he'd finally dozed off, his dreams had been fractured and muddled, his over-stimulated imagination mixing the investigation with his impending fatherhood. He'd awoken earlier than normal, with a feeling of disquiet.

Even after a second mug of coffee, the report still meant nothing to him and so he was forced to elicit the assistance of Ryan Jordan to interpret it; he called Moray Ruskin in to listen in on the conference call.

'They measured his blood alcohol level at 152 milligrams per millilitre, although there is some margin for error given the trauma he suffered before he died. That volume of alcohol would have made him a bit unsteady on his feet, but probably wouldn't have made him insensate.'

'What about the drugs tests?' asked Ruskin.

'The level of doxepin in his system was significantly higher than would have been expected if he had taken his prescribed amount, even allowing for the fact that Father Nolan was in the habit of ignoring medical advice and taking a nightcap to amplify its affects. However, I found fewer fragments of the pill's capsule in his stomach than I'd expect for such a large amount. I'd even hazard a guess that the fragments represent his prescribed dosage of one tablet.'

'Suggesting that he took his usual pill, but then additional capsules were opened and the contents poured into his drink?' suggested Warren.

'Entirely plausible. Doxepin is soluble in alcohol, and a lot of patients report dysgeusia, an alteration to their sense of taste, so he may not have noticed it. It also means that the drug would be absorbed much faster. That's why you shouldn't ever grind up pills unless told that it is safe to do so. Plenty of people have given themselves overdoses that way.'

'OK Ryan, cards on the table; would this combination of alcohol and drugs have left Father Nolan sufficiently mobile to get down to the chapel, largely under his own power, but rendered him compliant enough not to need restraint?' Warren held his breath.

Jordan sounded reluctant as he answered.

'I spoke to the forensic pharmacologist myself. She says that most people would have been on a steady downward spiral towards unconsciousness within thirty minutes to an hour after consuming that mixture. The rate would depend on the person's individual physiology, how quickly they drank it and how much they had eaten etc.

'It is possible that Father Nolan could have been confused enough to be led into the chapel, presumably by someone he knew, where he then slumped in the chair. The shock of the fire may have been enough to rouse him temporarily.

'It is equally possible that the drugs may have rendered him unconscious in just a few minutes, meaning he would have needed to be carried down to the chapel or transported another way.'

'Could he have taken himself down there, doused himself in petrol and then ignited himself with a box of matches, in the dark?'

The pause was even longer.

'When it comes to human behaviour, Warren, never say never, but I think it unlikely.'

57

Chapter 12

The decision the day before to change the cause of death for Father Nolan from suicide to homicide, led to an immediate shift in tempo. Murder investigations didn't come with a blank cheque – nothing did these days – but requests, in particular for forensics, were more likely to be granted than for suicides. Appeals for support from headquarters in Welwyn Garden City would typically be approved, and more colleagues could be co-opted to help speed up and expand enquiries.

However, Warren had already been assigned as Senior Investigating Officer to Nolan's suicide and DSI Grayson wasn't going to change that.

'Mags, I know that there is precious little CCTV on the site, but I want you to extend the seizure to cover all the cameras available, including internal areas. We have reliable sightings of Father Nolan, apparently alive and well, from after the evening meal that night. At some point he met his killer or killers. Did that happen in his room, or did they meet elsewhere in the grounds? Did he know them? They could have been waiting on site for him, so cross-reference visitors arriving that day with those leaving. There is a camera near the main entrance. It's unlikely that the murderer came in that way, but let's not miss the low-hanging fruit.'

'Could be a big job, sir. Ticket sales were a couple of hundred that day, and the cameras aren't great,' warned Richardson. 'The good news is that most visitors either have English Heritage membership or pay with a card. The regular parishioners coming to worship at the chapel are all known to the staff, and are let in for free. That should make identification of any unknowns a lot easier.'

'I'll authorise support from Welwyn. Focus on the day of the murder initially, look for anyone who comes in but doesn't leave. There's only one public entrance. The killer may also have visited before to recce the site, so pull in footage from the month preceding the murder, if it's available – that way we've got it if we need it.

'If they didn't use the entrance, then the killer had to get on site somehow, so widen the net around the abbey site to a mile, check if any of the nearby residential properties or businesses have CCTV. If the killer accessed the abbey by climbing over the wall, they may have been caught on camera. Prioritise video from immediately adjacent to the abbey and work backwards from the day of the murder. Again, we'll look at the wider area if needed.

'Get traffic to pull in ANPR cameras from the previous month and have them cross-reference the plates with locals. If the killer did arrive by car, he or she may have parked a few streets away.'

'Got it,' replied Richardson.

'Hutch, I need you to go back and re-interview all the residents, staff and volunteers from the abbey. It looks as though somebody may have spiked Father Nolan's drink with his own medication. That person may well have been in his room with him, which suggests that he may have not only known them but will have been comfortable enough with them to have them in his room. I'll get DSI Grayson to authorise some extra bodies and sign off on any overtime. This murder wasn't some chancer, or a robbery gone wrong. It took planning and forethought; whoever did it is not only smart, they also had a motive. Nobody is universally loved – not even the Chief Constable – so let's see who might have had a grievance with our victim.'

'I agree, sir. But what if the motive has nothing to do with Father Nolan himself?'

Warren could see where the experienced detective was headed.

'That's where DS Pymm comes in. Rachel, I want you to trawl the records and see if there is anything beyond Father Nolan. Perhaps a person with a grievance with somebody else at the home, or a wider upset with the church as a whole.'

'Take a ticket, and join the queue,' grumbled Sutton. 'That list grows longer every day.'

Pymm nodded. She already had her notepad out, scribbling down ideas.

'Have a look at the PNC and see if anyone associated with the abbey has a file on the system. Whilst you're at it, cross-reference with the probation service and see if anyone interesting has either been released recently or moved to the area. Be creative, contact the Social Media Intelligence Unit for assistance.'

With that, the meeting broke up. Warren watched his officers leave with a touch of envy. Most investigative work was a repetitive, long slog. He knew from experience that the twentieth person he interviewed would become muddled up with the thirtieth, unless he took scrupulous notes. Similarly, a day staring at grainy CCTV footage would leave him with a headache – a week of it and even his dreams would take place in a jerky, faded world.

But there was no denying the sense of purpose that it brought. The feeling that you were at the very heart of the investigation, an essential part of a team and that what you stumbled across might just be the vital clue that moved the case forward.

Warren supposed he should count himself lucky. So many of his peers, upon reaching the rank of inspector or above, retreated into their offices, their time filled with meetings, budget reports and people management. That came with the job, and it was an essential role in modern policing. But he'd seen the wistful looks on his fellow DCIs' faces as he left the latest management away day, and headed back to his team, whilst they scurried to their next meeting.

This unusual position was a result of Middlesbury CID's unique history. Tucked away in the very north of the county, about as far from Hertfordshire Constabulary's headquarters in Welwyn Garden City as it was possible to be and not cross the county borders, Middlesbury CID had remained a local first-response unit dealing with issues as they arose in Middlesbury and the surrounding towns and villages. The unit had survived the consolidation when Hertfordshire and Bedfordshire moved all of their major crime units into a single building in Welwyn Garden City.

Maintaining Middlesbury's independence had been the personal mission of Warren's predecessor, DCI Gavin Sheehy. Unfortunately, the man's uncompromising attitude had won him as many enemies as admirers, and when he was arrested for corruption, many saw that as vindication of the view that Middlesbury needed to be disbanded and absorbed into the main unit in Welwyn.

Whether DSI John Grayson had been appointed to save or bury Middlesbury CID was still unclear four years on. Tony Sutton maintained that the fate of Middlesbury CID was directly related to its usefulness in securing Grayson's next promotion and corresponding final salary pension; Warren felt that whilst his theory wasn't entirely without merit, it was a bit unfair to the man.

Of course, none of this was made clear to Warren as he was parachuted in to fill the vacancy left by Sheehy. Warren's first weeks as a newly promoted DCI had seen him walk unprepared into a maelstrom of politics that he'd been forced to deal with as he headed up his first major murder investigation. Over the next few months, Warren had found himself chasing a serial rapist and murderer, and embroiled in a cold case that had soon become all too personal. That investigation had led to the resolution of many of the issues surrounding the death of Warren's father when he was a teenager, but had led to new and unexpected betrayals.

When he had been interviewed for the role, Warren had made it clear that he wanted to use his time at Middlesbury to segue from an active Senior Investigating Officer to the more managerial role that a senior officer such as a DCI would typically fulfil. Grayson, it turned out, was more than happy to pass over anything investigative to Warren, assigning him as SIO to everything that came their way. Grayson, for his part, spent much of his time down at Welwyn.

On a good day, Warren was grateful that his Superintendent shielded him and his team from much of the administrative side of policing; on a bad day, Warren wished the man would do a bit less schmoozing, play a little less golf and actually get his hands dirty, instead of simply taking all the credit for the team's hard work.

That aside, there was one aspect of the job that Grayson could keep to himself. Unfortunately, that wasn't going to be possible today. With a sigh, Warren slipped on his best jacket, checked his hair in the mirror, and headed for the car park.

He hated press conferences.

Chapter 13

'I've been going through all of the past reports on the system that mention the abbey,' Rachel Pymm had a list in her hand covered in a multitude of different coloured fluorescent markers. For the briefest of moments, Warren had a flashback of Gary Hastings; despite the man's expertise with a computer, he'd still liked nothing more than a ream of paper covered in coloured pen.

He swallowed the lump in his throat. 'Take me through what you've got, Rachel.'

The press conference had been relatively brief, with little in the way of details. Doubtless the tabloids would focus on the more sensational aspects of the death, but at the moment the team wanted to keep the fact that Father Nolan was likely to have been murdered to themselves.

'The abbey and its surroundings are a bit of a crime magnet, so I decided to limit my search to the past five years. I can go back further if you want me to.'

'No, I'll defer to your judgement for the time being.'

'Well most of the offences can be classed as low-level vandalism and anti-social behaviour.'

'From the priests?'

'Less than you'd expect,' she said with a smile. 'It's mostly kids;

reports of graffiti tagging, broken windows, large noisy gatherings etc. They had a spate of damaged headstones about two years ago, and someone tried to nick lead off the chapel roof. They scarpered empty-handed when Rodney Shaw turned up. There's been no real pattern, other than a general increase after dark in the winter and a bit of a spike around October.'

'Well, thanks for looking into that, Rachel.'

'There is one report that might be worth looking at further.'

'Hit me.'

'On the ninth of January this year, Deacon Baines called the police after a man climbed over the wall and came into the grounds, shouting and being abusive.'

'Abusive in what way?'

'It's hard to be sure exactly. He was drunk, possibly high, and likely had mental health issues. The officers involved weren't able to talk him down and he was eventually arrested and stuck in the back of a police van. The report says that by the time he got to the nick he was ready to sleep it off.

'The next morning, he was fit enough to be charged with being drunk and disorderly, but the abbey declined to press charges over the minor damage done to the wall. It was dealt with by caution.'

'What do we know about him?'

'Lucas Furber. 35 years old, of no fixed abode. A couple of historic convictions for drugs, but nothing recent.' She passed across a headshot, taken in custody. Furber looked younger than his stated age, and poorly nourished. His skin was blotchy with acne, and his dark beard was straggly and matted, as greasy as his long hair. The bags under his bloodshot, blue eyes were like dark, purple bruises. The end of his nose was reddened. Drug use or a cold?

'Hmm, it could be just what it seems,' said Warren, 'but I'd like to know what he was ranting about. Did he know Father Nolan or was it aimed at someone else at the abbey? Was it a general dislike of the church, or had he just read the latest Dan Brown novel? Or was it something else, or nothing at all? We should definitely try to eliminate him. See if you can track him down. In the meantime, Deacon Baines was the one who confronted him. Let's see if he can tell us a bit more.'

* * *

Deacon Baines did remember the incident, when Warren called him.

'Ah, yes, that poor young man, clearly a very disturbed individual. Such a shame we couldn't help him more.'

'Can you tell me what happened?'

'Nothing too exciting, as I recall. It was late evening, shortly after we'd finished for the day. The last visitors had gone and the main gates had been locked. One of the sales assistants in the gift shop spotted somebody climbing over the wall as she walked back to her car – close to where those young people climbed over Friday night. We really need to get those spikes replaced, but there isn't any money.'

'And then what happened?'

'She phoned Rodney Shaw, who called me as he went to confront the man.'

Shaw again; it could be a coincidence. Nevertheless, Warren scribbled the man's name down on his pad.

'The reports said he was abusive.'

'Yes, he was being foul-mouthed and shouting at Rodney, who was trying to calm him down. When he saw me, he picked up a stick and started waving it about. That's when we called the police.'

There had been nothing about violence towards Baines or Shaw in the police report.

'It wasn't really worth mentioning; neither of us were in any danger, we just wanted the young man to get the help he needed. He dropped the stick when the police arrived.'

'Can you tell me what he was shouting about?'

Baines paused. 'Nothing really. This and that, he was clearly disturbed.'

'Can you be more specific?'

'Not really, and I'd rather not repeat the man's language.'

'OK. Thanks for your assistance, Deacon Baines. You're probably right, it was likely nothing.'

Warren hung up.

Baines clearly didn't want to discuss the incident. Until this point, the man had been open and helpful. Why was he suddenly so vague? It also sounded as though the intruder had become more agitated when Baines had arrived upon the scene. Was that significant, or was the man just feeling an increased threat now that there were two men confronting him?

Warren drummed his fingers on the table, before getting up and heading into the main office.

'Rachel, any luck tracking down Lucas Furber?'

'The custody report said that Furber was going to the Middlesbury Outreach Centre when he was released. They might be able to tell us where he is.'

'We'll send someone down there, but before they go, can you track down the arresting officers? It's a long shot, but they may remember what he was shouting about. I'd also like to speak to the person who witnessed him clambering over the wall. Find out who she is and arrange for her to come in.'

'Will do.'

Warren continued his circuit of the office.

'Hutch, what have you found out about our victim?'

'Apparently, Father Nolan was a man of simple tastes,' stated Hutchinson. 'He walked into town a couple of times a week to The Cock and Lion, where he liked a pint and caught the footie on Sky. He was also known to have the odd flutter on the horses.'

'Could he have had a gambling problem?'

'There's nothing in his bank accounts to suggest that he had any issues, but he could have been using cash. We don't know

66

where he placed his bets, so we'll need to wear out some shoe leather,' said Sutton. Warren remembered his conversation with Mags Richardson about the missing cash from the gift shop takings. Could there be a link?

Warren pictured his bulging in-tray. The arresting officers for Lucas Furber had clocked off, so he wasn't expecting a call before the next day.

'Leave it with me.' He moved onto the next desk.

'Moray? Fancy some fresh air?'

Chapter 14

Walk a few minutes from Middlesbury Abbey and the fairly affluent neighbourhood overlooking the historic ruins soon turns into a far less salubrious area. Father Nolan's favoured pub, The Cock and Lion, occupied the corner of Hanover Street and Tudor Avenue.

Ruskin described it as a typical 'old man's pub'; warm beer, cheap food and football on the TV. The sort of place where you could make a pint of bitter and a newspaper last all afternoon and nobody minded. Warren tried not to feel slighted; he rather liked the look of the place.

The landlady, a friendly woman in her mid-thirties with a West Country accent, didn't need to think twice before confirming that Father Nolan had been a regular. She shook her head. 'So sad. Suicide, they said in the paper.'

News that they were now investigating a murder had not yet been released to the public; Warren wanted a couple more days before the killer was tipped off that their attempts to cover up the killing had failed.

She shuddered. 'And what a way to go.'

'How well did you know Father Nolan?'

'Not very well, he was pretty quiet.' She tipped her chin towards a corner table, strategically placed to give the best view of the large TV opposite. 'He'd usually sit there and either watch the footie or read the newspaper. He'd say hello and make polite conversation, but wasn't exactly a chatterbox. To be honest, I wouldn't know what to say. I mean what do you talk about with a priest? I failed GCSE RE and have barely been inside a church since my first Holy Communion.'

'Did he speak to anyone else?' asked Warren.

'Not really. Most of the regulars knew him, and he'd express an opinion on whatever match they were watching, but he mostly sat on his own. Once or twice he came down here with other priests, but not often.'

'I don't suppose you noticed any change in his mood, recently?' asked Ruskin.

'You mean, like if he was suicidal?'

'It probably wouldn't be that obvious,' cautioned Warren.

She thought for a moment before apologizing. 'I just didn't know him well enough.'

'What did he usually drink?' said Ruskin.

'He'd usually have a go of whatever guest beer we had in, otherwise whatever bitter we have on tap.'

'And was he a big drinker?'

She laughed. 'I wish. Two pints was about his limit, and a packet of cheese and onion crisps if he was feeling peckish.'

'Would any of your regulars be likely to have noticed anything?'

She thought for a moment. 'Hard to say. I can ask around if you like.'

'We'd appreciate that,' said Ruskin.

'Why don't you come back for a drink in a couple of days and I'll let you know what I've heard?'

Warren hid a smile, as Ruskin politely deflected the offer and passed over a card with his number.

'Blimey Moray, and you weren't even in uniform,' teased Warren as they stepped back out onto the street.

The burly Scot shrugged. 'Not exactly my type. And I'm spoken for, remember.'

'Let her down gently.'

* * *

If, as Hutchinson had suggested, Father Nolan liked to place the odd bet before his pint, he didn't have far to walk.

There was something especially sad about a bookmaker's on a weekday afternoon, decided Warren, as they left the third shop in a street barely two hundred metres long. The woman behind the reinforced glass partition hadn't recognised Father Nolan's photograph. Neither had any of the punters, although most of them – scruffy men of varying ages – had barely been able to tear their eyes away from the galloping horses on the banks of wall-mounted TVs, or shift their attention from the ubiquitous fixed-odds betting terminals gobbling money at a rate far faster than the player could possibly earn it.

'They're like a bloody cancer,' muttered Ruskin, as they walked the twenty paces to the next establishment. According to Google Maps, there were another four within half a mile of their current location.

'You won't get any argument from me,' agreed Warren. 'They're just a tax on the poor and desperate.' He waved his hand vaguely towards the surrounding streets. 'Most of the folks around here haven't got a pot to piss in, yet these big companies can set up shops opposite each other and there's still enough business to go around. Tells you everything you need to know about their ethics and in whose favour the odds are stacked.'

'What is a bloke of working age doing in a bookie in the middle of the day on a Tuesday anyway?' asked Ruskin.

'I think it's fair to say that if you are in that position, life isn't going to plan.'

The two officers finally found what they were looking for in the fourth bookie they visited. So far, almost all of the main chains had been represented in a single stretch of road, with the remainder all within easy walking distance.

The inside of the shop was just a variation on the others they'd already been to. The wall to the left was covered in flat-screen TVs, some showing live horse racing, others a constantly updating series of betting odds and news flashes. The wall opposite was papered with pages from the *Racing Post*, with desk space below for gamblers to complete the pre-printed betting slips using one of the stubby blue biros. Unlike banks, the shop didn't feel the need to secure the pens to the desk with a chain, simply supplying containers filled with them. Probably a reflection of the profits made by a typical bookie compared to major high-street banks, Warren thought, his cynicism towards the betting industry having risen steadily over the past half hour.

For those unwilling to miss valuable gambling time by hand-delivering their slip to the assistants safely locked away in their reinforced glass cubicles, bets could be placed directly onto a computer terminal. And if studying form and actually awaiting the outcome for a race was too much, then each of the four fixed odds betting terminals would happily swallow money at a rate of £300 per minute. It was clear to see why they placed a chair in front of the machines.

The person behind the till, a man in his early twenties with a name badge saying 'Martin', nodded as soon as they passed the glossy photograph to him.

'Oh yes, I recognise him. He was a regular.'

'How regular?' asked Warren.

'Probably about twice a week. I work here most afternoons, after lectures finish. He used to come in late afternoon, then head off for a pint.'

'Was he a big gambler?'

The man paused. 'Look, do you have a warrant or something? I'm not sure I can just give out information about customers without their permission. You know, data protection and all that.

My manager is on his lunch break, perhaps you can call back later?'

'Father Nolan's dead,' said Warren, his eyes flicking towards the copy of the *Middlesbury Reporter* sitting on the desk next to the cashier; a different, but still recognisable, picture of Father Nolan took up half of the front page.

The man followed his gaze, then looked back at the photograph. 'Oh... shit, that was him? Guess it doesn't matter, then.'

'What sort of a punter was he?' repeated Ruskin.

The teller glanced over his shoulder, as if expecting his manager to suddenly materialise, then lowered his voice.

'Just a bit of a flutter. He'd spend a while reading the *Post* and then put a couple of quid either way on the favourite. He'd stay here for three or four races, if that.'

'So no more than, ten, fifteen quid?'

'Probably about that.'

'Did he pay by cash or card?'

'Cash.'

'Was he lucky?'

'No more or less than anyone, I'd say.'

'When was the last time you saw him?'

'Probably about a week ago. I had wondered why I hadn't seen him for a while. I never thought... shit. Burnt himself to death, they said. Poor bastard.'

'Did you notice anything different about him? A change of mood, perhaps?'

'Nothing, but he never really said much. He was polite, and he'd enquire after my health, but it was just chit-chat you know? I can't say I knew him.'

'Was he friendly with any of the other regulars?'

Martin snorted. 'It's not really that sort of place.' He discreetly pointed towards a man of about twenty, wearing a baseball cap, a rolled-up cigarette behind his ear, loading money into a gambling machine. He lowered his voice even more. 'Take that guy. Has two kids and still lives at home with his mum. You can tell when he's had his dole money because he goes and gets his rings back from the pawnbrokers. He won't be wearing them by the end of the week. I only know about him because his brother's the same and I overhear them talking sometimes. You try not to judge, but the guy's a complete failure and he knows it.' The young bookmaker sighed. 'To be honest, this place is pretty depressing. I'm only here because the money's better than stacking shelves and I'm doing an accountancy degree. I can't wait to leave.

'Customers like Father Nolan, who just come in for a flutter and know when to stop are pretty rare. "When the fun stops, stop", the adverts say.' His laughter was mirthless, as he angled his chin towards another customer. 'The fun stopped for most of these guys years ago.'

Dressed the same as the youth at the gambling machine, the man could easily have been forty years older. His face was a mass of deep creases, and his half-open mouth, with its tongue stuck out in concentration, had less teeth than his right hand had fingers. At his feet, the thin plastic of a white carrier bag did nothing to hide the two unopened cans of extra-strength lager, or the two others crushed in the bottom.

'Take that bloke over there. He self-excluded from here for six months last year; broke down in tears as I helped him fill in the form. Reckons he sold his grandkids' Christmas presents. It took three attempts to get him to bring in a passport photo; he knew he should do it, but his heart wasn't in it. I tried to get him to do it for the full five years, but he just said he needed to get back on track. Thing is, I'd still see him coming out of the shop across the way, so what was the point? As soon as the ban expired he was straight back in here. Prefers the atmosphere, apparently.'

'Did Father Nolan try and offer any, I don't know, pastoral care to customers?' asked Warren.

'No, he pretty much kept himself to himself. To be honest, I doubt it would be received very well. I don't think he ever really spoke to anyone.' He paused. 'Actually no, tell a lie, a few weeks

73

ago, he was in here a bit later than usual, and he recognised one of the regular after work crowd. The guy seemed a bit surprised to see him here. A bit embarrassed, actually.'

'Do you know the man's name?'

The young man's face screwed up, 'No, sorry, I can't remember. I haven't seen him since. I think he was a bit ashamed to be seen in here. A pity really, he was one of our regulars. Not a great judge of form, if you get my drift.'

'Can you be more precise about when you saw him?'

'After the new year, maybe a month ago?'

'Can you describe him?'

The man glanced upwards, as if the answers were written on the ceiling.

'Middle-aged, grey hair, white. Skinny build, I guess. Sorry.'

'What about his clothing?'

'Jeans, T-shirt. Sometimes he wore a fleece. Green, I think. Sorry, I'd know him if I saw him, but like I said, he hasn't been in since.'

'Well, thank you for your time, Martin. If you remember anything else, please call me on this number.' This time Warren handed over his card.

As they headed out, Martin suddenly called out, 'I've just remembered, he had a name badge on with the logo from the abbey. That must have been where he knew the priest from.'

'Can you remember what the name badge said?' Warren held his breath. If Martin couldn't recall the name, he'd ask him to come down the station and look at some headshots.

The young teller suddenly clicked his fingers. 'Got it, I remember now because you don't see that name very often. I guess it was because of that old comedy, you know, *Only Horses…*'

'*Only Fools and Horses?*' asked Warren.

'Yeah, Rodney was his name.'

* * *

'What are the odds that two different people called Rodney are at the heart of the same investigation?' asked Warren.

The question was rhetorical, but Ruskin couldn't resist suggesting that they ask the next bookie that they entered.

According to Google, there were several more bookmakers within walking distance for a reasonably fit older man, including more branches of chains that they had already visited. None of them recognised the photo of Father Nolan.

'Should we ask if anyone recognises Rodney Shaw?' asked Ruskin.

'No, let's keep it to ourselves for now. If word gets back to Shaw that we've been asking questions about him, it may spook him. Besides, I doubt we'll get much out of them without a warrant and it's still looking a bit circumstantial at the moment.'

'It seems a bit strange that Father Nolan was so open about going to the bookmaker's. Isn't gambling a sin?'

'According to what I've read on the internet, apparently not. As long as it is a true game of chance, and there's no cheating, then gambling itself isn't prohibited. Besides, if they took a blanket approach to banning gambling, church fetes would make a lot less money, and the manufacturers of raffle tickets would go out of business.'

Ruskin smiled politely, but Warren could see the young man was troubled.

'I can't believe the government doesn't regulate the industry more. Surely the taxes aren't worth the suffering it causes? I mean, fancy selling your grandkids' Christmas presents.'

'Like I said before, it's a tax on the poor and desperate. Cheap business rates aren't the only reason these places set up shop in the poorer parts of town, rather than the wealthier.'

Wednesday 25th February

Chapter 15

PCs Harper and Ballard had been the officers that arrested Lucas Furber after he'd climbed into the abbey grounds.

'Yeah, I remember it,' PC Harper said when Warren called him mid-morning, after dropping Susan back home from their clinic appointment.

The harvesting of Susan's eggs had been scheduled for 9 a.m. that morning, precisely thirty-seven hours after Susan had injected herself with the triggering hormones. Warren had also supplied a sample. The whole procedure had taken far less time than they anticipated, and before they knew it, the two of them found themselves sitting in the carpark feeling almost shell-shocked.

'I still can't believe it,' said Susan. 'Somewhere in that building is an incubator where our future child is forming.'

Of course, both of them knew that this was only the latest step in a sequence fraught with uncertainty and doubt. Much could go wrong over the next few days; there was no guarantee of success, even having got this far. The next morning's phone call might tell them that none of the eggs retrieved that morning had been successfully fertilised.

But now wasn't the time for such thoughts. Susan took another bite of the sticky pastry Warren had bought from the clinic's canteen. It was hardly her usual breakfast, but she hadn't eaten or drunk anything since the previous night and she was ravenous. Besides which, she deserved it. Warren just wished he could do more; could take a bigger role in what they were going through.

Warren forced his attention back to the matter at hand.

'He was certainly the worse for wear,' continued Harper. 'Definitely drink, probably drugs, but he was also clearly mentally ill.'

'And who was there when you turned up?'

Warren heard the rustling of paper in the background.

'The complainant was Deacon Gabriel Baines; he was the one who called it in. Furber was there, obviously, and the groundsman, Mr Rodney Shaw. There was also a Miss Bethany Rice who'd originally seen Furber climbing over the wall.'

'Can you remember what Furber was shouting about?'

There was a silence at the end of the line, before Harper replied.

'I can't remember the details exactly, it was mostly stream-of-consciousness. He clearly had something against the church. I remember he called them a bunch of hypocrites at one point.'

'Any indication why he may have said that?'

'No, most of what came out of his mouth was just incoherent shouting. I haven't heard the F-word used so much since I went to see Billy Connelly live. Unfortunately, he lacked the Big Yin's eloquence or wit. Mind you, I was too busy trying to decide if pulling my baton was necessary or would likely escalate things to pay that much attention. PC Ballard might remember, she's usually better at engaging them in conversation than me.' His voice became muffled again as he moved the telephone handset away from his mouth and handed it over.

'Yes, sir, I remember him. Certainly drunk, probably high and definitely not in touch with reality.'

'Can you remember what he said?'

'Mostly a string of F words and C words. And something about them being hypocrites.'

78

'Nothing else?'

'No… oh hang on, he shouted something at Deacon Baines. Something about forgiveness of sins.'

'You mean he was asking for forgiveness?'

'No, I don't think it was for him. I think it was aimed at Deacon Baines.'

* * *

'The metal petrol can from the scene of the fire has been positively identified as one stored in the groundsman's tool shed. He used it for the lawn mower,' said Andy Harrison, his voice echoey over the briefing room's speakerphone.

'I've sent a sample off for petrol branding, to check that the fuel in the can was the same kind that was used to start the fire. We found three different sets of prints on the can. One set match the head groundsman, Rodney Shaw, who we already had in the system from his previous convictions, another set corresponds to the prints taken from the deceased's personal belongings.'

'Suggesting that Father Nolan handled the can at some point, fitting the narrative that he did pour petrol over himself,' interrupted Warren.

'Yes. The final set are currently unknown, but we are waiting exclusionary prints from the young lad who is apprenticed to Shaw. He mows the lawn as well, and presumably fills the mower with petrol when needed.'

'If the scene was staged, that implies that the killer made Father Nolan hold the petrol can, I'm assuming that he didn't help mow the lawn,' said Sutton.

'Father Nolan did work in the abbey gardens,' interrupted Hutchinson. 'He helped tend their vegetable patch. The tools are stored in the same shed as the lawnmower.'

'In that case, he might just have moved the can out of the way of his tools and transferred his prints that way,' suggested Warren.

'That might also explain why his fingerprints are on the key to the tool shed padlock found at the scene,' said Ruskin.

Warren tapped his teeth thoughtfully.

'We're pretty certain that it was murder staged as suicide. If the unknown prints match the apprentice groundsman, then he has an alibi. He's seventeen and he was at home with his parents and siblings in front of the TV. That leaves only Rodney Shaw or an unknown killer who took care not to leave his or her own prints at the scene.'

'If the killer wasn't a regular user of the tool shed, he could have left trace evidence behind when collecting the petrol. The shed doesn't have electricity, so the killer may have been stumbling around in the dark,' said Harrison.

'OK, take some prints and do a preliminary search of the premises. We'll work up a list of everyone who legitimately used the shed and make sure we have prints and DNA. The tool shed is a short walk from the chapel, so look for footprints. Cross-reference anything you find with the findings from Father Nolan's room. If we can work out the sequence of events that night, we'll be a step closer to finding who did it.'

'We'll do what we can, but I'm not sure what you're expecting to find, sir. It's been a few days now, and not all the pathways were locked down immediately.' Harrison's tone was cautionary.

'I know. Give it your best shot, Andy. Aside from the chapel and Father Nolan's room, the shed's the one place that we know the killer is likely to have been.'

Chapter 16

'Moray, fancy a trip to a homeless shelter?' called Warren.

'You've seen what I earn then?'

'Funny man. We need to interview the locals at the Middlesbury Outreach Centre, to see what else we can find out about Lucas Furber.'

'I'll get my coat.'

Tony Sutton sidled up next to Warren. 'Can I have a quick word, Boss? In private.'

'Of course. Moray, I'll be with you in a moment.'

'What's the problem, Tony?' asked Warren when the door closed.

Sutton looked uncomfortable.

'It's about Moray.'

Warren was surprised.

'Is there a problem? I thought he was doing really well. He's on track to complete his probationary training well within the two years, and his paperwork is in a far better state than mine was when I was at his stage.'

'He is. That's the problem.'

'You've lost me.'

Sutton sighed. 'Sir, you're a DCI. Why are you traipsing around bookies and homeless shelters with a DC?'

'I've always been hands-on, Tony, and willing to get out of the office, you know that. It's what I like about Middlesbury, most officers my rank spend half their time in meetings.'

'That's not what I meant.'

'Moray's a probationer, he's still learning the ropes. He'll be a fine officer one day and I want him to get the support he needs. I learnt a lot from my own DCI, as I'm sure you did.' Warren paused, as he remembered the history of their respective senior officers, but decided the point still stood. 'Look, this is a fast-moving investigation, with a lot of different threads. If you think Moray would benefit from spending a bit more time working with Hutch or Mags, or even you, then I'll take your advice, you've done a lot more mentoring than I have recently.'

Sutton sighed, he could see that Warren either wasn't getting the hint, or quite possibly was ignoring the uncomfortable truth.

'Chief…' he started, before pausing and starting again, 'Warren. Moray isn't Gary.'

Warren felt as if he'd been slapped.

'What do you mean?'

'I mean that you can't keep him wrapped in cotton wool.'

Warren was dumbfounded; Sutton ploughed on quickly.

'What happened to Gary affected us all, I still miss him every day. I spent twenty minutes comforting Mags after we marked his birthday last month, and Hutch wasn't much better. I can only imagine how you must feel, sitting next to him as it happened—'

'That's right, you can only imagine, and I'd rather you didn't,' snapped Warren.

'It wasn't your fault,' insisted Sutton. 'Professional Standards know that. I know that, as does everyone in that office, even Karen knows it.'

'I think you've said enough, *DI Sutton*.'

Sutton ignored him.

'You can't undo what happened to Gary by being overprotective of Moray. He needs room to grow. He may be a probationary

DC, but he was a very well-regarded uniform constable before he transferred over.'

'I said that's enough!'

'He's more than capable of asking a few questions in an outreach centre. And look at the bloody size of him, he can take on two normal people and not break a sweat.'

'Gary Hastings had a black belt in *Jiu-jitsu*, and that was fuck all use in the end.'

The moment he said it, Warren wished he could take the words back.

'I'll see myself out,' said Sutton, without waiting to be dismissed.

The thin partitioned wall rattled as the door slammed behind him.

Warren slumped into his chair, anger coursing through him.

How dare Sutton speak to him like that? Not since the two men had butted heads when Warren first transferred to Middlesbury, had the two men argued in such a way. Matters of friendship aside, Warren was still Sutton's superior officer. He knew that if he'd spoken to Bob Windermere like that back when he was an inspector, he'd not only have ended up with a written warning on his file, he'd have found himself giving crime-prevention presentations to little old ladies at the local community centre.

He stared through the window into the office beyond.

After Gary's death, they'd rearranged the layout. It was a small gesture, but nobody would have been comfortable taking his old desk, next to his girlfriend Karen Hardwick, on medical leave since his death and now entering the last few weeks of her pregnancy. On the other hand, leaving his desk empty would have been just as bad, not to mention impractical.

And so one evening, when the number of people in the office was at a minimum, Tony Sutton and Warren had rearranged everything. John Grayson, upon hearing the sound of scraping furniture had emerged from his own office. He'd said nothing, just put down his cup of coffee, rolled up his sleeves and given them a hand.

Gary's death had hit them all hard. In Warren's opinion, the small, close-knit nature of the team at Middlesbury was one of its biggest strengths, but it also meant that the loss of a team member was perhaps more closely felt than it might be otherwise.

That was the view of the counsellor Warren had been assigned following Gary's death. The nightmares had decreased in frequency in recent months, but he'd had another the night before – the third since the fire at the abbey. Should he report them? The counselling had been helpful, no question, but did he really have the time? He was already taking personal time out to accompany Susan to the hospital. There was a strict no phones and do not disturb rule at the counsellor's office. Could he afford to be uncontactable during such a critical and fast-moving period of the case?

He thought back to his last session. He'd been warned not to ignore other signs of PTSD. Was that why he was being overprotective towards Moray Ruskin? It wasn't hard to see the parallels between Gary and Ruskin, his direct replacement. Was he letting his guilt towards what had happened to Gary Hastings colour his interactions with Ruskin?

It was hardly fair; so far, the man had impressed Warren and everybody else with his competence. He still had plenty to learn, as his sometimes naïve questions indicated, but did he require the level of direct supervision that he'd been receiving? Particularly, did he need the second most senior officer in the building breathing down his neck? Worse, was it compromising the effectiveness of the team? He and Ruskin could have visited all those bookmakers in half the time if they'd split up; that sort of routine enquiry was far more suited to a constable – detective or otherwise – than the Senior Investigating Officer.

When Warren emerged from his office, the rest of the team were busy. He spied Ruskin sitting next to Rachel Pymm, discussing something on her screen.

'Moray?'

The bearded Scotsman looked up.

'Something's come up. Are you OK to go visit the Middlesbury Outreach Centre on your own?'

'Sure, no problem.'

The eagerness with which the young detective jumped to his feet confirmed everything that Sutton had said. Warren looked over and caught the man's eye. He gave a small nod. After a pause, Sutton nodded back.

Enough said.

Chapter 17

Moray Ruskin pulled himself out of the tiny Fiat 500, the car lifting slightly as he removed his eighteen-stone bulk. Alex had bought the car before meeting Ruskin and it was definitely not suited for someone of his size. Unfortunately, Ruskin's own car was having its service and MOT, so he was stuck with his partner's for the next couple of days.

The Middlesbury Outreach Centre, known also as the Phoenix Centre, had been in its current location for over thirty years, according to the plaque outside. Sandwiched like an ugly duckling between newly completed luxury apartment blocks and prime office space, Ruskin wondered how much money they'd turned down from developers for the land it stood on. He and Alex had looked at buying a so-called 'affordable' one-bedroom flat in the new complex and decided to hold off until one of them won the lottery.

Ruskin's parents never failed to mention how cheap houses were back in Scotland whenever he rang home. However, despite the pair meeting at Dundee University, Alex had always planned to move back to England to take advantage of the increased job opportunities near London. As living in the capital was a complete non-starter financially, they'd compromised on Middlesbury, barely thirty minutes by fast train from central London, and where Ruskin had – in the words of his parents – turned his back on his university education and joined the police. His parents still didn't believe that these days the police was a largely graduate profession.

The inside of the outreach centre was painted a soothing blue, the walls covered in pin boards advertising services ranging from substance abuse counselling to HIV testing, free adult education classes, and support groups for victims of abusive relationships.

The reception desk was behind reinforced glass, a bank of monitors showing alternating views from cameras situated inside and outside. A sternly worded sign warned that verbal or physical abuse of staff, volunteers or other users would not be tolerated, with the police called if necessary. The caution was repeated in a half-dozen languages. The ubiquitous red and white No Smoking signs had been supplemented with similar prohibitions on alcohol, drugs and weapons.

Despite all this, the door to the reception desk had been propped open with a wastepaper basket and the place had a relaxed, pleasant vibe to it. Music came from a nearby open door, along with the clack of pool balls.

'Hello officer, how can I help you?'

The young woman behind the reception desk wore a dark-blue headscarf and a badge identifying her as 'Nadia – counsellor'.

'That obvious, eh?'

'Practice. We haven't reported anything, and there's only one of you, so I'm guessing you aren't here to arrest anyone?'

'No, just a chat about one of your clients, if you don't mind.'

'We're quite strict about what we say without a warrant,' she warned. 'We need to be otherwise our clients won't trust us.' She paused. 'I'm due a break. Let's go somewhere a bit more discreet.'

The staffroom was locked with a mechanical keypad, so Ruskin had to hold both plastic cups of coffee as Nadia let them in.

'Who can I help you with?'

'Lucas Furber.'

She frowned slightly. 'We don't always know our clients' full names. Do you have a photo?'

Ruskin passed over a copy.

'Oh yes, I know him.'

'He was arrested by Middlesbury Police for being drunk and disorderly back in January. The arresting officers were concerned that there may be mental health issues.'

'Well, before we go any further, you should know that I'm not prepared to discuss Lucas' mental or physical health without a court order.'

'That's fair enough, I just want to talk to him. Do you know where I can find him?'

'To be honest, I haven't seen him for a while.'

'It's really important that I speak to him. Can you think of any places that he might be?'

She pulled her lip. 'The last time I saw him was before Christmas. He said he'd got a room in Purbury Hostel. I've no idea if he is still there, they are quite strict about behaviour and have zero tolerance for drugs and alcohol.'

'And you think that might have been a problem for him?'

'I wouldn't be surprised,' she sighed. 'Like I said, the last time he visited it was at the end of December, and he was clearly full of the Christmas spirit if you get my drift. We don't allow drinking or drug-taking on site, but we're realists, especially that time of year, we know that they may have been drinking or using before they arrive here. We usually have a quiet word and if that fails tell them to go home and sleep it off. As long as they aren't violent or abusive, all is forgiven next time they turn up. It normally works; one of our regulars gets sent home about once a month. He always comes back the next day to apologise. Usually with a bunch of flowers he's pinched from somebody's front garden.'

'But Lucas didn't come back?'

'No. To be honest, it wasn't a big deal at first. He was apparently a bit noisy and kept on trying to start a sing-song, which was annoying everyone. Reverend Billy was upstairs and he came down to have a word and Lucas called him a… well, I'm not going to use that word. It all got a bit heated and in the end we threatened to call the police if he didn't leave. He hasn't been here since.'

'I assume Reverend Billy is a priest?'

'Baptist minister, actually. I'm told that's a bit different.'

'Would I be able to speak to him?'

'I don't see why not, I think he's doing a literacy class.' She glanced at the clock. 'Wait here, he'll probably be down in a few minutes.'

* * *

Reverend Billy was a short man in his fifties with a firm handshake and a ready smile. His sweater, a bright red and green affair, was almost literally eye-watering and clashed horribly with his purple shirt. He wore a white dog collar.

'I lost a bet with a parishioner, and I have to wear this jumper for a whole week, unless I'm in church.'

Ruskin liked him already.

'It was a shame about Lucas. He was a troubled young man, but there was a lot of promise beneath all that anger.'

'Do you know why he was so angry?'

'Sadly, no. He didn't speak to me very often. I got the feeling that this—' he pointed to his collar '—made him uncomfortable.'

'Do you get that a lot?'

'Hardly ever to be honest. Most of our clients are happy to speak to me, particularly when I make it clear that I've no intention of talking about religion to them unless they want me to.'

'So what happened the day that Lucas was kicked out?'

Reverend Billy winced.

'That's not really what happened. Lucas had clearly been

drinking before he turned up mid-afternoon. The weather was quite poor, so a few of our regulars were in here sheltering from the rain, watching the TV, reading the paper or using the computers. Lucas was very hyper and he put the radio on really loud and started dancing to it.

'One of the lads asked him to turn it down as he was trying to watch the news. Lucas turned the volume up. The song was Band Aid's "Do they know it's Christmas?", so he started singing along and then grabbed one of the women on the computers and tried to make her dance with him.

'By the time I got downstairs, he was standing in the middle of the floor shouting that it was "effing Christmas" and we should all be celebrating. Another ten seconds and I reckon he was going to get lamped by someone.'

'So you asked him to leave?'

'Not immediately, no. I tried to settle him down a bit, but he called me a C U Next Tuesday. You know, I hear a lot of bad language here – I've got a bit of a potty mouth myself at times – but nobody has ever called me that before. That's when I asked him to leave. I told him he could come back the next day if he sobered up and behaved himself.'

'How did he take that?'

'He started shouting that "we're all same" and that we'd all "burn in hell". I lied and told him I had called the police, and that was when he finally left, after kicking a couple of chairs over.'

'Any idea what he meant by that?'

'I've really no idea. I like to think it was the drink and the drugs talking, but you know what they say, "*in vino veritas*", so who knows what he was going on about?'

'Any idea where he went after that?'

'No idea. If you do find him, detective, can you let him know that there are no hard feelings and that he's welcome back here?'

Ruskin assured the man that he would, before heading back to the car.

Somebody had keyed a scratch along almost the full length of the left wing. He looked around at the empty street. The arcs of the CCTV cameras above the door didn't cover the car. He sighed. Alex would not be happy.

Chapter 18

Warren had to wait until Bethany Rice's father was free, before she was able to attend the station for an interview. A few weeks shy of her eighteenth birthday, Bethany Rice was a sixth-form student who worked at the abbey on weekends. Strictly speaking, she didn't need an appropriate adult present, since she wasn't under arrest and was seventeen, but Warren had learnt to choose his battles wisely, and he needed her cooperation.

Apparently her father had been present when she was originally interviewed about Father Nolan's death. He had reportedly been unhappy about her having her fingerprints taken for exclusionary purposes, and had insisted on going over her witness statement before she signed it, whilst helpfully explaining the rules regarding the retention of biological samples to the twenty-year veteran constable conducting the interview. The man had clearly been on Wikipedia before bringing his daughter in.

'She's doing really well, at school,' her father had told Warren as they'd walked down to the interview suite, clearly flattered on his daughter's behalf that she was being interviewed by a DCI. For his part, Warren was already wishing he'd passed her off to somebody else, but he had been free and wanted her interviewed sooner rather than later.

By the time they reached the interview suite, Warren was already fully up-to-speed about the medical school interviews that Rice had recently been for, and the work experience at Addenbrooke's hospital that she'd completed, even though her school hadn't been as supportive as they could have been and they'd been forced to engage a tutor to help compensate for the poor teaching. Throughout this, Rice had said nothing, mostly looking at her shoes.

Things did not improve when Warren started the interview. Mr Rice had clearly assumed that his daughter had been called in as a vital witness in the death of Father Nolan. It then transpired that Rice hadn't told her father about the intruder in the abbey grounds.

'If I'd had any idea that the site was so unsecure, I never would have let my daughter work there.'

This last comment seemed to be aimed squarely at Warren, although quite what the man thought he could do about it was unclear. It also explained why Rice had chosen not to share the incident with her father.

'I'd just finished my shift in the gift shop and I was walking back to the staff car park,' said Rice, making eye contact for the first time.

'We bought her a car after she passed her test first time,' interjected Mr Rice. 'Much safer than letting her catch that bus, especially when it's dark.'

'Carry on, Bethany,' said Warren, pointedly ignoring the man's interruption.

'I saw somebody climbing over the wall along from the main entrance, in front of the graveyard. He sort of flopped over and hit the ground with a really loud thump, so I went over to see if he was OK.'

Next to her, her father's eyes bulged.

'You went over?'

'Yes, I thought he might have hurt himself.' Her tone was defiant.

'But he could have had a knife or anything,' spluttered her father.

'Well, he didn't. I asked him what he was doing and when he didn't answer, I told him I was going to call security, so he'd better leave now.'

'What did he say?'

'He called me an interfering bitch and told me to fuck off.'

Whether her father's shock was at the words that had been aimed at his daughter, or the matter-of-fact way that she repeated them wasn't clear. Regardless, Warren had to ask him to let his daughter continue her story uninterrupted.

'I called Rodney and told him what was happening. It took a couple of minutes for him to get there, so I kept the man talking. He was obviously drunk or on drugs, but I think he was also a bit confused and disturbed.'

Mr Rice looked horrified. Warren was impressed at her peace of mind. She'd do well in a busy A&E department on a Friday night.

'Anyway, I managed to get him to tell me his name and asked him why he was here.'

'What did he say?'

'He was a bit unclear, but he kept on saying he wanted to speak to the priests and ask them why they did it.'

'Why they did what?'

'I don't know. Rodney turned up and he got really agitated. He started shouting, "you all knew about it" and "why didn't you do anything?"'

'Then what happened?'

'Rodney started trying to calm him down, asking him why he was here, but he got really abusive, shouting and calling names. Rodney unlocked the front gate and told him that the police were on the way, so he should leave.

'The man started to walk up the path towards the house, so Rodney stood in his way. There was a load of fence posts by the gate, and Rodney picked one up and he told the man to "fuck off, or he'd get some". That was when Gabriel, that's Deacon Baines, arrived.'

There had been nothing in either the arrest report or Baines' statement about Shaw brandishing a weapon.

'What happened when Deacon Baines arrived?'

'He also tried to cool things down, but the man kept on saying "you're one of them". He picked up a branch and I thought Rodney was going to attack him. Then the police arrived, which seemed to quieten things down a bit. Both Rodney and the man threw their weapons away when the police came in the main gate.'

'What happened when the police came?'

'They tried to reason with him, but it was obvious he was going to end up in the back of the police van.'

'Did he say anything else?'

'Mostly swearing, but when he was being arrested, he did stop and shout specifically at Gabriel and told him to "seek forgiveness for his sins", which seemed a bit weird.'

'Do you have any idea why he shouted that?'

'I don't know. He was clearly a bit mad and off his face on drugs and booze.'

'What did Deacon Baines and Mr Shaw say after the police took the intruder away?'

'Not a lot. Gabriel asked if I was OK, and Rodney offered to give me a lift home if I didn't have my own car. I said "no thanks" because my car was in the staff car park. When I left, Gabriel was telling Rodney how they had to get the wall fixed to stop the nutters getting in and that next time they might not be so lucky.'

'Have there been other incidents like this?'

Rice glanced at her father, who still looked annoyed that he hadn't been told about this before. According to the police report, Bethany Rice had been little more than a passive spectator, her name taken as a witness, but never contacted again. But it seemed that they'd underestimated her importance in the drama. Judging from what he'd seen of her father, he got the feeling that a lot of people underestimated Bethany Rice.

'I don't know if they've had to call the police before, but I heard that somebody was made to leave the abbey grounds a few months ago when he was caught up by the house.'

None of the reports filed previously about trespassers had mentioned anyone getting caught near the house. Was it the same person, or someone else? And why hadn't Baines mentioned it? Despite the man's apparent openness, Warren was starting to suspect that he would not offer any information unless asked directly.

After determining that Rice had nothing else to offer, Warren thanked them both for their time. Mr Rice got up quickly, leaving the interview suite. His daughter lingered. It was clear that she had more to say, and would rather her father didn't hear it.

It wasn't what he expected.

'Are you Mrs Jones' husband?'

Damn. He'd had no idea that she was one of Susan's pupils. He thought for a second, but couldn't think of any obvious conflict of interest.

'Yes. I assume she teaches you biology?'

'Yes.' She glanced over at the door and lowered her voice. 'Ignore what Dad said, Miss is a really good teacher. Even with a tutor, I'm just not, you know—'

'Come on Beth, I need to get back in time for a conference call to New York,' her father called from the corridor outside.

'That's very kind of you to say.' Warren could see no harm in passing on that little bit of praise to his wife; he knew she'd be touched.

Rice glanced over her shoulder and lowered her voice even more.

'I'll be eighteen soon. Do the police offer work experience?'

* * *

Purbury Hostel was on the far side of town to the Phoenix Centre. Ruskin decided to park around the corner and walk. The car was out of his direct sight, but hopefully nobody would realise it belonged to him and add to the petty vandalism.

'How can I help you officer?' asked the apparently teenaged security guard in the tiny security cubicle in the lobby of the apartment block. He looked excited; no doubt a visit from the police would be the highlight of his shift.

'Am I wearing a badge or something?' asked Ruskin.

The man shrugged.

Ruskin pushed a copy of Furber's photo under the glass partition.

'Oh yeah, I know him, Lucas. He was here for a few months before Christmas. Managed to get himself kicked out in January.' He lowered his voice conspiratorially. 'Between you and me he probably should have been given the boot before then, but I wasn't going to kick a bloke out before Christmas.'

'Why was he asked to leave?'

'The usual, booze and drugs. They're not supposed to take either in their rooms. Strictly speaking, they shouldn't even smoke in there, but we gave up that fight long ago. I smelt weed a couple of times and told him to knock it on the head, just friendly like, but he wouldn't listen. I couldn't turn a blind eye though when one of the cleaners found a bong in his room.

'So you told him to leave?'

'Yeah, no choice really. There's a waiting list for a room.'

'Any idea where he went?'

'No, I don't usually deal with that side of things, I'm just security, but the manager, Sunil, reckons Lucas got the hump, grabbed his bag and disappeared before we could try and arrange for a place in one of the emergency shelters – not that there are any places these days, but you never know...'

'So he's homeless? Sleeping rough?'

'Probably. You could try one of the homeless shelters, or one of the street teams. Have you tried the Phoenix Centre?'

Ruskin confirmed that he had.

'Not a lot else, I can suggest, sorry.'

Chapter 19

'Results are back from traffic about Rodney Shaw's alibi on the night of the fire.' Mags Richardson was excited. Warren and Sutton hurried over to her desk.

'They picked up his licence plate on numerous ANPR cameras, as well as several CCTV cameras that evening.'

On one of her monitors a detailed street map of Middlesbury was marked with the location of the abbey and Shaw's flat. Blue dots showed the location of junctions with working cameras.

'This is his journey to the abbey after he was called on his mobile phone.' A red dotted line appeared on the map, joining up several blue dots, each of which had a time stamp next to it.

'Well, despite what he claimed when he was interviewed, he clearly wasn't home in front of the news when his phone went off,' said Sutton immediately.

Sure enough, the red dotted line started in the south of the town, with the first sighting of the car on an ANPR camera three and a half miles south east of his flat, eight minutes after he received the call about the fire.

Warren squinted at the map. 'I can't see any way that he could have got to that part of town from his house without going past at least one camera. What time did his car arrive there?'

'He drove there immediately after work.' Richardson clicked the mouse and an irregularly shaped area of the map was shaded in grey. 'All we can say, location-wise, is that his car stayed somewhere within this area for almost the next five hours, from 5.19 p.m. until seven minutes after he was phoned at five past ten.'

'It's a pretty large area,' said Sutton. 'We'll need to narrow it down. Mobile phone records?'

'He's clearly lied about his whereabouts that night, I'd say that is enough justification for a warrant,' said Warren.

'How far is it from the abbey?' asked Ruskin, who'd just arrived back in the office.

'The one-way system increases the journey length, but assuming quiet traffic that time of night, then by car it would take between thirteen and eighteen minutes at normal speed, depending on where he started from within this area. But we know that he didn't use his own car, as it wasn't spotted on cameras again until after he was called back because of the fire,' said Richardson.

'See if any of the other cars that were in that area are related to Shaw,' instructed Warren. 'He could have borrowed a friend's car. Check if his wife has her own car.'

'I'll also get onto the bus companies and cab firms and see if they picked up Shaw,' said Richardson.

'That's if he used public transport,' cautioned Richardson. 'It's only between 1.2 and 1.6 miles as the crow flies and Shaw's a pretty fit man. He would have been able to easily cover that distance between the fire being set and his car re-appearing on the cameras.'

'But why did he park his car there?' asked Ruskin.

'Presumably he didn't want to park too near the abbey in case he was spotted, and his flat was too far to walk from,' said Richardson.

'Probably, but why here specifically? And what was he doing in the almost five hours between him driving there and going to the abbey?' asked Sutton.

'Location data from his mobile phone should help narrow down his exact position. In the meantime, get Rachel to compile a list of local businesses within that area. Knowing his proclivities, he could have spent some time in a local bookie or had some Dutch courage in the pub.'

Thursday 26th February

Chapter 20

It had been over five days since Father Nolan had been set on fire. Unusually, the murder was still being reported as a suicide, with limited information released to the public. The decision to do so had been justified on the grounds that the killer probably assumed that they had got away with it, and would therefore not be on their guard. Hopefully, this would increase the likelihood that they would slip up. How much longer the subterfuge would be allowed to continue was a decision well above Warren's paygrade.

However, although Warren and Grayson ran a tight ship at Middlesbury, the number of seconded officers involved was rising rapidly, increasing the risk of a leak that the death was suspicious. And if the investigators themselves didn't let something slip, how long would it be before members of staff and residents at the abbey started to question the ongoing presence of so many police and forensics officers?

In those five days, a lot had been accomplished, but after the first flurry of activity, the team was starting to get into a routine. It would be unfair to say that they were in a slump, but Warren knew that they could end up that way if he wasn't careful. Fortunately, this morning's briefing had two new, exciting leads.

Warren passed over to Moray Ruskin.

'This is Lucas Furber, a new potential suspect. On January the ninth he gained entry to the abbey grounds and threatened both Deacon Baines and Rodney Shaw. He was clearly intoxicated and may have been suffering from mental health problems.

'Significantly, he seems to have something against religion, specifically Christianity, although we have no evidence either way about his views on other religions. Witnesses reported that he was shouting about them all being "hypocrites". It is also claimed that he accused them of "knowing about it" and "doing nothing" and telling them to "seek forgiveness". We don't know as yet what he was referring to.'

'Are we sure it's specific to religion and not just authority generally, or the world at large?' asked Hutchinson.

'Priests wearing dog collars seem to be a specific trigger for him. Apparently, the confrontation in the abbey grounds escalated significantly when Baines arrived on the scene – the arresting officers have confirmed that his dog collar was visible. A minister at the Middlesbury Outreach Centre told me that Furber seemed uncomfortable when he wore his collar, and that he too had been abused by Furber when he was under the influence. Again, he said that he would "burn in hell."'

'We should look into his past and see if there are any links between him and some of these cases of abuse that are becoming public knowledge,' said Sutton.

Was it Warren's imagination, or did he look satisfied that his stated distrust of the church might actually be justified?

Warren gave himself a mental shake, ashamed at even thinking such a thing.

'Well, he certainly sounds like someone we should be interviewing,' said Richardson. 'Any idea where he is?'

'Unfortunately, no,' replied Ruskin. 'The last reported sighting was early January, when he was kicked out of his accommodation. Assuming he's still in Middlesbury, he's either sleeping rough or using one of the shelters. I've organised a team of community support officers and homeless outreach volunteers to try and track him down.'

'Excellent work, Moray,' said Warren. 'Next up, the groundsman Rodney Shaw. He was already a person of interest given his previous convictions and unconfirmed reports that he was heard arguing with Father Nolan. That wasn't much more than gossip, however a witness in a bookmaker frequented by both men reported an uncomfortable meeting between the two of them; CCTV footage from the bookie is being processed to confirm this. It's possible that Shaw was ashamed to be seen there and might have tried to silence Father Nolan.'

Warren looked around the room.

'So far it's pretty tenuous, but last night Mags found that he was lying about his whereabouts on the night of the fire. It's far too soon to pull him in for questioning yet, we don't want to tip him off, but I want to know what he was doing that night and why he lied about it.'

'Could he and Furber have been working together?' asked Pymm.

'Interesting idea, look into any links between the two men,' said Warren

'Shaw has historic drug convictions, perhaps they know each other that way?' suggested Pymm.

'Maybe,' conceded Warren, 'although witnesses to the confrontation in the abbey grounds gave no indication that they knew each other then. In fact, it seemed to be quite a violent encounter. However, that was nearly two months ago; much can change in that time.'

Chapter 21

'We've been trying to figure out what Rodney Shaw might have been doing during the unaccounted for period between him leaving work on the evening of the fire and his car re-appearing on the ANPR cameras eight minutes after he received the call about the fire and headed back to the abbey.'

Mags Richardson had moved her laptop next to Rachel Pymm's workstation and there was a substantial pile of printouts on the desk between them.

'I'm promised the records from his mobile phone any minute,' interjected Pymm.

'In the meantime,' continued Richardson, 'we've looked at the area within that ANPR dead zone, and for a few streets either side of it. It's not great news, sir. Even in a small town like Middlesbury, there are a lot of homes and businesses in that vicinity that he could have visited. There are twelve public houses, two restaurants, nine fast-food takeaways and two bookmakers. He could even have been getting his car serviced or picking up some dry cleaning. I imagine if he did visit "Nelly's Nails" it wasn't for a manicure.'

'Start canvassing the area if the phone data doesn't give us any more clues,' ordered Warren. 'He lied about his whereabouts in the initial interview, I presume that there was a reason for that, but it doesn't mean he was doing anything we're bothered about. Let's see if anyone can provide an alibi for some of that time so we can discount him.

'Are there any interesting residents in the area that he could have been meeting?'

'Define interesting,' said Pymm, before answering her own question. 'Thirty-eight addresses within that zone have occupants with at least one recordable offence on the PNC. That's a bit above the average for an area of that size in Middlesbury, but it's hardly a den of criminality.

'The data has its limits, though, as it records addresses at the time of the offence. If we decide to go to town on this, we'll need to cross-reference the latest electoral roll data with the PNC, and perhaps even benefits and tax records.'

'File the appropriate requests for that information, but hold off on the analysis unless we get nowhere with the phone records. What type of offences are we talking about?'

'Mostly low-level, or historic, but two properties have received multiple call-outs for domestic violence, another person served a six-month term for assault occasioning actual bodily harm and another resident has been convicted twice for possession of class B drugs with intent to supply, the last offence being eighteen months ago.'

'I presume the domestic violence had no link to Mr Shaw?'

'As far as I can tell. I've had a look at the reports filed and there's no mention of a third party involved.'

'Put them on the bottom of the list then. What about the dealer? Could Shaw be using again?'

'Possible, although if she is his supplier, she's moved up in the world. Both previous convictions were for possessing enough cannabis for several joints. The people she was supplying to were her boyfriend and a couple of friends at university, there was no suggestion that she was earning any money from it, and there's nothing recent.'

106

'Put her to one side and see if she comes back into the picture when we get his mobile phone records. What about the assault?'

'A drunken brawl in a bar in Brighton back in 2007; the defendant broke the victim's jaw and then took a few swings at the bouncers and passers-by, before trying to head butt the arresting officer. Nothing recent or before then.'

'Sounds unlikely, unless Shaw is a friend. What else have you got?'

'I looked at the ANPR records for the cameras surrounding the area for the previous forty-eight hours. Shaw's car doesn't appear during the preceding two days. I've requested records going back further to see if he made the trip regularly. In terms of the cars that left or entered the area within that time, no car both exits and re-enters.'

'So it's unlikely that he borrowed someone else's car to go to the abbey without being seen?'

'Not unless he arranged to leave it somewhere else,' said Pymm.

'What about other cars exiting or entering – could they have dropped him off, or picked him up from near the abbey?'

'Thirty-two cars exited the area within the unaccounted time period. Since he would probably have needed to have arrived at the abbey at least an hour before the fire was set to drug Father Nolan and get him down to the chapel, and assuming he had no accomplice, then we can immediately trim that to twelve cars that would have given enough time to do what he needed to. Ten of those cars travelled away from the abbey; it would make no sense for him to have got in those cars, unless he was performing some sort of elaborate doubling back exercise to build his alibi.'

'Not impossible,' commented Warren. 'But put them to one side. Tell me about the two cars that headed towards the abbey.'

'One could have passed within a half mile of the abbey, the other just over a mile. The cars are registered to residents within that area.'

'Put them on the list, they could have given Shaw a lift. We'll pull them in for questioning if necessary. What about returning cars?'

'Again, assuming that he needed to leave after we believe the fire was started, and unless he had an accomplice, four cars entered the area in the time before his car exited. None of them came from the direction of the abbey, although it looks as though a minicab may have picked up a fare within a mile of the abbey grounds. I've put in a request for their records.'

'What about buses?'

'The 562 has a stop right in the centre of the zone of interest, and another stop four streets over from the abbey's main entrance. Four buses passed through the area between him driving into the zone and the time of the fire, but there were no return journeys between the fire being set and Shaw's car re-appearing. I've already requested the CCTV from Stagecoach.'

'OK, so no obvious reason for Shaw visiting that area or indications why he may have lied about it. It looks like we need to wait for his mobile phone records then, to see if he called anyone associated with that area or failing that to pinpoint his whereabouts more precisely. Get on with that as soon as the records appear. In the meantime, speak to Hutch about a priority list for door knocking, so we're ready to hit the ground running as soon as possible.'

'On it,' responded both women simultaneously.

Chapter 22

Warren had planned on sneaking away early to surprise Susan when she returned from school; if nothing else, tonight was likely to be their last chance to have a glass of wine together for the foreseeable future.

And so he was torn when Andy Harrison called to update him on the search of the tool shed.

'We were nearly done, after examining most of the surfaces and the handles of the tools most likely to come in contact with somebody stumbling around in the dark. We've got plenty of stuff to process and compare against what we've already got.'

'Good work, Andy.' Warren was keen to leave, but he wasn't distracted enough to miss the satisfaction in the veteran CSI's voice. And the man was an experienced Crime Scene Manager – he'd hardly be phoning Warren for a pat on the back for doing what he was asked.

Harrison took that as his cue to continue.

'There was an old cupboard at the back of the shed, filled with the usual crap you'd expect, including a rusty souvenir shortbread tin.'

'Dare I ask what was in it?'

'Screws, plastic wall plugs, insulating tape.'

'Anything else, Andy?'

'Two hundred and sixty pounds in used twenty-pound notes. And plenty of nice, clear fingerprints.'

* * *

With his plans to leave early scuppered, Warren headed back into the office.

'We have the mobile phone records for Rodney Shaw,' said Pymm.

'We're processing the numbers dialled at the moment, but so far we have calls from Deacon Baines at the time he phoned to notify him of the fire. He called that number regularly, with lots of short duration calls and texts between nine and five most days. If I had to guess, I'd say that he and Baines kept in touch during the working day by mobile phone.'

'That should be easy enough to confirm.'

'The next most common number is registered to his wife, Yvonne Shaw. They speak at length about once a week, with occasional short duration calls and texts at other times.'

'That seems a bit strange for a married couple, why can't they talk at home?' asked Warren.

'Could their marriage be in trouble?' suggested Pymm.

'Look into it,' ordered Warren. 'Now, what about the night of the fire? Any suggestions where he spent the hours before being called back to work?'

'That's where we are struggling. Shortly after leaving work, he called an unregistered pay-as-you-go phone. It wasn't the first time he's called it, he does it at infrequent intervals roughly every two weeks. Short duration, about five seconds.'

'An unregistered pay-as-you-go phone,' mused Sutton. 'Perfectly legal to own, but is anyone else's nose twitching?'

'Definitely,' agreed Warren, 'what do we have in terms of location data?'

'We have cell-tower triangulation for his phone that entire day. To start, the phone is at his registered address overnight until about seven-thirty, when it moves along his expected route towards the abbey. It then remains within the abbey grounds until just after 5 p.m.'

'So he didn't leave for lunch?'

'No, and it moves around a bit, suggesting he carries it with him rather than leaving it in a locker – which would make sense if he uses it to communicate with Baines during the day. We don't have good enough resolution to narrow it down to precise locations within the grounds, but it doesn't appear to go to the end of the complex where the chapel is located. However, he does spend the last hour of his day around the retirement home.'

'Which gives a legitimate reason for any trace evidence that may be found at the scene,' interjected Sutton.

'Then what?'

'The phone moves along the route taken by his car, travelling into the camera dead spot where we lost sight of the car itself. A few moments later, the phone appears to stop moving and then remains stationary for the next few hours, until shortly after he receives the call about the fire when it starts moving along the route that we tracked back towards the abbey. There's no indication that the phone moved any appreciable distance at walking pace or in a moving vehicle, during those five hours.'

'So that leaves us with three possibilities, either he was visiting a location within that area; he sat in his car for five hours…'

'Or he left his phone in the car and disappeared off to do whatever he was doing before returning to the car sometime before he drove it to the abbey,' finished Sutton.

'What's in that area?'

Pymm switched to a more detailed map. A large red dot was surrounded by two concentric circles.

'The resolution from cell-tower triangulation in that part of town is between fifty and one hundred metres, which covers

111

this inner area, with a decreased probability of it being within this wider perimeter. There was a little movement, but only a few metres, and within the error range for a stationary phone. In total, it includes about four streets, no bookmakers, and one pub. There are two other small businesses, a newsagent and an off-licence, the rest of the properties are residential.'

'Right, use the electoral roll and any other records you can find to work out exactly who lives in those houses, then liaise with Hutch to prioritise door knocking. The pub, the newsagent and the off-licence may remember him or his car, especially if he did sit in it for some time.'

'What about the houses? If Shaw was visiting a resident there and up to no good, the last thing we want to do is go knocking on that house and warn him off,' said Richardson.

'By the same token, that person could also eliminate Shaw from our enquiries,' said Sutton.

Warren mulled over both comments for a few moments.

'Let's play the odds shall we? See if we can find a few houses occupied by little old ladies with nothing better to do than stare out the window all day and notice strange cars.'

'Dog walkers and curtain twitchers, every detective's best friend,' commented Sutton.

112

Chapter 23

The whiteboard in the main CID office now had a second name in the suspects column, beneath Lucas Furber.

'Rodney Shaw, head groundsman at the abbey. He has historic convictions for violence and drug possession, supposedly clean since leaving prison in 1986. Everyone at the abbey was aware of his past, and regarded him as a poster boy for the power of redemption.'

It was 6 p.m. and Warren was with Tony Sutton briefing DSI Grayson on the team's progress so far.

'Motivation is circumstantial at the moment, but there are unconfirmed reports that he was heard violently arguing with our victim a couple of weeks prior to his death. We don't know what the argument was about, but it is possible that he has substituted his drug addiction for a gambling problem. He has been known to frequent at least one bookmaker in town, where he was described as an unlucky gambler. The same bookie was also a regular haunt of our victim, and a worker there saw them meet, and felt that Shaw was ashamed of being seen by Father Nolan.'

'Killing Nolan to hide his lapse seems a bit much,' opined Grayson, indicating he had been at least half-listening as he scrolled through emails on his phone.

'Ordinarily, I'd agree,' said Warren, 'however, there has been an unexplained loss of money over the past few weeks, they believe twenty pounds each day. The abbey management were reluctant to consider that there might be a thief on site, but it looks pretty obvious that they have a problem and that the person in question has access to the money before it is deposited in the bank. Shaw pretty much has the run of the place, and has been in the office plenty of times when the takings are placed in the digital safe. It wouldn't be too difficult to memorise the code, which hasn't been changed for years.

'This afternoon Forensics found a significant number of twenty-pound notes in a tin, in the communal tool shed used by the grounds men and the volunteer gardeners. There were fingerprints from both Father Nolan and Rodney Shaw on the tin.'

Grayson put down his phone, his attention fully on Warren now.

'I assume your working hypothesis is that Father Nolan bumped into Shaw in the bookmakers and confronted him over his gambling. At some point he found the biscuit tin in the shed and realised that Shaw had been stealing to support his habit? Shaw then killed Nolan to stop him from revealing this and covered up the murder by making it look like a suicide?'

'That's about the size of it. Obviously the exact sequence of events is yet to be determined.'

Grayson puffed his lips out.

'It's tenuous, Warren.' He looked over at Sutton. 'What do you think, Tony?'

'I agree it's not much, but we've plenty more circumstantial evidence. I think he's at least worth a closer look, and I'd like to see what he has to say for himself under caution.'

Grayson scowled and took a sip of his coffee. He'd recently upgraded the coffee machine in his office to a new model that took individual capsules. Warren felt slightly guilty every time he had a cup; Susan had shown him an article explaining how the capsules were a disaster for the environment. But it was still the best coffee in the building…

'What else have you got?'

'So far, no alibi for the night in question. He claims to have been home alone when the murder took place. But we now know that's untrue.'

'Go on.'

'In terms of opportunity, he admits to having his own set of keys to the chapel and the undercroft, so he could easily lock the door again from the outside and leave the communal keys inside with Father Nolan. He is trusted implicitly and he doubt-less knows that the majority of CCTV cameras are fakes. He is also familiar with the retirement home; he has access to keys for all the doors and would be able to slip in and see Father Nolan easily enough without being seen by anyone else. Even if he was seen, nobody would think anything of it. He could have tampered with the alarm on the fire exit at any time in the previous six months since the last fire brigade inspection.'

'Have Forensics found any evidence that he was in Nolan's room yet?'

'None so far.'

Grayson looked torn.

'It's flimsy, Warren. He's lied to us about his whereabouts that night, so we could arrest him and justify a search warrant. But unless he confesses immediately, or we find something unequiv-ocal, we'll probably end up bailing him. Do we want to run the risk of spooking him? Officially it hasn't even been publicly declared a murder yet.'

'There is another way,' suggested Sutton. 'Arrest him over the missing money, and see if he confirms our theory about his gambling addiction. Then see if we have enough to justify a search on those grounds. The money in the biscuit tin is a few hundred pounds less than the discrepancy noted in the abbey's takings, so assuming he hasn't already pissed it up the wall at the bookie, it could be at home.'

'It would take some clever wording on the search warrant, to ensure anything we find is admissible in court,' warned Warren, 'and it would seem a bit suspicious if the officers in charge of Nolan's supposed suicide suddenly start pursuing a bit of missing cash.'

'There is also the small matter of no thefts being reported at the abbey,' added Grayson.

'I'm sure we can persuade Deacon Baines to report the thefts, and we can use different officers that Shaw hasn't met before to conduct the actual interviews,' insisted Sutton.

Grayson picked up the golf ball that sat on the end of his desk, and absently threaded it through his fingers. Almost a minute passed.

'OK. Go and speak to legal, and see if you can knock together a warrant that won't get thrown out by a defence solicitor for over-reaching. If they can craft something, then come back and I'll make a decision then.'

It was hardly a ringing endorsement, but Warren would take it.

Chapter 24

It was late evening before Warren received his reply from legal about the wording on the search warrant for Rodney Shaw. In the meantime, he had convinced Deacon Baines to file a report about the missing money, thus allowing them to open a legitimate investigation. Since the murder, the abbey had been closed and so there had been no opportunity to see if the thefts had continued. Despite the late hour, Warren was determined to celebrate with his wife and had texted her to put a bottle of prosecco in the fridge; they could drink it in bed if necessary.

'We can execute a section eight search warrant for evidence pertaining to the stolen money, as long as the dominant reason for the search is the thefts. However, once we've gained access to the property, we can seize anything else that may be evidence of unrelated criminality under section nineteen.'

Grayson pinched the bridge of his nose.

'Christ, Warren, it's a potential legal nightmare. If we do find something and his defence team argue that the dominant reason was not the investigation of the stolen money, then anything you find could be inadmissible.'

He drummed his fingers on the table top.

'Right, you need to plan this very carefully. Coordinate Shaw's arrest and interview with the execution of the search warrant and fully brief Scenes of Crime. I want you physically present leading the search. Tony and I can monitor the interview by video link and maintain an open channel with you. If you find anything that looks as though it may be related to the murder but not the stolen money, then call it in and await further instructions. If necessary, I'll arrange a second warrant and if needs be further arrest Shaw to keep his lawyer happy.'

'Will do, sir.'

'Who will do the arrest and conduct the interview?'

'Mags Richardson will arrest, with a couple of uniform for back-up.'

'What about Moray Ruskin? God knows the lad's big enough to handle himself.'

Warren frowned. 'I'd rather not. He's been working with me quite a bit, I don't want Shaw to link us. Mags has been coordinating from here, he won't make the connection to the fire investigation.'

'And the interview?'

'I was thinking Mags Richardson and Rachel Pymm. Rachel's been itching to get away from the computer.'

Grayson shifted uncomfortably. 'Is she up to it. You know...'

'I know what you mean, sir, and she is a very competent and experienced DS,' said Warren firmly.

'Of course. No question,' said Grayson quickly.

Friday 27th February

Chapter 25

With much of the abbey grounds still sealed off, Rodney Shaw was temporarily a man of leisure. He was dressed in jeans, T-shirt and slippers when DS Mags Richardson and a uniformed constable appeared on his front doorstep shortly after 8 a.m. He seemed bewildered when she arrested him on suspicion of theft and came quietly.

Rodney Shaw hadn't been in trouble with the law since his convictions for drug possession and wounding with intent over thirty years previously. Nevertheless, he'd learnt his lesson from that experience and after regaining his composure refused to say anything until the duty solicitor arrived.

As agreed in the operational briefing, Warren was supervising the search on site. Any actions or discoveries would be reported to Warren first, and he would then relay them to John Grayson and Tony Sutton, who would also be watching Shaw's interview by video-link.

Shaw lived in a small, two-bedroom, ground-floor flat on the outskirts of Middlesbury. Travelling to the abbey would involve either driving directly through town, or in rush hour via the longer, but less-congested, bypass. In Shaw's earlier statement about the night of the fire, he had claimed that because of the hour, he'd taken the more direct route through town, something that they now knew to be a lie.

The execution of the search warrant had been easy, with Shaw simply leaving his keys behind as he was bundled into an unmarked car. The residents of the flat above had already left for work, but the sudden appearance of white-suited CSIs had quickly aroused interest from the neighbours across the road; the shadowy forms of a couple were clearly silhouetted in the downstairs windows. Upstairs, a young woman had thrown open her window and was hanging out of it filming the whole scene on her mobile phone. It was doubtless already on Facebook, Twitter or whatever social media sites she favoured. It probably wouldn't be too long before somebody remembered that Rodney Shaw worked at the abbey and started to question if the death of Father Nolan was really suicide.

The press office had been clear in their instructions: Warren's team could refuse to answer questions (which would only serve to heighten speculation) or tell a version of the truth – but not lie outright. Consequently, the carefully crafted press release truthfully claimed that a search warrant had been executed in relation to an investigation unrelated to the death of Father Nolan.

Warren only entered the flat after it had been videoed, temporary plastic flooring had been laid down to preserve any trace evidence in the carpet or on the kitchen floor, and the flat had been secured – after all, regardless of the stated legal basis for the search, Rodney Shaw was a suspect in an especially brutal arson and murder. Warren had no desire to end up on the wrong end of a booby trap, especially when wearing a plastic-coated paper suit

By this point, Shaw's solicitor had arrived and he had been led into interview suite one. Rachel Pymm was already present, setting up the PACE tape recorder that supplemented the two colour video cameras, positioned either side of the room to ensure that there were no blind-spots.

At the other end of the building in the main CID office, DSI

Grayson and DI Sutton sat either side of a large computer monitor showing a live feed from the digital recorders.

After everyone had introduced themselves for the tape and Shaw had been reminded of his rights and the reason for his arrest, Shaw's solicitor insisted on making a statement.

'My client wishes to cooperate fully with the police, but would like it to be made clear that he has no knowledge or involvement in any thefts from his employer. Furthermore, he has no access to, or involvement with, the money taken by the abbey, and is unsure why he has been arrested.'

Richardson acknowledged the statement and suggested that they started at the beginning.

Back in the CID office, Grayson and Sutton watched the video feed intently.

'Well he's certainly a cool customer,' noted Sutton. 'He still looks more confused than guilty.'

Shaw sat with his hands loosely folded on the table. A fit looking man with a slim build, he still had the remnants of a summer tan; his skin leathery and lined from years of outdoor working, the blue tattoos on his muscled forearms faded and indecipherable. His full head of hair was more white than grey, the ends curling slightly. A couple of days' worth of silvery stubble covered his chin. His age could have been ten years either side of the 51 listed on his police record.

'Well, if he is our man, he slopped petrol over a helpless priest and set him on fire. That takes a special kind of psycho, if you ask me. The threat of a bit of jail time for theft isn't likely to bother him too much,' said Grayson.

On the screen, Shaw was confirming his hours and duties at the abbey.

'This time of year it isn't light until about seven, and it's getting dark around five-thirty, so I tend to work eight to five, most days. I'll probably start working a bit later when the clocks go forward next month.'

'And what would your duties normally entail?' asked Pymm.

'I'm the head groundsman. I'm primarily in charge of keeping the grounds tidy. I maintain the lawns, look after the flower borders and make sure the graveyard is fit for mourners and visitors.'

'What about the vegetable gardens?' asked Richardson.

'I do a bit of the heavier work, such as turning the soil with a rotavator, but most of the general tending is done by the priests.'

'Such as Father Nolan?'

'Yes, and Fathers Lewis and Pascutti.' He smiled slightly. 'They work for free and it means we can use it as a selling point when we advertise our produce; one of Gabriel's ideas.'

'How would you describe your relationship, with Deacon Baines?' asked Pymm.

Shaw shrugged. 'Pretty good. Technically he's my boss, but we've known each other too long for that to really matter.'

'Do you do any work in the house?'

'Yes, I do some odd jobs. Basic maintenance, that sort of thing.'

'Do you have access to the vestry?'

Shaw sighed. 'Yes, Sergeant. Pretty much everyone does. And to pre-empt your next questions, yes, I know where the safe is and no, I don't know the code.'

'So you don't have access to the takings from the shop?'

'No.'

'What about when they are transported from the shop to the safe?'

'Nope, not my job. Gabriel does that in the evening when the visitors and volunteers have gone home. And again, before you ask, yes I am familiar with the routine for taking money to the bank, but no I am not involved.'

'So if we were to look at the safe for your fingerprints, or look at the carpet in front of the safe for your boot prints, we wouldn't find either?' asked Pymm.

For the first time since the interview started, Shaw paused.

Seated in front of the live feeds, Sutton and Grayson held their breath.

'No.'

Grayson looked at Sutton. 'I'd say we have a legitimate reason to seize his work boots and any other footwear. If his footprints are in front of the safe, we've caught him in a lie.'

Sutton agreed and relayed the instruction to Warren.

'We've got some sturdy looking work boots on the back porch, a pair of trainers, some wellies and some smart leather shoes,' responded Warren.

'Seize the lot,' instructed Grayson. 'It won't take long to take impressions of the soles and swab for petrol residue or trace evidence from Father Nolan.'

Back in the interview room, Shaw was starting to get irritated.

'Yes, I have previous convictions for burglary, possession of a class A drug and wounding with intent. Is this why you've pulled me in? Some money goes missing, so the obvious suspect is the ex-junkie. It doesn't matter that I was barely 20 years old back then, that I haven't had so much as a parking ticket in thirty years and been clean of drugs since the day I was sent down. It's never going to go away, is it?'

'We are pursuing a number of lines of inquiry...' started Pymm, but Shaw was now on a roll. He pulled his sleeves back.

'There you go. Take a good look. Those track lines are thirty years old. Get me a plastic cup and I'll piss in it for you.' He plucked at his head. 'Here, I haven't had a haircut since the summer. Take a strand and look for traces of recent drug-use.'

He slumped back in his chair and folded his arms.

'For Christ's sake, I've been clean more than half of my life. Gabriel and I run workshops and visit local schools to try and stop kids from making the same mistakes that I did. Bishop Fisher and the priests in that home gave me my life back. They trusted me and believed in me when I confessed my sins. I owe them everything, I could never steal from them.'

He lapsed into silence.

'We are all well aware of my client's previous history,' said the solicitor as the silence started to drag on, 'but it is clear that he has successfully turned his life around. His story is an inspiration to many, especially young people who are heading towards the life that Mr Shaw turned his back on. I would like to suggest a short break.'

The two officers agreed and terminated the interview.

After Shaw had been led away by a custody sergeant for a comfort break, Sutton and Grayson joined Richardson and Pymm in the interview suite. Richardson took a swig of her water, whilst Sutton presented Pymm with a glass of her favourite tea.

'I dredged a ditch out the back, because I know that's just the way you like it.'

Pymm said nothing, merely extending her middle finger as she took a long mouthful.

'Warren has seized his footwear to see if we can catch him in a lie about him being near the safe,' said Grayson.

'What should we question him about next? His gambling, or should we go straight for the tin of money in the shed?' asked Pymm.

'Go for the gambling, there's no rush. Besides, the search team have made some interesting discoveries,' instructed Grayson, passing over a page from his notepad.

Richardson raised an eyebrow. 'You aren't kidding.'

* * *

Shaw was calm again by the time he returned, and even apologised for his outburst.

'You have a job to do, let's just get on with it, shall we?'

'Tell me about your wife, Rodney,' started Pymm.

'I hardly see what Mr Shaw's private life has to do with this situation,' rebuffed his solicitor.

'If you wouldn't mind answering the question,' said Pymm.

Shaw shrugged. 'If you insist. I imagine that your search team have drawn their own conclusions. My wife and I have been living apart for the past six months.'

His admission confirmed the impression gained by Warren and the CSIs, both from his phone records and the search of his house. The small flat was covered with framed pictures of Shaw and a striking woman a few years younger in a range of poses. In more recent photos, the couple were joined first by a baby, then a toddler, and finally a gangly pre-teen, all three of them wearing T-shirts from the 2012 Olympics.

However, the master bedroom was best described as functional, containing nothing but a cheap double-bed, with plain bedding, a flimsy-looking flat-pack wardrobe, and an upturned crate pulling double duty as a bedside table.

'What about your daughter?' asked Richardson.

'She lives with her mum on the other side of town. We still all get on OK and she's fifteen now, old enough to make her own mind up. She doesn't like to see her old man lonely, so she stays over at the weekend. Even bakes a cake sometimes.' His voice softened. 'She's a good kid.'

That also confirmed the search team's observations. The rear bedroom had a single bed, with a bright pink *Hello Kitty* bedspread. A chest of drawers was covered in make-up and a large mirror. Unlike her father's room, the walls had been painted and decorated with posters of bands and singers that Warren had never heard of.

'What does your wife do for a living?' asked Richardson.

'She's an estate agent. Bloody useful to be honest, she found me the flat and got me a decent rate on the rent.'

'Why have you and your wife split up?' This time Pymm asked the question.

Shaw's eye twitched slightly, and for the first time he looked evasive.

'Just grew apart, I guess.'

'That's it? No affairs or major disagreements?' pressed Pymm.

'No.'

'I don't see the relevance of this line of questioning,' started Shaw's solicitor.

Pymm ignored her.

'What about money? Any financial problems?'

'Not really.'

'Is that a yes or a no?' asked Richardson.

Shaw scowled. 'We argued about it sometimes.'

'About your gambling habit?'

Shaw gave a start, before looking over at his lawyer.

She maintained a neutral face.

'I like a bit of a flutter,' he admitted finally, 'but I'd hardly call it a habit.'

His body language was as defensive as his tone of voice.

Pymm cleared her throat and pulled over the list supplied to her by Grayson.

'You left your wallet behind, and our search team executed their right to examine it. In it we found a pile of receipts from bookmakers. We also found some more in a box by your bed. I'm guessing you kept them because you won. Maybe a good luck charm?'

Shaw remained stony faced.

'Not too bad. Fifty pounds on a four-to-one at Newmarket, thirty pounds on a favourite at two-to-one.' She skimmed down a bit further. 'This one did all right, although it was only six-to-four. Is that why you risked a hundred quid on that one?'

Shaw said nothing.

'The thing is, I know for a fact that nobody keeps up the winning over a long stretch. To mix my gambling clichés, "the house always wins". We found forty-six winning betting slips, showing total winnings of about three-and-a-half thousand quid. How many betting slips did you screw up in disgust when your horse limped home fourth or didn't even make it? Three grand in winnings, versus how many thousands lost?'

Shaw fixed his gaze on the wall behind the two officers.

'The dates on here are quite interesting,' continued Pymm. 'Some weeks there are slips from two or even three days. That suggests to me that you were a pretty frequent visitor. If I said that you visited most days, would that be fair.'

Shaw licked his lips.

'Probably.'

His voice was so quiet that the two officers could barely hear it. Fortunately, the high gain microphones on the recording equipment were more sensitive than a typical human ear.

'How much money have you lost, Rodney?'

'Dunno.'

'Is that why you and your wife no longer live together?'

He nodded, unable to meet either officer's gaze.

Pymm glanced at Richardson, who gave a tiny nod.

'Rodney, there were a number of red demands under your bed. Council tax and electricity mostly, although there was a receipt to show that you had caught up with some outstanding rent arrears.' She paused. 'I'm guessing they were hidden because you didn't want your daughter to find them?'

Shaw nodded; he looked on the verge of tears.

'The betting slips are mostly from a bookmaker's on Stuart Lane, but the latest ones are a couple of streets away. Why did you switch?'

'Fancied a change,' Shaw mumbled eventually.

'Really? Was that it?'

Shaw said nothing.

'Did you meet anyone in the bookie? Perhaps someone you knew?'

Shaw stared at the tabletop.

Richardson leant forward, her voice soft.

'It's an addiction, isn't it? You know there are organisations that can help you, don't you?'

128

Shaw nodded.

'You kicked the drugs all those years ago. I'm sure you can kick this habit. What have Bishop Fisher and the priests said?'

Shaw mumbled again; this time Richardson asked him to repeat himself, she wasn't sure that even the microphones would have heard him.

'I haven't told them.'

She feigned surprise. 'Why ever not? They forgave you before and showed you love and acceptance. Don't you think they'd do it all again?'

Shaw's response was too muffled to hear all of it, but the two officers got the gist.

'You're too ashamed?' said Pymm.

'So, nobody from the abbey is aware that you have been gambling?' asked Richardson.

Shaw said nothing. Richardson let the pause stretch for a few seconds more, but it was clear he didn't want to say anything more.

'Why did you switch bookmakers?' repeated Richardson.

'Like I said, I just wanted to try somewhere different.'

'Really? That was it? You see, I have a theory. I reckon you met someone in that bookmaker's. Someone you knew.' Pymm said.

'Who did you bump into that made you switch bookie?' asked Richardson.

'Don't know what you mean,' mumbled Shaw.

'Come on, Rodney, we know something happened to make you move bookie,' said Richardson.

'We can work it out from the shop's CCTV,' said Pymm, 'but you can save us a lot of time and it will look good if you cooperate with us.'

'My client still denies that he is guilty of these thefts, and you have yet to show me any evidence otherwise, so talk of his cooperation looking good for him is premature.' Shaw's solicitor's voice had an edge to it.

'Father Nolan,' muttered Shaw.

'Father Nolan?' Pymm injected a note of surprise into her voice. Shaw nodded miserably.

'Why didn't you want to tell us?'

'Why do you think?' For the first time, Shaw made eye contact with two officers. 'Father Nolan supposedly committed suicide last week. Suddenly you arrest the only abbey employee with a criminal record over some missing money. Why am I really here? Am I under arrest for his murder?'

Up in CID, Sutton and Grayson held their breath.

'Careful...' muttered Grayson. Pymm and Richardson were treading a fine line. They couldn't flat out lie, yet they needed to avoid tipping off Shaw that he was a suspect in a suspicious death that hadn't even been announced as one yet.

'As previously stated, you were arrested on suspicion of theft...' Pymm paused. 'Unless you have information that you wish to share about the death of Father Nolan. Do you wish to make a statement at this time?'

'No, of course not!'

'Nicely done, Rachel,' said Grayson. Sutton agreed.

'Do you know if Father Nolan told anyone at the home about meeting you?' asked Pymm, the interview back on track.

'I don't think so. Nobody said anything.'

Back upstairs in CID, Sutton and Grayson were leaning so close to the screen their noses were practically touching it.

'Either he's been lying all this time, or he's telling the truth,' said Sutton.

'If he has been lying, he's the best I've seen in a long time,' pronounced Grayson.

Back in interview suite one, Richardson and Pymm had suggested another break; Grayson and Sutton hurried to join them.

'It'll give him a chance to have a think. He might cop to the thefts, if he thinks it'll get us to back off about any involvement in the fire,' said Richardson.

'Even if he doesn't, he's admitted that Father Nolan met him in the bookie and he's made it clear that he's ashamed of his problem,' said Pymm.

'Ashamed enough to kill anyone who threatens to reveal his secret?' asked Sutton.

'People have killed for less,' said Grayson.

'Anything more from the house search?' asked Hutchinson.

'They've seized a bunch of keys, including some that look as though they would fit the chapel and the undercroft. We'll identify the rest, although he's already admitted to having access to most of the house,' said Sutton. 'We'll check with Deacon Baines to see if he has any keys he shouldn't.'

Grayson looked at his watch.

'When he comes back, give him the opportunity to confess to the thefts. If he does that, then play it by ear and ask him if he thinks anyone suspected anything. It'd be great if he suggests a motive for killing Father Nolan, but I doubt he's that daft. Either way, we still have plenty of time left before we need to release him or charge.'

'What about the biscuit tin with the money in it? It also had Father Nolan's fingerprints, suggesting that Father Nolan discovered the money and potentially confronted him. Should we bring that up if he doesn't confess?'

Grayson rubbed his chin.

'Bring up his fingerprints, but don't mention Father Nolan's yet. We need something to keep his solicitor sweet, pretty soon she's going to start asking very loudly what justification we have for pulling him in here, other than his previous convictions. We can always mention Father Nolan's fingerprints down the line, if we get as far as disclosure.'

* * *

Hopes of any sort of confession were in vain.

'My client has admitted to a problem with gambling that he

131

has realised needs specialist help. He is also willing to consider telling those that care for him at the abbey about his problem, in the hope that they can help him overcome his addiction.

'That being said, he wishes to repeat his earlier statement that he knows nothing about these alleged thefts. Furthermore, you have yet to disclose any evidence, beyond Mr Shaw's past conviction, that lead me to believe that this is anything more than a fishing expedition.'

Richardson opened the manila folder that had sat on the table since the interview started.

'Do you recognise the object in this photograph, exhibit 2015/02/NH4352-1?' she asked.

For the first time since the interview had begun, Shaw picked up the reading glasses on the table in front of him.

'Yes. I think it's the shortbread biscuit tin from the tool shed.'

'Could you tell us what is in it?'

Shaw looked up at the ceiling briefly. 'Bits and pieces, screws and stuff.'

'Would anybody else be likely to use them?'

'I doubt it. I use them for odd jobs. Repairing broken window catches and things like that.'

Richardson pushed another photograph across the table.

'This is a photograph of the inside of the tin, exhibit 2015/02/NH4352-2. It can be clearly seen that in addition to screws and wall plugs, there is a wad of twenty-pound notes held together with an elastic band. Total amount, two hundred and sixty pounds.'

Shaw's breath caught in his throat.

'Can you tell me how this money got in the tin?'

He shook his head vigorously, 'No idea. It's nothing to do with me.'

'The tin has your fingerprints on it.'

'My client has already established that he has handled the tin previously, therefore that is not conclusive.'

Pymm ignored the solicitor.

'I think we can guess what has happened here, but it would be a lot better coming from you, Mr Shaw.'

Shaw looked pale. 'No, definitely not. I wouldn't steal from them, you have to believe me.'

'Did anyone else know about your habit, Mr Shaw? Did anyone else know that you were helping yourself to the takings from the till to fund it? Perhaps somebody else was working with you?'

'No. No, I wouldn't do that.'

'Then how did you fund your habit, Mr Shaw? And please don't tell me you never lost. Nobody wins in gambling except for the bookie.'

'I sold my wife's jewellery.' It was almost a shout. 'I pawned my wife's favourite necklace and her father's gold watch.' The tears were now flowing down his cheeks. 'I was down a few hundred and I'd missed some mortgage payments. I just needed a good win to sort myself out. So I borrowed the jewellery temporarily to raise some cash. I had a great tip on a thirty-to-one outsider that was under-priced. If it came in, I'd be able to buy back the jewellery, pay off the mortgage and still have enough left for my wife's birthday. I couldn't lose.'

'But you did, didn't you?'

'It stumbled on the last furlong. Dropped from first place to fifth.'

'Then what happened?'

'I had no choice. I told Yvonne that night what I'd done. She managed to buy back the jewellery, but that was it. The money we'd been saving for our summer holiday and Christmas cleared the mortgage debt.

'The thing is, she knows my history. She knows that I have an addictive personality. She says she can handle that. It's the lying that she couldn't live with. Yvonne was worried that I could really screw things up if I didn't stop gambling. She's an estate agent, she's seen what happens when people don't keep up with their mortgage. It really frightened her.

'I agreed to move out for the time being and give up access to the joint accounts. If I can successfully keep a roof over my head and get help, then she may take me back.'

'And are you getting help?'

Shaw stared at the table top again, before shaking his head.

'I wanted to. But I can't,' he raised his eyes, 'everything in my life is so shit right now, the buzz is the only thing that keeps me going. I'm worried that if I lose that buzz, there'll be a hole. And I'm scared of what I'll fill it with.'

* * *

Warren had returned from Rodney Shaw's house, leaving the CSIs to finish up. After watching the recordings of Shaw's interview he agreed with the rest of the team and DSI Grayson's assessment.

'He doesn't feel like a killer.'

'He comes across as open and honest throughout the interview, even admitting that he needed help with his addictions,' offered Richardson.

'But then psychopaths are often charming individuals who understand human nature – he could be playing everyone,' countered Sutton.

'We clearly can't arrest him as a suspect in the murders yet,' decided Warren, 'but let's keep him on the suspects board, at least until we've confirmed his alibi. We'll get Forensics to process everything we seized; I think we've reached the limits of the search warrant and we'll need more before we can get a new one.'

'What about the thefts?'

Warren tapped his teeth thoughtfully. 'Most of what we have is circumstantial, and his lawyer is right that his fingerprints could have found their way quite innocently onto the biscuit tin. It's going to take time for the twenties to be fingerprinted. If his lawyer knew that Father Nolan's fingerprints were also on the tin, I'm sure she'd be drawing the obvious conclusion.'

'If Father Nolan stole the money,' said Ruskin, 'how would that fit with his murder?'

'It might not,' suggested Pymm. 'It could just be a coincidence.'

'Bail him?' asked Richardson.

Warren agreed. 'We won't get any results back before the custody clock runs out tomorrow, and we've no grounds for an extension. His solicitor is probably already wondering why he's still sitting in a cell three hours after his interview terminated. You did a good job of deflecting his suspicions, but let's not push our luck. If he is our killer, we don't want him thinking he's under suspicion for anything more than some missing cash. Hopefully he'll slip up.'

Saturday 28th February

Chapter 26

Saturday morning marked the start of the second week of the investigation. Furthermore, a new tranche of officers from Welwyn had been seconded to the team, and so Warren decided to hold an extended 8 a.m. briefing.

'We identified twelve suitable properties to visit in the area where Rodney Shaw's mobile phone was stationary for so long on the night of the fire, as well as a pub, newsagent and off-licence,' stated David Hutchinson. 'Neither the offy nor the newsagent recognised the photograph of Shaw. The tills for both businesses are at the rear of the shop, away from the entrance, so they've no idea if his car was parked outside.'

'CCTV?' asked Warren.

'Seized from both, but they cover the shop, not the pavement outside. I'll fast forward through the period of interest later on and see if they missed him, but they're sole traders and pretty much only serve the locals.'

'What about the pub?'

'One of the bar staff thought he might look familiar, but couldn't be sure. I have their CCTV also.'

'What about the neighbours that you canvassed?'

'All little old ladies, you'll be pleased to hear, so unless Shaw has been buying surplus Temazepam from them, I can't see them tipping him off that we've been asking questions about him.'

'This isn't Glasgow, so we're probably OK on that score,' said Sutton.

'Hey, watch it with the stereotypes,' said Ruskin. 'My gran and her friends only sell good quality homemade crystal meth.'

'Anything from those houses?' asked Warren after the laughter had died down.

'Nothing much. One woman thinks that a strange car matching Shaw's may have been parked up that evening, a couple of doors down from the pub, but she can't be sure, and she has no idea if anyone was sitting in it. Nor did she see the driver.'

'Any idea about the time?'

'No, she thinks it was getting dark.'

'So, still no idea why, or even if, Shaw was there when the murder took place,' summarised Warren. 'Thanks Hutch. We'll see what Forensics come up with.' He flicked over his pad to the list he'd scribbled.

'We're still awaiting forensic document analysis of Father Nolan's note. I've authorised fast-track for it, so we should hear back soon. Any news back from Forensic IT, Rachel?'

Pymm pushed her glasses back onto her nose.

'The retirement home is set up for wireless broadband, and some of the residents are keen computer users, including social media. Father Nolan wasn't. He didn't own his own computer, or a smartphone. On the rare occasions he needed computer access, he used a communal desktop PC in the lounge, which Pete Robertson and his team have finished analysing. There's no record of who was using it at any particular time, but the internet browsing history shows nothing suspicious. It's pretty much the sort of thing you'd expect a group of elderly priests to be accessing: BBC News, a few theological websites and sports pages. The hard drive is largely empty, mostly Word documents of sermons or personal correspondence.'

'Is there any indication that he borrowed anyone else's computer?' asked Sutton.

'Not that anyone's admitted. From what we've heard, he wasn't especially technically minded.'

'What about his mobile phone?' asked Ruskin.

'We've got his records. Like I said, it's not a smartphone and apparently he rarely took it out with him, so the location data never shows it leaving the house. He only phoned a half-dozen numbers, which we've identified as a cousin back in East London, and some others back in Ireland. The remainder included his local GP surgery and his dentist. You can count the number of text messages he's sent in the five years he's owned the phone on the fingers of both hands and the toes of one foot.'

'It doesn't sound as though he had many friends,' commented Ruskin.

'That fits with the description of him,' said Hutchinson. 'Pleasant enough, but quite a self-contained, quiet man.'

'What about the initial forensics report from the search of Rodney Shaw's house?' asked Warren. 'Please, tell me it's good news, and that he's our man.'

'Sorry, Chief, it's inconclusive at best,' replied Pymm, passing over her iPad.

Warren skimmed the reports from the tests, reading aloud as he did so.

'No traces of petrol on his work clothes or work shoes. The keys all fit locks around the site, including the chapel, undercroft and vestry but Baines has confirmed that it was perfectly legitimate for Shaw to have those keys.'

Warren scrolled further.

'Impressions of his boot prints match prints found around the chapel and the undercroft, as well as the fire exit. However, Shaw does a monthly fire inspection of the house and all buildings on site, including the chapel and undercroft. According to the log, his last inspection was six days before the fire – no violations found.

139

The weather has been poor enough that he would probably have left footprints. Since the fire exit next to Father Nolan's room is at an unused end of the corridor, it is only cleaned occasionally, so the footprints could have been there for some time.'

Warren continued scrolling, he could feel the increasing disappointment in the room.

'No conclusive evidence of Shaw's footwear in front of the vestry safe, although there are too many overlapping shoeprints to be conclusive. The digital key pad is negative for his fingerprints.'

'Bugger,' said Sutton. 'He works all over the site, so there's nothing here that rules him out or rules him in for either the murder or even the stolen money.'

Warren agreed. 'What about his background? Is there any overlap between him and Father Nolan before they met at the retirement home? What about his school days?'

'Nothing yet. He did go to a Catholic school, but it wasn't even in the same diocese as any that Father Nolan worked at,' said Pymm.

Warren considered everything that had been said. Sutton was right, the evidence was still circumstantial, but by the same token, they still hadn't managed to clear him from the investigation.

'His name stays on the board whilst we keep digging.'

Chapter 27

Later that afternoon Crime Scene Manager Andy Harrison swung by the office, on his way home from Welwyn. He declined a cup of coffee, saying he needed to go to sleep as soon as he got in, ready for his next early shift.

'We've got our forensic document analysis back for the suicide note found on Father Nolan's dresser,' he stated, handing over his iPad.

'What's the conclusion?' asked Warren, preferring the team to hear the CSI's summary, before going through the report in detail.

'First of all, the examiner believes that based on the hand-writing samples submitted for comparison, the author of the note was indeed Father Nolan. However, the writing shows some evidence of impairment.'

'Such as alcohol and drugs?' asked Sutton.

'The examiner wouldn't be drawn on specifics – he said that's straying into the realms of forensic graphology and he'd rather stick with science – but he would be willing to speculate off the record and say that the handwriting strayed markedly from Father Nolan's typically neat and quite pedantic style.'

'What else is there?' asked Warren.

'The paper was probably torn from the A5 spiral-bound pad

141

on the dresser. The fibres match, indicating that they come from the same batch of paper. Chromatography tests on a small sample of the ink match that of a biro also found on the dresser.'

'What about fingerprints?'

'They used alternate light sources on the paper, the pad and the pen, and found latent prints matching Father Nolan, but nobody else.'

'Could it have been wiped clean? Surely there would be finger-prints from the shopkeeper or other customers that handled it before he bought it?' asked Ruskin.

'That's a good question, but this type of pad comes wrapped in disposable plastic wrapping, so we wouldn't expect anyone else to have touched the actual paper other than Father Nolan.'

'What else?' asked Sutton.

'There are a total of eleven leaves missing from the pad. Two were found elsewhere in the room; a shopping list in the back pocket of a pair of trousers, and a list of what we've confirmed are horse-racing fixtures from a couple of months ago down the back of the bedside table. There was no sign of the nine missing leaves, however there were impressions left on the pad, and this is where it gets interesting.' He opened a series of images on the iPad, each showing the same piece of paper, but under different filtered light.

'Using alternate light sources again, they found indentations matching the suicide note, and they also found two other attempts at it. Both were in Father Nolan's writing, but both had mistakes.

'Because he was drunk?'

'We can speculate. But there's more. A third set of indentations, with the same words 'Forgive me Father, for I have sinned', but printed in block capitals and in a different person's handwriting.'

There was a pause whilst the team digested that thought.

'So basically, what we are saying, is that Father Nolan was made to write his own suicide note; but he was so inebriated that somebody else had to write the words down for him to copy?'

'Yes. There were also traces of petrol caught in the paper fibres, where the pad and the note had been handled; there were no such remnants on the sheets found in his room. The concentration was too low to suggest that paper had been doused in fuel, or even had any spilled on it, more likely Father Nolan had traces of petrol on his hands from handling something with petrol residue.'

'Such as the petrol can found at the scene?'

'Entirely possible.'

A disturbing picture of Father Nolan's last hours were starting to emerge.

What had initially looked like a tragic suicide, was now appearing much more sinister. The priest had drunk whiskey laced with his own medication. He had then been escorted, probably semi-conscious, to the undercroft where he had been made to write his own confession, before being doused in petrol and set alight. His killer then returned to his room and placed the note prominently on the man's dresser.

The degree of planning alone gave Warren pause for thought.

* * *

Warren was sitting with Sutton in Grayson's office again. Unfortunately, Grayson was due to brief Assistant Chief Constable Mohammed Naseem in the next few minutes, and so hadn't offered either man a cup of his coffee.

'Take me through what we have.'

Warren quickly brought him up to speed on the latest forensic developments.

'So the killer probably returned from the chapel to place the suicide note on the dresser in Father Nolan's room? And did so without being seen by the two kids that reported the fire?'

'Yes, which narrows the potential routes that killer must have taken. They couldn't have exited the chapel by the front door without being seen, so must have left via the rear entrance near the altar, which means they could then have walked unseen back to the house. It isn't possible to exit the undercroft directly.'

'And Rodney Shaw is still the main suspect?'

'Yes. We are also trying to find a homeless person called Lucas Furber who was arrested for causing a disturbance in the abbey grounds some months ago, and who seems to have issues with the church, but Shaw is looking the most promising. His alibi for that night is collapsing around his ears as we speak.

'We also know that the killer used a second set of keys to relock the chapel and the undercroft, so that they could leave a set with Father Nolan and make it seem as though he locked himself in there. Rodney Shaw has his own set of keys. On top of that, he has full access to the retirement home and can move around largely unnoticed. His footprints have been found around the fire exit that we believe Father Nolan was taken through.'

'Circumstantial, and easily explained away by defence counsel,' warned Grayson.

'I agree. However, we might now have a sample of the killer's handwriting, that we may be able to match to him. I'd also like those missing sheets of paper, but they could have been disposed of in any one of a dozen ways by someone like Shaw.'

'What's your plan?'

'Full forensics on the likely routes between the house and the chapel. If Father Nolan was stumbling around drunk and drugged, he and his killer may have left fibres and other trace evidence along the route. We have samples of some of Shaw's clothes from the search in relation to the thefts for comparison.'

'What else? You have enough to arrest and question again, and to do another search explicitly to look for evidence in relation to the murder, but unless he confesses I'm not seeing enough to charge. If you need to bail him at the end of the interview, you've just tipped him off.'

Warren gave a sigh.

'You're right. We've seen no signs that he's planning to flee,

144

or that he thinks his previous arrest was for anything other than those thefts, so I don't think he's a flight risk. Let's continue testing his alibi. We should also be able to find a sample of his handwriting for comparison purposes.'

'Are we going to tell the church that it's now a murder case?' asked Sutton. 'It's all very well us not wanting to tip our hand by arresting Shaw, but the killer is still out there. The residents of that home – or the community at large for that matter – could be in danger here.'

'A fair question,' said Grayson; he looked troubled. 'That's a decision for ACC Naseem to make, I think, but I'll pass on your concerns.'

Grayson looked at his watch and stood up.

'I'll tell Naseem that we have two potential suspects. Let's talk again tomorrow and decide if we should arrest.' He paused. 'Of course there's still one more unanswered question. Of all the things to make Father Nolan write on his suicide note, why "Forgive me Father, for I have sinned"?'

Sunday 1st March

Chapter 28

The rattling of Warren's phone against the bedside table was enough to awaken him from his slumber. Beside him, Susan mumbled something before rolling over.

A quick swipe quietened it. 'One moment,' he whispered as he disconnected the charger and tiptoed out of the room.

'Sorry to disturb you, sir.' Warren didn't recognise the voice at the end of the line; he glanced at the phone's screen: 5.30 a.m.

'Not to worry, the alarm goes off in half-an-hour anyway.' At least, it did for him; Susan liked a lie-in on a Sunday.

'There's been a body found.'

Warren felt a surge of excitement, mixed with dread, his tiredness suddenly evaporating.

Generally speaking, there were plenty more officers further down the food chain than Warren who would be called to attend a scene before him, unless there was reason to suspect foul play, especially at such an early hour, on what was technically Warren's rest day.

'I'll be right there.'

* * *

147

Hastily erected mercury lights illuminated the scene, chasing away the remnants of the night's darkness; the rattle of the portable generators shattered the early dawn quiet.

'A group of students found him at about two-thirty. They were staggering back from town and decided to take a short cut.' The uniformed sergeant pointed to a group of four young people huddled next to a police van. Dressed for a night out, rather than an early morning on a riverside towpath, the two women and two men shivered under police-issue blankets. All four of them had swapped their shoes for plastic booties and were sipping hot drinks from a thermos flask.

'Have they been processed?'

'Yeah, they're still a bit pissed but the adrenaline and cold have sobered them up enough for a preliminary statement.'

'Take me through it and then we can run them home. Let them get some shut eye before we get them back in later.'

The officer flipped back through his notepad.

'As I said, the witnesses were walking along the riverbank after a night out. They're third-year students living in digs up by the Chequers estate. It's not the safest route home, but it's a significant shortcut and they were in a group of four.

'One of them, they're not sure who, spotted something lying underneath the bridge. When they realised it was a body, the two lads clambered down the bank, whilst one of the lasses phoned an ambulance. The water's not very deep, but it was moving quite quickly. When it became obvious that the body was face down in the water and probably dead, they gave up trying to get to it. Probably sensible, otherwise we'd be dealing with three fatalities, not one.'

'Then what?'

'I arrived, along with PC Abis. He secured the scene and took preliminary statements, whilst I saw the body recovery team in.' He motioned towards the van parked on the verge then checked his notebook again.

'They arrived at quarter past four, and sent a team in to secure the body; it was wedged between some rocks, so it isn't going anywhere. They're waiting for full light before they retrieve it. Scenes of Crime reckon that any evidence that was going to be washed away will have already been lost, and another couple of hours won't hurt.'

The Crime Scene Manager was no doubt correct – and they needed to keep their team as safe as possible – nevertheless Warren chafed at the delay. He could imagine fibres, DNA and other clues disappearing down the river.

'They managed to have a look at the body and saw it was an elderly, white male. When they spotted the dog collar, I figured we'd better call it in to you guys right away.'

Chapter 29

The body in the river had undergone preliminary identification by 10 a.m.

Alarm bells had started ringing when Father Gerry Daugherty failed to appear at breakfast, and then missed Sunday service. Bishop Fisher turned an unhealthy grey colour, and Warren had to take his arm and lead him to a chair when Baines confirmed the priest's absence.

Warren had already seen a photo of the deceased man in the river and it was clearly the same person in the photograph on Father Daugherty's bedroom wall.

More damning was the note, sitting on the wooden dresser.

'Forgive me Father, for I have sinned.'

'Another suicide? Why?'

Warren said nothing. It was clear that the time was approaching when it would be necessary to reveal to the public that Father Nolan's death was a murder rather than a suicide, but that wasn't Warren's call to make. In the meantime, it was important to treat this as he would any other unexplained death, leaving open the possibility of suicide, murder, or as unlikely as it seemed on the face of it, accident or natural causes.

Baines also looked shaken.

'Can you think of any reason that Father Daugherty might take his own life?' asked Warren.

Both men shook their heads.

'Father Nolan had a history of depression and mental illness. What about Father Daugherty?'

Fisher paused. 'Father Daugherty was taken ill a few years ago with nerves.'

'Was that before or after he became a resident here?'

'Before.'

Warren looked at the retired bishop carefully.

'Was that the reason he retired?'

The brief snapshot of the late priest's life, relayed to him by Baines, suggested that like his former colleague Father Cormac Nolan, he was younger than normal when he gave up his ministry.

'In part,' allowed Fisher.

'The death of Father Nolan was a tremendous blow to our community,' said Baines. 'It is always possible that those already depressed or in spiritual pain may have been more affected than was first obvious.' He looked toward Fisher. 'I'm very sorry, Your Grace, I should have prioritised the care of our community, rather than wasting my time chasing this supposed thief.'

Warren decided not to acknowledge the sly dig in his direction.

Fisher dismissed the man's apology with a wave of his hand. 'We have all been failing in our pastoral duties.'

* * *

The additional afternoon briefing was packed, not least because DSI Grayson was the person who'd called it.

'I've just been on the phone to Assistant Chief Constable Naseem. There is obviously going to be speculation from the public about the circumstances surrounding the death of Father Daugherty and any possible link to Father Nolan last week.

'The identity of Father Daugherty has not yet been released

151

to the press, but the fact that the victim is a priest has already made it onto social media, no doubt courtesy of the students who found him.

'Currently, Father Nolan's death is still being portrayed as a suicide.' He paused. 'For operational reasons, that will not be changing in the immediate future.'

Around the room, officers shifted uncomfortably. Warren couldn't blame them. He'd been a silent party to the conference call between Grayson, ACC Naseem and the press office earlier that day and there had been a vigorous debate about whether they had a duty to inform the public that a murderer was likely within their midst. On the one hand there was the public safety aspect; on the other, the potential benefits from not tipping off the killer. Added to that, the complication of how exactly to answer direct questions from the press.

In the end, a compromise had been agreed upon: Father Daugherty's death would be described as 'unexplained' for the time being, until a likely cause had been established. Questions concerning any link between the two deaths would be deflected for now, however, the true nature of Father Nolan's death would be released to the public in the next twenty-four hours.

That gave Warren and the team another day where the killer might still think that he or she had got away with it. He was determined not to waste it.

'Rodney Shaw doesn't usually work weekends. Find out what he was doing last night, and if he has an alibi.' Mags Richardson nodded her agreement. 'Again, pull in any CCTV and ANPR records,' Warren continued, 'and cross-reference with the data from the night of the fire.

'Hutch, you and your team have got to know the retirement community pretty well, and the surrounding neighbourhood. See if you can find out anything new, but bear in mind what DSI Grayson said, make sure the team don't let the cat out the bag about any suspicions.'

'Will do,' promised the Geordie sergeant.

'Rachel, start scrutinising Father Daugherty's past. Look for any overlap between the two men, besides their place of residence. Chivvy along the Social Media Intelligence Unit and get them to prioritise searches related to either man or the retirement home.'

'I'll get right on it. I was expecting a preliminary report soon, I'll ask them to extend the search parameters.'

'Moray, did the students who found Father Daugherty have anything else to contribute when you interviewed them earlier?'

'Nothing, sir. They were all pretty hungover when I spoke to them and couldn't remember anything new.'

'Probably a bit of a stretch,' admitted Warren. He remembered the state they had been in that morning. With that he dismissed the team and headed back to his office. On the way, Tony Sutton joined him. The older man looked at Warren carefully, but waited until the office door had closed before saying his piece.

'It wasn't your decision to make.'

There was no need to elaborate on which decision he was referring to.

Warren sighed. 'I know, Tony. But I could have said more during the conference call with ACC Naseem.'

'Don't take this the wrong way, Chief, but I think you're too far down the pecking order for your opinion to have carried much weight.'

Warren smiled briefly. 'Thanks. I think.' His tone sobered. 'The problem is that I can't help wondering if the killer of Father Nolan has struck again, because he thinks he got away with it the first time. And if that's the case, and we don't announce a murder investigation soon, will the killer will strike again? Inside that retirement home are a couple of dozen vulnerable, elderly people. Are we gambling with their lives?'

Chapter 30

The press conference had been unusually busy for a Sunday evening. Held at Welwyn HQ, there had been no unoccupied seats.

It wasn't surprising. The death of Father Nolan had been gruesome and tragic and involved an organisation often viewed by the public with both fascination and suspicion. News of a second death had editors scurrying to cover the story, no doubt hoping for something similarly juicy.

So far they had been disappointed. DSI Grayson had followed the script, merely confirming that the cause of death was as yet unknown and stating that they were keeping an open mind as to any link between the two deaths. When asked directly about the investigation into Father Nolan's death, his answers had been non-committal and devoid of any substance. He'd again appealed for any witnesses to come forward.

Much to Warren's relief, he hadn't needed to attend. Warren's appearance at the previous press conference for Father Nolan had established that he was SIO of that investigation; having him sitting next to Grayson would run the risk of prematurely confirming a link between the two cases. Besides which, it meant that Grayson got all the attention, a fact snidely pointed out by Tony Sutton.

Despite the paucity of new information, the assembled reporters had pounced on every detail and the conference was headline news on every news bulletin that night, and the top story on every newspaper website. By the time Warren checked his email one last time before going to bed, there had been two reports of freelance photographers being detained for trespass, after they were caught scaling the abbey's perimeter wall. In addition, some enterprising reporters had worked out Warren's likely email address and contacted him directly for a quote, bypassing the press office. One of the grubbier tabloids had even hinted at a willingness to 'compensate him for his time' if he took them up on their generous offer for their paper to enlist their readers in helping the police.

He deleted the chancers and forwarded on the attempted bribery to Professional Standards, copying in DSI Grayson; he doubted they would do much more than rebuke the paper (who would immediately apologise and blame it on an over-eager junior reporter), nevertheless he didn't want any suggestion that he had colluded with them. Doubtless Grayson would remind the team of their ethical and legal obligations the next morning in case anyone else had received a similar offer.

Monday 2nd March

Chapter 31

'This is what we know about Father Gerry Daugherty, so far.' Tony Sutton was presenting the morning briefing. Behind him on the wall screen, a picture of a clean-shaven man in his sixties, with a shock of silvery hair, smiled at the camera, the head shot clearly showing the traditional black shirt and the white collar of a Roman Catholic priest. At the back of the room, Warren covered his mouth, stifling a yawn. Neither he nor Susan had slept properly the night before; today was a big day for them.

'Born in 1947 in Cardiff to second generation Irish parents, he moved to Liverpool when he was three years old. He went to St Cuthbert's College in Ushaw, Durham to train for the priesthood in 1965 and was ordained in 1971. He was a parish priest back in Liverpool for the next fifteen years, then when his parents retired in 1986 and moved down to South Cambridgeshire to be closer to his father's family, he decided to make the move also. He wound up just over the border in Hertfordshire, where he took on the role of school chaplain at Saint Thomas Aquinas Catholic Comprehensive. He reportedly stayed there until retiring in 2005 on the grounds of ill health – likely mental health related – and moving to St Cecil's.'

'Father Nolan was also a school chaplain, could they have known each other?' asked Hutchinson.

'It's not impossible that their paths crossed from time to time, but they trained at different seminaries and so far, we have no evidence that they knew each other before they met at the retirement home.'

'What sort of relationship did they have?' asked Richardson.

'Nobody we've spoken to mentioned anything notable,' said Sutton. 'They were neither close friends, nor did anyone ever see them arguing. They had different hobbies and supported different football teams. Like Father Nolan, Father Daugherty rarely used the communal PC and didn't own a laptop or smartphone. I've requested his mobile phone records, but everyone I've spoken to say that he rarely used it.'

'How was he regarded by the other residents and staff?' asked Pymm.

'With great affection from what I can tell. Father Nolan was largely regarded as a pleasant, but quiet man. Father Daugherty on the other hand was a bit of a character. The kids at school nicknamed him Father Scouse on account of his accent, and he loved to live up to the stereotype; he was very witty. As far as anyone was aware, nobody disliked him.'

'Do we know how he took Father Nolan's death?'

'The whole community were shocked obviously, and Father Daugherty was said to be especially quiet. He was usually a source of humour and wit, but he was supposedly very down about the death, particularly its very violent nature.'

'Both Father Nolan and Father Daugherty took early retirement on the grounds of poor mental health, could there be a connection?' asked Hutchinson.

'They were both registered at the same GP practice, but it's the nearest one to the home, so that would be expected. We're currently applying to get their medical records released.'

'What about family and friends outside the home?' asked Richardson.

'No wife and kids obviously, but he had a niece and a nephew on his father's side, both of whom lived in Devon, and he was reportedly very fond of their children. He would visit a few times a year, particularly around Christmas and Easter. Outside the home, like Father Nolan, he was also a football fan – Everton – and he frequented the Duke of Wellington pub, which is in the opposite direction to the Cock and Lion where Father Nolan drank. There's no indication that he was a gambler.'

'We should get someone to question the landlord, to see if there were any notable changes in his behaviour, or if he mentioned any worries,' said Warren. 'Do we know why he was on the bridge that night, or how he got there?'

'Well, he was in the habit of taking an evening constitutional,' said Sutton. 'He'd usually head out after evening meal, for an hour or so between seven and nine. It was a regular thing, even in winter or when it was raining. He enjoyed the peace and quiet. The last person to see him was Sister Clara, who said she saw him putting his coat on before heading out at about seven.'

'Could he have seen something the night of Father Nolan's death? If the killer thought Father Daugherty saw him acting suspiciously, he could have decided to kill him to keep him quiet,' suggested Ruskin.

'He didn't mention anything when he was originally interviewed over Father Nolan's death,' offered Hutchinson.

'Nevertheless, it's a good suggestion,' said Warren.

'Would his walk have taken him to the bridge?' asked Hutchinson.

Sutton shook his head and switched slides to a plan of the abbey grounds. Hand-drawn, the title proclaimed it to be from the fourteenth century.

'Doubtful. The bridge over the river Herrot dates back to the original abbey, when there used to be a water mill just inside the abbey perimeter. The bridge was a convenient way to transport wheat to the mill house. A gate next to it was wide enough to allow a fully laden horse and cart into the grounds, and provided easy access to the gardeners and cook's quarters that existed at the time.'

He switched slides, this one a modern plan of the abbey grounds.

'You can see how things have changed. The water mill and the mill house are gone, as are the old cook and gardener's quarters. The house that eventually became the retirement home was built on the land that the infirmary once stood upon. The bridge has remained, as has the gate, however it's now made of metal, padlocked and rarely used.

'It's quite possible that Father Daugherty's wanderings may have taken him along the inside of the perimeter wall, perhaps even to the gate, but unless he had a key to the padlock, he's unlikely to have been able to walk out on to the bridge. We've yet to find one on his body, but if he had it in his hand when he fell, it could be downstream. We'd need to dredge the river to find it.'

'I'll let you suggest that to DSI Grayson, Tony.'

'Was the padlock locked?' asked Ruskin when the chuckles had died down.

'Yes, although he could easily have locked it after himself, without a key, by reaching through the gate and snapping it shut. Forensics are dusting for prints.'

'Who would have access to the key?' asked Pymm.

'As usual, they were hanging up in the vestry. We'll do another audit of the keys, although if he was murdered, the killer may have returned them since.'

'If they didn't use those keys, then we all know someone who probably has a copy of his own,' said Richardson, darkly.

'We'll check out Rodney Shaw's whereabouts as a priority,' promised Warren. 'In the meantime, Forensics are busy going over Father Daugherty's room and looking for signs that he was taken to the bridge against his will. The bridge has stone walls about four feet tall, so he won't have been able to fall over either accidentally, or even after a helpful shove. He either climbed that wall of his own free will, or somebody lifted him over.'

Chapter 32

'What have you got for us, Prof?' asked Warren.

Today was the day of the egg implantation procedure. Warren had planned on taking the day off, but Susan had insisted that as her appointment wasn't until late afternoon, she would be going into school first thing to set cover lessons for the remainder of the week. Warren had no choice therefore but to go into work himself. As the hour of the procedure had drawn closer though, Warren had found himself increasingly distracted. In the end, he'd decided to travel down to Ryan Jordan's laboratory at the Lister Hospital in Stevenage, since he had to head in that direction for the clinic anyway.

'Preliminary tests indicate drowning,' said Jordan. 'He had head injuries consistent with a fall from that height onto the rocks below, but his lungs were filled with water, with the changes in the fluid around his lungs indicating fresh water drowning. There are signs of damage to his brain tissue indicative of hypoxia; I'll know more when the slides come back from histology.'

'What about alcohol or drugs?'

'Blood alcohol is only fractionally above zero – roughly what I'd expect if he had a glass of wine some hours before his death. I'm still waiting for toxicology, but there are no fragments of any pill casings in his stomach.'

'He probably had a glass with his evening meal. I don't suppose that could be used to give a time of death?'

Jordan said nothing, just raised an eyebrow.

'Sorry, teaching my grandmother to suck eggs.'

'In answer to the question, no, not with any certainty. Judging from the state of the food in his stomach, death occurred a couple of hours at least after his last meal, but when it comes to the rate of digesting food and metabolising alcohol, everyone is different.

'His core temperature was close to ambient when the CSIs first waded in to check he was dead and secure his body, but he'd been lying face down in cold running water. It's impossible to be any more precise than suggesting he probably died more than an hour before he was found.'

'So we're talking death occurring sometime between a couple of hours after his evening meal and an hour before the CSIs stuck a thermometer up his backside?'

'Probably.'

* * *

The appointment at the clinic was at 2 p.m. Warren had simply marked it in his online work calendar as 'busy'. He met Susan in the car park.

'It feels as though we're having some sort of clandestine affair,' joked Warren after pecking his wife on the cheek.

'It's not dingy enough,' said Susan, 'I like my affairs sordid.'

'I'll remember that in future.'

It had been a year since the couple had started attending the clinic, and by now the staff on the reception desk were a familiar, friendly sight. Despite this, Warren still dreaded his visits. Ever since he'd found out that the cause of the couple's problems were due to his low sperm count, rather than any issues with Susan's fertility, he'd felt a failure. He felt as though he was judged every time he walked in there; that everyone from the nurses and doctors to the health care assistants and receptionists looked in his notes and sniggered.

Absolute madness.

He knew that and Susan, a biology teacher by profession, knew that. And she told him that every time he was foolish enough to bring it up.

Over the last few weeks, as the couple had decided to embark upon the procedure, Warren had forced himself to stop complaining out loud. In the grand scheme of things, he had nothing to whinge about. For two weeks Susan had injected herself daily with powerful hormones, and trekked to the clinic every other day for ultrasound scans of her ovaries. Then she'd undergone the egg collection procedure, with nothing stronger than paracetamol to numb the discomfort. Yet she had never uttered a word of complaint. To his chagrin, Warren realised that he'd been so self-consumed with his own feelings of inadequacy, and by the rapidly unfolding case, that he hadn't even asked if she was in any pain.

He really had nothing to complain about; twenty minutes in a cubicle with some adult literature and a plastic cup had been his entire contribution to the process.

'It'll be fine,' said Susan. 'They phoned again at eleven to say the eggs are still dividing normally.'

As usual Susan had seen right through him. Warren worked with liars every day, but next to his wife he felt a mere amateur when it came to spotting somebody concealing the truth. Her reputation for making guilty pupils give up their secrets was well known amongst pupils and staff, and the science department had the lowest detention rate in the school. The threat of 'being sent to Mrs Jones' held a significant level of currency amongst the students. It was a talent she had inherited from her mother.

'And we'll be fine,' replied Warren. 'The procedure will go swimmingly.'

If Susan spotted the doubt in his voice, she chose not to say anything. She also generously ignored Warren's awful attempt at a pun.

* * *

Warren had been right. Everything had gone swimmingly, and by early evening, he and Susan were driving home. Despite Susan's protestations, Warren had insisted that they leave her car at the clinic and both go home in his. He'd pick her car up the following day.

The cost for parking overnight had been eye-watering, but he'd fibbed and said that they'd already been at the clinic long enough to pay the 'up to twenty-four hours' charge anyway, so he may as well pick it up on the way to work. If the human lie-detector sitting next to him had seen through his deception, she didn't say anything.

When they got home, Susan was insistent that she wasn't an invalid. Warren ignored her, lifting her school bag out of the car for her and demanding that she sit on the sofa with her feet up.

'Why is your bag full of marking? I thought you just went in this morning to set cover for the rest of the week?' called Warren as he placed her bag in the dining room.

'I'm waiting for an egg to implant, not recovering from open-heart surgery,' she replied from the living room. 'It'll be quite nice to reduce the backlog without having to deal with naughty kids or the senior leadership team banging on my classroom door every half-an-hour.'

'Yeah, those pupils really get in the way of you doing your job.' It was a running joke between them. Warren said similar things about the criminals he dealt with; nothing derailed a well-planned day like an unexpected murder, he'd found.

Warren poured the tea, then loaded up a saucer with some of the nice Marks and Spencer biscuits he'd secreted behind the never-used bread maker. He'd booked the remainder of the day off, and was looking forward to spoiling his wife for a change.

Pushing the door to the living room open with his foot, he stopped in his tracks. Susan lay across the sofa, eyes closed. A soft snore escaped her open mouth.

* * *

The tea was long cold by the time Susan woke up from her nap, later that evening. Warren had studiously avoided the temptation to check his work email. He knew that if anything desperately important happened, he'd be phoned.

The phone call happened at seven that evening as Warren was boiling pasta.

Tony Sutton.

For a long moment, Warren stared at the phone, willing it to stop ringing.

'It could be important,' called Susan from the living room, her sharp ears having picked up the phone's vibration on the kitchen counter.

With a sigh, Warren swiped the phone, answering just before it was due to switch to voicemail.

'Are you going back into work?' asked Susan, when he finally returned to the living room.

'No. It's nothing Tony can't handle. I've blocked the evening out in my schedule. Tonight I'm all yours.'

Tuesday 3rd March

Chapter 33

Warren arrived at work over an hour before the 8 a.m. briefing. He'd been as good as his word the night before, leaving his phone on vibrate only and not checking his emails, spending the evening with Susan in front of a film, before going to bed early. By unspoken assent, neither had mentioned the elephant in the room, but he doubted that she could describe the plot of the film any more than he could.

It was still dark when he finally gave in to a nagging conscience and got up. What little sleep he had managed had been punctuated with unpleasant and uncomfortable dreams that he couldn't remember, but which left him feeling depressed and demoralised. After a short cab journey back to the clinic to pick up Susan's car and pay its ransom he eventually found himself sitting in his office, slurping his second coffee of the day, still feeling out-of-sorts.

By the time he'd finally dealt with the bulk of his inbox, it was time for the meeting, his renewed focus on the case pushing the clouds to one side.

Moray Ruskin started the briefing by describing the previous afternoon's visit to Father Daugherty's favoured local, The Duke of Wellington.

'He was well known in there, according to the landlord. He

wasn't a big drinker, but he had a big personality. The locals also used to call him Father Scouse. He always had a couple of new jokes to share, and he usually watched the football, especially if Everton were playing. He'd take his dog collar off if his team were playing badly, in case anyone overheard his language and reported him to the pope. The landlord said everyone was very shocked to hear what had happened.'

'Did he go there with any other residents or staff from the retirement home?' asked Sutton.

'Not very often. A couple of the locals reckoned they might have seen someone else with him wearing a dog collar once or twice, but it certainly wasn't a common occurrence. I showed them photos of Rodney Shaw and Father Nolan, but nobody recognised either of them.'

'Did he have any regular drinking partners?' asked Hutchinson.

'Again, not really. Pretty much everyone knew him, and most had shared a few jokes with him, but there was nobody that the landlord would describe as a close friend, or who he always made a bee-line for'

'What about changes in mood?' asked Sutton.

'A couple of the locals said that he didn't come in at the beginning of the week and when he did come in on Thursday evening to watch the Europa League game, he was quite subdued, even when Everton won 3-1. The landlord expressed his condolences over Father Nolan's death when he saw him, and said that Father Daugherty was clearly quite upset over it. He had expected to see him Sunday, because Everton was playing Arsenal in the Premiership, but obviously that didn't happen.'

'So could Father Daugherty have been depressed enough over the death of Father Nolan to have killed himself, or is his death another murder disguised as suicide?' asked Richardson.

'That's the big question,' conceded Warren. 'Let's hope the forensics can tell us either way.'

Chapter 34

The first results from the CSIs investigating Father Daugherty's drowning came through mid-morning from the Crime Scene Manager Meera Gupta, Andy Harrison's deputy. Gupta promised a formal report within the next day or so, but in the meantime Warren made scribbled notes in his notebook. As soon as the call ended, he summoned the rest of the team to an impromptu briefing.

'Father Daugherty's fingerprints have been found on the padlock on the gate between the bridge and the abbey grounds,' he started.

'Were there any other identifiable prints?' asked Sutton.

'Some partials, but nothing good enough to run through the database,' said Warren. 'In anticipation of your next question, I asked specifically about a match to Rodney Shaw. The official answer is that they aren't nearly clear enough. Unofficially, they share enough common features with his prints for him not to be excluded at this stage.'

'What about cause of death? Is it a suicide, or something more suspicious?' asked Ruskin.

'It's early days,' cautioned Warren, 'so I'm keeping an open mind for now. The PM confirmed that his injuries were consistent with taking a dive from the bridge and landing headfirst on the rocks his body was found on. The CSIs went for a paddle and found traces of what appears to be his hair, and some blood embedded in the rock, so they're supporting that interpretation for now.

'They also found traces of fibres similar to material from the jacket he was wearing on the top of the bridge's wall and traces of stone dust on the coat, suggesting he rubbed against the wall as he went over. There were also black cotton fibres that match the shirt he was wearing.'

'I know that we have to rule out suicide before we declare it as murder,' said Ruskin, 'but if he did top himself, why would he put his coat on? Surely the last thing he'd be worried about is catching his death of cold?'

'It's a good thought, Moray,' said Sutton, 'but it could simply have been habit. It's not uncommon for people who jump from tall buildings to remove their glasses first so that they don't get broken.'

'There is another question, of course,' said Pymm. 'If Father Daugherty was wearing his coat, how did he transfer black cotton fibres from his shirt to the wall?'

'Which is exactly why I've persuaded DSI Grayson to categorise the death as suspicious; he's agreed that in the light of what happened to Father Nolan it's better to resource the investigation as a potential murder from the outset and down-grade if necessary later—' Warren smiled grimly '—which means that if this was just a tragic suicide we need to prove that quickly, before we burn up too much money and end up having to justify ourselves to the bean counters.'

A sympathetic murmur rippled around the table; nobody in the room envied Warren that conversation.

'Forensics have also found some dried seeds embedded in his coat,' continued Warren, dragging the briefing back on track, 'and along long the brick work on the bridge there were green, wax-coated fibres from a Barbour-style jacket.'

'Could that give us an indication of the route he was dragged?' asked Richardson.

'Quite possibly. They've been sent off for formal analysis, but CSM Gupta has also taken high resolution photographs that she's going to have run through a botanical database. It won't be good enough for court, we'll need the expert testimony for that, but it'll be a lot quicker and it might tell us where to look for more evidence.'

'What about inconsistencies?' asked Sutton. 'Aside from the question over fibre transfer, if it was a murder then the killer has done a good job at making it look like a suicide so far.'

'They're still investigating. But so far they haven't found the key to the padlock on his person, which raises the question about how he got on the bridge and why his fingerprints were on the padlock.'

'He could have touched the padlock, realised he didn't have a key and then walked around the long way,' suggested Hutchinson.

'Perhaps.' It sounded unlikely to Warren. 'Mags, see if there are any CCTV cameras outside the grounds that may have picked him up.'

Warren flicked to the next page in his notebook.

'There are also some questions over how he made it over the bridge wall. It's about four-foot tall and the marks on his coat and fibres on the brickwork are consistent with him scrambling over, but Gupta would have also expected some scuffs on his shoes and/or rubber marks from his soles on the wall. It's hardly conclusive, but worth noting.'

'Speaking of soles, what about footprints?' asked Hutchinson.

'Two partial footprints that matched Father Daugherty's were identified on the bridge. Unfortunately, the weather was not ideal, and they were just transfers from dirty shoes. There was also another partial that doesn't match Father Daugherty's. In answer to the obvious question, there isn't enough detail to match the impressions to the unknown prints found by the fire exit in the house.'

171

'What about Rodney Shaw?' asked Pymm.

'Again, not enough detail to match them to any of the shoes seized when we searched his house. Besides which, his work boots are still sitting on the shelf next to Andy Harrison's workspace, so if it was him, he was wearing a different pair.'

* * *

The phone rang as Warren was headed out of the office to brief Grayson on the latest findings. The DSI was now fielding daily calls from Assistant Chief Constable Naseem, who was himself on the speed dial of a number of high-profile parties, including the current Bishop of Hertfordshire and Essex. One unexplained death at a priest's retirement home was a tragedy; two was starting to look suspicious, and the force needed to control the flow of information and limit speculation until they were certain of what was happening.

'Is it urgent, Professor? I'm on my way to a meeting.' Warren had known the pathologist long enough to know that the man wouldn't be offended by his abrupt tone.

'Father Nolan didn't drown in that river.'

'The meeting can wait.'

* * *

'Diatoms. Microscopic, waterborne creatures with hard silica shells.' Warren had called an urgent briefing for everyone available.

Sutton nodded his head in understanding, as did Richardson and Pymm. Moray Ruskin looked blank.

'Basically, the little critters are ubiquitous. Freshwater or seawater, even tap water, all contain them. There are at least fifteen-thousand known species and the type and abundance varies depending on the source of the water. When someone drowns, the diatoms migrate through the lining of the lungs and into the bloodstream, from where they are then deposited in organs around the body. It only takes a few seconds, as long as the heart is beating of course. Histologists can identify them easily when examining tissue samples under the microscope.'

'Let me guess,' said Sutton, 'no diatoms?'

'Close enough. The number of diatoms throughout his solid organs were far too low, and the diatoms that were present were the wrong species. Wherever Father Daugherty was drowned, it wasn't in that river.'

A murmur travelled around the room.

David Hutchinson was the first to ask a question.

'How confident are we that the conclusion is sound?'

'The science is well respected, and peer-reviewed. Include all the discrepancies that the CSIs found at the bridge, and I think we're definitely looking at murder.'

Wednesday 4th March

Chapter 35

The decision had been made to go public with the belief that the deaths of Fathers Nolan and Daugherty were murder, not suicide. A press conference had been scheduled for midday, but Warren thought it important that the residents and staff at the retirement home be briefed first thing, before the press were informed. The only space big enough for everyone was the dining hall.

The huge room was dominated by a massive open fireplace. Red flocked velvet wall coverings spoke of the Langton family's wealth back in the eighteenth century, and the tiled, wooden floor gleamed under the lights suspended twenty feet above the gathered crowd.

Most of the original paintings had been removed to storage or local museums, and the subsequent spaces covered with appropriate paintings and iconography, including portraits of the most recent popes, a tasteful rendering of the virgin Mary with child, a painting said to be of St Cecil – the retirement home's namesake – and a near life-size crucifix.

The simple trestle tables that the priests typically dined at had been folded away after breakfast, to create more space, so that everyone could have a seat.

The room was filled with a low-level buzz of conversation as the residents and staff filed in. Beside Warren, Deacon Gabriel Baines discreetly ticked attendees off on a sheet; anybody absent would be an immediate suspect – or worse, the killer's potential next victim. Warren estimated that he had personally met about one third of the people in the room during the recent investigations. Rodney Shaw was the last to enter.

'Everyone is accounted for,' Baines told Warren quietly; even Fathers Kendrick and Ramsden had been brought down in their wheelchairs, along with their carers, including the three sisters. Aside from the brief flash of grey cloth, glimpsed when Sister Clara informed them that Father Cormac Nolan was missing from his room, it was the first time Warren had clapped eyes on the resident nuns.

Nobody in the assembled crowd was a fool, and it was clear from snatches of overheard conversation that everyone assumed that they would only have been gathered, with the SIO of the two deaths, if the fatalities had been ruled suspicious.

Bishop Fisher stood up and cleared his throat. Immediately the room fell silent. After a short prayer for the souls of their two deceased friends, and a request for the Lord to give strength and support to Warren and his team, Fisher passed the floor to Warren.

The news might not have been unexpected, nevertheless it was clearly a shock and upsetting to all of those present. There was also a degree of anger.

'DCI Jones, I believe I speak for many of us here when I say that I find it disturbing that we have been left in the dark about these killings, and our safety put at risk.' The speaker was a relatively young priest, Father Angus Boyce, who helped provide care for some of the priests.

'I think it is clear from the degree of ongoing police activity that you knew – or at least had suspicions – that the death of Cormac Nolan was more than a suicide. Yet you did nothing to warn us. Perhaps if Gerry Daugherty had thought that there was a killer on the loose, he may have taken precautions and still be with us?'

The speaker had a point, and from the nodding of heads and general murmuring of assent, it was a widely shared view. The best that Warren could claim was that for operational reasons he was unable to go into specific details about an active investigation and appeal for their patience and continuing assistance.

From the continued mutterings, it was clear that no one, including Father Boyce, was satisfied with that answer. For his part, Warren had a suspicion that there was a serious case review likely in the coming months, and that every decision made by his team would be scrutinised.

'Are we in any danger?' asked somebody else. Again, Warren recognised the speaker; Father Owen Merricks was a red-cheeked Welshman whose broad shoulders and upright posture belied his 78 years.

Before Warren could respond, one of the health care assistants, a tall, man in his mid-thirties, with a broad Black Country accent, also spoke out. 'Shouldn't we have armed guards, until this maniac is caught?'

'Perhaps we should evacuate the home, until this all blows over?' suggested his co-worker, a petite, Asian woman.

'Where would we go?' asked Father Merricks.

'At present we have no evidence to suggest that there is a specific threat to your safety, and there is no need to close the home or move any residents out.' Warren had to raise his voice to cut through the rising chatter. 'We will be posting police officers at the entrances to the home to ensure that no unauthorised persons enter the house. In the meantime, we urge you to remain vigilant; to report anything suspicious to one of our officers or Deacon Baines or Bishop Fisher, and to take care when outside the home, especially after dark.'

Nobody seemed particularly satisfied with his answer, least of all the two health care assistants. Warren wondered if either of

177

them would appear for work the next day, given that neither of them stayed in the house overnight.

'Do you have any suspects?' asked Father Boyce, when the muttering died down.

'We are pursuing a number of lines of enquiry,' hedged Warren. Despite studiously avoiding looking at Rodney Shaw, he could feel the groundsman's eyes burning defiantly into him.

'What about a motive?' This time the speaker was one of the nuns that shared a room and helped look after the priests' needs. Her grey habit covered her hair and made judging her age difficult, but Warren placed her age at about 40 years old. He couldn't recall which of the three sisters she was.

'Again, we are following a number of different leads, Sister…'

'Clara,' she supplied.

Warren addressed the room again.

'If any of you have any ideas about why Fathers Nolan and Daugherty might have been targeted, please, let me or one of my team know your thoughts, in confidence if you prefer.'

* * *

After addressing the residents of St Cecil's, Warren headed straight for the press conference at Welwyn. This time, the press conference was beyond full. Most of the chairs had been removed, to squeeze more people in. The story had now grown beyond local and national interest, with several reporters from international agencies also in attendance.

Grayson, as usual, was revelling in the attention. As a DSI, he would typically be expected to dress in plain clothes, but unlike many of his peers, Grayson usually wore his uniform around the office. For press conferences, he also wore his jacket; freshly dry-cleaned, his medals gleaming. His white shirt, on closer inspection, was made of tailored Egyptian cotton, rather than the multipack supermarket shirts that most uniformed officers wore each day, and even though he was sat behind a table emblazoned with the force's logo, his shoes would have passed the strictest of inspections at police training college.

Next to him, even in his smartest suit – the one usually reserved for weddings and funerals – and wearing the dark-blue silk tie that Granddad Jack had bought him for Christmas, Warren felt underdressed. His hair, whilst not untidy, had lost its freshly-cut sharpness; by contrast, Grayson's hair could have sliced cheese. More than a week of sleepless nights and stress had left Warren with bags under his eyes; Warren strongly suspected that Grayson was wearing make-up. Tony Sutton reckoned it was so he looked good in close-up on high-definition TVs. Even the man's after-shave smelt good.

The press conference was carefully choreographed. First came the revelation that both deaths were being investigated as suspected homicides. Next came more specifics about each death; as always, the precise details were chosen carefully, with as much care taken in deciding what not to release as to what was actually disclosed. Appeals for more information, for which a dedicated hotline had been set up, alongside the usual force numbers and the anonymous Crimestoppers help line, typically resulted in a flurry of calls from timewasters and fantasists. A few carefully chosen questions about details not yet released could usually weed those out.

The questions from the press were as predictable as Grayson's answers.

'Are the two murders linked – are we looking at a serial killer?'

'At the moment, we are keeping an open mind.'

'Are the general public in any danger?'

'We currently have no information to suggest that the public should be worried, but we would urge people to remain vigilant and report any suspicions to the police.'

'Will you be posting officers to protect the priests in the retirement home?'

'I'm afraid I cannot disclose operational matters.'

'Do the police have any idea why these particular priests were targeted?'

'We are pursuing a number of lines of inquiry.'

'Should priests be concerned about their safety?'

'Again, we have no specific intelligence to suggest that priests are in any particular danger, but we will be issuing guidance to churches about increasing their vigilance.'

'What about other faith groups? Could the killer be targeting religious leaders generally?'

'We have no indications that that is the case, but again we would urge worshippers to take extra care.'

Finally, the questions started to dry up and a number of reporters started to slip out the back. The clock at the rear of the room ticked over to 1 p.m. and Grayson called an end to the briefing.

As they filed out of the room, Grayson murmured out of the corner of his mouth.

'Conspiracy theorists. Start your engines...'

Chapter 36

'I've got an identification for those seeds found embedded in Father Daugherty's coat.' Deputy CSM Meera Gupta called Warren on his mobile as he headed back to Middlesbury. Grayson had opted to remain in Welwyn for meetings, which suited Warren fine. Grayson was an impatient traveller, and where possible he would engage the quickest police driver available to get him from A to B. If that wasn't possible, he drove himself, at high speed, often holding an animated conversation on his hands-free kit; quite how he had avoided the accumulation of multiple points on his license was a mystery to Warren.

Either way, Warren preferred not to travel with the man.

'Closest match looks like strawberry, you know the little seeds on the outside of the fruit?'

Pulling into the station car park, Warren thanked her and hung up.

Impatient to see if an idea he had been developing since the phone call was correct, Warren used the internet browser on his phone as he waited for the lift to CID. Opening the website of Middlesbury Abbey, he navigated to the gift shop. By the time he entered the main office he'd found what he was looking for.

For an eye-watering price, one could purchase a 340g jar of jam made from the abbey's home-grown strawberries.

* * *

'It's a bit early in the season for this year's strawberries to be ripe, but the floor of the greenhouse is covered in dried seeds from previous years. Anybody spending a significant amount of time in here would pick up a few of them.'

Gupta and her team were already on site and so it had been the work of moments to seal the greenhouses occupying the south-facing wall of the walled garden.

'There's access to running water from a standpipe, with a hose attached,' she continued. 'According to Professor Jordan, a preliminary report from the limnologist suggests that the diatoms found in Father Daugherty's tissue correspond to our local tap water.'

'What else have you found?'

'A wooden garden chair and a balled-up towel. It's no longer wet, but it's stiff, as if it was allowed to dry in that position. The concrete paving slabs surrounding the chair are also cleaner than the rest of the greenhouse.'

'Suggesting they were washed down?'

'Possibly, although I think it more likely that it was just caused by over-spilling water.'

It took a moment for Warren to put together the clues. When he did, he could scarcely believe what he was saying.

'Are you suggesting that Father Daugherty was water-boarded?'

'I wouldn't bet against it.'

Warren was stunned. Waterboarding involved placing a towel over a victim's face and then pouring water onto it, simulating the feeling of drowning. The US Army euphemistically referred to it as an 'enhanced interrogation' tactic; to everyone else it was torture.

Father Cormac Nolan had been burnt alive; now Father Gerry Daugherty had been subjected to torture. Whoever the killer was, they were a sadist and he or she needed to be taken off the street and locked away.

Warren's musings were interrupted by a call from the other end of the greenhouse.

'You need to come and see this, Meera. Bring DCI Jones with you.'

Warren followed the CSI along the plastic boarding. The far end of the greenhouse opened into a brick-built shed. A chipped porcelain sink with a dried cake of soap stood in one corner. The rest of the space was taken up by watering cans, trowels and other tools that Warren vaguely recognised, but couldn't name. Even through the mask, Warren could smell the familiar scents of his childhood; Granddad Jack had been a keen gardener and Warren had loved the warm, damp smell of his greenhouse and the dry, earthy scent of his shed.

The CSI triumphantly held up a pair of work boots. Turning them towards Warren and Gupta, he pointed out the black marker pen on the ankle.

'R.S.'

'Looks as though the boots we took from Rodney Shaw weren't the only pair he owned,' said Warren.

'And that's not all we've found.'

He pushed back the shed door. Hanging on a hook was a mud-covered, green wax jacket.

Thursday 5th March

Chapter 37

At 5 a.m., when Rodney Shaw was arrested for the second time, he was still in his nightwear. Despite his protestations, he was given a police-issue tracksuit and his hands were covered in plastic bags to preserve anything caught beneath his finger nails.

With Shaw safely placed in the back of a police car, the crime scene investigation team were free to enter the flat he had occupied since he and his wife separated. This time the search warrant stated clearly that the house, his car and any relevant outbuildings were to be searched for material relating to the murders of Fathers Nolan and Daugherty. A similar search warrant was also being executed at his family home. This time there was less need to ensure that the search didn't over-stretch its original remit and so Warren was happy to leave the searches to be supervised by Sergeants Richardson and Hutchinson.

* * *

Shaw opted to stick with the same duty solicitor as his previous arrest. After setting up the PACE recorder, reminding Shaw of his rights under caution again, and introducing Tony Sutton, Warren got down to business.

'First of all, as you are aware, you are under arrest on suspicion of the murder of Father Gerry Daugherty. Before we start, is there anything you wish to tell me?'

'I didn't kill him.'

'Mr Shaw, please could you tell me what you were doing on the night of Saturday the twenty-eighth of February until the early hours of Sunday the first of March?'

The approach to interview had been decided upon the previous night. They already knew that Shaw was lying about his movements the evening that Father Nolan had been murdered. Consequently, Warren decided to put the first murder to one side. Revealing that they knew about his lies from then might make him clam up and start 'no commenting', a cycle that could be hard to break someone out of.

'I was on my own, watching TV. Then I went to bed.'

'So you have nobody who can vouch for your whereabouts?'

'No, I was alone.'

'What about your daughter? I thought she visited you on the weekend?' asked Sutton.

Shaw scowled. 'Funnily enough, her mum was reluctant to let her come over after you lot came crashing in last week. God only knows what she's going to think after you appeared at their house this morning.'

Warren ignored the implied rebuke.

'What did you watch on TV?'

He shrugged, 'I think I watched the news, then stayed up for *Match of the Day* and the *Football League Show*.'

'Who played?'

'I dunno. Fulham and Derby County, I think.' He paused. 'Yeah, Fulham won two-nil. Both goals in the first half.'

Warren made a note to get that checked out, however he knew it was hardly conclusive. Shaw could easily have recorded the match or looked up the highlights online. Besides which, that only accounted for the latter part of the evening. Father Daugherty's body had been found at 2.30 a.m. and he'd last been seen at about 7 p.m., before he headed out for his post-dinner walk. That left a window of seven or so hours.

'What did you do in the hours before then? Did you go out?'

'No, I stayed in all day and pottered about the house.'

'Doing what?'

'Just stuff.'

'What sort of stuff?'

Shaw flushed.

'I dunno, I can't remember.' His voice rose. 'can you remember what you did all day Saturday? It was my day off, and I'd had a shit week, thanks to you lot. I just didn't feel like going out or doing anything.'

'OK, let's move on. I believe that you keep a number of keys to various locks around the abbey grounds in your house. Why do you do that?'

'For safekeeping and in case I get called out during the night. I also have some on my own keyring for locks that I use every day.'

'Such as?'

'The main tool shed and the greenhouse, as well as the visitor centre and toilet blocks.'

'And what keys do you have at home? For safekeeping.'

'You already know this. You took them last week.'

'Remind me.'

'The main front gates, rear gate and visitor side gate, the chapel and the undercroft. Also, the front door and rear doors to the retirement home, the gift shop and the ticket booth.'

'What about other keys?'

'I don't have copies of them, they're hanging in the vestry. As you already know.'

'Do you have a copy of the key to the padlock to the gate down by the old mill house that lets people through the gate by the bridge?'

'No, I can't remember the last time it was even opened. The key for that should be in the vestry.'

Warren made a show of writing that down.

On cue, Sutton opened the folder in front of them.

'Do you recognise these boots?'

He passed the colour photograph across the table. Shaw squinted at it.

'Yeah, they're my spare ones. I keep them in the greenhouse.'

'And what about this jacket?'

Sutton pushed a second photograph across the table.

'Looks like the one hanging up in the greenhouse. It's an old one I use if the weather's really crap, or I'm going to be doing something really dirty.'

Sutton thanked him and put the photographs back in the folder.

'Does anyone else borrow these clothes, Mr Shaw?'

'I doubt it. My apprentice has feet like canoes, he'd never get into my boots and he's not been here long enough to do any really dirty jobs.'

Warren also wrote that down. The unknown fingerprints found on the petrol can used in the arson on Father Nolan had already been matched to the apprentice, and his alibi for that night was sound; he'd get someone to confirm that the boots couldn't fit the lad, but the teenager had been all but ruled out of the enquiry.

Shaw shifted in his seat, his face was a mixture of irritation and nerves.

'When was the last time you wore these boots, Mr Shaw?' asked Warren.

'I've no idea. I usually wear my other work boots, but I haven't seen them since you took them last week.'

'So what shoes have you been wearing at work?'

'Well first of all, I've barely been to work. Even when I've not been wasting my time sitting in here, on trumped up charges, there's been hardly any point going in. For most of the past ten days the whole bloody place has been covered in police tape. In case you haven't noticed, it's spring and I've got stuff that needs doing.'

'Which shoes have you been wearing?' repeated Warren.

'My trainers. You know, the white ones you took last week and gave me back covered in black fingerprint powder.'

Warren made another note.

Shaw's eyes flicked towards Warren's notebook. Warren casually closed it before Shaw could read what he had written.

'Tell me about your relationship with Father Daugherty.'

'Everyone loved Gerry. He was a lovely man. Very funny.'

'What about you? Did you speak to him very often.'

'Sure. I'd often see him around the house if I was up there doing a job.'

'What about in the grounds? Did you ever work together in the gardens?'

'Gerry? No chance. He could kill a plastic Christmas tree.'

'So he never helped out in the greenhouse?'

'No. I doubt he ever set foot in there.'

'Father Daugherty was found face down in the river, but the gate to the bridge was locked with a padlock. Have you any idea how the killer might have been able to open those gates?' Sutton asked.

'With a key presumably.'

'Where would he get the key?'

'From the vestry, I suppose.'

'The key is still hanging in the vestry.'

'So the killer must have returned it.'

'That's a bit risky, don't you think?'

'The whole thing sounds risky.'

'Do you have a copy of the key?'

'I already said I don't.'

'Well, presumably the padlock came with two keys when it was bought. Where is the second one?'

Shaw's forehead creased.

'I think they're both on the hook in the vestry.'

'We found only one, so where is the second key?'

'I dunno, I guess the killer must still have it.'

Warren made another note.

'OK. Let's go back to the jacket hanging in the greenhouse. You only wear it in bad weather?'

'Yes.'

'When was the last time you wore it?'

'A few weeks ago, maybe? Some fencing blew down. Eventually I had to go out and fix it, even though it was raining.'

'And you haven't been down to the river in it?'

'No.'

'In that case, could you explain why there are fibres from this coat at the scene of Father Daugherty's murder? Also, why is there dust from the wall that Father Daugherty was lifted over on the coat, and on the soles of your spare work boots, footprints from which have been found next to the bridge?'

Shaw's mouth dropped open.

Warren opened the folder again and removed a second photograph. A close up of a padlock key.

'This key fits the padlock to the gate by the bridge over the river. It is the matching key to the one still hanging in the vestry. It was found in the inside pocket of your wax jacket.

'I am going to ask you again. Were you involved in the murder of Father Gerry Daugherty?'

Chapter 38

'We've got him on the back foot over Daugherty,' started Warren.

It was now coming up to 8 a.m. and Shaw had requested a break, after again denying the murder of Father Daugherty.

Since he'd been dragged from his bed at 5 a.m., they couldn't say no. Not that Warren wanted to. Between drafting the request for a warrant and picking it up from the duty magistrate on the way to Shaw's, Warren had managed only a few hours of sleep himself.

Tony Sutton looked similarly tired, his skin grey, his hands shaking from too much coffee. Moray Ruskin looked as fresh as a daisy; he wasn't even wet from the unexpected rainstorm outside. Unfortunately, the same couldn't be said for Rachel Pymm, who had been unable to hold her umbrella properly whilst using her walking sticks. Her hair was stuck to her forehead and her glasses were steamed up. She was not in a good mood.

'I've got Shaw's mobile phone records from the night of Father Daugherty's murder. Unfortunately, it matches what he says. His handset didn't leave his house all day Saturday or Sunday.'

'He could have remembered to leave it at home this time,' said Sutton. 'Anyone who watches TV must know that we can track their movements if they carry it with them.'

'What about calls?'

191

'Nothing much. The last call is to his wife, late on Friday evening, and a text to his daughter immediately after.'

'Which would match what he said about her refusing to let him see his daughter over the weekend,' said Ruskin.

'What about his car? Any sign of it on traffic cameras?'

'I'm afraid not, Chief,' responded Richardson. 'Nothing on any of the static ANPR cameras near the abbey, or from the junctions closest to his house. As far as we can tell, his car didn't leave the vicinity of his house all weekend.'

'That might not mean anything,' said Warren. 'We found a mountain bike at his flat Everything that was used to kill Father Daugherty was at the scene of the crime, including his jacket and boots. He could easily have travelled there by bicycle.'

'Could his bike fit in the back of his car?' asked Ruskin, suddenly.

'Good question, that could explain how he travelled to Father Nolan's murder undetected,' said Sutton.

'His car is a Volvo estate,' said Warren. 'If he took the wheels off it might.'

'I'll get the CCTV team to look for bicycles on their footage,' said Mags Richardson.

'We should also get Forensics to check his tyres for mud and trace evidence,' suggested Sutton. 'That might indicate if he cycled into the abbey grounds.'

'Good suggestion. Meanwhile, any luck with his computer?' asked Warren. One of the first things the CSIs had seized was Shaw's rather elderly desktop PC.

'It's with Pete Robertson down at Welwyn. He's looking at it as we speak,' said Richardson.

'Good. Interrupt us if anything relevant turns up.'

'I think we've pushed the death of Father Daugherty as far as we can at the moment,' said Sutton. 'His solicitor is going to claim all the evidence so far can be explained away as circumstantial. We don't even have his fingerprints on the padlock key.'

'I agree. Let's come back to it when we have more forensics, we've got plenty of time. Speaking of which—' Warren looked at his watch '—I think he's had a long enough break. Let's see what he has to say about Father Nolan.'

* * *

Rodney Shaw looked less nervous, and more annoyed when the interview resumed. His solicitor opened the proceedings.

'This is the second time that my client has been arrested on spurious charges with only circumstantial evidence to back up your claims. Even if your forensics team have successfully placed Mr Shaw's spare jacket and boots at the scene of Father Daugherty's death, those items of clothing hang in an easily accessible greenhouse. You have yet to show me any convincing evidence that Mr Shaw was the person wearing those clothes, or that he placed that padlock key in the pocket.

'It's clear that you don't have anything substantial on my client. In fact, I'd go as far as to say that you're getting desperate to be seen to be doing something. Well, my client objects to being used in this fashion. I insist that you either charge Mr Shaw or end this charade and release him.'

Warren waited until the solicitor had finished.

'What was your relationship like with Father Nolan?'

Shaw blinked, clearly nonplussed by the change of subject.

His solicitor spoke up, her irritation clear in her tone.

'I thought there was something a bit fishy last time. I've never seen that sort of treatment for a simple accusation of theft.' She paused. 'Rest assured, DCI Jones, I will be going over that previous search to make certain you didn't overreach yourself. I will also be reviewing the transcript of the interview, paying particular attention where your officers denied that the arrest was in relation to the murder.'

Warren ignored her bluster; Pymm had been careful in her choice of language.

'Again, what was your relationship like with Father Nolan?'

'Fine. He was a quiet man; kept himself to himself like, but he was friendly enough.'

'I believe that you mentioned in your previous interview that he often helped with the garden?'

'Yes. He was quite a keen gardener. He tended the vegetables.'

'And you never had a falling out?'

'No, we got on fine.'

'What about after he caught you in the bookmaker's?'

Shaw scowled.

'He didn't "catch me". I've broken no laws. I'm perfectly entitled to spend my time in a bookmaker's.'

'My apologies, I misspoke. Let me rephrase the question. Was your meeting Father Nolan in the bookmaker's the cause of the argument that witnesses overheard between the two of you?'

'What argument? Father Nolan and I got on just fine.'

Warren looked at the man carefully. He seemed genuinely bemused. The question had been a gamble, designed to elicit some sort of response from Shaw. It didn't seem to have been successful.

'Fair enough. We'll come back to that later.'

Warren made a show of leafing through his notes.

'Why did you lie to us about your whereabouts on the night that Father Nolan was killed?'

This did elicit a response. It was a few seconds before Shaw was able to answer.

'What do you mean?'

'You lied to us. In your original witness statement taken the day after Father Nolan's death, you claimed that you received a call about the fire from Deacon Baines at five minutes past ten. That was the first you knew about the fire.'

'Yes, that's right.'

'And that you were at home, watching the BBC News, preparing for an early night?'

194

Shaw was clearly conflicted. Would he admit his original lie, or try and brazen out?

He tried to brazen it out.

'Yes.' His voice cracked slightly and he took a sip of water.

'I think you're lying. Why don't you tell me what you were really doing when Deacon Baines called you.'

The silence stretched.

'No comment.'

Warren mentally punched the air. Up unto this point Shaw had answered everything they put to him.

'Are you sure about that, Mr Shaw?'

'No comment.'

Warren opened the folder again. Shaw's eyes tracked his movements. From his perspective, nothing good had ever come out of that folder. He had to be wondering what else was in there.

Warren took his time, angling the folder slightly so that neither Shaw nor his solicitor could see the sheets as he removed them. Or the fact that more than half the bulk of the folder was taken up by a blank A4 pad, a trick that had worked well in the past.

'We know that you didn't receive the call at home. That is quite clear from the mobile phone triangulation data that I have in front of me.' He pushed the printed map across the table.

Shaw swallowed hard, but said nothing.

'This is several miles from your flat. Yet you said that you were at home when you received the call.'

Shaw licked his lips.

'I made a mistake. I popped out for some milk, I must have received the call whilst I was in the shop.'

'Which shop? It was five past ten.'

'That was why I was in that shop. It opens late.'

It was getting painful. Warren wondered how much longer Shaw would keep up his lies.

'There is a newsagent within that radius,' pointed out Sutton.

Shaw relaxed slightly.

'Unfortunately, it closes at 8 p.m.' Sutton had no idea if that was true, but it didn't really matter; everyone in the room knew Shaw was lying.

'I hadn't realised.' Shaw's tone brightened slightly. 'That's why I didn't have any milk on me when I turned up at the fire.'

'Seems a bit of a gamble to drive all that distance, when there's a late-night garage less than one hundred yards from your flat,' said Sutton.

'I didn't know it was open until midnight. I've only lived there for a few months.'

'Well you would have had to drive past it to get to this newsagent. Didn't you notice the blazing lights on the forecourt.' Shaw blinked helplessly. 'And I don't recall saying it was open until midnight, just that it was late-night. Am I right DCI Jones?'

'I believe so. We can rewind the recording if you'd like, Mr Shaw?' Shaw slumped in his seat.

'Is this your car, Mr Shaw?'

Warren pushed a photograph across the table. He could just have read out a description and the licence number, but he felt a photograph of the Volvo on a low-loader, surrounded by CSIs, would have more of an impact.

'Yes.' His voice was barely a whisper.

'According to Automatic Number Plate Recognition cameras, your car left Middlesbury Abbey just after 5 p.m. It then drove across town, arriving in this part of town at approximately twenty-past. Phone mast records confirm that your phone followed this same route, at the same time. And we know that you had your phone on you because you answered it at five past ten. Your phone then remains more or less stationary until that call came in, when you drove straight to the abbey.

'Now I would really like to know what you did in the almost five hours between you arriving here and leaving to drive to the abbey.'

Shaw looked sick.

'No comment.'

Chapter 39

'What do you think, Moray?' asked Sutton. Ruskin had been watching the interview of Rodney Shaw over a video link. Shaw had again denied the murder of Father Daugherty and then requested a break to speak with his solicitor.

'He's lying,' stated the young constable.

'Everybody lies,' said Sutton. 'I don't think there's a person who steps inside that room who doesn't lie. And that includes us.'

'Bit of a cynical view, don't you think?' said Ruskin.

'Not at all, it's a simple fact of human nature. Everybody lies. All the time. The question is, do the lies matter? Are they important to us or this case?'

'So you reckon that he might be lying about something that has no bearing on our investigation?'

'Perhaps. People lie because they are ashamed of something, or because the truth might get them into trouble. Sometimes they lie because they think that something innocent could be taken the wrong way, or sometimes just because they don't think the answer is any of our damn business. It's your job to decide which lies are important and which aren't. Which lies do you pursue and which do you let go? Which ones do you let slide then pull them up on later? If we can catch them in a lie in one area, it can strengthen our hand in another. Sometimes it's the little, prov-able lie that gives us enough justification to get a search warrant. You've seen how it works.'

'I suppose it's true what you say. I certainly saw that when I was in uniform. I remember arresting one guy who'd been accused of shoplifting. We made him empty his pockets, and he copped to the two bottles of vodka he'd concealed in his tracksuit bottoms. But the security guard reckoned he might have some-thing else in his underwear, because he was sitting funny. The bloke swore blind that there was nothing down his undies, and that he couldn't sit right because he had really bad piles. Anyway, we didn't believe him, he was definitely lying. So when we took him back to the nick, we arranged for him to be strip-searched. He made a right fuss, and we were like, "mate, you've already been done for nicking the vodka, just admit to it. Kicking off isn't going to make things any better".

'Eventually we persuaded him to remove his trousers and it turns out he's wearing his wife's frilly knickers. They were so small his balls were practically blue, no wonder he couldn't sit properly.'

'What did you do?'

'Took ourselves outside, had a bloody good laugh, then did him for the stolen vodka. We decided not to mention his lack of cooperation.'

'Exactly. It was a lie that didn't matter. You know DS Pymm lied to my face first thing this morning?'

Ruskin was shocked.

'Yep, a straight up lie.'

'What did you do?'

'I let it go. Not important.'

'What was it about?' asked Ruskin, without thinking.

'Well, not that it's any of your business, but when she came out of the lift this morning, I asked her how she was and she said "fine".'

'Oh.'

'I knew she wasn't fine, because she'd just walked across the carpark after some thoughtless idiot parked in the disabled bay because they didn't want to get wet. She's been doing overtime and isn't even due in today. Yet here she is.

'This morning she lied to my face, and said she was fine. I let it go, because I know that she doesn't want anyone to make a fuss – she has too much dignity to accept help unless she really needs it – and because I trust her judgement.'

'I see what you're saying, sir.'

Ruskin stood up and reached for his wallet and keys.

'Where are you going?'

'I'm going to move my car and buy Rachel a slice of her favourite cake.'

'Good lad, I knew you'd get the hint. When you're done, go and check out some of Rodney Shaw's lies.'

Chapter 40

'The press conference has stirred up a fair bit of interest. Several dozen calls already,' said Rachel Pymm as Warren came back into the office after his interview with Rodney Shaw.

'Go on, give me the highlights.'

'So far we've had calls blaming everyone from radical Islamists to a rogue IRA cell and the illuminati. Lots of helpful folks have asked if we've considered it might be revenge for historic child abuse – although none of them actually had anything helpful, they'd just seen it on the news. We've also had four confessions, all from our frequent fliers, including our best friend Colin the Crank.'

'Well, he supposedly stitched up Lord Lucan when he was only three years old, so bumping off a couple of elderly Catholic priests should be easy for him.'

'Quite. Maybe we should just arrest him and accept his confessions – we'd clear half the high profile cases from the past twenty years.'

'Anything more worthy of our attention?'

'A couple of people think they may have seen suspicious characters hanging around the abbey, we're sending someone over to take a statement. But this one is a bit more interesting. Vernon

Coombs, a former journalist on the *Middlesbury Reporter*. He asked for you by name.'

'Don't they always? Refer him to the press office,' said Warren.

'He's not after an interview, he claims to have information that could help us. Besides which, I doubt he's looking for his next big scoop.'

'Why do you say that?'

'He's given his address as Goldfinch Hospice up on Osprey Close. He says to pop by tomorrow morning. I wouldn't wait too long, it doesn't sound as though he's long for this world.'

* * *

The interview with Rodney Shaw resumed in the late afternoon. Warren had spent the intervening hours waiting for forensics from the search, and scanning old articles on the *Middlesbury Reporter* website, written by Vernon Coombs.

The final article under Coombs' by-line was dated approximately eighteen months previously, which corresponded with the small article about his retirement from the paper after twenty-two years. The accompanying picture was of a smiling, robust man with neat grey hair.

Scrolling through the other articles attributed to the reporter, they matched what the short notice about his retirement had stated. His articles primarily dealt with so-called local and community news. It seemed that he was also something of a history buff, particularly when it concerned Middlesbury's past.

Little of his previous work seemed to be crime-related, and he wasn't credited with reports on any of Warren's own cases. There was no clue as to why he thought he could provide insight in the abbey murders. Warren would have to wait until the following morning to see what the man had to say for himself.

'Shall we start where we left off, Rodney? What were you doing in the almost five hours between leaving work and receiving the phone call about the fire?'

'No comment.'

'Are you sure about that, Rodney? We have evidence that you were not where you said you were on the night of the fire. Juries can be a forgiving lot, but they really don't like a liar.'

'No comment.' His voice was firm.

'Do you recognise this mobile phone number? You called it the evening Father Nolan was killed, before you were informed of the fire.'

Shaw barely glanced at the number. 'No comment.'

'You call it quite regularly. Every couple of weeks.'

'No comment.'

'The night that Father Nolan was killed, he left his room by the ground floor fire exit. In addition to his footprints, we also found traces from your work boots around that door. Can you explain why his footprints and your footprints were down there?'

'I don't know why Father Nolan's prints were there, but I did a fire inspection a few weeks ago. They could have been from then.'

Warren made another note. Shaw didn't seem nearly as nervous as before. In contrast, Warren was starting to feel that they were going nowhere. They really needed to know what Shaw was doing the night of the fire, but so far they had no evidence that he had even left that area whilst the fire was being set.

Similarly, they still had no evidence that Shaw was anywhere other than his flat the night Father Daugherty had been killed.

The interview was stalled until they had more forensics.

'Don't go anywhere, Mr Shaw,' instructed Warren as he terminated the interview.

* * *

'We're still lacking a smoking gun,' said Warren. It was late afternoon and Warren was starting to feel the effects of several early starts and late finishes in a row.

'What are you still looking for?' asked Grayson. At least he'd put some coffee on.

Rodney Shaw had been arrested at 5 a.m. that morning. Warren was beginning to wish they'd gambled and held back; that way the custody clock would run out at a more civilised hour. At the same time the following morning, Shaw had to either be released, charged or an extension to custody applied for.

'I can get you another twelve hours,' said Grayson, 'but you know you haven't enough for a magistrate to grant the full ninety-six based on what you have so far. You need to come up with the goods by 5 p.m. tomorrow or he walks again.'

'Ideally we need evidence of him leaving the ANPR blackspot and returning within that time period. We're awaiting CCTV and witnesses for that. Unfortunately, in this case a lack of evidence doesn't rule him out, it's easily within walking distance,' said Warren.

'What about his mobile phone?'

'It's essentially stationary during that time, but he could have just left it in his car.'

'You're going to need more than that.'

'I know.' Warren was too tired to keep the frustration from his voice. 'We're awaiting more detailed records for an unregistered mobile that Shaw called at half past five that evening. He calls it regularly, every couple of weeks. Short duration.'

'What about the night Father Daugherty was killed?'

'We'll know that when we get the records back.'

'What about his movements the night Father Daugherty was killed?'

'He claims not to have been out all weekend. So far his phone records match his account and his car wasn't picked up on ANPR cameras. His neighbours weren't around much that weekend and so can't provide an alibi. He has a bicycle and we are looking for CCTV footage of cyclists in the vicinity of both murders, and forensics on its tires to see if we can place it in the grounds.'

'This isn't looking good,' said Grayson.

'We've got some more forensics pending. Professor Jordan found fibres inside Father Daugherty's nostrils. They have been positively matched to a towel that we found balled up on the floor in the green house, beside a hosepipe and garden chair. He believes that Father Daugherty was essentially water-boarded, and died when it went too far. We're looking at Shaw's wardrobe to see if we can find any fibres from the towel. We've already found a couple on the wax jacket.

'The chucking him off the bridge was a clumsy attempt to make it look as though he'd killed himself. That might explain why Shaw left the padlock key in the pocket of the coat instead of returning it to the vestry. If he wasn't expecting Father Daugherty to die in the greenhouse, he might have panicked.'

'Anything else?'

'Document Analysis are looking at the note left on Father Daugherty's dresser. If we can link it to Shaw we have a case.'

'Fingers crossed,' said Grayson. He placed his cup down carefully. 'What if Shaw is innocent? Who else are you looking at? What about that disturbed young man that turned up at the home unannounced after Christmas?'

'We've got teams looking for Lucas Furber and trying to track his whereabouts.'

'Well, don't put all your eggs in one basket, Warren.'

* * *

It was already late when Warren arrived home that night. He'd seen from the drive that the bedroom light was turned off, and knew that Susan would already be in bed at this hour on a school night. He'd sleep in the spare room again.

She'd left some pasta and Bolognese sauce in a Tupperware container. The note beside it read 'For tea tonight or lunch tomorrow. Don't work too hard. Sxx.'

This was what he hated most about these sorts of cases — policing was a twenty-four-hour business, and as SIO, no matter how hard he tried, he'd end up working silly hours that didn't overlap with his wife. In the past he'd gone whole weeks communicating with Susan by text message, even though they shared the same bed.

That would have to change in the future. When he was a child, his father had been away a lot when he and his brother were growing up. If Niall MacNamara had known how his life would suddenly be snatched away when Warren was only 13 years old, would he have made the effort to be around more often?

Alone in the kitchen, waiting for the microwave to ding, Warren found himself dwelling on everything his father had missed, both before his death, and after his death. The school nativity play that Warren had sung a solo in at primary school. The sports day where he'd unexpectedly won the hundred metres. His graduation from university. His graduation from police training college. His wedding to Susan. And, God willing, his first grandchild.

Warren vowed to be there for all of those events for his own child, no matter what sacrifices he would have to make professionally. He refused to miss those special, life-changing events the way that his own father had.

And the way that Gary Hastings would.

Friday 6th March

Chapter 41

Over the years, Warren had visited many different hospices and they varied enormously. From dismal places where time stood still as the occupants and their loved ones simply waited for the Grim Reaper to make his appearance so they could free up the bed, to more cheery places, where death was an inevitability, but what life remained was celebrated.

Thankfully, Goldfinch Hospice was of the latter variety, Warren had spent too much time in the former.

The twelve-hour extension to Rodney Shaw's custody had been authorised and served the night before; Warren and his team had until 5 p.m. that evening to find enough evidence to either charge him, release him on bail, or extend his custody. Warren had swung by Shaw's cell first thing that morning to see if a night in the station had loosened his tongue. It hadn't.

Vernon Coombs' room was on the ground floor, and was spacious and well-lit. The early morning spring sunlight streaming through the windows from the pretty gardens outside complemented the pale, yellow walls and the bright bed spread. Those same walls were covered by family photographs and scenic watercolours from the Lake District.

'That's where I've asked for my ashes to be scattered,' said

Coombs after the care assistant had shown Warren into the room. 'My daughter painted those for her GCSE art, would you believe?' He laughed, a rumbly, chesty rattle. 'Probably the only time we ever got her to take homework away with her on holiday.'

He pointed to a garish stick figure painted in bright primary colours on the opposite wall, 'Get well soon Granddad' had been neatly printed, with a couple of sloppy crosses underneath. 'That masterpiece was painted by my Lilly, she's only three – I reckon she'll take after her mother.'

To Warren's untrained eye, Rachel Pymm had been correct. Coombs was almost unrecognisable as the smiling journalist featured on the *Middlesbury Reporter* website, just eighteen months ago.

He'd clearly lost significant weight; everything from his clothes to the wing-backed armchair he was sat in seemed several sizes too large. His skin, an unhealthy yellow colour, hung off him like a limp bedsheet. His neatly combed, full-head of hair was entirely gone.

Clear plastic tubes snaked out of a cannula on the back of his left hand to a machine on the bedside table. A small plastic unit with a red button was clipped to his shirt pocket, a cable running to the machine. Warren recognised it as a patient-administered morphine pump.

'Prostate cancer,' explained Coombs. 'I started having a bit of trouble with the old waterworks a couple of years back. I ignored it obviously; figured it's just what happens as you get old, besides I was busy and if I'm honest, didn't fancy some doctor's index finger up my arsehole.

'Any way, about twelve months or so after I retired, I finally figured, I've got no excuses left and went to the GP. Turns out there's a fucking blood test, you don't even need a finger up your bum unless the results are dodgy.

''Course, by this point my PSA test is off the scale. They whipped my prostate out immediately and started me on chemo

208

and radiotherapy, but the bastard had already spread. They gave me two months at the outside.'

'I'm sorry to hear that.'

'Don't be, that was last October, so I'm already well into injury time. Didn't think I'd live to see Lilly's next birthday, but she turns four this weekend.'

'You said that you had some information that might help in our investigation.'

Coombs fingered the button on the pump, before clearly thinking better of it.

'Makes me drowsy,' he explained.

'I can come back later, if you are uncomfortable,' said Warren. He could see the pain shadowing the man's eyes.

'No, you've come all this way and I need to speak to you.'

Coombs reached over to a small coffee table. A thick, lever arch folder sat upon it. He rested his hand upon it.

'When you get to this stage in life, there are things you regret. Not going to my GP is obviously top of the list, but other than that it's not only the things you should have done, but also the things you won't do.'

Warren said nothing. He'd gone to bed the night before with his late-night musings in the kitchen weighing heavily on his mind. Coombs' ruminations were a little too close for comfort.

'I don't believe in miracles, DCI Jones. I know I'll never see my Lilly grow up and get married. My next trip to the Lake District will be in an urn, and England will never win the World Cup again in my lifetime. But one of the things I regret the most? I'll never see this published.'

He slid the folder towards Warren.

'My complete history of Middlesbury Abbey. It was my retirement project. I had hoped to get it finished in time for the 800th anniversary.'

Warren was nonplussed. He couldn't see what a partly written history book had to do with the murders of the past few weeks.

Nevertheless, he kept quiet, letting the man continue. It was clearly very important to him, and Warren had no intention of denying a dying man one last chance to feel relevant.

'I've been fascinated with the abbey since I was a kid. One of my first memories was my grandparents taking me around there on a summer's day. We had ice cream and coke – a real treat, my mum and dad didn't have much money to spare back then.

'Next time I visited was in primary school and we had a tour of the place by one of the priests. They must have thought I was a right weirdo; all my classmates wanted to do was go and buy a rubber or a leather bookmark from the gift shop, but I kept on asking all these questions, until it was time to go home.'

He coughed and reached for his morphine pump, again stopping himself.

Warren watched with concern.

'Well, I never stopped finding it interesting. I dragged my own kids around there, and in later years joined the Friends of Middlesbury Abbey. The most frustrating thing though was that unlike some of the more famous abbeys, like Tor Abbey down in Torquay or Bury St Edmunds, nobody ever wrote a book about it. The free guidebook is a stapled collection of black and white sheets written in the late Nineties. I promised myself that when I retired, I would write that book. I've been taking photographs there for years, some of them pretty good, and I've even travelled to Spain to visit where the founding order of monks originated.

'There was also a lot of unpublished material that I could use. The monks in the abbey were highly literate and they recorded much of their daily life. Many of them wrote detailed diaries, and included the good, the bad and the ugly. Why they did that, I guess we'll never know, although they wrote in Latin, which suggested they regarded them as some sort of official record. They were never published or made available to the public, however when they abandoned the abbey in 1539, they left them behind in the old undercroft.

'Most of the rest of the buildings fell to ruin of course over the next couple of hundred years, but the undercroft was dry and stable, and they were written on high quality paper, and so they survived until the site was taken over by Sir Howard Langton at the start of the eighteenth century.

'He paid for the diaries to be translated from the original Latin and catalogued. His plan was to one day open a museum, maybe even write a book himself. Unfortunately, when he died the work stopped and so again the diaries were left ignored, this time in the basement of the house, rather than the undercroft.'

'Until you came along?' filled in Warren. So far, Coombs had confirmed what Deacon Baines had told Warren as he'd shown him around the retirement home. He still had no idea where this was leading, but he decided to let the man continue.

Coombs nodded. 'I became aware of their existence after a private tour given to the Friends of Middlesbury Abbey back in 2008. I mentioned that one day I would like to write the history of the abbey and Bishop Fisher offered to arrange access to them. I started visiting the archives on a regular basis in about 2010. Other priests in the house became interested in what I was doing and I soon had a couple of regular helpers.

'I'm hoping that someone may decide to carry on my work and finish the book,' he sighed. 'I'd love that to be my legacy.'

'And you think that may have some relevance to the murders that I'm investigating?'

'Tell me DCI Jones. This Father Nolan, he was burnt to death in the undercroft?'

'Yes.' That much was easily read in the newspapers.

'And he was doused in something to set him on fire?'

'Yes.' That wasn't public knowledge yet, but was a reasonable guess.

'He wasn't restrained, but he was dead drunk, so he didn't wake up?' That definitely wasn't in the public domain.

'I'm afraid I can't discuss the exact details of the case,' said Warren carefully.

211

Coombs grunted.

'No mind, although I'm not sure who you think I'm going to tell, and I'm sure the man upstairs knows all the important details.'

Warren said nothing; the man used to be a journalist, the last thing he wanted was for confidential details to become the topic of conversation the next time one of his old colleagues dropped by with a bunch of grapes.

'Now, the second death – drowning, the papers said. Face first in the river?'

Warren nodded cautiously.

'But I'll bet he didn't drown in the river, did he? I'll bet he drowned somewhere else and the killer dumped the body in there.'

Despite his best efforts, Warren's expression must have given him away.

Coombs gave a mirthless smile.

'Feel free to ask to see my medical notes if you're considering placing me on the suspect list.'

It was true, the man was in no state to murder the two priests. Warren even doubted he could have been a witness; it didn't look as though he'd been out of the little room for some time. Nevertheless, he appeared to know intimate details about the case that the team had deliberately kept under wraps. A leak wasn't inconceivable, but Warren was mystified as to how a terminally ill, bed-ridden, former reporter would have come across them.

'Now, tell me about the suicide notes. More of a confession than a note, I assume?'

"Forgive me Father, for I have sinned," recalled Warren silently. The seven words were all that had been written on the notes left on the two priests' dressing tables. It wasn't impossible that the person discovering the empty rooms had unfolded the notes and the information had found its way to Coombs. Otherwise, the only other people that were aware of the contents of the supposed suicide notes, aside from the investigative team, were Bishop Fisher and Deacon Baines. Had they told Coombs? And if so, why?

'Before you start worrying about an information leak, DCI Jones, don't worry. I didn't hear it from anyone alive.'

Before Warren could ask what he meant, the sick journalist started coughing.

Warren reached for a glass of water on the bedside table, but the man was spluttering so hard it just sprayed everywhere. Warren noticed a couple of tiny flecks of blood on the tissue Coombs ineffectually used to dab his chin.

When the coughing didn't subside after a few seconds, Warren jogged quickly to the door, 'I need assistance, immediately.'

Chapter 42

Warren's sharp tone brooked no argument and within a few seconds two healthcare assistants were by Coombs' side. It took all of Warren's self-control to remain out of the way, knowing that he was more likely to hinder than help matters.

A few worrying moments passed before the coughing subsided and Coombs' breathing returned to normal. One of the assistants carefully placed an oxygen mask over his face.

'I'll give you a dose of morphine, to make you more comfortable,' he said, reaching for the button clipped to Coombs' shirt pocket.

To the surprise of everyone in the room, Coombs stopped him. When he spoke, his voice was wheezy and muffled by the mask.

'No. Not yet. I must talk to DCI Jones.'

'I'm not sure that's sensible...' started the other assistant.

'No. I need to speak to him.'

Both assistants turned to Warren who shrugged helplessly. There was no question that he wanted to speak to the man more than ever now, but having a witness die on him mid-interview would be awkward to say the least.

'OK,' said the first assistant eventually, 'but if it happens again, pull that cord, it's what it's there for.'

With a final glare in his direction, the two assistants left.

When he spoke again, Coombs' voice was noticeably stronger, although he didn't remove the mask.

'Let me tell you a story,' he started. 'It's supposedly a deathbed confession, but I've cross-referenced with some of the diaries of the monks living at the abbey at the time and they seem to confirm that the key events happened as described.'

Coombs coughed again, although he waved Warren away before he could summon help. When he continued speaking, his voice was stronger.

'The story dates back to 1522, when the abbey was in its heyday. By then, the community had grown to almost fifty brothers, led by an Abbot Godwine. Similar to now, the abbey paid for itself through growing produce, some of which they sold at market. In addition to the brothers working in the gardens, they also employed cooks and cleaners and a groundsman from the nearby town.

'The groundsman was a man by the name of Francis Scrope. He had two sons, and had been widowed during the birth of the younger son. The elder son, Simon Scrope, was apprenticed to his father, whilst the younger son, Matthias, joined the abbey at the age of twelve to begin training for the priesthood.

'By all accounts, they had a pretty good life, when compared to their contemporaries in the town. Francis Scrope and Simon Scrope earned a good wage by the standards of the day, and they had a house and free food. Both boys were taught to read and write and perform basic arithmetic by the brothers, which they probably wouldn't have been able to afford if they were simply peasants. Joining the priesthood was also a prestigious occupation for the younger brother.'

'I'm guessing this isn't going to be an entirely happy ending,' said Warren passing over a glass of water.

'Yeah, it starts to get pretty dark,' Coombs agreed after a long swallow.

'It seems that even back then, the church's instinctive response to any whiff of scandal was a cover-up. The description in the confession and in those diaries that mention the events are typically circumspect, but it seems that the younger son attracted the wrong sort of attention from some of the older brothers.'

'Abuse?'

'Of the worst kind, apparently. According to the confession, Matthias wasn't the first to be attacked in this way. It may even have been tolerated as one of those things that came part and parcel of being accepted into the community.'

'Christ,' breathed Warren; even five centuries on, the crime still shocked him.

'I doubt *He* had a very high opinion of what had happened,' stated Coombs. 'Anyway, Matthias told his father what had happened and Scrope went to see Abbot Godwine. As to what happened next, we only have the word of the older brother to go on, who is himself recounting it secondhand, years after the fact, but it seems that the abbot simply bought the father off.'

'He bribed him to let it go?'

'Five pounds – the equivalent of a year's salary – plus as much wine as he could drink; an apparently irresistible sweetener for the father. He also supposedly made it clear that if any more was said on the matter, the father would lose his job and with it his home, the older brother, Simon, would lose his apprenticeship and Matthias would be excommunicated.'

'What happened to the monks involved in the abuse?'

'Apparently nothing. I suppose if they had been kicked out or disciplined too harshly then there was always the chance that word would get out and the abbey itself would come under the scrutiny of the mother church. The beginning of the sixteenth century was a period of great upheaval and some of the church's less godly behaviours were being challenged. These events took place when the established church was coming under pressure from Martin Luther on the continent and King Henry VIII in England. The abbot would have wanted to keep his head down.'

'So what happened?' The story was fascinating, in a morbid sort of way, but Coombs had yet to link those events to the present day murders, although Warren was starting to have his suspicions as to where it was heading.

'Well, Matthias was never the same again after that, and neither was his father. He couldn't accept what had happened, and supposedly ended up blaming his son for bringing it on himself; he couldn't understand why they chose his son unless he did something to encourage them. Sixteenth-century victim-blaming to use the latest terminology.'

'It's an attitude that some still hold five hundred years later,' noted Warren, thinking back to some of the cases he'd dealt with over the years.

'All this time, Simon Scrope was apparently ignorant of what had happened, as his brother was too ashamed to tell him. But it all came to head a few months later when Matthias tried to kill himself by throwing himself off the abbey roof.

'By some miracle he survived for almost a week. At that time of course, suicide was considered a sin, and so the boys' father refused to speak to him. Matthias told Simon what had happened a few hours before he finally died, reportedly saying that all he wanted was for those involved to admit what they had done and seek forgiveness for their sins.

'And did they?' It was a hypothetical question.

'What do you think, DCI Jones? Matthias was buried in an unmarked grave outside of the abbey grounds, supposedly because his suicide brought shame on the abbey community and his family. When his brother confronted his father over what had happened, his father reportedly said that he only had one child, and even blamed Matthias for the death of his mother in childbirth.'

Coombs took another swallow of water, and closed his eyes,

his hand straying towards the button again. Again, he stopped himself.

'Please, have a rest,' said Warren.

Coombs shook his head slowly, before opening his eyes. When he spoke again, his voice was firm, but noticeably weaker.

'Plenty of time to rest in the not too distant future. Where was I?'

'Simon Scrope had just confronted their father after the death of his younger brother.'

'Oh yes. Well it seems that Simon felt racked with guilt for not having spotted his younger brother's distress earlier and so he decided to get revenge on all those who had been complicit in his abuse and to fulfil his dying wish to confess their sins.

'The first person that he killed was his own father. It was poetic justice I suppose, he made it look like a suicide; and nobody suspected otherwise until Simon Scrope made his deathbed, confession, thirty years later. He claimed to have waited until his father was drunk one night and then made him confess to what had happened, before covering him in tar and setting him on fire. The confession was pinned to the abbey gate and reportedly read by a number of the more literate townspeople before it was taken down. Nobody suspected a thing, they assumed he was so wracked with guilt at the death of his son that he'd taken his own life. Nobody questioned who had actually written the note, even though the father was supposedly illiterate and could only write his name. Take a guess where he was burnt alive?'

'The undercroft,' whispered Warren.

Coombs nodded.

'Next he started targeting the monks who had committed the abuse.' Coombs started coughing, but again ignored Warren's pleas that they take a break. After a few moments, his breathing returned to normal.

'As I am sure you are aware, they were pretty creative in the medieval period when it came to torture. Scrope claims to have waited in the shadows until the monks were on their way back from vespers – evening prayers – before setting upon one of them. He was a pretty big lad by all accounts, used to hard, physical work, so it wasn't too hard for him to subdue the much smaller monk.

'Back in those days, the ducking stool was a real crowd pleaser. It was used primarily to humiliate those who had committed minor crimes, or punish scolding or gossiping housewives, but it was also used to elicit confessions and punish crimes such as witchcraft. Scrope says he had witnessed its use in town and he figured if it could make a person admit to being a witch, it could make them confess to what they had done to his brother.

'He tied the man to a chair and repeatedly submerged his head until he eventually agreed to write a confession. He doesn't say whether he drowned the man deliberately, or if it happened by accident, but after he died, he carried the body out to the bridge by the mill house and threw him over. These days we call it waterboarding and everyone thinks the Americans invented it in Iraq, but Medieval Europeans were centuries ahead of them.

'After that, he again pinned the suicide note to the abbey gates where it was read by the townsfolk before being taken down and presumably destroyed. Again, everyone believed it was a suicide, probably brought on by guilt and triggered by the death of Francis Scrope.'

Warren sat back in his chair, stunned. It seemed to be too fanciful to be true. As if reading Warren's thoughts, Coombs reached over and patted the lever arch folder on the coffee table, and then pointed shakily towards the closet.

'It's all in here, and there are photocopies of the original documents in the wardrobe, you can easily check them out for yourself.'

'Where did the drowning take place?' asked Warren. They still hadn't located where Father Daugherty had been killed before he was dragged to the bridge. If the present-day murders were following the same pattern as the ancient killings, then it was possible that he had been drowned in the same place. The location could contain vital forensic evidence.

'It doesn't say. Simon left it too late to start writing his confession; I've seen the original document and his handwriting deteriorates markedly towards the end, before finishing abruptly with his signature.' Coombs smiled humourlessly. 'I can sympathise with his poor timing.'

He coughed again, and Warren passed him his water. He sipped it gratefully, before starting to choke, water dribbling down his chin.

'Shit.' Warren had become so carried away with the man's story he'd forgotten how ill he was. Reaching over he went to slap the man's back, before hesitating. The man was stick thin, could he take a pounding? Remembering the carer's admonishment, Warren pulled the red cord that dangled by the bed.

The assistants appeared within seconds. Yet again, Warren found himself standing helplessly to one side.

'I think that's enough for today,' said one of the carers as they firmly pressed the button on the morphine pump. Warren agreed.

'I'm not going anywhere,' rasped Coombs, a trace of humour in his voice. 'Call tomorrow.'

'Call ahead,' warned the carer.

Suitably chastened, Warren nodded and headed toward the door. Already Coombs' face was softening, as the powerful sedative worked its magic.

'DCI Jones?' Warren stopped, Coombs' voice had a dreamy quality to it, and his eyes were closed.

'There was more than one monk involved in Matthias' abuse.'

Chapter 43

'Wow.'

Everyone around the briefing table, including DSI Grayson, agreed with Moray Ruskin's assessment of the story Warren had brought back from Vernon Coombs.

'If you read that in a novel, you'd say it was too far-fetched,' said Sutton.

'I agree,' said Warren. 'It'll have to be checked out obviously, but the whole thing seems a bit elaborate for someone that ill to have made up. I imagine a man in his position has more pressing things to do with his remaining time than string us along on a wild goose chase. Not to mention the fact that he drew parallels with information that shouldn't be in the public domain.'

'He could know the killer,' suggested Ruskin. 'Maybe it's some elaborate ruse to throw us off the scent?'

'Perhaps, but I think the point about the effort required to make it all up still stands. And how does it throw us off the scent? There's still a killer out there.'

'Rather more concerning is the fact that he said there were other monks involved,' said Grayson. 'It sounds rather like he's suggesting that there could be more killings. Did he give any indication as to how many there were?'

'No, he said that the original confession ended very abruptly, I don't know if he found any more evidence in the other diaries. He's not a well man to say the least, and I didn't want to press him too hard. I'll ask him when I next see him. We should also try and get a copy of his manuscript and the original research, to see if we can glean any more clues to the killer's method ourselves.'

'And perhaps even an idea of what he may do next,' said Sutton.

'Of course this also suggests a potential motive,' said Warren.

'The Catholic Church covering up sexual abuse is hardly unheard of,' stated Sutton.

'I agree, it's a route that we definitely need to follow up,' said Grayson, 'but let's not blind ourselves to other possibilities.'

'Nothing came up on our PNC check about convictions for abuse, so we are going to need to dig a bit deeper,' said Warren. 'Rachel, liaise with the sexual exploitation unit in Welwyn, see if you can find out anything relevant. I think I also need another chat with Bishop Fisher, but I don't want to tip him off. If something is being covered up, it's likely to involve higher-ranking clergy. He could well be in on it.'

'I agree. See what else we find, before you go speaking to Fisher,' said Grayson.

'How might this link to Rodney Shaw or Lucas Furber?' asked Richardson.

'Well, an obvious parallel, if we buy into the premise that the killer is following the pattern of the historic crimes, is that Rodney Shaw is the modern day counterpart of Matthias' father, the groundsman,' said Sutton.

'Then shouldn't Shaw have been burnt to death himself?' asked Ruskin.

'Perhaps, Shaw is doing what he thinks his predecessor should have done at the time?' countered Sutton.

'Like some sort of cosmic justice? Sounds a bit nuts,' opined Rachel Pymm.

'The whole thing is nuts,' agreed Sutton.

'Well, let's keep an open mind, for the time being,' cautioned Warren.

'Of course, there's another question we should be asking,' said Grayson. 'Who else knows the story of the abbey? If Coombs is to be believed, he's the first to write about it for five hundred years. So I'd like to know who has been helping him in the archives.'

Chapter 44

'The forensic document analysis of the note found in Father Daugherty's room has come back and it makes for interesting reading.' CSI Gupta stifled a yawn.

'Go on, Meera,' Warren urged as he positioned his desk phone more comfortably in the crook of his neck.

'Unlike with Father Nolan, there is no indication of impairment.'

'That fits with what we know from the autopsy. Father Daugherty wasn't drunk, or under the influence of drugs. Did you find a source of the same paper in his room?'

'Yes, this one was easier. It had been torn out of a Moleskine notebook, full of his own writings. The pad was covered in his fingerprints. The paper fibres match, and the ink corresponds to a black fountain pen, also covered in his fingerprints. What doesn't match is the handwriting.'

'Come again?'

'According to the report, the person who wrote the note has had a stab at mimicking Father Daugherty's handwriting, but it's full of tiny errors and lacks fluidity. The writer also made at least four attempts, presumably practise runs, before tearing them out. The notepad is missing five pages in total, with no evidence that Father Daugherty had previously removed pages from the notepad.'

'So Father Daugherty didn't write that note?'

'The examiner is pretty confident. As an aside, I've looked at the positioning of fingerprints on the sheet left on the dresser and they aren't necessarily where you would expect them to be for someone writing on that page. If I had to speculate, I'd say that Father Daugherty's fingers were pressed onto the page to make us think he'd handled it.'

'I don't suppose you have some magic trick that can tell us if that happened pre or post-mortem?'

'I'm afraid not. If he'd been dead a couple of days when the impressions were made, we might have found chemical evidence of putrefaction or there may have been some skin slippage, but it's unlikely in this case. That being said, the notebook and the suicide note had a couple of small spots of dried water, and the very edge of the writing touches one of the spots. Looking at the way that the ink has spread, I'd suggest that the paper became wet before it was written on, rather than after.'

'So the note was again written at the scene and taken back to the room, rather than written before hand?'

'That I can't say, sir. The spots of water could have occurred within his room.'

Warren thanked her and hung up. His gut was telling him that they weren't going to get everything they needed to keep Shaw for much longer.

* * *

The custody clock was ticking loudly. The team had two hours to either charge Shaw, release him, or extend his custody. Shaw's solicitor reminded him of this as soon as they sat back down again.

At this moment, Warren would be happy with enough evidence

to extend his custody, but before he did so, he needed the answer to one specific question.

'What can you tell me about Vernon Coombs?'

Shaw shrugged.

'No idea who you're talking about.'

Warren pushed a photograph of the retired reporter taken from the *Middlesbury Reporter*'s article about his retirement. He figured that Coombs had probably stopped coming to the house when he got too ill, and the treatment started to take its toll on his appearance.

'Oh, yeah, the historian guy. I think he was writing a book or something.'

'What was your relationship with Mr Coombs?'

'I didn't have one. I saw him around the house sometimes coming out of the basement where they keep the archives. I haven't seen him for months. I think I heard he was sick.'

Warren made note.

'Let's go back to the night of Father Nolan's killing. You lied about going home after work. Instead, you drove in the opposite direction to your flat, before parking your car in the vicinity of Guest Road. This is within easy walking distance of the abbey grounds.

'When you pulled up, you phoned this pay-as-you-go mobile phone number. A number that you phone every couple of weeks. Why don't you tell me who this phone belongs to?'

'No comment.'

'This doesn't look very good for you at the moment, Rodney,' said Sutton.

'Look, we don't care what you were doing after work,' said Warren. 'It's none of our business if you've been knocking boots with someone other than your wife. We don't even care if you are paying for it. If you've had a little lapse and were getting back into drugs, that doesn't bother us either. Give us something so we can eliminate you from our enquiries, then you can go home and have a decent night's sleep in your own bed.

'What were you doing in the hours between leaving work and receiving that phone call?'

Shaw's eyelid fluttered. He looked towards his solicitor, sitting Sphinx-like beside him. He licked his lips.

'No comment.'

Warren gave an elaborate shrug.

'You can't say we didn't give you a chance.' He and Sutton stood up. 'Interview suspended. Stick around, eh?'

* * *

Ninety minutes remained on the custody clock. Significantly less when you factored in the time necessary to persuade a magistrate to sign an extension on a warrant.

'What have you got?' asked Warren. He didn't want to sound desperate, but they needed something – anything – to hold Shaw further

'They're still fingerprinting the twenty-pound notes found in the shortbread tin, but they're a real mess, and they aren't hopeful. The CCTV from the number 562 bus doesn't show any passengers matching Shaw's description within the time period we're interested in. We're still waiting for CCTV from the bus routes close to Shaw's flat for the night of Father Daugherty's murder,' said Richardson. 'Sorry, I couldn't get it analysed any quicker. We're still tracking down the owners of cars near the abbey that night. The window of opportunity is much wider than on the night of the fire.'

It was an understatement. Theoretically, Shaw could have gone to the abbey at any time over the weekend and simply waited for a chance to ambush Father Daugherty. Every hour that the timeframe was widened resulted in dozens, if not hundreds more vehicles that they needed to trace and several more buses that needed their CCTV footage analysed, not to mention increasing the number of hours of video surveillance from static cameras in the vicinity of the abbey and along Shaw's likely route to the abbey.

'What about cyclists?'

'Nothing yet. Middlesbury's a pretty cycling friendly town, so there's a lot to look at,' said Richardson.

'Fair enough. Anything back from the forensics on his bicycle tyres?'

'Early days, but inconclusive so far,' said Pymm. 'Even if they do find evidence that the bicycle was in the abbey grounds, surely it's circumstantial at best? He worked there, he might have cycled there if the weather was nice.'

'It's a long shot,' agreed Warren. 'See if witnesses can tell us if he cycled to work or not. Hutch, what have you got?'

'Sorry, boss. we've tracked down all of the drivers of the cars in the vicinity that we were interested in on the night of the fire. None of them admit to even knowing Rodney Shaw and all had plausible reasons for their journey that evening. I traced the cab driver that we saw heading away from the abbey. He didn't recognise Shaw's picture, but he admits that he sees a lot of fares.'

'Thanks. Rachel?'

'Nothing immediately helpful, sir, but it's certainly suspicious. I've got the records back from the unregistered mobile. Shaw didn't call it over the weekend that Father Daugherty was killed.' A series of groans rippled around the table.

'What's suspicious then?' asked Warren.

'The phone is turned off most of the time, except between approximately 4 and 6 p.m. most days. In that time, the phone is present only at that location. There are about two dozen numbers, most unregistered, that call the phone typically every couple weeks. Like Shaw, the calls rarely last more than a few seconds.'

'That is suspicious. Anyone got any thoughts?'

'Drugs?' said Ruskin immediately. 'They could be arranging a pick up.'

'Possible,' said Warren. 'Although Shaw seemed fairly confident that he was clean – he offered to be tested.'

'He could just be dealing,' said Ruskin.

'Maybe that's what he was arguing with Father Nolan about, rather than the gambling?' suggested Hutchinson.

'Again possible,' conceded Warren. 'But how would Father Nolan know about it? We have evidence that they had an awkward meeting in the bookie, but how would Father Nolan get wind of the drugs?'

The table lapsed into silence.

'It could be literally anything,' said Hutchinson. 'The number could belong to a prostitute who only sees clients that time of evening.'

'Rachel, pass what you have onto Welwyn,' said Warren. 'Hopefully, if the number is already known to them they'll get back to us, if only to tell us to mind our own business.'

'We could always try calling the number,' said Ruskin. 'We could even use Shaw's own phone so they don't hang up.'

'What happens when they don't recognise Shaw's voice?' asked Hutchinson, beating everyone else in the room to the question.

'And if it is a part of someone else's investigation, they aren't going to be impressed if we come crashing in and wreck their operation,' said Pymm.

Ruskin's face fell.

'We'll see what Welwyn have to say about the number, then have a think about our next step,' said Warren encouragingly.

'Anything else? What about the suicide notes?'

'We got a sample of Shaw's handwriting for comparison, to see if it matches the handwriting that attempted to fake Father Daugherty's on his note,' said Pymm. 'Unfortunately, the attempts to emulate Father Daugherty's handwriting also serve to disguise that of the true author. We'll have to wait for a deeper analysis. We know that Shaw's fingerprints are not on the document.'

'What about the note from Father Nolan's room?'

'Again, nothing conclusive. The note written by the killer for Father Nolan to copy was in block capitals. The indentations were clear, but the analyst has said that they won't be able to

229

determine if it's a match unless we can get Shaw to rewrite the exact wording under controlled conditions, and in block capitals.'

Warren looked at the clock, 'I doubt we'll have time to arrange that before the current extension runs out.'

The door to the briefing room opened and Tony Sutton entered.

'I've got the forensics back from the search of Shaw's flat.'

Saturday 7th March

Chapter 45

It was now two weeks since the fire at the abbey and Warren felt as though the investigation was stalling.

It wasn't of course, there were dozens of different avenues being chased even as he drove in that morning. His own small team at Middlesbury was only the tip of a very large iceberg. Dozens more officers and specialists were beavering away day and night down at headquarters in Welwyn Garden City. Thousands of hours of CCTV footage were being analysed and dozens of phone records were being trawled through, in the hope of finding a pattern that could explain either the behaviour of Rodney Shaw or throw up new suspects for the whiteboard.

The sun was still low in the sky this time of the morning and Warren pulled the sun visor down to shield his eyes.

Specialist teams were still canvassing the town's homeless population and those that interacted with them, in the hope that at the very least the whereabouts of Lucas Furber could be pinned down on the night of both murders. So far, he had largely disappeared. Warren was beginning to worry that he may not even be in Middlesbury anymore.

The atmosphere in the office had taken a dip the previous

evening after Sutton had delivered the preliminary results from the search of Shaw's house, and his car.

'No traces of the fibres from the towel used to smother Father Daugherty have been found on the clothes in Shaw's laundry bin, or in his car.'

It wasn't a death blow to the case, by any stretch of the imagination. Alongside the mysterious Lucas Furber, Rodney Shaw was still their number one suspect. Unfortunately, the lack of evidence meant that there was no longer reasonable grounds to hold Shaw in custody and Warren had bailed him ten minutes before the custody clock ran out.

Shaw had left the building without so much as a glance over his shoulder. A perfunctory objection to the bail conditions imposed by Warren had been summarily dismissed. Rodney Shaw would either be staying with his estranged wife or making other arrangements – his flat was still being searched, but Warren wasn't hopeful that they'd find anything incriminating.

'Good morning everyone. I'm sure you are all up to speed on yesterday's events.' Warren injected a note of positivity into his tone. He didn't want the malaise that he was feeling to take hold within the rest of the team.

'As you are aware, yesterday I had a meeting with a retired journalist with an interest in the history of Middlesbury Abbey. He told a pretty fantastic tale about historic murders disguised as suicide. Nevertheless, he seemed to know plenty of details that are supposedly not in the public domain. I'm hoping to speak to him again later today. He's not a well man, and I suspect my time with him will be limited, so I'd like suggestions for questions to put to him.'

'Who helped him research the documents that he used in writing the story?' suggested Hutchinson.

'What is his relationship with Rodney Shaw? Shaw denied any connection with him yesterday,' said Sutton. 'If he does know him, that's another lie we've caught him in.'

'For that matter, does he know Lucas Furber?' suggested Pymm.

Warren acknowledged the suggestions, scribbling them on his pad.

'He said that there were other abusers of Matthias Scrope. Does he know how they died? If the killer is mimicking these historic deaths there might be more to come. Perhaps we can prevent them?' said Richardson.

'All good questions. In the meantime, we need to look at some of these ourselves. DSI Grayson will be looking into the best way to ensure the Church's cooperation.'

'You mean the least awkward way of ensuring their cooperation,' muttered Tony Sutton.

Warren ignored the interruption.

'The rest of you continue looking into the private lives of Fathers Nolan and Daugherty, as we discussed yesterday. Let's also elicit the help of the sexual exploitation unit, they may have some insight that can help us.'

'If the killer is emulating the historic killings, then that might explain why they were disguised as suicides,' said Sutton. 'The question is whether the killer ever intended us to realise they were murders. Matthias Scrope's older brother only ever confessed to hiding the murders as suicides on his death bed.'

'But Simon Scrope also pinned the abuser's confessions to the abbey gates so that everyone knew what they had done. The two notes found so far simply say "Forgive me Father, for I have sinned." There are no details of their supposed sins,' countered Hutchinson. 'This whole thing could just be a coincidence or about something entirely different.'

'Well, the similarities between the two deaths are enough that we can't dismiss them out of hand. Let's hope Vernon Coombs can help us out.'

* * *

234

Warren's hopes of getting a quick answer to the questions raised by his meeting with Vernon Coombs were thwarted.

'Your visit yesterday really did him in,' said the carer who answered the phone. 'He's still asleep. Try again tomorrow.'

Warren hung up, feeling guilty.

His next call didn't make him feel much better.

'We've been through Rodney Shaw's computer. It was easy enough, he just used a basic password, no fancy encryption or anything.' Pete Robertson's tone of voice indicated what he thought about the security afforded by such simple measures. He promised a more detailed report by email later in the day.

'Anything suspicious?'

'There wasn't much to look at, to be honest. A folder of family photos, a bit of music and a folder full of paperwork. We've had a look at them and there's nothing obviously amiss. I'll send you a copy of his email inboxes for you to look at. He keeps his porn in a folder marked 'Work stuff', presumably to stop his daughter stumbling across it.'

'Anything interesting in there?'

'It's not to my taste, but there's nothing illegal or particularly kinky. Boobs and bums, mostly.'

'What about his browsing history? Particularly on the night Father Daugherty was murdered.'

'Again, nothing illegal or suspicious. News, sports and some gardening and estate management forums. On the day Father Daugherty was killed, he spent some time logged onto a few gambling sites and his favourite porn site.'

'What time?' Warren pulled over a pen and paper. If Shaw was accessing those sites when Father Daugherty was likely to have been killed, then it could provide him with an alibi.

'Gambling-wise, he spent the afternoon following the horse racing from about 1 p.m to about 5 p.m; that's when he closed the browser window. I can't be sure if he was actively using the site, or it was just open on his computer. He also accessed an online poker site just after 11 p.m. and that was open until half past one. Again, we can't be sure if he was active during that time.'

Even if Shaw had been using the sites, there was a window of six hours in the middle when he could have killed Father Daugherty.

'What about the porn site?'

'It's a free webcam streaming site. Performers in their skimpies doing stuff in front of the screen. He opened the window at 6 p.m. and didn't close it for about four hours.'

'That coincides with Father Daugherty's time of death.'

'Well, don't rule him out on those grounds. Again, the website is fully contained within its own browser window. I have no way of telling if he was actually interacting with the site, or if it was just open, perhaps even minimised.'

'So he could have logged onto the website, then just left it playing in the background whilst he went and did something else?'

'I'd almost guarantee it. He was on that site for four hours, that's an incredible feat of stamina.'

'A good point,' conceded Warren.

Robertson's call hadn't helped account for Shaw's whereabouts at all that evening, and left Warren no clearer as to his involvement in the murder. On the one hand, it explained his reluctance to say what he was doing that night. They knew that he was ashamed of his gambling habit. Warren imagined he was probably even less willing to admit to something as personal as his use of pornography.

On the other hand, maybe he was setting up an alibi? Even a casual viewer of TV would know that these days, the first thing the police do is seize a suspect's computing devices. He could easily have logged onto his computer, then left it on when going to kill Father Daugherty, thus creating a false electronic account of his whereabouts.

Warren thanked Robertson and hung up. If Shaw had manufactured an alibi, it pointed to an unexpected level of sophistication. They would need to take that into account when they dealt with him in future.

236

Sunday 8th March

Chapter 46

Sunday morning was like any other morning of the week in Middlesbury CID when there was a major case underway. The unit was filled with additional officers from headquarters in Welwyn, and Warren spent some time chatting to them; a case this complex might drag on for months or years and he needed the newcomers and Middlesbury's permanent officers to integrate fully as one team. Technically, Warren was on a rest day, but he wanted to speak with Vernon Coombs and keep abreast of any new developments. He'd promised Susan that he'd be back in time for lunch.

Despite it being the weekend, most of his own core team were also present. At the moment, Warren was happy to authorise the overtime for anyone willing to put in the extra hours. Their experience with the case made them more valuable to Warren than a comparative newcomer from Welwyn, who might have only been assigned to the case a few days ago. Besides which, his officers could probably use the extra pay – he knew that Moray Ruskin and his partner were desperately scraping together a deposit for a flat, but he needed to keep an eye on the hours they were working. He didn't want his officers becoming ill from overwork – it was a poor manager that worked their staff so hard in the short-term that they went off sick in the long-term.

Warren called Goldfinch Hospice during his morning break. A different carer answered the phone. After explaining who he was and why he was calling, there was a short pause.

'I'm very sorry, DCI Jones. Vernon passed away this morning. He fell asleep on Friday, shortly after you left and never woke up.' She paused. 'It was very peaceful and his family were with him at the end. It's just a shame he had to die on his granddaughter's birthday, without saying goodbye.'

* * *

'Bloody hell, Warren, it's hardly your fault,' said Sutton. The two men were sitting in Warren's office. Sutton looked even greyer than he had earlier in the week and Warren had ordered him to go home after lunch and get some rest.

Warren sighed. 'I suppose not, it's just I was the last person he spoke to, which seems really sad.'

'By all accounts, he'd been circling the drain for some time. It was going to be sooner rather than later.'

'Beautifully put, Tony.'

'Sorry, you know what I mean.' He paused. 'At the risk of being even more insensitive, what do you think has happened to his manuscript and all of his notes?'

'I suppose his family have them.'

'You realise that if they don't want to part with them, we might need to get a warrant to seize them?'

'Bloody hell, Tony. Let's at least ask nicely first.'

Monday 9th March

Chapter 47

Monday morning's briefing was halfway through the third week of the investigation into the deaths at the abbey.

Warren broke the news of Vernon Coomb's death to those who hadn't heard.

'His story, crazy as it sounds, is certainly worthy of serious consideration. So far, we have no evidence that Fathers Nolan or Daugherty were involved in child sexual abuse, and the sexual exploitation unit have nothing on them, but given the Catholic Church's previous form on this, it is being actively pursued as a line of enquiry. In terms of motivation, it would certainly seem more plausible than something as seemingly trivial as Rodney Shaw's gambling problems.'

'So are we dismissing Rodney Shaw?' asked Ruskin.

'Not just yet. We're still trying to work out what the hell he was doing the night that Father Nolan was killed.'

'What about this Lucas Furber character?' asked Grayson. 'He must be at least as strong a suspect as Rodney Shaw.'

'Nothing yet,' Ruskin said, frustration in his voice. 'The search teams are under instructions not to give away too much about why he's of interest to the police, so they're having a hard time getting people to admit they even knew him, let alone tell us his whereabouts. I guess they don't want to get him into trouble.'

'Well keep at it,' encouraged Warren.

'What about Vernon Coombs' notes?' asked Pymm.

'I'm glad you asked that question, Rachel. I'll be needing someone to trawl through them, to see how closely they match what he told me, and to see if there are any clues as to our killer's future plans.'

'Well, I love a bit of local history, so count me in,' said Pymm, as Warren had suspected she would. 'When can I expect them?'

'I'm going to see his family this afternoon.'

Hutchinson let out a low whistle.

'That's a bit quick, don't you think? He's barely been dead twenty-four hours.'

'I don't disagree, Hutch, but we need to move quickly on this. And the last thing we want is for those notes to be chucked in a bin when they empty his room.'

Warren just hoped that the family chose to cooperate. The thought of intruding on them so soon left a sour taste in his mouth and he prayed that Sutton's warning from the previous day didn't come to pass. He really didn't want to explain to a magistrate why he needed to serve a warrant against a grieving family who hadn't done anything wrong.

* * *

'Please accept my deepest condolences,' Warren started, as he sat down in the small, cramped lounge.

His meeting with Coombs had left him with far more questions than answers and the former journalist had hinted that there may be more deaths to come. So far the tale he had told, though fantastical, had also included allusions to details that shouldn't have been in the public domain. At the very least, Warren needed to look at the manuscript that he had been working on and the research that he had uncovered. He just hoped the original sources had been translated. A single year of Latin, twenty-five years previously, had left Warren with little more than the ability to proclaim that the main protagonist in the course textbook they had used 'was in the garden'.

Coombs' eldest daughter was an olive-skinned woman in her mid-thirties. She shared her father's sharp features, although hers lacked the extra definition brought on by his dramatic weight loss. A photograph on the mantelpiece was almost certainly the famous 'Lilly'; she'd inherited her mother's dark hair, rather than her grandfather's lighter colouring, but even at such a young age, the cheek bones were all Coombs.

She nodded her thanks; doubtless she had heard dozens of variations on the words over the past twenty-four hours.

'Dad had been ill for months of course, but he had been doing so well, we didn't expect the end to be so sudden…' Her voice tailed off. 'I'm told that you were the last person to speak to him.'

It wasn't a question.

Warren chose his words carefully. Her tone was flat, neutral and he couldn't be sure of her thoughts on the matter. There was no question that Warren's visit had been more exhausting for the man than he'd realised, even then. Would she blame him for hastening her father's death? Warren wasn't sure he could fault her if she did.

'Yes, we spoke about his research.'

'That bloody book.' Her tone was more fond than the words suggested. 'He was obsessed with that abbey. My earliest memories are of me attending some lecture or other.' She smiled, 'Don't ask me why. I was about two years old and Dad was looking after me whilst Mum was in hospital expecting my brother. Apparently, he used to take me there when I was a babe in arms, and I'd sleep through. Nobody told him toddlers aren't quite as compliant.'

Warren returned the smile. 'I can imagine. He told me that his

243

own interest in the abbey and its history could be traced back to his childhood. From what he's told me, it clearly has a past more interesting than many similar ruins.'

'Yes, he uncovered some blood-curdling stories...' Her voice broke off, her eyes narrowing.

'I am such a fool.'

'Sorry?'

'Here I was, wondering what an earth a Detective Chief Inspector was doing visiting my father on his deathbed. When the hospice told me about your visit, I assumed you were an old friend; he used to have an occasional drink with police officers back when he did more crime reporting. But unless you're a lot older than you look, he left that beat before you even joined the police.

'You were there badgering him about those murders.' Her voice started to rise. 'What on earth do you think he could tell you about the goings on at that abbey? He hasn't been outside that hospice since before Christmas.'

'I'm very sorry, he contacted the hotline, I had no idea...' started Warren. But she wasn't listening.

'The carers told me that he was distressed when you left, but I didn't think anything of it. I thought to myself "at least he was with a friend when he was taken ill."'

'I'm really sorry, he called us to report some information he thought might be relevant to our investigation.'

'Well, unless you've decided to try and charge someone with those murders from five hundred years ago, I can't believe he had anything worth telling you about.'

Warren couldn't really defend himself against her accusation, without revealing details he'd rather keep quiet.

'The moment you saw how ill he was, you should have left.' She stood up abruptly.

'I'm very sorry, I—'

'Stop saying sorry, and save your explanations for the Chief

244

Constable, DCI Jones. I'm sure that he will be very interested to read newspaper stories about how his officers are so desperate they've taken to harassing people on their death bed. You can see yourself out.'

Tuesday 10th March

Chapter 48

Warren had barely taken his coat off before his first visitor of the day presented herself at his office door. He quickly rose to his feet and moved around his desk, snagging a chair as he went past. As a matter of courtesy, colleagues usually went to Rachel Pymm's desk rather than the other way around. It must be important for her to travel across the office.

Warren leant her sticks against his desk, as Pymm sat down.

'What can I help you with, Rachel?'

'I'm so sorry, sir. I've made a mistake.'

'Go on.' Warren perched on the edge of his desk.

'You asked me to cross-reference the abbey staff and residents against the PNC. I did, but as soon as we got a hit on Rodney Shaw, I got side-tracked and stopped probing.'

'So there were other criminal records on the PNC?'

'Not exactly. There was nothing on the national computer. Nobody else had any recordable offences, but I forgot to check the local forces' systems. As you know, not everything gets uploaded to the PNC. When I dug further, I found that Father Daugherty had a "No Further Action" against his name, dating from 2005.'

Warren thought back. 'When he was a school chaplain?'

'Yes. There are almost no details, just a comment about him

247

being questioned over allegations of improper behaviour towards a minor. No further action taken.'

The importance of the information hit Warren like a hammer blow.

Seeing the look on his face, Pymm started to apologise again. Warren stalled her with a raised hand.

'Rachel, you are doing a sterling job. You know how information trickles into an investigation in dribs and drabs. The important thing is, we've got it now.

'You say that the NFA was recorded in 2005, that's not that many years ago. I wonder if the investigating officer remembers the case?'

Pymm handed over a page from her notepad.

'I have the officer's name. He's still with Herts Constabulary, based at Hitchin nick. Here's his direct line, he's back on duty tomorrow morning.'

* * *

'Stay away from Guest Road,' said Grayson.

Warren blinked in surprise. Pymm had left only moments before and he still hadn't finished booting up his laptop.

'Sorry?'

Grayson flopped down into the recently vacated visitor's chair. He also rarely visited Warren's office.

'The exact words of Chief Superintendent Brigstocke from Serious and Organised Crime. It turns out they've had their eye on number 68 Guest Road for the past few months.'

'Why? What on Earth is Shaw mixed up in?'

'It is believed to be an illegal gambling den, plus a hangout for drug dealers, pimps and other charming individuals.'

'Well, that accounts for Shaw's interest, although I didn't think he was that big a gambler,' said Warren.

'He's probably not, she'd never heard of Shaw. Brigstocke said

248

that it's a pretty amateur affair, however the gang that run it have aspirations to join the big league. Brigstocke's team are looking at ways of infiltrating it whilst it's still a small player and seeing if they can use it as a way into the wider network.'

'Hence the warning to back off.'

'Exactly. Brigstocke even suggested that Shaw might be useful to them, although I persuaded her to hold fire until we know if he's actually a double-murderer first.'

'Glad to hear it,' said Warren. 'I could really do without organised crime breathing down my neck, alongside everyone else.'

'I'll do what I can to keep them at arm's length,' promised Grayson.

Warren sighed philosophically. 'Even if they could supply Shaw with an alibi, I'm not sure I'd believe them. Hell, the buggers could even have assisted him.'

'Well if that's the case, our investigation will take precedence,' said Grayson. 'In the meantime, how did yesterday's visit to Vernon Coombs' family go?'

'Not well.'

By the time Warren had finished describing the visit, Grayson looked pained.

'If you really need that research, then I'll back you in obtaining a warrant to seize it. If necessary, we can use the fact that he appears to have access to confidential information as an indication that he may have closer links to the murders than would be expected.'

'You mean treat him as a suspect, or a person of interest?' said Warren.

'If necessary.'

Warren puffed his lips out. 'I agree that we could go in mob-handed, but that's pretty dangerous. I did a bit of poking around and it turns out that she wasn't making an empty threat; her husband is a reporter for the *Mercury*. We could find ourselves splashed across the front page.'

'She's right that the Chief Constable won't be very impressed, but he's a realist, it'll blow over soon enough.'

'I'm not worried about that, I'm more concerned that any story may speculate about a link between those fake suicides from the middle ages and the present-day murders. If Coombs is right, then our one advantage over the killer is that he doesn't know that we are aware of any such link. If, as Coombs hinted, there were more killings to come, then not only might we be able to prevent more deaths, we might also be able to catch the killer in action.'

'What do you suggest?'

Warren gave a sigh. 'A fulsome apology and your smartest suit, sir.'

* * *

You could say what you liked about DSI John Grayson, but when he wanted to turn the charm on, he was a master. It also helped that Vernon Coombs' granddaughter, Lilly, was present when Warren and Grayson next visited. Grayson had just become a grandfather himself, and was by all accounts a doting uncle to several nieces and nephews of a similar age to Lilly. It was another glimpse at the man behind the façade he usually presented at work.

'It's my granddad. He's in Heaven,' the little girl pronounced, when Grayson asked her what she was drawing. To Warren's surprise, Grayson took the poignant statement in his stride. 'I'm sure he's very proud that you are such a good artist.'

Having at least passed that test, Warren and Grayson were allowed to say their piece, again apologising for Warren's intrusion into her father's final days and reiterating that they had only visited by invitation.

By the time they left it was getting dark and Coombs' daughter had to switch on the security lights as the two officers carried three large boxes of research, and the lever arch folder containing the partially written manuscript, out of the garage. Warren also had a memory stick in his pocket that he'd promised to copy and return immediately.

'Well, at least we won't be needing this,' said Grayson with satisfaction as the car pulled away, removing the search warrant from his inside jacket pocket.

* * *

'Are you having a laugh?' asked Rachel Pymm, when she saw the three boxes of photocopied research from Coombs' room sitting on the table that had been moved next to her usual desk.

'Hopefully, much of what you need will already be in the manuscript.' Warren patted the lever arch folder. 'Or failing that, in his computer files. Coombs' daughter was unsure how complete the first draft was, so I suggest you read this first.'

'And if it isn't?'

'I'm sure DSI Grayson will be happy to authorise the cost of a small team to go through the raw research.'

Pymm pulled the file over. 'Remind me what I'm looking for?'

'In the first instance, the deathbed confession of Simon Scrope. It should detail the ways in which he supposedly killed those that abused his younger brother, including his father, who apparently held the victim at least partly responsible for his own abuse.

'Check for similarities between the murders of Father's Daugherty and Nolan and those described in the manuscript. Let's see if Coombs was correct, or if he was imagining things.

'Then, see if you can find any other deaths. Coombs said that there were multiple abusers. If our killer really is re-enacting deaths from this story, then there may be clues to future killings. Scrope's confession apparently ends abruptly, so if there is more to be found it's likely to be recorded in the monks' diaries.'

'No pressure then.'

Warren smiled sympathetically. 'I'll speak to DSI Grayson about authorising a team to help you.' He turned to leave. 'Oh, one more thing. When handling the photocopied sheets, wear gloves. If Coombs is to be believed, he is the first person to delve into this story for hundreds of years. But it sounds as though at least some of the research was done with the help of others. Put anything that seems relevant to one side and we'll get Forensics to see if anyone else handled the sheets. It's a long shot, but we might find something.'

'Great, sweaty hands as well,' grumbled Pymm.

Wednesday 11th March

Chapter 49

Sergeant Archie Ingram, the school liaison officer when Father Daugherty was accused of improper contact with a child, remembered the incident well, and agreed to come over to Middlesbury for a chat first thing.

'I've gone through my original notes.' He produced a dog-eared notebook. 'You're lucky. Another three months and I've done my thirty years. I'll be sailing off into the sunset – or at least moving to Devon.'

Sergeant Ingram was a large man in his early fifties. Easily six feet two, his uniform shirt barely covered his pronounced beer belly.

'Back then I was link officer to a number of schools in the town. I remember this one really well, because it was unusual.'

'How so?'

Ingram sighed and leaned back in his chair.

'The one part of the job I won't miss is child protection. Over the years, I've seen and heard some really shitty stuff. Unfortunately, by the time these things reach me, they've usually been going on for some time. The real kicker though is that often there just isn't enough evidence to proceed. Where possible, I'll escalate it and get outside organisations involved, but usually

254

nothing happens. The child ends up on a register as vulnerable, but the alleged perpetrator denies everything and it becomes the kid's word against theirs. And you know how that goes…' His tone darkened. 'Sometimes I read the evidence and question both parties and I just *know* the bastard did it. And he knows that I know. And he just smirks…' Ingram's fists clenched. 'And I'd give anything to wipe that smug grin of his face.'

'So what happened in this case?'

'Nothing.'

'I saw that, "No Further Action".'

'No, I mean literally nothing. Nothing happened.'

'You mean it was a false allegation?'

'Yes, she withdrew it when she realised the consequences of her lies on Father Daugherty.'

'So something may have happened, but she changed her mind, or was persuaded to change her mind?'

If that was the case, then perhaps they had their motive. Had the girl – now a young woman – spent the intervening years dwelling on the injustice of what had happened to her? Was the murder of Father Daugherty an act of revenge? And if that was the case, what was the connection with Father Nolan? Despite their best efforts, they'd found no evidence that the two men knew each other before becoming residents at the same retirement home.

Were they even connected? Or was the death of Father Nolan a mistake?

Ingram shook his head.

'No, you don't understand. Literally nothing happened. That's why it stuck in my mind. True malicious allegations are really rare. As you well know, not enough evidence to proceed isn't the same as the offence never happened.'

'So how do you know that it was definitely malicious?'

'To put it bluntly, the girl wasn't very bright and had a history of saying things that were untrue. Teachers – especially male teachers – were under instructions not to be alone with her.'

'Unreliable witness?'

'No.' Ingram looked annoyed. 'Look, I'm sorry, sir. I realise that the track record of the authorities in believing vulnerable, abused victims is woeful – trust me, I've seen it firsthand – but in this case, it really was untrue.'

'Sorry, Sergeant, I didn't mean to sound judgemental. Take me through what happened.'

'I got a call from the school safeguarding lead to tell me that an allegation had been made against a member of staff, and could I attend for a preliminary interview?

'The child, a 14-year-old, year-nine pupil, had gone to her form tutor and claimed that Father Gerry Daugherty had touched her inappropriately when she was in confession. She said that he had threatened to go to her parents and tell them what she had confessed, unless she touched him back. And that when she did that, he'd unzipped his trousers and made her pleasure him. She declined to tell us what she had supposedly confessed.'

'So then what happened?'

'Well, the most important thing to do in these circumstances is to ensure that no young people are in any danger, so after the interview was concluded, I went to see Father Daugherty, with a view to escorting him off site whilst the allegations were investigated.

'I took him back to the station and he offered to give a voluntary statement. He claimed that he had threatened to speak to the girl's parents, but that it had nothing to do with confession. In fact, he'd caught her smoking cannabis around the back of the church car park. He was concerned that she was hanging around with the wrong crowd and he was going to have a word with her parents, who were parishioners, with a view to helping her. He said that she then completely lost her temper and told him that if he did, she'd make him sorry.'

'So did he tell her parents?'

'Ironically, no. He didn't get a chance. One of the other parents of the kids she was with told them. But she must have assumed that he was involved and gone through with her threat.'

'So how did you know it was untrue?'

'Well, she was clever enough to claim the assault happened several weeks before, and that her school uniform had been laundered since, so there would be no forensic evidence. But she wasn't clever enough to think up a plausible date when the attack could have occurred. Father Daugherty was away on a walking holiday with his nephew's family in Devon for a week either side of when she claimed the attack occurred.'

'She could have got her dates mixed up, the event would have been very traumatic,' countered Warren.

'You're right, but by this time I think she was starting to think through the repercussions of what she had done. Obviously, since Father Daugherty was cooperating voluntarily and hadn't been arrested, his name hadn't been released to the papers, but the girl had told her best friend, who told her friends... after about a week, the entire school knew what had allegedly happened, with the story growing in the retelling. Parents were ringing the school and gossiping amongst themselves – fortunately, social media wasn't really a thing back then. His car was vandalised, and "paedo" was sprayed on the church doors. In the end, he had to take a leave of absence.'

'Then what happened?'

'With the support of her parents, the girl retracted her accusations. Unfortunately, because of the nature of the allegations, the school was unable to give anything more than a brief statement, as they couldn't release any information that might identify the child – although everyone knew her identity by all accounts – so a lot of the school community declared it a cover up; no smoke without fire and all that.'

'What happened to Father Daugherty?'

'Well he'd never been arrested, so from our point of view, it was recorded as NFA. But in the end he went off with stress and the last I heard he'd retired, the poor bastard.' Ingram shook his head. 'It was a real shame. I knew him as part of the wider community and he was a really nice man. He would do anything to help those kids, that's why he was going to speak to her parents. He was worried about her. There were never any similar allegations made against him, not even historic accusations where more alleged victims came forward after all the publicity.'

'What happened to the girl?'

'Nothing in the end. There was some talk of a managed move to another school for a fresh start, but a statement from Father Daugherty claimed that he forgave her. The school decided that to exclude her would not only identify her, it could be seen as punishing someone who the whole school saw as the victim, as well as discouraging real victims from coming forward in the future.'

'Are you still in touch with the accuser?'

'Nah, never heard another peep from her. Eventually the whole thing blew itself out. To be honest, until you called me about it, I hadn't thought about it for years. The saddest thing was what happened to Father Daugherty. A couple of the local muckrakers, who as usual knew bugger all about what had really happened, claimed that he had been sacked for child molestation, although I don't know if anyone really believed them. Still, it ruined the reputation of a good man, it's no wonder he never came back to the school.'

Chapter 50

'I've finished reading the printed manuscript in the lever arch folder,' said Pymm. Her tone was reproving. 'It was a bloody mess, if I'm honest, nowhere near a complete first draft, and it was covered in red pen.'

'What have you found out?'

Pymm shifted slightly in her chair.

'First, the good news. In amongst far more than I ever wanted to know about the funding model for a thirteenth-century abbey, and some admittedly cool plans showing priest holes and escape tunnels, there was the deathbed confession that Vernon Coombs told you about.'

'And did it match his account?'

'Well, the way it was told in the manuscript was the same as the way you said he relayed it to you. He also cites other accounts from diaries around the time it occurred. Fortunately, he is a great believer in the numbered footnote, so my next job will be to pull out those references from the cardboard box mountain that is blocking my sunlight.'

'What's the bad news?'

'It looks as though that was the chapter he was working on when he became too ill to write any more. He only names one of the alleged abusers, the one that was drowned. IT have finished scanning the computer files on the memory stick you supplied for malware and emailed me a copy. I'm going to see if he has any more complete drafts that he hasn't printed out yet, but it won't be quick. He wasn't the most organised worker, everything is in separate numbered files that don't correspond to the chapter numbers in the printed manuscript.'

'Do what you can. I presume that you are here to ask for more help?'

'Yes please. Those boxes are filled with reams of copied documents and scanned pictures. I had a look inside and they're numbered, but they aren't in order and the photocopier wasn't the best.'

She held her hands out; the fingers shook slightly. 'I don't have the dexterity to go rooting through these boxes, especially if I'm wearing gloves, and I can't deal with that much paper sitting down.'

'Of course, I completely forgot. I'll arrange that team immediately,' said Warren, embarrassed that the welfare of a member of his team had slipped his mind.

'Thanks, Chief.' Pymm gave a small smile. 'I'm working from home tomorrow as I have a hospital appointment in the middle of the day. I'll tackle the computer files, assuming the remote access server isn't down again.'

She heaved herself to her feet as Warren handed over her crutches.

'Well, don't overdo it.'

'Don't worry, sir, I know my limits.' She paused. 'Sorry, I get a little snappy when I'm tired.'

Warren took the hint. 'I'll put in the request to HR immediately.'

Thursday 12th March

Chapter 51

7.30 a.m. and Warren and Tony Sutton were updating Grayson before the general 8 a.m. briefing. Grayson was wearing a freshly pressed uniform. Immediately after, he was meeting with several members of the force's most senior officers and Bishop Fisher's successor, the current Bishop of Hertfordshire and Essex.

The appointment was both a courtesy to assure the church that the murders were being taken seriously, and a means of forging links with the diocese to ensure their full cooperation with the investigation. Warren's gut was telling him that the case was likely to uncover some uncomfortable truths and that they were going to need as much assistance as possible.

Warren's interview the previous day with Sergeant Ingram indicated that sexual misconduct might not be the motivation behind the two priests' murders, nevertheless, he wasn't prepared to entirely dismiss the idea. Especially given Rachel Pymm's confirmation that Vernon Coombs' tale of sixteenth-century sexual abuse seemed to be correct.

'It's a hell of a story,' said DSI Grayson, 'but it seems pretty far-fetched. Sometimes coincidences do happen. Look at anything hard enough and you'll start to see connections that don't exist.'

'I agree that the murders are similar to the methods supposedly used by Simon Scrope to avenge his brother's mistreatment,' said Warren, 'but we can't find any evidence that either priest was involved in sexual abuse. Sergeant Ingram was adamant that Father Daugherty was falsely accused and that the student eventually withdrew the allegation. As for Father Nolan, we haven't found anything at all.'

'All that tells us is that the motive or the reason these men were chosen were different to the original murders,' interjected Sutton. 'I still think that the killer is familiar with the stories about the abbey's past. I think we need to continue looking at who else might have had access to the same sources as Vernon Coombs.'

'The question is how do we do that without showing our hand? Ideally the killer won't know that we suspect a link, but I don't know if Vernon Coombs had told anyone of his suspicions before he met me – although obviously, he didn't tell anyone afterwards.' Warren cringed inwardly at how callous his words sounded. He still felt sad that he was probably the last person to have a meaningful conversation with the dead reporter.

'Perhaps he made a note in his files, so that he could acknowledge their assistance later?' Grayson's words were clearly more optimistic than he felt.

'Perhaps, but Rachel says the work was pretty disorganised. She and her team are looking for anything that might help.'

'What about this supposed false accusation against Father Daugherty?' asked Grayson.

'From what we've heard from the school liaison officer that dealt with the original complaint, it was likely to be just that. I've asked Hutch to dig a little deeper and see if the No Further Action was justified, and also track down the complainant's whereabouts, to see if they have an alibi. The Social Media Intelligence Unit are looking at her social media posts, to see if she has expressed any strong views about the Church's recent problems, or if she has any ongoing links to people in the local community that could have been involved in the killings.'

'Good work, keep me posted.'

Chapter 52

Moray Ruskin looked even more keen than usual when he appeared at Warren's office door.

'We have a report back from forensics about the padlock key found with Father Nolan's body.'

'Oh? I thought they'd already done the fingerprints and other trace evidence,' said Warren.

'They had, but Andy Harrison noticed some scratches on the key and followed what he called a "hunch".'

'Go on, Andy's hunches usually lead somewhere interesting.'

'He reckons that the scratches could indicate that the key has been clamped, for example in a key copying machine.'

'OK, but we know that the key is a copy; Rodney Shaw has the master key. The spares are kept in the vestry and Shaw has the masters for safekeeping.'

'Well, not quite. The padlock to the tool shed is relatively modern, probably only about ten years old, so the key in the vestry is actually one of the original two keys supplied when the lock was bought. Technically, both the key in the vestry and Rodney Shaw's copy are masters.' Ruskin looked smug.

'So what you are saying is that the key found with Father Nolan – which we believe is the one from the vestry as it has that blob of paint on it – was itself copied?'

'It's not conclusive but it looks that way. And furthermore, CSM Harrison thinks it was copied recently. Something about the cleanliness of the scratches and the lack of oxidation.'

The importance of the revelation struck Warren immediately.

'If that's true, then it raises the question, why would Rodney Shaw need a second copy of a key he already has? And if it wasn't Rodney Shaw who made the copy, then who did?' Was this evidence that Shaw was not the killer? Or was it an elaborate ruse to throw them off?

'Is there any way that we can find out where the key was copied?' Warren felt he probably already knew the answer, but he needed to ask anyway.

Ruskin shook his head.

'No, I asked that as well. The scratches don't really carry any meaningful information. If we had the very same key cutting machine in front of us, Andy said he may be able to match the scratches to whatever imperfection on the clamp caused them, but even then he's not convinced. As for the key and padlock, it's a generic brand that has been sold for years everywhere from hardware stores to large supermarkets. It isn't a security key, so you can walk in off the street without any questions asked and have it copied whilst you wait.'

'I'm not even going to ask how many key cutters there are in Middlesbury, let alone the rest of the county.'

The excitement of the find had all but gone. It was possible that the murders had been planned for months, even years. They key could have been cut at any time in that period. If they had a hard suspect, Warren supposed they could always show a photograph of them to staff in those shops, but they must see dozens of customers each day, and there was nothing especially memorable about the key.

Perhaps the killer paid using a card – an oversight for sure, but not impossible – they could trawl through all of the cutter's sales for the past couple of years and see if any familiar names jumped out.

If the killer had the key cut relatively recently, they could always look through any CCTV footage that hadn't already been recorded over. Combining the time stamps for sales of cut keys – they wouldn't need to rely on credit card sales, cash would also be recorded – would allow them to narrow down the amount of video that needed to be examined, but it would still be considerable. It also relied on the cutters having a modern till that recorded the type of each sale.

It would be a mammoth job and extremely expensive. Would DSI Grayson be prepared to sign off on it?

'I had another thought, sir.'

'Go on.' Warren braced himself for even more expense.

'Well, I figured tracking down who copied the padlock key might be a bit of a stretch. But then I got thinking. If they needed a copy of that key, then presumably they also needed a copy of the keys to the chapel and the undercroft.'

'Have they been copied?' Warren perked up immediately. Those keys were over a hundred years old. Surely they'd stick in the memory more than a modern padlock key?

'Impossible to say, the keys are covered in all sorts of dings and scratches.'

Warren's excitement faded.

'But then I went into the key cutter's pop-up shop in the supermarket and he reckons that keys that old wouldn't be cut by a regular key cutter. They only do mass-produced keys, as they have to use a commercially available blank. If you want a key like that copied, you would need to use a specialist locksmith.'

Ruskin's excitement was infectious.

'Brilliant work, Moray. Get on it.'

Friday 13th March

Chapter 53

The village of Copperston had been home to Fullbright and Sons Locksmiths for over two hundred years. The village was only eighteen miles from Middlesbury, but first thing in the morning, it took over an hour to cover that distance. The shop opened at 8 a.m. and so Ruskin had decided to drive there before work. By the time he arrived back at his desk it was late morning, and he was in a foul mood.

'Why the hell do the dustbins need to be collected in rush hour? Seven until nine is the busiest part of the day on the road in literally every town and city in the country; you've got people going to work and parents doing the school run, so which idiot in the local council thinks it's a good idea to block the roads with a sodding great bin lorry? What is so urgent about collecting bins that it can't wait until when the traffic has died down?'

'Productive trip, Moray?' asked Pymm mildly. She pushed an open cake tin across her desk. 'Joey wanted to make cupcakes for his friend's birthday. This is the first attempt; they're a funny shape, and an even funnier colour, but they taste OK.'

'Thanks, Sarge.' Ruskin chose a bright green one. 'Alex has decided to go sugar free for Lent, so there's bugger all worth eating in the cupboards at home.'

'I had no idea Alex was religious,' said Pymm.

'He's not. He just wants to look his best for our wedding.'

'What did you find out?' asked Warren, who'd heard Ruskin's rant from across the office and come over to investigate. He helped himself to a purple cake.

'The good news is that the cutter remembers the keys. They were custom jobs and he had to take a mould because the customer couldn't leave them for the time it would take to get them made.'

'That fits with him needing to return them to vestry before anyone noticed they were missing,' said Pymm.

'I suppose it's too much to hope that we have a name or a description?' asked Warren.

'I'm afraid not. He says that the customer was a man, but he doesn't recall any other details. However, he was able to track down the order. It was placed on Friday the sixteenth of January and collected a week later on Thursday the twenty-second, paid for in cash. The name given by the customer was Bob Smith, but there's no way to be sure that was his real name. He did give a mobile phone number as a contact, for when the keys were ready for collection. I'll send it to you, Sarge, to see if you can do anything with it.'

'Well, fingers crossed,' said Warren, although he suspected the phone was probably unregistered. The killer had left precious few clues so far.

'Was there an invoice or any other paperwork that the killer might have touched?'

'No. The owner is pretty old school. He writes down his orders in a ledger and then transfers them to a spreadsheet once a week. He gives the customer a ticket, but doesn't retain it when they come back in. The customer doesn't need to sign anything.'

'The keys were cut almost two months ago,' said Warren. 'What are the chances that any CCTV footage is still available?'

'None for the locksmith's, he doesn't have any cameras. There are a few more shops nearby, but I didn't have a warrant to go demanding footage.'

'Get Mags on that. Ask her to send some officers over to secure what they can, plus any traffic camera footage from either of those two dates and CCTV from the train station. If we can place any suspects in that area, we've got the start of a case against them.'

'Anyone we should be looking for straight off the bat?' asked Pymm.

'Rodney Shaw is an obvious one, as is Lucas Furber, although I doubt he has access to a car. Otherwise, cross-reference licence plates with any vehicles associated with the abbey.'

* * *

'The Social Media Intelligence Unit have found something that might be useful,' said Pymm. She was leading the afternoon briefing.

The wall-mounted screen changed to that of a web browser. The website was basic but functional. The banner image at the top of the page was a stylised black and white image of a small child, head down, hugging their knees, a teddy bear on the floor next to them. A single line of text below stated, 'we believe you'.

'Survivorsonline.net. It's a website for survivors of sexual abuse. It skirts pretty close to the edge in terms of libel, as it isn't afraid to name alleged abusers or publish unsubstantiated rumours. Unfortunately, it's hosted overseas so shutting it down isn't possible and they aren't silly enough to name anybody with enough clout to take them on in court.'

Pymm selected a link.

'The site is essentially a collection of chat forums, moderated anonymously. There are sections for survivors of childhood abuse, adult abuse, elder abuse and also advice for those still under-going abuse or harassment. They also have a specialist sub-forum

270

dedicated to those abused by religious organisations, including the Catholic Church generally, and Catholic institutions such as schools and orphanages.

'The site won't appear on most web searches, because its robot. txt file has a "disallow command" to ensure mainstream search engines skip over it and don't index it. However, once you've found it, it's not too difficult to join and take part.'

'So how do abuse survivors find it?' asked Ruskin.

'Mostly by invitation. Current members hang around in publicly available chatrooms or social media pages and they send the link privately to those that they think they can help.'

'So what is the link to our victims?' asked Warren.

'We've got a hit on Father Cormac Nolan.'

'What have you got?'

'Looks like hearsay mostly, but it claims to be from an actual victim, going by the username 'Victimnomore'. The allegations date from 2004 or 2005, and name Saint Andrew's school in Hertfordshire.'

'That's a year or so before Father Nolan took early retirement from there on the grounds of ill health. What does the victim allege?' asked Warren.

'He claims that he sang in the school choir and that Father Nolan would sometimes take him and other boys away for the weekend to sing in competitions. At the time it happened, he says that his parents were alcoholics and physically abused him and his sister. Father Nolan was very kind to him and he was flattered by the attention. When he got into trouble at school over a playground fight, he says Father Nolan intervened and stopped him being expelled. Of course, he now realises that he was never going to be expelled, the fight wasn't serious enough.'

'Classic grooming,' muttered Sutton. 'Pick on the most vulnerable and show them the love that they crave.'

'It looks that way. Anyway, he said that the abuse happened twice. The first time, he was waiting backstage for a competition

271

to start. He was on his own as he was singing a solo. He was nervous and he said Father Nolan had come backstage to try and calm him down. As they were talking, he placed his hand on his knee and asked him if he had a girlfriend. The boy was a bit embarrassed and confused, as he was only twelve at the time. Father Nolan then started mumbling something about how he had never wanted a girlfriend, but that the priesthood could be very lonely. He thinks he may have been drunk.

'They called his name to get ready and he said that Father Nolan stood up really quick and seemed very flustered. Looking back on it, he reckons Father Nolan was trying to hide an erection.'

'Christ,' whispered Sutton.

'The second time was more serious and took place on a weekend trip to Blackpool about six months later. There were an odd number of boys in the choir so most of them were paired up to share a room, except for the poster.'

Warren closed his eyes briefly; it was all too clear where the story was leading.

'The boys all went to their rooms about ten o'clock. A few hours later – he isn't sure exactly as he fell asleep – he woke up and found Father Nolan sitting on the end of his bed. He was so scared he didn't move. He then alleges that he felt Father Nolan's hand move under the covers and start stroking his crotch. It was then that he realised that Father Nolan was also pleasuring himself.'

'Bastard,' muttered Ruskin.

'Anyway, he must have moved or made a noise, as Nolan stopped what he was doing and jumped up and fled the room. Again, he thinks that Nolan had been drinking.

'The following day, Father Nolan cornered him and told him not to talk about it to anyone. He said that he'd been able to feel how much the lad had enjoyed it. When the boy said he was going to tell his parents, Father Nolan had told him that if he did nobody would believe him and that he'd be kicked out of the school. Remember, he'd already convinced the victim that he had the power to stop him being expelled, it wasn't too hard to convince him that the opposite was true.'

'So what happened between the alleged incident and Father Nolan retiring? Assuming the dates are correct, there is a time lag of up to two years,' asked Warren.

'The poster alleges that Father Nolan tried to avoid him wherever possible. When his voice broke later that year, he left the choir and stopped serving on the altar and that was the last he spoke to Father Nolan. However, he claimed that it was open knowledge that Father Nolan liked a drink and that, eventually, he retired to some retirement home for priests.'

'There's the link. There aren't many priest retirement homes, I'm sure it couldn't have taken much detective work to track him down,' said Sutton.

'None at all. On the twelfth of April 2014 a different user, named Angryman80, simply asked for the name of the home, to which Victimnomore replied the "Middlesbury priest retirement home" – obviously, he must have meant St Cecil's.'

'Bloody hell. Well, let's list both users as potential suspects. I suppose it's a bit much to hope that either of them filled in any personal information on their profile?'

'No, sorry. We can't even be certain of their gender.'

'I presume that requesting their IP address from the website, so we can narrow down their physical location, is a non-starter?'

'I'll speak to IT, but the website is physically hosted in Bulgaria and everyone posts anonymously, I doubt they'll pay any attention to a court order.'

'OK, well get the Social Media Intelligence Unit to see if they can build a profile from their posts and interactions on the site. Their usernames are distinctive, see if it they appear anywhere else on the internet.'

Warren used a marker pen to scrawl the two usernames into the suspect column on the whiteboard.

'Is there anything else on the site of any interest?' asked Sutton.

'Potentially, but without direct access to their archives, Social Media Intelligence are limited to the site's own search facility. They are already concerned they may be blocked for suspicious activity if their searches lead to an unexpected spike in site traffic.'

'Well, do what you can,' said Warren. 'See if there are any references to St Cecil's retirement home or Father Daugherty.'

'I'm afraid I've some bad news,' said Pymm. 'More people might know about the original abbey murders than we thought.' Pymm projected a Word document on the screen.

'I found this on the memory stick Vernon Coombs' daughter gave us.' She scrolled to the top of the document, highlighting the title.

'Murder and cover-ups: The dark history of Middlesbury Abbey,' read Sutton out loud.

'They appear to be notes from a public lecture he gave to the Friends of Middlesbury Abbey. The file creation date was July last year.'

'Damn. Depending on who was in attendance, that could really widen the suspect list. How much detail does it contain?' asked Warren.

'The notes are only bullet points, so it's hard to tell exactly what he shared with the audience, but he does mention the death bed confession given by Simon Scrope.'

'Which means that the details of the murders that inspired the killings of Fathers Nolan and Daugherty were in the public domain,' said Ruskin.

'According to his notes, he finished up with a question and answer session, so who knows what else he revealed?' said Pymm.

'I don't suppose he had a list of attendees?' asked Warren hopefully.

'No. And neither do the Friends of Middlesbury Abbey,' she said. 'I looked them up online, and spoke to the secretary of the organisation. He said the talk was hosted in the chapel, and was fairly well attended, both by members of the society as well as a fair number of local priests, including some from the retirement home, even a couple of the sisters.'

'Any idea who they were?'

'He can't recall. He thinks Bishop Fisher was there and Deacon Baines, plus a few others. I've downloaded the members list for the Friends of Middlesbury Abbey, so we can cross-check with our records.'

'I don't suppose he remembers if Rodney Shaw was there?' asked Sutton.

'He is listed as a member of the society, so he may have been, but when I asked if any members of the abbey staff were in attendance, he couldn't remember. To be fair, it was eight or nine months ago.'

Warren looked across the room at the suspects' board. Rodney Shaw's headshot stared back at him. Why couldn't they clear that man?

Chapter 54

Moray Ruskin's expression told Warren that all wasn't well.

'Come in, Moray. Take a chair and tell me what the problem is.'

Ruskin sagged into the visitor's chair opposite Warren's desk.

'They've found Lucas Furber.'

'Where?'

'In a derelict garage on the Wheatsheaf estate. It's sometimes used as a squat by homeless people. Looks like a drugs overdose.'

'Who found him?'

'They aren't sure. There was an anonymous call to 999 from someone claiming to have found the body. It sounds as though he's been dead for some time.'

'Bugger, he was our best lead.' Warren stopped. 'Sorry, that was a bit insensitive, are you OK?'

Ruskin let out a puff of air.

'Sorry, I'm being silly. I didn't even know the guy.'

'But you felt like you did,' supplied Warren. 'You've spent ages tracking him down, trying to learn about him. It's natural that you became attached to him.'

'Yeah, but it's more than that. What if I helped cause his death?'

'Moray, you can't think like that.'

'I know, I know. But I've been stomping around town in

my size thirteens asking who's seen him. Maybe word got back to him that the police were looking for him and he, I dunno, decided to end it?'

'I doubt that. If that was the case, he'd probably just lie low or disappear. And if he was involved in the murders, then you can hardly hold yourself responsible for his guilty conscience.'

'What if he was an accomplice to the murders, and my poking around meant that the other killer decided he was a liability?'

'Again, not your fault.'

Ruskin sighed again; he still didn't look convinced.

'I suppose you're right.'

'Of course there could be another explanation.'

Ruskin looked hopeful.

'He could just be a drug addict who took an overdose.'

* * *

The garage where Lucas Furber's body had been found was one of a half-dozen on the edge of the Wheatsheaf estate.

'The garages were originally assigned to a block of flats. When the flats were condemned and knocked down, the garages were abandoned.' Tony Sutton pointed towards a building site nearby.

'The original flats are being replaced with a mixed-usage residential and business complex, due to open in about eighteen months. The garages will be flattened and a car park built on the site, but that phase isn't due to start until next year.'

Warren and Ruskin had met Sutton at the end of the road leading to the garages. The three men walked up to the police tape.

'You'll need to wear a suit if you want to go any further, sirs,' warned the constable holding the clipboard with the scene log.

'We can see what we need to from here,' said Sutton.

The garage where Furber had been found was the third from the left. The metal up-and-over garage door had been propped up, so that white-suited technicians could easily move in and out.

277

'The site is supposed to be secure, but there's a hole in the fencing. Local residents have been complaining for months that it was being used by rough sleepers and needed to be fixed, but apparently the developers didn't do anything about it.'

'How did he get into the garage?' asked Ruskin.

'The locks are pretty old, they've all been broken open,' said Sutton.

'Were the other units in use?' asked Warren.

'It looks like they might have been once. Two at the end have even had the wall knocked through to make one big unit. I guess who ever lived there must be a fan of DIY TV shows.'

'Any suggestion as to how long ago they were occupied? If there were others living here, then they might be witnesses,' said Ruskin.

'It's hard to say. The CSIs are bagging food packaging and rubbish to see if anything has a date on it we can use, but most of them have leaking rooves, so they might have been abandoned some time ago. I've been on the phone to the rough sleeping unit, and they reckon that there aren't many that sleep down here, because there are better spots closer to the soup kitchen, and there's a problem with rats. I saw one earlier; damn thing was the size a small dog, I thought it was going to attack one of the CSIs.'

'Makes you wonder why Furber opted to sleep down here then,' said Warren.

'I'll ask the rough sleepers unit, they're the experts.'

'What about CCTV?' asked Ruskin.

'Doubtful. The only cameras we've tracked down are on the building site, to stop thieves. None of them cover this area and there's no reason to walk past them to get here.'

'The locals complained about rough sleepers, so maybe somebody saw Furber coming in and out. Maybe they saw someone with him?' the Scotsman suggested.

Warren sincerely hoped so. So far, Friday the thirteenth had mostly brought bad luck; they could do with some more leads.

Saturday 14th March

Chapter 55

Moray Ruskin had insisted that he wanted to attend Lucas Furber's autopsy. Warren decided to go along with him; the death had hit the young probationer hard, and Warren was concerned about him. It was a decision he regretted almost the moment they arrived at the morgue. He'd completely forgotten that it was Granddad Jack's birthday party that afternoon. Now he'd have to get changed again before he jumped in the car with Susan for the journey back to Coventry.

'He was dead for some time, and the body has been disturbed by wildlife,' warned Professor Jordan. Warren decided a second shower might also be in order before Susan picked him up.

The body on the gurney looked like a poor Hollywood prop. The skin was a dark, bloodless grey, slightly puffy from the early stages of decomposition that Warren's nose told him was taking place. The body was nude, and it was clear to see that Furber had been malnourished. In addition to his prominent ribs, the man's pelvis was clearly outlined, and his knees were the same width as his upper thighs.

Mercifully, the Y incision had been completed and the chest sewn back up before Warren and Ruskin had arrived.

Often the recently deceased looked peaceful. In the case of

Furber, it was impossible to tell; Ryan's warning about wildlife held true.

'Poor bastard.'

Ruskin's voice behind his mask was thick-tongued. Warren looked at him with concern, but the burly Scotsman showed no signs of being ill.

'They go for the soft, exposed flesh first,' said Jordan. 'Fortunately he was wearing tight-fitting underwear and jeans. Rats can crawl through the smallest of gaps.'

'They only go for dead bodies, right?'

'Not always, if the person is deeply unconscious, they might take an exploratory nip. If they don't get swatted away, then they might carry on.'

'Jesus. He wasn't…'

Jordan took pity on the young constable.

'No, he was quite dead, when they started.' He pointed at the hole where Furber's nose had been. 'No blood.'

Ruskin said nothing behind his mask, but his shoulders relaxed.

'Any indication of cause of death?' asked Warren.

'Almost certainly an overdose of opiates. I'll know more when I get the toxicology results back, but he was found with a needle and syringe still inserted in his left median cubital vein. The remains of the drug inside the syringe tested positive for opiates. Again, we'll know more about the specifics of the drug when I get the results back.'

Jordan turned the inside of the man's arm over. A small hole was visible at the crook of his elbow, surrounded by what appeared to be dark blood.

'He passed out with the needle still in his arm, which caused the tearing you see.'

Jordan pointed to a discoloured band of skin around the bicep. 'Marks from the tourniquet. It was still attached, although loosened when he was found.'

'Was he a habitual user?' asked Ruskin.

'Certainly in the past. There are scars on the inside of both elbows, as well as dotted around his body.'

'But nothing recent?'

'Not that I could find.'

'So why did he start using again?' asked Ruskin.

It was a rhetorical question, and nobody answered.

'What else have you found?' asked Warren.

'He was malnourished and in poor health, obviously. In addition, he had scrapes and bruises, but nothing that stands out. There was a significant volume of what appears to be super strength lager in his stomach, although I won't know his blood alcohol levels until the results come back from the lab.'

'Any indication that he had been restrained, or beaten?'

'No. At this stage, it looks to me like an accidental overdose; not uncommon in recovering addicts, especially if they have drunk a lot.'

'How long ago?'

'That's a bit more tricky. Some time ago, obviously, you can tell by the fact that he has started to decompose. Other than that, I can't tell. The weather has been cold, but he was well sheltered in that garage and wrapped up warmly, with decent clothes and quite a thick sleeping bag.'

'What about maggot larvae?' asked Ruskin.

'Eggs will have been laid pretty much as soon as he died. We could get a forensic entomologist in to have a look.'

It was a good suggestion, but Warren doubted DSI Grayson would be willing to authorise the expense for what appeared to be a simple overdose. Forensic entomology worked on the principle that flying insects such as blow flies laid their eggs on dead bodies, within hours of death. The eggs then developed over the course of the next few days, weeks or even months to hatch into juvenile flies.

The individual developmental stages of the larvae's growth were well-characterised and the process was temperature-dependent.

As long as the temperature of the area where the body had lain was known, a forensic entomologist could obtain a fairly accurate indication of when the deceased died.

The problem was the cost. Forensic entomologists were typically employed as freelance consultants who usually held a day job at a university or other research institute. Furthermore, there was always a backlog of cases.

However, if they could narrow down when Furber died it could potentially rule him out of Father Daugherty or even Father Nolan's deaths and answer once and for all his role in recent events. But was the expense justified, when other methods might be just as accurate, at a fraction of the expense?

'Can you preserve the samples in case we decide to pursue this at a later date?' asked Warren.

'Yes, I can freeze the eggs in liquid nitrogen.'

'Do it.'

Chapter 56

Warren's final job before taking off for the weekend was to stop off at the press office. It was sad, but the death of a homeless drug addict was never going to fill a press conference like the murder of an elderly priest. Without explicitly linking Lucas Furber to the ongoing investigation into the murders – which Warren was reluctant to do at this stage – the best they could hope for was for a half page in the *Middlesbury Reporter*, with an appeal for information. The prominence of the article and accompanying photo depended entirely on the other stories deemed newsworthy that day. Warren prayed that Middlesbury's long-standing Member of Parliament didn't finally decide that today was the day to announce his intentions for the upcoming general election.

Therefore, it was well after lunch before Warren was finally able to drive home, shower, change and meet Susan. Consequently, it was late afternoon before they made it to Coventry.

Granddad Jack's front garden was as immaculate as always, although he had bowed to the inevitable and allowed Warren and Dennis, Susan's father, to transfer plants to more easily maintained raised pots; 90-year-old knees don't cope with weeding as well as they once did.

The windowsills and front gate had been freshly painted by

Susan the previous summer and the vibrant red was one of the few splashes of colour in the street.

'Oh look, number twenty-six is up for sale. That must be why he's finally tidied the front garden,' commented Susan as they climbed out of the car.

'Probably just as well, I can't imagine that rusty old Ford Escort added much to the house price. Come to think of it, getting rid of it probably raised the value of every other property in the area,' said Warren as he locked the car and took his overnight bag from Susan.

The front door was opened by Jane, his second cousin. Warren had his own keys of course, but it didn't feel right just walking in.

Warren's apology for not getting there sooner was met by the usual stiff smile that he'd grown to expect. Jane was a stay-at-home mother, who lived barely two miles from Granddad Jack, but still seemed unable to understand that it was harder for Warren and Susan, who lived a hundred miles away and worked full-time, to visit than it was for her.

'We started without you.'

'Of course, that's fine,' said Warren as he hung his coat up. 'Where are the kids?'

'They've gone home. It'll be bath time soon and we don't want to disrupt their routine.'

'Oh, that's a shame,' said Warren, meaning it. He hadn't seen his niece and nephew since Christmas, although even then Jane and her husband's infamous 'routine' had curtailed their visit to just a couple of hours on Boxing Day. It was a marked contrast to the somewhat more free-wheeling parenting style of Susan's sister Felicity and her husband Jeff whose gaggle of kids typically ran riot wherever they went.

Warren hoped for a happy middle ground if – when – he and Susan finally had children. On impulse, he reached over and gave Susan's hand a squeeze. The plan for the weekend was to forget about Monday's pregnancy test and simply enjoy themselves. Not a chance. The two had barely said a word to each other during the two-hour journey, and if Susan's state of mind was anything like Warren's, not even the pressures of work could distract them for long.

The first round of pleasantries over, Warren disengaged himself from Jane's perfunctory hug and he and Susan headed into the small lounge.

'How's the birthday boy?' asked Susan.

'All the better for seeing you,' replied Granddad Jack, as he struggled to his feet to embrace his granddaughter-in-law. Behind her, Warren couldn't help but compare the old man in front of them with the person who'd still managed to hold court in the Lime Tree social club during his surprise ninetieth birthday party the year before.

An inch or two shorter from an increasing stoop, his shoulder blades were sharp under a loose hanging jumper that had fit him perfectly twelve months ago. How much more weight had he lost?

That being said, the beaming smile and shining eyes were a promising sign. The death three years ago of Nana Betty had left him depressed for a spell and Warren couldn't help assessing his mood every time he called or visited. Touch wood, he seemed to be his old self.

'Can I get you two a drink?' called Dennis from the kitchen. Susan's father had clearly been busy. Since finally retiring full-time, he'd thrown himself into his favourite hobby, cooking. Now, no visit was complete without a filled Tupperware box or two. The kitchen table where Warren had spent so much of his adolescence, was covered in food, all freshly baked. His stomach growled loudly.

In recent months, Dennis had even encroached into his wife Bernice's traditional territory, baking, and Christmas had required a degree of diplomacy as two, beautifully iced cakes had been presented to the assembled guests. With that in mind, Warren decided it would be safer not to enquire who was responsible for the impressive birthday cake. The rest of the fare on offer was clearly down to Dennis.

'Just a Coke for me,' said Warren. It was still late afternoon and although he and Susan planned on staying overnight, he wouldn't feel relaxed enough to have a drink until late evening when he knew that it was unlikely that he'd be forced to drive back to Middlesbury.

'Any news?' asked Dennis quietly, when he could be sure that Bernice was out of earshot.

Susan's mother had made it abundantly clear that she disapproved of the couple's decision to ignore the Catholic Church's official position on assisted reproduction and embark on IVF. In recent months she had relented somewhat, unwilling to jeopardise her relationship with her daughter, and any future grandchildren, but it was still a subject best left untouched in her presence.

'We'll find out either way Monday,' said Warren.

Dennis clasped his shoulder; it was about as expressive as he ever got.

'I saw you on the news,' said Jane as Warren re-entered the living room.

'Terrible business,' said Bernice. 'Those poor men. They spend a lifetime selflessly serving the good Lord and their community and they can't even live out their retirement in peace. What sort of society do we live in where that sort of thing can happen?'

'Any indication why they were targeted?' asked Jane.

'We're pursuing a number of lines of inquiry,' hedged Warren.

'I bet it was one of those satanic cults that you read about,' said Bernice primly.

Susan rolled her eyes.

'I reckon they were paedophiles getting their just desserts,' said Jane. 'You know what they're like. You're always hearing about them. Priests touching altar servers and all that.'

'What a terrible thing to say,' said Bernice. 'Those men dedicated their life to doing good and as soon as they can't defend

287

themselves people start saying such horrible things about them.'

'Well, whatever the reason, I'm sure Warren and his team will figure it out,' said Susan, her tone suggesting the conversation was over.

* * *

'Sorry to interrupt the party, sir, but I thought you'd want to know right away what I've found out about Olivia Mason, the girl who accused Father Daugherty of inappropriate behaviour. I'm on a rest day tomorrow.'

'That's fine, go ahead, Hutch.' Warren closed the kitchen door. Even with his hearing aids, Granddad Jack needed the TV turned up so loud that the living room door alone wasn't enough to block the sound.

'I tracked down the school's safeguarding lead from the time that the complaint was made, a Mrs McCulloch. She still works there. She confirmed that the NFA was appropriate. Apparently the girl already had a history of trying to avoid punishment by making false accusations and had been caught in a lie a couple of times previously. Fortunately, the incident with Father Daugherty was the last time she tried it. She was said to have been very upset when she realised the effect it had on him.'

'Do we know what she's doing these days? Is she still living in the area?'

'Apparently the family were originally from Australia; her mother was a university lecturer. Olivia arrived at the school halfway through year eight, and they moved back after Olivia finished her exams at the end of year eleven. Some of the behaviour was probably due to the disruption. Apparently, Olivia was angry and upset about being uprooted from her friends and school in Australia, and found it hard to settle and make friends after arriving during the middle of a school year.'

'Can we be sure that she isn't back in the UK?'

'She remained an Australian citizen, and according to UK Border control, neither she nor her immediate family have been back here in the past four years. We know that she had friends that she met whilst she was here, the original poster on Survivorsonline claimed that she knew her personally, so she could have incited someone from afar. But it seems unlikely, and there is certainly nothing suspicious in her public social media posts.'

'Well, as alibis go, I think that's pretty strong. Thanks Hutch. Enjoy the rest of your weekend, you've earned it.'

As had many of the team; Warren realised that he'd forgotten to check the overtime logs to make sure nobody was working too many hours. He resolved to do that as soon as he got back.

In the meantime, there was one more name off the suspect column.

289

Chapter 57

It was late evening, and Warren had decided to have a beer. The likelihood that he'd be called on to drive back to Middlesbury was now quite slim. Dennis and Bernice were getting ready to depart; Dennis had produced two large Tupperware boxes that he'd crammed with leftover food, so that was lunch sorted for the next week.

Warren was just peeling back the tab on a can of lager when his phone rang. He stopped in his tracks.

The caller ID showed the main CID switchboard. He placed the can down on the sideboard and answered.

'Sir, I have Professor Jordan on the line. He says it's urgent.'

'Put him through.'

There was a pause as the line went dead, before the background noise changed.

'Sorry to call at this late hour.'

'Not at all, Ryan, I appreciate it.'

'I've got the toxicology results back from Lucas Furber.'

'Tell me what you've found.'

'First off, I was right. It was an opiate overdose that killed him.'

'Good.' Warren waited, Jordan wouldn't have been so

insistent in speaking to him if he was just confirming what they already suspected. An email or a voicemail would have been sufficient.

'I sent a sample of the drug residue of for testing. It came back as heroin. But not just that, it also had hospital-grade morphine mixed in.'

'Which presumably increased the drug's potency?'

'You'd think so. But actually it's not that clear cut. Plus, morphine isn't very soluble in water. It's one of the reasons that diamorphine – heroin – is sometimes used in hospitals.'

'But he still died of an overdose?'

'Yes. In fact, it was a massive overdose. Probably exacerbated, in part, by a blood alcohol concentration of 212 milligrams per millilitre. From what I can tell, Furber had been clean of heroin for several months. In that time his tolerance for the drug would have decreased markedly; I imagine he could still withstand a bigger dose than either you or I, but if he used the same amount of drug as he used previously, it would probably have killed him. It's what happens to all those celebrities that OD after being clean for a long period of time. The amount he took was already much higher than necessary to kill him, there was no need to doctor the drug.'

'What do you mean doctor the drug? Are you saying that drug he took wasn't street heroin? I thought they mixed all sorts of crap into it?'

'They do, but usually it's low-cost filler to increase their profit margins. Hospital grade morphine is expensive, compared to the stuff they usually use. According to the person I spoke to at the drugs unit, it's extremely unlikely that they would have wasted high quality morphine in street heroin. He can't recall ever seeing it.'

Warren took a few moments to digest what Ryan had said.

'So the heroin that Furber decided to take – despite months of being apparently clean – was cut with a drug that would have

291

likely reduced its potency, and is too expensive to make financial sense for a street dealer to use?'

'As far as I can tell, that's about the size of it.'

'That doesn't make any sense, unless he was killed by someone who knew little or nothing about the drugs they were supplying to him.'

'That sort of speculation is beyond my remit, obviously, but it seems the most logical explanation. Unless you're involved in that sub-culture or know habitual drug users, that information isn't as easy to come by as you might think. You can't exactly find it on Wikipedia and the specialist internet forums where users share tips like these are blocked by a lot of internet service providers. To be fair, ask a hundred people on the street if mixing high quality hospital morphine with crappy street heroin would increase or decrease the potency and I reckon most would guess that it would increase it.'

Warren agreed with his assessment.

'So next question, where could the killer have got the morphine?'

'The immediate answer these days is the internet; so-called dark websites that don't get picked up by the regular search engines.'

Warren was familiar with the idea of the deep or dark web – the 90 per cent of the internet that was hidden from the sight of the casual user and even 'surface' search engines such as Google or Bing. He'd been to a number of workshops on the increasing use of this part of the web by criminals. Not everything on the dark web was illegal of course. Many legitimate businesses kept the non-public part of their internet presence hidden out of site, whilst citizens of oppressive regimes used the anonymity that often came with such sites to live their online lives free from persecution.

The example that immediately sprang to mind was Survivorsonline. Warren wasn't sure if simply instructing search engines to skip over the site and not index it counted as the dark web, but it implied that the killer, who very likely used the victims' forum, was at least familiar with the concept.

Warren said as much to Ryan.

'That's well outside my area of expertise, Warren. Of course, there's a simpler way of obtaining hospital-grade morphine. A hospital.'

Sunday 15th March

Chapter 58

First thing Sunday morning, Warren and Susan drove Granddad Jack to church for the Lent mass. Neither of the Jones had been to church since their excruciating annual visit to midnight mass. The priest had again thanked Mr Potter for making the accompanying carol service so memorable and again speculation in the car on the way home had centred around how the hapless organist managed to butcher the same carols every single year, without any evidence of improvement.

Warren had been so pre-occupied with the case that he'd almost forgotten that Sunday also marked Mother's Day. A reminder from Susan the previous evening gave him enough time to buy a bunch of his mother's favourite flowers to place on her grave. He'd also bought some of Nana Betty's favourite blooms, to spruce up her plot.

The bidding prayers opened with a general request for the Lord's help and protection for those who did God's work, and a more specific appeal for His assistance in finding those responsible for the murders in Middlesbury. Warren doubted that the prayers were inspired by his presence – he imagined similar petitions were being made up and down the country – nevertheless, Warren's face had been on television and there were enough members of the congregation who knew him, for him to keep his eyes down-turned, avoiding any curious gazes. He imagined he could feel the curious stares burning into the back of his head and he resolved not to linger any longer than was necessary when the service ended.

The service passed in a blur, the readings and gospel forgotten as soon as he heard them. The familiar routines of the Catholic litany, usually a source of familiarity and comfort for even an occasional church-goer like Warren, seemed hollow and insincere. The message boards on Survivorsonline contained allegations about dozens of priests, but surely they were only the tip of the iceberg? And whilst it appeared that Father Daugherty had been the unfortunate victim of a malicious allegation, that was certainly the exception rather than the rule. Warren had been to too many seminars and briefings about abuse to be under any illusion that the majority of victims were telling anything but the truth.

He found himself staring at the priest's back as the elderly celebrant prepared the altar for the Eucharist. How many apparently normal priests were secret paedophiles? How many led clandestine second lives, exploiting the shame and embarrassment of their helpless victims and the wilful ignorance of their fellow church members to commit such despicable acts?

Surely it was only a small percentage? According to some reports, the proportion of abusers in the church broadly reflected the proportion of abusers in the general population; but such data was hard to verify.

But that wasn't really the point.

Warren had been brought up like all Catholic children, to regard priests as God's representatives on Earth. After all, if you couldn't trust a priest, who could you trust?

As an adult, he'd learnt that even priests are fallible. The things he'd witnessed in the line of duty had left him cynical when it came to human nature. He'd long grown out of such childhood naivety. And yet here in his childhood church, surrounded by people he had known all his life, enveloped in familiar comforting rituals, he felt transported back to that childhood.

The betrayal made him feel sick, and it made him angry.

Around the world, over a billion people had been baptised as Catholics. Some, like Bernice, followed the church's teachings, barely questioning them, whilst others paid lip-service at best.

So why were he and Susan even here? They rarely, if ever, attended Sunday service, unless with her parents or with Granddad Jack. Were they here for their own sake, or just because it was 'what was expected of them'? Were they being hypocrites?

He remembered the six months before they got married; they'd attended church every Sunday thus ensuring the church wedding that both of them had dreamed of. How many times had they been back since then?

He knew without question that their children would be baptised. But would they be doing it because they wanted them to become full members of the Catholic Church, or again, because it was expected of them? Or because the nearest primary school to their house 'Required Improvement', but the Catholic school further down the road had been rated as 'Outstanding' by OFSTED?

A cynic might shrug and say, 'so what?' Play the game to get what you want. Giving up an hour every Sunday morning was a small price to pay for a beautiful church wedding. Attending a few classes and having a priest pour water over your bewildered child's forehead was worth it to get them a decent education – and a damn good excuse to have a party afterwards.

But what about those other expectations? The automatic assumption that a priest and his actions were, by definition, sanctioned by God, and that even questioning them was sinful, was what had allowed abuse to flourish in an organisation that should have been on the forefront of preventing it.

Then there were the implacable dictates that even married couples avoid contraception, or shun IVF, even though neither option had even been conceived of two thousand years ago.

Warren still felt angry at the pain Susan had gone through over the summer when Bernice had described their plans to use IVF as 'ungodly'. Bernice had eventually apologised, after Susan had made it clear that she would play no part in her future grandchildren's lives if she didn't back down. But they still avoided broaching the subject with her.

Warren was angry, because if ever there was a time that Susan needed her mother's support it was now, and he resented the unnecessary barriers that inflexible doctrine had built between them.

At the pulpit, the priest was talking about God's mercy and his love for all of his children. Warren tasted bile in his mouth.

If God loved all of his children then why had He allowed Gary Hastings, himself a practising Christian, to come to such a brutal end, leaving an unborn child that would never know their father's touch, and a fiancée who would never walk down the aisle with the love of her life? If it was all part of some master plan, too divine for man to comprehend, then count Warren out.

Looking around the church that he had grown up in, Warren found himself coming to a sobering realisation.

This might be the last time he set foot in here.

And he didn't know whether he should be upset or relieved.

Chapter 59

'Andy Harrison here.' The announcement wasn't really necessary, given that the crime scene manager's name appeared on Warren's phone screen. And if that didn't work, Warren couldn't think of any other men he worked with that had such a broad Yorkshire accent. The retention of his native inflection was remarkable given that the man had worked in this corner of Hertfordshire for well over half his life.

Assuming that his accent was still authentic, of course; Warren recalled an uncle from Liverpool who'd seemingly kept his Scouse accent for the fifty-plus years he'd lived in Birmingham. It wasn't until the mourners were several pints into his wake that one of his sisters, who'd remained in the North West, admitted she couldn't understand a word her brother had said towards the end of his life. 'It was like watching a film full of Hollywood actors who learnt the accent by watching reruns of Harry Enfield.'

'What have you got for me, Andy?'

It was 2 p.m. and Susan was driving the couple home, leaving Warren free to answer and make calls. Ordinarily, they'd have enjoyed a long, leisurely lunch, followed by a lazy afternoon, with slices of birthday cake washed down with multiple cups of tea, but Warren had been too busy to linger.

299

Saying goodbye to Granddad Jack so early had been harder than Warren expected. He was 91 years old – how many more birthdays would they have with him? Would he even live to see his first great-grandchild? Granddad Jack would be the first to know if Warren and Susan's appointment the next day yielded good news, Warren vowed.

Warren pushed the thoughts away; he recognised the signs. Overwork, lack of sleep and so many dead bodies always conspired to make him maudlin. When it was all over, he resolved to take Granddad Jack away for a bit of a holiday. Easter was only a few weeks away, and with the overtime he was accumulating he should be able to take a few days off over the school holidays with Susan.

'We may have a window for the timing of Lucas Furber's death,' said Harrison. Warren had already ascertained that nobody had seen Furber coming or going from the derelict garages where his body had been found.

'Brilliant, take me through it.'

'The site was full of rubbish. It looks as though he'd been here for some time. I called Professor Jordan and he confirmed that Furber's last meal was a Sainsbury's cheese and broccoli quiche, probably consumed within six hours of death.'

'Sounds delicious.'

'Amongst the rubbish, we found the packaging. The quiche had a use by date of Monday March the ninth.'

'That narrows things down. Do we know how long these quiches stay on the shelf before they reach their use by date?'

'Even better. The barcode had been replaced by a reduced-to-clear sticker. Fifty pence. I contacted the shop and they reckon that the sticker and that level of reduction is only applied towards the end of the day that the food expires. Assuming that he bought it at the nearest store to the garage, that particular store marks food down after about 7 p.m. A number of the local homeless community know this and tend to pop in then to see if they can snag a bargain. As long as they don't harass staff or customers, the manager doesn't do anything to discourage them.'

'That's fantastic, Andy. There's no guarantee he ate it immediately, but it gives us a last time that he was reliably seen. I'll get Mags to seize the CCTV from all the Sainsbury's in the area to see if we can pick him up.'

Warren hung up then immediately dialled into the office, passing on Harrison's information. Assuming that Harrison was correct, this meant that Furber had died several days after both Fathers Nolan and Daugherty had been killed, leaving his name on the suspect's board.

It also meant that Rodney Shaw had been released from custody some days before Furber's death. Based on what Professor Jordan had told him about the doctored heroin, could he have been Lucas Furber's killer? Shaw had supposedly been clean of drugs for decades, and was no longer part of that scene. Might that explain why he was ignorant of the effects of mixing hospital-grade morphine with street heroin?

But if Shaw was the killer, what was his motive?

Chapter 60

The Social Media Intelligence Unit had been busy over the weekend, sending Rachel Pymm several interesting snippets that she'd asked to share with Warren and the team after Susan dropped him off at CID.

'They found a reference to Father Daugherty on Survivorsonline. It didn't come up immediately because the poster had misspelt his surname D-O-H-E-R-T-Y, and the website's search engine isn't very sophisticated.' Pymm had drained her latest cup of nettle tea, leaving what appeared to be a pile of sodden leaf-litter at the bottom of her mug. She noticed the direction of Warren's gaze and glared at him, as if daring him to comment. He decided not to rise to the challenge. He already knew that the suggestion he was going to make at the end of the briefing wasn't going to be received well, and he didn't want to antagonise her before he even broached it.

'Well, we've got it now, what did they find?'

'There is an ongoing discussion about "priests who got away with it". The original thread is ancient, it was started about eight years ago, shortly after the site first went live. Somebody claiming to have been at Saint Thomas Aquinas school, at the time of the alleged incident, posted the story about Father Daugherty about five years ago. They don't claim to have been abused by Father Daugherty themselves – according to their other posts they were on the site for unrelated reasons to do with an abusive relative – but they reckon they knew the girl who made the allegation.'

'I assume from the title of the thread that they don't believe she made it up?' said Sutton.

Pymm's slightly frosty tone when she replied made Warren wonder if Sutton had already commented on Pymm's beverage before he had arrived.

'No, the poster claimed it was successfully covered up by the church and the school. The account is riddled with factual inaccuracies, not least the spelling of his name, and the poster admits that they don't remember all the details, but it's similar enough to what we know happened to definitely be the same event. At the end of the post, they said he had been moved to a retirement home.'

'Could that be the connection? Is that how the killer is targeting his victims?' asked Warren. 'Searching the website for priests that have retired?'

'I can't imagine it would be too difficult,' said Sutton. 'How many priests listed on this site are coming up in posts with keywords related to "retirement home"?'

'And with that in mind, how many retirement homes dedicated to retired clergy are there likely to be? Presumably all the residents in the home are on the electoral roll?' asked Pymm.

'Good point,' said Warren. 'A few seconds online would reveal if they are registered at the home for voting and council tax. Check that out please, Moray, also see if they are on the public electoral roll or if they've ticked the box to avoid being included; that might help narrow down who would be easily able to track them down. In the meantime, what were the responses to that original post, Rachel?'

'In the days immediately following the post, there were a handful of replies – mostly of the "another bastard's got away with it" variety and the thread was buried in the archives. In total the website's software records it as having been viewed eighty-six times. Without access to the website's server logs though, we can't know if those were unique views, or the same few people viewing the thread multiple times. We also don't know if the page views were recent or from years ago.'

'So that leaves a number of potential suspects,' summarised Warren. 'Firstly the original poster, themselves a survivor of abuse, who claims to have known Olivia Mason, the girl who accused Father Daugherty. If they truly believed that Father Daugherty "got away with it", they could be evening the score on her behalf.

'Then there are the people that viewed and replied to the post. Make a note of any usernames from people that replied and scan their usage history, cross-reference the usernames of those replying to the posts and see if any names come up on both.

'Tony, look at raising a warrant to see if we can persuade the website owners to release their server logs so we can identify users that viewed the post but didn't contribute.'

'Don't hold your breath,' cautioned Pymm.

'It's also possible that our killer doesn't use the same username each time,' said Sutton. 'He could have multiple identities to disguise his tracks.'

'Let's hope not; if we can't actually link a username to a real-world person, it isn't much use to us,' said Warren.

'The abuse allegations about Father Daugherty were posted five years ago. What triggered them to start killing now?' asked Ruskin.

'Many abuse survivors keep silent for decades,' pointed out Pymm.

'I agree, but there must have been some sort of incitement,' said Sutton.

'Carry on digging, maybe that will give us a clue to their identity,' ordered Warren. 'Of course, there is one connection that is glaringly obvious; both of these priests took early retirement for mental health reasons and Bishop Fisher approved them moving into the home. We should speak to the diocese to see if any other residents moved to the home on the say-so of Bishop Fisher because of mental health concerns.'

'I think we've got more chance of persuading a Bulgarian internet service provider to comply with a search warrant, than getting the Catholic Church to cooperate with that sort of request,' replied Sutton.

'Well, we won't know if we don't ask,' said Warren trying mightily to keep his tone light-hearted. 'In the meantime, Rachel, get onto the social media team and ask them to replicate that search to see if any other priests are coming up. They might be in danger,' ordered Warren.

'Already ahead of you,' said Pymm. 'Their search is ongoing, but another name has already popped up. Back in April 2014, some-body calling themselves "Innocencelost1980", posted a request for information about a Father Wilfred Dodd, that the poster claims worked at the Venerable Thomas Tichborne School for Boys, a Catholic boarding school for boys in Essex in the Nineties. The school closed down a few years ago. One of the replies claimed that he had retired when the school closed.'

Warren flicked through his notebook.

'Are you sure about that name? There's no Father Dodd listed as being resident at the home, or working there as a volunteer for that matter.'

'That's what it said. This post was also less than a month before the one questioning what had happened to Father Nolan. The posters had different usernames, but they could still be the same person.'

Warren tapped his teeth thoughtfully; finally a concrete lead, rather than some enigmatic online persona that may not even truly exist.

'If the school only closed a few years ago, I wonder what the head teacher is doing these days?'

Monday 16th March

Chapter 61

It was Monday, the first day of a new week. Most of the team sitting in front of Warren had been in at least one day over the weekend. Warren had been right the day before; Rachel Pymm had not been impressed when he'd told her to take some of her rapidly accumulating annual leave. She was vital to the success of the team, but useless to them if she ended up sick. He'd have to convince Sutton to take some time off also, the man looked exhausted.

Despite this, Warren always felt there was something symbolic about a Monday morning briefing; a chance to regroup, recap and reset.

Helped by doughnuts, naturally.

Several paper bags had already been torn open and the table top was covered in a crust of sugar.

'Lucas Furber's death has finally been published in the *Reporter*.'

Warren held up the copy of the weekly paper he'd bought along with the doughnuts.

'Luckily for us it's a slow news week, so we've got the front page, along with a picture. I also spotted it on the billboard outside my local newsagent. I checked online and it's top of the page on their website. Let's hope it jogs a few memories. I'm told there are plenty of posters up in homeless shelters and outreach centres, so hopefully we'll hear something soon. Mags, what have you got for us?'

'I've got a list of the licence plates for all the cars in the vicinity of the locksmith's on the days that the keys to the chapel and the undercroft were copied. Twelve cars were seen on both days, none of which have any obvious links to the abbey or anyone associated with it. According to the DVLA, eight of them are registered to local residents, and were photographed at traffic lights on the main thoroughfare travelling one way in the morning rush hour and the opposite direction in the evening.'

'Commuters, by the sounds of it,' suggested Sutton.

'Three others look to have been doing the school run, and the last one is registered to a sandwich delivery firm, it shows up all over the place for about twelve hours each day.'

'Damn. So the killer didn't drive there?'

'Not in his own car, no. However, there are a handful of private hire cab firms that operate in the area, and several of them crop up.'

'Get their records. Maybe the killer used a cab so that his own car doesn't appear in the area.'

Warren looked thoughtfully at the suspect board. Only two names really stood out; Rodney Shaw and Lucas Furber. Warren wasn't sure about either of them. Sometimes Warren thought Shaw was their man; other times he seemed on the cusp of being ruled out. As for Lucas Furber, he had been alive at the time of both priest's murders and seemed to have a deep dislike, even hatred, aimed at clergy, but now he was dead himself, probably murdered. It could just be by chance, of course; Furber had lived on the edges of society, who knew what he had got himself into? However, Warren didn't like those sorts of coincidences. Which therefore meant that even if Furber had killed one or both of the priests, somebody else was also involved. On the other hand, perhaps Furber had nothing to do with the priest's deaths, but had known who the killer was. Was his death a way of silencing him?

Chapter 62

Dr Ethan Massey was a robust man in his late sixties.

'I spent the last six years of my career as head of St Joseph's, but my fondest memories will always be of Thomas Tichborne. I started there as a newly qualified teacher back in 1970, would you believe? Teacher of history, then head of department. A few years at St Philip as head of sixth form and deputy head, and then finally back to Thomas Tichborne in 1998 as headmaster; it's hard to imagine when I look back on it.'

Warren was sitting opposite Massey in the man's living room. The former teacher clearly had a fondness for antiques, the room was filled with aged wooden furniture, including a tall grand-father clock with a glass front, exposing a swinging pendulum. The time on the clock's face reminded him belatedly that he and Susan had an appointment at the clinic later that afternoon. Warren had already calculated how long he could stay before he absolutely had to leave. He berated himself for not delegating the interview; unless Massey was a little less long-winded, he'd have to leave before the interview finished or phone Susan to tell her he'd be late. Given that she'd reminded him not once, but twice the evening before, neither option was attractive.

'Of course, things were different back then. We were almost

exclusively a boarding school when I started, about 90 per cent of the boys lived on site, at least during the week. But times change and throughout the Eighties our intake grew rapidly, with the increase almost exclusively day pupils. At our peak, the day pupils outnumbered the boarders about two-to-one.'

'Was that why the school eventually closed?' asked Warren, before taking a sip of his tea.

It hadn't been hard to track down Dr Massey. The Venerable Thomas Tichborne School for Boys may have been closed for almost nine years, but it had an active online alumni association, with many former pupils and even teachers taking part in everything from annual old boys rugby games to monthly meals and even holidays. Dr Massey was, by all accounts, still highly regarded, and largely remembered with affection. When Warren had contacted him via the email address given on the site, the man had been intrigued and invited him over to his house in Hitchen.

'In part,' Massey sighed. 'Boarding schools aren't nearly as popular as they once were, and it's an expensive investment. Thomas Tichborne was an excellent school, but it was no Eton or Harrow. We were better known for producing candidates for the priesthood than Downing Street. Our boarding school pupils brought in more funding per pupil than our day boarders, which was a perfectly serviceable business plan back when we started two hundred odd years ago, but we really should have started changing the model decades earlier than we did. By the time I was appointed as head, in part to help address the issue, the rot had set in.

'Unfortunately, the empty boarding houses were in the centre of the school grounds, so selling them off to real estate developers wasn't practical, and there's only so much money you can make flogging off the playing fields.'

He drained his tea, before refilling both men's cups, unbidden, from a large, china teapot.

'The twentieth of July 2006. The day that 214 years of outstanding education came to an end. You know, the school opened within twelve months of the Roman Catholic Relief Act of 1791 that effectively decriminalised Catholicism? And it ended on my watch,' he cleared his throat.

'What happened to the pupils?' asked Warren.

'Fortunately, we knew almost a year in advance that the school was doomed. Our day pupils were absorbed by local schools in the area, and were still able to maintain friendship groups. Unfortunately, our boarders were scattered far and wide, sometimes returning to where their parents lived, other times to other boarding schools here and even abroad. Thank goodness for the internet, at the last count there were over twelve hundred Tommy Tichers on the alumni Facebook page.'

'And what about the staff?'

'A similar story. Some filled local vacancies, others, especially younger teachers who lived on site and had few roots in the area, moved away. A couple more retired or decided to pursue other careers.' He paused. 'It really was the end of a community. Some of our housemasters had lived there for twenty years. They lost their family home, as well as their job. It was very sad.'

'And what about Father Wilfred Dodd?'

Massey eyed Warren over the rim of his tea cup.

'What is this about, DCI Jones? As much as I enjoy reminiscing about my days at Thomas Tichborne, I can't believe that's why you've come to see me.'

'Just some routine enquiries.'

'Enquiries into those sickening murders up at St Cecil's retirement home? I looked you up on the internet, DCI Jones, and saw the press conference you gave.'

'I can't go into details,' said Warren.

'Surely Father Dodd can't be a suspect?'

Warren ignored the question.

'What happened to Father Dodd?' he repeated.

'He retired. To St Cecil's I believe. But then I'm sure you already knew that.'

311

'From my understanding, Father Dodd was below the usual retirement age for priests. Do you know why he retired so early?'

Dr Massey looked at Warren for a long moment, before finally sighing.

'Somehow, I doubt I am doing any more than confirming your suspicions. Yes, Father Dodd was rather young to have retired, and to the best of my knowledge, he was in excellent health. In fact, he was hoping to take up a new position as school chaplain at St Philip. Father Anderton, their previous chaplain had died suddenly the previous year and they had been relying on local priests to fill the vacancy. It seemed as though it was all going to work out perfectly.'

'So why didn't it?'

'It's a question that I've often wondered about. As far as I knew, he was due to take up the position in the new school year, but then I heard that it wasn't happening and that instead, he was taking early retirement.'

'On what grounds?'

'I don't suppose it really matters now. Mental health, although I was unaware of any issues. Mind you, you never can tell, can you?'

Chapter 63

'Another priest taking early retirement for mental health issues, then moving into Bishop Fisher's retirement home. Nothing suspicious about that at all.' Tony Sutton took a bite of his pastry, taking care to brush the resulting crumbs off his trousers and onto the floor of Warren's office.

Warren bit his tongue.

He'd only just made the appointment at the clinic, and now, two hours later, he was sitting back in his office, knowing he should be at home with his wife, but also knowing that when she said she needed her own space, she meant it.

Over the past few years, Tony Sutton had become one of Warren's closest friends. It was an indication of just how all-consuming his job had become that his friend was also someone he spent most of his working day with.

Should he tell Tony what he and Susan had been told?

Immediately he recoiled from the thought, recognising his own foolishness even as he did so; thousands of couples needed help conceiving, and for many of those couples the root cause of their problems was the man's sperm. It was certainly nothing to be ashamed of, no matter what his mother-in-law may imply.

Yet to admit such a personal thing to Sutton... Warren

couldn't bring himself to do it. Would he feel the same if the outcome of this afternoon's appointment had been different? If the consultant delivering the results of Susan's pregnancy test had told them the implantation had been successful, and that in a little under nine months' time, God willing, they would finally become parents? When it finally became time to show his colleagues and friends the first black and white images of their unborn child, would he have nonchalantly mentioned that they had needed a bit of help to achieve this miracle, or would he have smiled politely at the jokes about there 'still being life in the old dog yet'?

He really didn't know.

'I tell you, there's something dodgy going on in that place.'

Warren dragged his attention back to what Sutton was saying.

'I tend to agree,' he replied. 'Unfortunately, according to Dr Massey, he recalls no complaints against Father Dodd from when he worked at the school.'

Sutton snorted. 'What about rumours, then?'

'That's where he got a little cagey. He said that Father Dodd was rather old school and that his strict approach to discipline wasn't always appreciated by those in his care.'

'It's one thing to be a bit liberal with the detention slips, or even a bit enthusiastic with the cane or slipper before they were banned, but another thing entirely to be interfering with pupils,' said Sutton.

'I agree, but when I pushed him, Dr Massey became very defensive and claimed to be insulted at the implication that he'd covered something up.'

'How about an interview under caution?'

'On what grounds?'

Sutton placed his tea plate on the edge of Warren's desk.

'I suppose we could think of something if we really wanted to,' he said, but there was no conviction in his voice.

'I'm not against the idea, but everything is so wishy washy

314

at the moment. I'm already worried that our interest might tip off the killer.'

'Could Dr Massey be the killer?' asked Sutton.

'On what grounds?'

'Maybe he wanted to even a few scores? Perhaps fix a few wrongs?'

Warren thought about it for a moment.

'If he did, then he concealed it pretty well. There's nothing about any historic suspicious deaths at the retirement home on the PNC or, for that matter any suicides.'

'Father Dodd is also not on the list of current residents.'

'Meaning he's either died or moved on.'

'Or was never recorded as having lived there in the first place.'

Tuesday 17th March

Chapter 64

'Thank you for agreeing to visit me, Your Grace, it was kind of you to come here.' Warren was again facing the elderly bishop. This time however, he was on his own territory.

Warren had been tempted to take the morning off for personal reasons, but Susan would have none of it. The two of them had lain awake all night, although they had both pretended otherwise. When the alarm had sounded at its usual time, Susan had headed straight for the shower and was fully dressed in her school clothes and applying her make-up by the time Warren had emerged from the bathroom himself.

Her outward acceptance of the previous day's disappointing news about the failed implantation was surely an act, but he didn't know how to broach the subject without upsetting her. As he'd lain awake, he'd found himself racked by doubts. Maybe Bernice was right after all? The Catholic Church was opposed to IVF and he was now investigating the church, questioning the honesty of its most prominent adherents. Add to that his blasphemous thoughts at mass on Sunday, and you had to ask yourself if perhaps somebody upstairs was upset?

He recoiled from the thought in disgust at as soon as it formed, recognising it as the product of an over-stressed, overworked imagination. He'd discuss it with his counsellor when he finally had time to book an appointment.

'Of course, Inspector,' replied Bishop Fisher. 'You only have to ask. We are all keen to track down this disturbed killer and bring him to justice before he harms anyone else.'

'Thank you. You don't mind if I record this, do you? This is a voluntary statement and you are not under arrest. You are free to stop the interview at any time or ask for legal representation.'

Bishop Fisher gave a little shrug. 'Of course.'

'First, can you tell me what you know about a Father Wilfred Dodd? He wasn't on the list that you gave me of current residents and staff. Has he left?'

Fisher gave a sigh.

'In a manner of speaking, I suppose he did. He passed away a few years ago.'

'I see.'

'I can't imagine any link, however – he died of natural causes. A short battle with leukaemia after spending a few years with us.'

That confirmed what Warren and the team had managed to find themselves through public records.

'Why did he retire?'

'The school at which he was a chaplain closed down. Father Dodd took that as a sign from God that he had reached the natural end of his active ministry.'

'Again, he seems a little young, given the shortage of priests that the church is facing at the moment. He was a resident at St Cecil's for six years, yet you said he died of a short illness, which implies that he was healthy when he first entered the home.'

For the first time, Fisher paused.

'Would it be possible for me to get a glass of water, DCI Jones?'

'No problem.' Warren sprang to his feet, and poked his head around the door, relaying the request.

'The custody sergeant will bring one immediately.'

The total length of the interruption had been less than a

minute. Enough time for the clergyman to compose his thoughts, but hopefully not long enough for him to make up something too elaborate.

'According to staff and former pupils, Father Dodd had something of a reputation,' started Warren again.

It was a gamble that the team had discussed at some length; after all, they only had the vaguest of insinuations, from an anonymous source on the internet. However, Warren wanted to see Fisher's reaction and hear what he had to say.

'I'm not sure what you are implying, DCI Jones.'

'There were rumours of inappropriate conduct towards some of the pupils by Father Dodd.'

'I am not aware of any formal complaints made about Father Dodd. He was highly respected by his colleagues.'

'As I said, there were rumours. As bishop of that diocese at the time, are you saying that you were unaware of what was being said about him?'

Fisher sighed, removing his glasses and rubbing them on a silk handkerchief.

'There are always rumours. Any man that opts to work with children will have experienced them. School teachers, scoutmasters, swimming instructors, nobody is above suspicion.'

Was that a confirmation?

'And you believe that there was nothing to these rumours?'

At that moment there came a soft knock on the door.

'That'll be your water.' Warren stepped over to the door and took the plastic cup, passing it to the aged priest.

Fisher took a long swig.

'Where were we?' asked Warren, making a show of looking at his notepad. 'Oh yes. Tell me, why did you block Father Dodd from taking up a position as school chaplain at St Philip? By all accounts they were in desperate need of one and Father Dodd was very keen to take on the role.'

Bishop Fisher's reaction wasn't as dramatic as snorting water out of his nose, nevertheless Warren admonished himself; a second interviewee dying on him would be unfortunate to say the least.

'I beg your pardon, DCI Jones?'

'According to witnesses, Father Dodd was fit and healthy and looking forward to the challenge of working with a school who had been without a full-time chaplain for over a year. It seems strange that not only would you block him from taking up that role, but that you would insist on him taking early retirement, especially given the shortage of priests in the diocese at the time.'

Fisher shifted in his chair, the conflict on his face apparent. He took another sip of water. Warren said nothing.

'Father Dodd had some mental health issues that I felt would make it inappropriate for him to continue in his current role, and that he would be better served by taking retirement.'

'Another early retirement through mental health issues? Tell me, Your Grace, were any of these priests formally diagnosed?'

'I do not think it would be appropriate to discuss the medical histories of these people without consent.'

'Which may be tricky to arrange, given that they are dead. Don't worry, I'm sure that I can get a court order, if necessary.'

Fisher said nothing, his face impassive.

'Tell me, Your Grace, in a community so small, would one really expect such a high proportion of priests to have retired early on the grounds of mental health?'

The bishop's shoulders slumped slightly, as he relaxed.

'You are making the erroneous assumption that such a community is randomly selected, in which case your argument might be true. However, our community is not, by definition, a random selection.' Fisher leant forward in his chair slightly, his voice becoming firmer, and Warren was reminded again that the man in front of him had a formidable intelligence; you didn't gain a doctorate in theology and philosophy, and rise to such a prominent position, if you were an intellectual slouch.

'As I am sure you are aware, the normal retirement age for a

Catholic priest is 75 or older. Those that are blessed with good health may continue to serve the church and their community in some capacity for many years more. Those that do retire are often supported within the community, or in ordinary retirement homes. Many have extended family that can help care for them, or even a pension from a previous occupation.

'St Cecil's retirement home is specifically for those who do not have the luxury of that support, or whose needs are different. Sadly, the clergy are no more immune to the frailties of the mind, the body or the spirit than anyone else. We care for, and provide, a sense of community, for those that need us.'

'So, you are saying, that by its very nature, St Cecil's would expect a greater proportion of its residents to have retired early, perhaps through mental health issues?'

'Yes.'

'Tell me Your Grace, would you regard sexual attraction towards children as a mental health issue?'

The bishop gave a visible start.

'I… I don't know what you are implying, DCI Jones…'

'Father Gerry Daugherty was accused of the abuse of a child in his care, whilst he was chaplain at St Thomas Aquinas school. I believe that he then had a breakdown and you authorised his early retirement?'

Fisher again relaxed.

'That was an extremely unfortunate incident. If you look a little deeper into the case, you will see that all concerned are satisfied that the allegations made by that poor, disturbed girl, were false and that she later retracted the accusations.'

'That is not how the local community saw it.'

Fisher's lip twisted slightly. 'Unfortunately, the sensitive nature of the case means that Father Daugherty was unable to publicly clear his name.'

'And that was what caused Father Daugherty to undergo his breakdown?'

'In a nutshell, yes. Far be it for me to criticise those involved, they were only doing their jobs with the child's best interest at heart, but the whole situation placed Father Daugherty under a tremendous amount of pressure. I decided that it was in Father Daugherty's best interests that he take early retirement, and come to stay with us at St Cecil's.'

'Presumably, it also removed him from the community and placed him out of harm's way?'

'Yes, of course.'

'Were you keeping Father Nolan out of harm's way when you invited him to stay?'

'I'm not sure what you mean...'

'How much did you know about Father Nolan's transgressions? Were you contacted by the school? Did a parent or child tell you? We have no record of a formal complaint, and the school denies any knowledge of any incidents.'

'There were no allegations made against Father Nolan that I am aware of,' said Fisher firmly.

'So you are saying that Father Nolan did not engage in any inappropriate behaviour with children in his care.'

'As I said, there were no allegations made about his behaviour.'

Warren looked the bishop squarely in the eyes.

'That wasn't what I asked, Your Grace.'

Fisher said nothing.

The idea, when it came, formed so quickly that Warren barely had time to think it through before the question came tumbling out of his mouth.

'There weren't any allegations, were there? Father Nolan came to you himself.' Warren paused as the ideas crystallised further, the truth of his thoughts reflected in Bishop Fisher's eyes.

'He confessed his sins to you, didn't he?'

Chapter 65

'I'm afraid that what is said in the confessional must remain confidential, DCI Jones,' Bishop Fisher's voice was firm.

'That's exactly what happened isn't it?' continued Warren. 'Father Nolan confessed his sins to you, knowing that you could not say anything to the police and begged you for forgiveness?'

Fisher looked over at the PACE tape recorder.

'I would like to end the recording of this interview.'

Warren looked at the man carefully. Did this mean that the interview was over, or that Fisher wished to make an admission that he'd rather wasn't on tape? If necessary, Warren could still take notes, and these would still be admissible as sworn evidence, although Fisher hadn't been arrested and wasn't under caution.

Warren reached over and pressed stop.

'What did he tell you, Bishop Fisher?'

'As I have said, the seal of confession is absolute.'

'That retirement home – it has no links to the local schools, and the residents are largely separated from the community, except for the celebration of Mass and a bit of volunteering in the abbey grounds. You set it up to protect society from these men, didn't you?'

Fisher remained silent.

323

'That's why you blocked Father Dodd from taking up a new position as a school chaplain and insisted that he take early retirement, isn't it? You knew his past, he told you all about it in confession. Then what? Absolution? What was his penance, ten Hail Marys and a demand that he lock himself away in your special home?'

Fisher said nothing.

'You're a retired bishop. You don't need to be slumming it in a retirement home in the grounds of a ruined abbey. Why are you there, Your Grace? As a prison guard or an inmate? What sins have you committed, Bishop Fisher?'

'I think this interview is over.' The bishop's tone was icy.

'Not so fast. I need to know, do we have a home full of sexual predators on our doorstep?'

The recorder was turned off and Warren no longer cared what the bishop thought of him. The time for good manners had passed.

'There are over twenty residents in that home. Are they all paedophiles? Do the staff know? What about visitors?'

'Of course not,' Fisher snapped. 'That house is filled with good, holy men, who have dedicated their lives to serving God and the community and are now living out the remainder of their lives in peace and quiet.'

'How many more of those "good and holy me" have confessed to you that they are a danger to children?'

'I've told you that the seal of confessional is absolute. I cannot reveal what was said to me, without the penitent's express permission. That is the agreement that is entered into between the penitent, his confessor and God.'

'Three of the penitents are dead.'

'That does not matter; as far as the Catholic Church is concerned, life continues after death.'

'You realise that it is an offence to conceal a crime, such as this?'

'I will be judged by a higher authority than the courts, DCI Jones.'

'Maybe so, but whilst you are still in this earthly realm, you are subject to the court's authority. You have a moral and legal obligation to reveal what you know to help this investigation, uncover historic offences and protect the public.'

'I have an obligation to the oath that I swore when I accepted my ministry. Only the Holy Father himself can release me from this obligation.'

'If necessary, I will arrest you.'

'Then it looks as though I am going to prison.'

Bishop Fisher glared across the table at Warren, who matched the intensity of his stare with his own.

How on earth had it come to this? Standing head to head in an interview room with a bishop, who he had just threatened to arrest for perverting the course of justice? Had anyone ever done such a thing? Had using the seal of the confessional as a defence actually been tried in the courts? Warren couldn't remember.

Regardless, such a call was well above his paygrade. To say the shit would hit the fan if Warren followed through with his threat, would be an understatement of epic proportions; the Chief Constable would have a stroke.

Unbidden, an image of his mother-in-law Bernice sprung to mind. The Chief Constable had the power to make Warren's professional life an absolute misery if he misjudged this call. Bernice, as devout a Catholic as Warren had ever met, would make every other aspect of his life a living hell.

When Warren spoke, his tone was deliberately more concilia-tory.

'Your Grace. It is clear to us that a killer is out there, hunting down priests who have been accused of child abuse. Regardless of what these men were alleged to have done, they were tortured and brutally killed. We do not have the resources to protect everyone in your community indefinitely, we need to know who the next victims might be. That way, we can keep them safe and hopefully bring this person to justice.

'I am begging you, please at least give an indication of who the killer's next victim might be.'

When Fisher spoke again, his voice was also softer.

'I'm sorry, DCI Jones. When a person takes the sacrament of confession, they know that the seal is absolute.' He paused. 'There can be no exceptions. Perhaps the consequences of their actions are catching up with them.'

Chapter 66

'Arrogant bastard,' said Sutton after Warren filled in the team about his interview with Bishop Fisher.

Sutton had already made his thoughts on Fisher hiding behind the seal of the confessional quite clear, and Warren had no intention of going over that ground again.

'I have put in a request to the diocese to release details of which residents took early retirement and/or had their place at the home granted at the request of Bishop Fisher. If he has been using the home as a way of sequestering problem priests somewhere safe, this may give us an idea of who else could be a target.'

'And are they cooperating?' Sutton's tone was more belligerent than usual.

'So far. However, I have prepared warrants as well, I'm sick and tired of getting the run around.

Sutton grunted, apparently satisfied for the time being. Warren resolved to have a talk with him about his attitude.

'Where do we stand legally in forcing Bishop Fisher to give evidence regarding what he was told in confession?' asked Hutchinson

'I spoke to the CPS and strictly speaking there is no legal recognition for priest-penitent privilege in English civil law,' said

Warren, 'but it's never been fully tested in court. It's a moot point regardless, Bishop Fisher has made it absolutely clear that he isn't going to break that seal, and we won't get any support from the church so what's the point? It'll just create a shit storm.'

The look on Sutton's face suggested that he wasn't entirely adverse to that outcome, but he wisely kept his mouth shut.

'So, given what we now believe, who are our chief suspects?' asked Warren. The interview with Bishop Fisher had placed a whole new complexion on matters and he wanted to see what new ideas his team thought of. He resolved to stay mostly quiet for the time being and let his officers thrash it out amongst themselves.

'I still can't make my mind up about Rodney Shaw,' admitted Sutton. 'He has no alibi for either night, he's lied about his whereabouts, and he just keeps on cropping up.'

'Much of that evidence is circumstantial though,' Richardson pointed out. 'He's the groundsman, we'd expect his foot and fingerprints to be all over the place.'

'And what about motive? If he didn't know about Nolan's sexual proclivities, killing him because of a bit of pilfering and an embarrassing gambling problem seems a bit extreme,' said Hutchinson.

'We've all known people kill for less,' said Sutton.

'What about Father Daugherty? Why kill him?' asked Ruskin.

'He might have seen something he shouldn't. Father Nolan was taken down to the chapel around about the time that Father Daugherty usually takes his evening stroll,' said Sutton.

'He didn't mention anything when he was questioned,' Hutchinson reminded him.

'He might not have realised the importance at the time,' countered Sutton.

'Just to play Devil's Advocate,' said Richardson, 'if Shaw isn't the killer, then the real killer may well have known that he keeps his spare work boots and jacket hanging up in the shed.'

The team fell silent; from the mixture of facial expressions around the table, Warren could see that the team were torn, but nobody had dismissed Shaw completely.

'How does this morning's interview with Bishop Fisher change things?' prompted Warren.

'It still doesn't let Rodney Shaw off the hook,' said Sutton. 'What if he found out about both priests' past and decided to enact some revenge?'

'It's not impossible that he was abused himself when he was younger,' suggested Hutchinson, 'I don't want to generalise, but a lot of people turn to drugs to cope with shitty childhoods. Could that be why Shaw was a heroin addict?'

'That's a good point,' said Sutton, 'but if he was abused by priests when he was a kid, why would he seek out work with the church, and why wait twenty-odd years to start killing?'

Warren was pleased to see that Sutton was willing to raise objections to his own theory.

'Who says he was abused by priests?' replied Hutchinson. 'It could have been someone completely different. But imagine the sense of betrayal and anger if he found out that people he worked with every day were abusers?'

'But how would he find out?' asked Ruskin.

'Could he have been on Survivorsonline?' asked Richardson.

'We'll know when they finish looking at his computer, although if he was clever enough, he might have used a different machine,' said Warren.

'Would he have known about the historic murders?' asked Ruskin.

'It's entirely possible that he attended that talk given by Vernon Coombs,' said Pymm. 'The title of it certainly sounded interesting enough, especially if you've worked in the place for twenty years.'

'Good point. So we leave Shaw on the suspect board. Who else should be on there?' asked Warren.

'Bishop Fisher,' said Sutton immediately.

'Go on,' said Warren, his voice neutral. He wasn't in the mood

for another rant by Sutton about the bishop's refusal to cooperate fully.

'I think we can probably assume that Bishop Fisher knew about
Father Nolan and Father Daugherty's past. Perhaps he has taken
it upon himself to seek justice for their victims?'

'He's a bit old, don't you think?' said Ruskin.

'He could have been working with somebody else. He could
even be trying to hinder our investigation,' said Sutton.

'But why now? And what is the link to Survivorsonline? Surely
he doesn't need to look up the details if he already heard them
from confession?' said Richardson.

'The link to Survivorsonline could just be a coincidence,'
pointed out Hutchinson.

'As to why now, there could be any number of reasons,'
suggested Sutton. 'It could just be old age. Maybe he's worried
that if he doesn't sort things out now, he never will?'

'It also implies that he didn't believe Father Daugherty was
innocent of those accusations,' said Pymm. 'Or perhaps Father
Daugherty admitted to other offences during confession?'

'But why kill them? Why not just report them to the police?'
said Ruskin.

'"The seal of the confessional is absolute",' parroted Sutton.

'I doubt it's more absolute than "thou shalt not kill",' interjected Warren.

'If he did have help,' said Richardson, 'who could it have been?'

'Again, Shaw is the obvious choice,' said Sutton.

'Or Deacon Baines,' said Hutchinson. 'Most of what we've said
about Shaw could also apply to Baines. He has full access to the
grounds, he has known Bishop Fisher since before the retirement
home even existed and he has no satisfactory alibi for the night
of either killing.'

'He'd also be in the perfect position to frame Rodney Shaw
over the missing money,' pointed out Richardson.

'What about Lucas Furber?' asked Ruskin. 'The homeless

guy arrested for trying to break-in to the retirement home. He certainly had a grudge against religion, from what we've found out.'

'His time of death appears to have been sometime after Father Daugherty was killed. He could have done it,' pointed out Richardson.

'That raises a fair few questions,' said Sutton. 'Not least, how did he know about the historic murders? I can't imagine that he's a paid-up member of the Friends of Middlesbury Abbey or a local history aficionado.'

'That's a bit of an assumption, don't you think?' said Pymm. Uncharacteristically, it was the first contribution she'd made to the meeting, the single day off that she'd taken having done little to refresh her.

'Even addicts have interests and hobbies,' she continued. 'For all we know Lucas Furber could have been obsessed with history since he was a school kid.'

Sutton raised his hands. 'That's a fair comment, I take it back.'

'But that doesn't tell us how he got hold of the keys to the chapel and the undercroft, or even the padlock to the gate by the mill house bridge,' said Hutchinson.

'Or gained access to St Cecil's, for that matter,' said Sutton. 'The forensics suggests that Father Nolan was probably taken from the house after evening meal, whilst the killer had to somehow place the "Forgive me Father" note on Father Daugherty's dressing table. In both cases he'd have needed to enter the home, unseen. That's pretty risky.'

'So if Furber was the killer, it suggests that he wasn't acting alone,' said Warren, 'so who was he working with?'

'Any of the above,' said Sutton after a moment's thought.

'It also raises the question as to whether he was killed, committed suicide or accidentally overdosed on a batch of dodgy heroin,' pointed out Ruskin.

'Again, I'm thinking Rodney Shaw,' said Sutton, 'but if he's been clean for thirty years, would he know anything more about the current drug scene than anybody else?'

'He's been doing outreach work with troubled young people, could they have put him in contact with dealers?' said Ruskin.

'If we are assuming Shaw has specialist knowledge about drugs, then wouldn't we also expect him to know that medical grade morphine is unlikely to increase the potency of street heroin?' asked Pymm.

'Again, if he has been clean for thirty years, he might not have been up to date on the latest trends,' pointed out Sutton.

'Whilst we're on the topic, have there been any reports of medical grade morphine being stolen recently?' asked Warren.

Pymm flicked over a page in her notepad.

'There were at least eight thefts across England and Wales in the previous twelve months, so we know that the stuff is out there, but none were reported within Hertfordshire.'

'I'm sure the stuff gets moved around the country,' said Warren. 'It could have come from anywhere, which doesn't really help us.'

The team agreed.

'So with that in mind,' he continued, 'who else should we keep on the suspects board?'

'What about Dr Massey, the head teacher at Thomas Tichborne?' asked Sutton. 'Did you get any feeling that he knew what Father Dodd had been up to when he was working at the school?'

Warren pinched his lip, 'Hard to tell. He denied any knowledge and seemed surprised, of course, but he admitted to having Googled me before I arrived, so he had time to get his story straight.'

'If it is him, then there are a whole load of questions regarding whereabouts, motive and opportunity,' said Sutton. 'Not least why he waited until now, if he worked alone, and why he decided to kill Fathers Nolan and Daugherty when nature had already done the job for him with Father Dodd.'

'OK. Arrange a team to dig into his background. See if he

overlaps at all with any of our victims, or suspects for that matter. Get support from Welwyn. We'll make a decision either way based on what we find out,' ordered Warren.

'Have we definitely eliminated Olivia Mason, the girl who falsely accused Father Daugherty?' asked Richardson.

'She certainly won't have been physically involved,' said Hutchinson. 'She's been in Australia for the past few years.'

'And we're confident that it was a false allegation?'

Again, Hutchinson replied, 'Sergeant Ingram was pretty certain when he spoke to DCI Jones, and I spoke to the school's safe-guarding lead who said that she retracted everything and was upset at all of the trouble she'd caused.'

'And for what it's worth, Bishop Fisher seemed confident it was a false allegation,' chipped in Warren.

'Yeah, but not everyone was convinced he was innocent,' said Richardson. 'The allegations on Survivorsonline were from someone claiming to be a friend of hers. Not to mention the other users on the forum.'

'Where are we in terms of a warrant for the server logs?' asked Warren.

Pymm shrugged. 'The warrant has been drafted by the Social Media Intelligence Unit, but they've told us not to get our hopes up.'

Sutton had been pulling at his lip thoughtfully.

'I've had another thought about Bishop Fisher and his refusal to cooperate.'

'Go on,' said Warren, a slight edge in his voice. He didn't want to shoot down Sutton in front of the rest of the team, but he wasn't prepared to tolerate another debate about the rights and wrongs of priest-penitent confidentiality.

'I can't be the only person who has seen the parallels between Bishop Fisher and the abbot in charge of the abbey back at the time of the medieval murders?'

A few shrugs around the table suggested that few had given it much thought.

'Abbot Godwine was his name,' supplied Pymm.

'Well, what happened to him?' continued Sutton. 'Was he killed? Was he a suspicious death, or was he implicated in the abuse? There certainly seems to be a suggestion that he helped cover it up or at least dismissed the allegations.'

'A good question,' said Warren. He turned to Pymm, 'Rachel, carry on looking for any references to the fate of Abbot Godwine. He could be our next target.'

Pymm shook her head. 'We haven't found much reference yet to Abbot Godwine in the monks' diaries, but we're still less than halfway through the boxes you gave us; it's really slow going. However, I do know that he wasn't killed in the 1520s when these events took place. Amongst Vernon Coombs' notes were some photocopies from a textbook about the dissolution of the monasteries. Abbot Godwine is mentioned several times as having tried to negotiate with Thomas Cromwell and his deputies over the terms of the abbey's surrender, but he eventually gave up in 1539 and left, probably to return to Spain where the order originated.' Pymm gave a grim smile. 'It was probably just as well, given what happened to the abbots of Colchester, Reading and Glastonbury. Hanged, drawn and quartered for treason apparently.'

'So Godwine wasn't killed directly by Simon Scrope then,' summarised Warren. 'Of course, it doesn't mean our killer won't decide to murder Bishop Fisher anyway, so we can't rule out his being a target. In the meantime, keep on looking for clues to any potential further victims, Rachel. I have a feeling that the key to this case may lie somewhere in that pile of paper.'

Chapter 67

Warren left work as early as possible. The previous day had been bruising for both him and Susan and he still felt guilty for not taking the rest of the day off. Neither of them had really spoken when he'd arrived home that night, and he knew that whether Susan wanted to or not, they needed to talk about their disappointment before they could move on.

Their next implantation attempt was some weeks away, and so Warren decided a bottle of decent red from the Marks and Spencer service station, supplemented with a box of Susan's favourite chocolates, might help matters along. Flowers also seemed like a good idea, but as always, staring at the tub of bouquets, he had no idea what to get.

The first bunch was too bright and cheerful, almost celebratory. The one next to it looked suspiciously like something one bought if the date of your anniversary had slipped your mind. The bunch of red roses certainly communicated how much he loved his wife, but seemed a bit too much like date night and Warren was sure he'd heard somewhere that chrysanthemums were associated with funerals – which might match their mood, but would hardly help matters.

He thought about asking the woman behind the till, but

couldn't bring himself to say what was on his mind: that he needed a bunch of flowers to tell his wife that no matter what, he would always love her and even though they felt as if they had suffered a bereavement, they would lick their wounds and move on, and that this one crushing defeat wouldn't break them.

Eventually, he settled on some daffodils. Keep it simple – in the end it's the thought that counts, he decided.

Arriving home, he saw that Susan's car was in the driveway. The living room light was on and the curtains were still open. He stood on the doorstep, composing his features, readying himself for whatever awaited him. The previous day, Susan had been stoic. Almost matter-of-fact, citing probabilities of first-time success, talking about how transplanting frozen embryos was almost as successful as implanting freshly fertilised eggs and how they'd known they were in it for the long-haul. She'd flatly refused to take the day off.

'We've been trying for a baby for years. This is simply another failed pregnancy test, just like all the others. I can't take a day off every month.'

Warren hadn't believed her, but he knew that pushing the matter at that time wouldn't help, and that Susan would process her emotions at her own pace. He just worried that the building emotions could only be kept in check for so long and that he wouldn't be there when the dam finally burst.

Opening the door, he stepped across the threshold.

One look at Susan's face told him everything he needed to know; the dam had burst.

* * *

Ten o'clock and the dam, if not sealed, was at least only leaking now. Susan lay with her head on Warren's chest. The TV was off, quiet music played in the background. In front of them the remains of a pizza delivery were going cold and the box of

336

chocolates was nearly empty. The bottle of wine sat unopened in the kitchen, its chemical catalyst having proven unnecessary.

Susan had finally stopped apologising for being so emotional and accepted Warren's assurances that what she – what they – were feeling was normal. Then the apologies had started about her not taking care of herself properly; about rushing back to work too soon. Again, Warren had worked hard to soothe them away. It didn't escape his notice that he was saying the exact same things that Susan had said to him every time his latest clinic results had come back.

By the time they'd finished their pizza, the two of them were far more relaxed; the disappointment and sadness weren't gone – and Warren suspected that the feelings would make themselves felt again at the least expected times – but the two had resolved to continue with their battle.

'Tell me about your day,' said Susan.

'Nothing much to tell, really,' lied Warren.

'Now who's keeping things bottled up inside?' admonished Susan.

Warren sighed. She was right. The case was starting to gnaw away at him.

Warren thought back to Sunday's church visit and the conflict he still felt. Despite his growing ambivalence towards his faith, he hadn't been prepared for the crushing disappointment he'd felt as Bishop Fisher had sat opposite him and refused to help him right previous wrongs and even prevent future killings. And what if Bishop Fisher was involved in the murders? If he had somehow decided that the sanctity of the confessional was more important than the commandment not to kill? How could the church as a whole elevate the sacrament of confession to a point where keeping silent about what was said was more important than preventing harm to the most vulnerable in society?

That some members of the church were capable of such wickedness was hardly a revelation; the church had been beset by scandals for decades – centuries even, if Vernon Coombs' research was to be believed – but it still hurt, Warren realised.

As a child he had been taught that a priest's love was endless and that they could be trusted implicitly. He had fond memories of Father McGavin, the stoop-shouldered man who'd seemed impossibly old to a 7-year-old Warren, as he'd knelt in front of him confessing his sins, before later receiving his first Holy Communion from him. Father McGavin had been a natural with children. Able to still the most unruly child with a steely glare from the pulpit, in person he was warm and humorous. Who knew that a priest could tell jokes?

Granddad Jack still had the picture of Warren posing in his white shirt and red tie, next to Father McGavin and Archbishop Eddington, as he was confirmed in his final year of primary school. His sombre expression reflected the weight of expectation on his 11-year-old shoulders as he became a full member of the Catholic Church.

Things had moved on – Warren had moved on – but still he felt betrayed; the powerful feelings he had experienced in church had only intensified since his interview with Fisher.

Susan listened quietly as Warren stumbled through his explanation, articulating feelings that he hadn't even been aware that he had before now.

'You know these men only represent a tiny, perverted minority, don't you?' she said finally.

'Yeah, I know. I'd even be willing to accept that they are less prevalent than in society as a whole. What really upsets me is that the church's very structure seems set up to protect these men.' He snorted. 'And now I sound like Tony.'

Susan craned her neck to look at him more closely.

'What's happened with Tony?'

Warren sighed again and told her of Sutton's belligerent attitude towards Bishop Fisher and, it would seem, the church itself. Sutton clearly shared many of the feelings that Warren did

338

regarding confession, but there was more to it. He almost felt as though his friend was judging him for his beliefs, even though Sutton himself was a regular attendee at his local Anglican church.

'You need to speak to him,' said Susan. 'You have to clear the air. You've said yourself that he is expressing views that could be regarded as unprofessional if the wrong person overheard them.'

'I know, I just need to figure out how best to go about it,' said Warren.

'He's your friend. Do it privately. God knows he isn't afraid to speak his mind to you, when he wants to. Perhaps you need to do the same, you can't let this issue damage your friendship.'

Warren forced a smile and kissed his wife on the forehead.

'You're right as usual. I'll try and grab lunch with him, so we can have it out away from the office.'

'Were you ever in any doubt? Now do as you're told.'

Warren kissed her again, this time full on the lips. The clock on the mantelpiece showed just past 11 p.m. A lie-in mid-week was impossible, but he resolved not to get up and leave before Susan awoke the next morning.

Warren's phone had slipped down the side of the sofa, as they'd lain there talking; its vibration was muffled and barely audible.

Warren felt a stab of frustration at the interruption, followed by a nagging alarm. How many calls had he missed?

The number on the screen was an unknown mobile number, and it had tried to call twice before; it was clearly important, whatever it was. He stabbed the answer button, mouthing an apology to Susan.

A minute later he hung up.

'That was Jane. Granddad Jack's in hospital.'

Wednesday 18th March

Chapter 68

'There are three cab firms in Copperston,' said Pymm. 'The local council has been having a real crackdown on rogue operators, so they claim that none of their drivers are picking up passengers who hail them on the street.'

Tony Sutton snorted his disbelief at the taxi firm's assertion. He was due to take the morning briefing in Warren's absence and wanted to pass on her findings to the rest of the team.

'Well, that's what they claim,' continued Pymm. 'Anyway, it means that they do have records, and guess what?'

'The suspense is killing me.'

'Two different cab firms logged a pick-up from Stonehill Mews on the edge of the town and a drop off on Woodvale Road, about two hundred metres from the locksmith. Alpha Cabs did it on Friday the sixteenth of January and Premier Cars did it on Thursday the twenty-second. On both days, there were then pickups from Old Kiln Street – which is around the corner from Woodvale Road about half an hour after the original journey, both times dropping off within two hundred metres of Stonehill Mews. The cab firms were switched for the return journey, so Premier Cars did it on the sixteenth of January and Alpha Cabs on the twenty-second.'

'Impressive, but how do you know it was the same passenger?'

Pymm smiled and lowered her voice.

'Keep it to yourself, but I cheated. Customers are asked to leave a contact number. I just scrolled down the lists from the two firms and spotted the unregistered mobile number that Moray got from the locksmith.'

'Your secret's safe with me,' said Sutton.

* * *

Warren had managed less than three hours of fitful sleep on his cousin Jane's sofa. On the plus side, less sleep meant fewer opportunities to dream, which at the moment was a blessing.

'Warren, we have to face facts. He's 91 years old. Should he still be living on his own?'

Jane looked just as exhausted as Warren. The two of them were sitting at her kitchen table, drinking coffee. Around them, her two children squabbled and fought over nothing. They were too young to understand what was going on, but the unexpected appearance of their dimly remembered uncle in the middle of the night, and the tense atmosphere in the house, had unsettled them. Jane's husband, Hugo, had arranged to go into work late so that he could organise the nursery run, and allow Jane a lie-in, but she had been up at her usual time, unable to sleep any later.

'What did the doctor say?' asked Warren.

'He said that it all depends on how well Jack recovers after the operation. The break was a clean one, easily pinned, and Jack wasn't lying on the floor too long before he managed to trigger his alarm – at least he was wearing it.' Jack had taken a lot of persuading to wear the radio-operated alert around his neck – Warren was glad they had persevered.

'The doctor says that at the very least, if... when... Jack gets out of the hospital he'll probably need residential respite care for a few weeks or months until they are satisfied that he can live on his own again. Even then, he's likely to need regular home visits, and they're unsure how well the leg will support his weight.' She paused. 'Warren, Hugo has been offered a new job. In Nottingham. And we've already put an offer in on a house there.'

It took a moment for what she had said to sink in.

Nottingham was over fifty miles away. Close enough to drive there and back in a day, but too far away for Jane to visit daily, even if Hugo did the school and nursery run.

What about Bernice and Dennis? Susan's parents loved Jack dearly, regularly popping around, taking him shopping and to church, and down the local for a pint. But they were spending increasing amounts of time playing grandparents to Susan's sister's ever-increasing brood, a commitment that would only increase if Susan and Warren finally made them grandparents for the fifth time.

But Granddad Jack in a home?

Warren could barely imagine it. Yet wasn't it inevitable? He'd always known that this time would come. Granddad Jack was a fit and healthy man, with the heart and lungs of someone twenty years his junior, but Warren knew that at that age the clock was ticking ever louder and the rest of his body was succumbing to the inevitable march of time. He'd just found it easier to ignore it. How many times had he changed the conversation when it strayed too close to uncomfortable decisions?

'Home visits...' Warren couldn't bear the thought. They all knew what that meant. Overworked, underpaid strangers racing from appointment to appointment, with barely enough time to say hello to Granddad Jack before they helped him with his most intimate needs... No. He couldn't do that to him. Granddad Jack and Nana Betty had been Warren's *de facto* parents, helping his mother bring him up after his father's death, providing him with a quiet place to do his homework and later a bed whenever he needed to get out of the house to avoid the increasing arguments between his mother and his older brother, James.

Jane must have seen the look on his face. She reached over and took her cousin's hand.

'Let's not put the cart before the horse. We've got a few weeks to think about this and decide what's best, and we'll see what Jack's thoughts are on the matter. He may have his own ideas.'

Warren nodded numbly. He looked over at the clock.

'What time can we visit?'

'The doctor said that no news is good news. If we haven't received a call sooner, we can go in any time after nine. It's his first day on the ward, he'll want familiar faces.'

Warren looked at the clock again, working out in his head how long it would take to get to University Hospital, or whatever they called Walsgrave these days, vowing to be at the nursing station at 9 a.m. precisely. Granddad Jack had already been prepped for surgery by the time he'd arrived the previous night, and he had only Jane's assessment of how he was before he was put under. Groggy from the pain relief and confused had been her opinion.

Warren had been able to sit with him for a few minutes after he came out of surgery, as he slept off the anaesthetic. The surgeon had pronounced himself satisfied with the operation, but Granddad Jack had looked so small in the hospital bed, his face bruised and cut where he'd hit the floor as he'd fallen, that Warren had been shocked.

Jack's right wrist had been bandaged, swollen from where he'd tried to catch himself, but it was the broken left femur that had been the big worry. As much as Warren tried to fool himself when it came to Granddad Jack's health, he knew that such an injury was very bad news in one so old. The forced inactivity alone could lead to complications such as pneumonia. Despite the apparent success of the operation, Warren knew that it was far from a done deal that Granddad Jack would be coming home.

* * *

'Take however long you need,' said Grayson.

Warren was in the visitors' room off Granddad Jack's ward. His DSI, despite his faults, was a very family-oriented man; he'd been very understanding when Nana Betty had passed away a few years previously, taking Warren's especially close relationship with his grandparents into account and authorising additional compassionate leave. Nevertheless, Warren could hear the strain in the man's voice.

No investigation, especially one as wide-ranging and complex as this one, relied entirely on one person. Warren knew that if he was suddenly indisposed, he could be replaced immediately. But it wasn't an ideal situation, and he would rather not place the team in that position.

He rubbed the bridge of his nose and breathed deeply. His neck was stiff; whether it was from his awkward night's sleep on the sofa or was linked to the tension headache that paracetamol wouldn't dent, he was unsure. He felt as if he was being pulled in a dozen directions at once. Even though Tony Sutton had brought him up-to-date on the latest progress and assured him that everything was in hand, and Susan had insisted that she too was fine, Warren wanted to be there with them. Yet Granddad Jack was still asleep after his ordeal; Warren had no idea how he would be when he woke up and his heart told him he should be there, by his bedside until he was satisfied.

'I'll be speaking to the doctors and I'll see how Granddad Jack is when he wakes up, then I'll let you know when I'm coming back.'

'Good. Let me know when you arrive, we need a quick chat.'

Despite his preoccupation, Warren heard the slight edge in the man's voice.

'Is there a problem, sir?'

The end of the line was silent. 'We just need to speak,' Grayson responded eventually.

'About something in particular?'

Despite himself, Warren had to know. If there was a problem, he'd rather be forewarned.

This time the pause was longer. Eventually Grayson sighed.

'I shouldn't have said anything, you've got enough on your plate.'

'Well, you may as well tell me now,' said Warren.

'Your interview with Bishop Fisher has ruffled a few feathers. I've been asked to discuss the matter with you.'

'I see.'

'It's not a big deal, and you're not in any trouble.'

'I'll let you know when I'm back,' Warren said, before hanging up.

Could the day get any worse?

* * *

Granddad Jack was confused, but coherent when he finally woke up a little after 10 a.m. Fortunately the restorative powers of a cup of tea helped ease the situation, and within twenty minutes, he was able to tell them what had happened.

'Bloody leg went to sleep.' Granddad Jack's voice was hoarse, but steadily gaining strength. 'I was dozing in front of the TV and I must have been sitting awkwardly. When I woke up, I needed the bathroom. I got up and the damn thing just gave way underneath me. I managed not to hit the coffee table when I went down, but I heard it go snap.' He grimaced.

Warren shuddered. Granddad Jack's legs were hidden under the sheets, but the huge bulge on that side spoke of the extensive framework that supported the pinned bone.

'Luckily, I had that necklace thing on.' For the first time since Warren and Jane had arrived, a smile ghosted across the old man's face. 'Feel free to tell me you told me so.'

The lump in Warren's throat stopped him from saying anything.

* * *

346

By lunchtime, Granddad Jack was able to eat a small sandwich. Afterwards, he drifted off to sleep.

Warren and Jane spoke to the doctor in charge of his care.

'He's remarkably tough for a man of his years. I normally expect far more confusion at this stage, and he seems to be adjusting well to his pain relief. I've seen no sign of any infection. His chest is clear and his vitals are pretty good – I wish I had his blood pressure.'

'Any idea of his longer-term progress?' asked Warren.

'Far too early to say. In the short term, we need to get that bone healing and as soon as possible get him mobile again. Muscle wasting happens at an alarming rate at this age, so we'll want to minimise that.'

'How long do you think he'll be in here?' asked Jane.

'Again, it's difficult to say. I suggest we take it day by day for now.'

With Granddad Jack apparently settled, Warren had a decision to make. Much to his surprise, it was Jane that pushed him to return to work.

'You heard what the doctor said, he's stable. There's nothing you can do for now. Bernice and Dennis are coming over this afternoon, and they've stopped by Jack's house to pick up a few things for him.'

'But I can't just leave him,' Warren protested.

'We've been watching the case on TV and Jack has been following it in the papers. We all know what you're dealing with in Middlesbury. You're needed down there; I can fit hospital visits around the school runs for a few days. I'll keep you updated and I'm sure you can get back here quickly enough if you need to.'

'I don't know…' started Warren.

'Just bugger off and go back to work,' came a weak voice from the bed. Granddad Jack's eyes were closed, but he had a faint smile on his face. 'I'm not going anywhere.'

Chapter 69

The drive back to Middlesbury was surprisingly stress-free, both the M6 and the A14 had been clear of heavy traffic, and so Warren made good time, arriving back at CID by late afternoon. He quickly texted Susan and Jane to let them know he had arrived safely; Jane replied that Jack was awake again and talking to Bernice and Dennis. Taking a deep breath, Warren headed for Grayson's office.

Grayson offered him a steaming mug of coffee, which Warren inhaled gratefully. Usually, when a bollocking was in order, Grayson dispensed with the hospitality. However, the day was an unusual one, and so Warren couldn't read the signals. After inquiring about Granddad Jack's health, he told Warren to take a seat.

'First of all, I have been assured that the diocese of Herts and Essex is keen to cooperate in any way that they can, including the release of any necessary documents. Obviously, they are very concerned about the two murders. They are also worried about the potential links to previous abuse scandals. It's something the church as a whole is wrestling with at the moment and they are remaining open-minded as to the motive for these killings.'

'But?'

Grayson paused.

'Your questioning of Bishop Emeritus Fisher yesterday was... robust.'

'Has he complained?'

'Not directly, but Bishop Fisher's presence here did not go unnoticed.'

'Then who complained?'

'Assistant Chief Constable Naseem has been under significant pressure from above to ensure that this case runs smoothly. And by the book. Without any unnecessary drama.' Grayson raised a hand slightly. 'His words, not mine.'

'Above' in this case could only really mean one thing; the Home Office, perhaps even the Home Secretary herself.

'If you review the recordings, you will see that the interview was conducted under PACE and that I was professional at all times,' stated Warren.

'I have watched the recordings, and I agree that you were doing your job correctly. There is no cause for complaint about your conduct in that interview. ACC Naseem agrees with that assessment.'

Shit, thought Warren. Naseem had directly reviewed the recordings?

'We also both believe that your suggestion that Bishop Fisher was aware of the alleged offences through confession with the priests concerned, but chose not to reveal them, has merit.'

'I'm pleased to hear it,' responded Warren, his tone a little more sarcastic than normal.

Grayson paused for a moment, before deciding to ignore Warren's manner and continue.

'However, we are concerned about what might have been said *after* the recording was terminated at Bishop Fisher's request.'

'Oh, for—'

'Warren.' The sharp edge to Grayson's voice cut him off. 'According to the CCTV outside the interview suite, you and

Bishop Fisher didn't leave the room for seven minutes after the interview recording was stopped. Bishop Fisher looked agitated when he left. The custody sergeant reported that raised voices were heard.'

'You aren't seriously suggesting that I behaved inappropriately towards Bishop Fisher after the recording ended, are you?' Warren couldn't believe what he was hearing.

'Of course not, don't be bloody silly. And neither is ACC Naseem.'

'Then what are you getting at? You can read my notes; I wrote down exactly what was said after the meeting.'

Grayson stood up and walked back over to the coffee machine, topping up both of their mugs without asking. When he sat back down, his voice was quieter.

'This case really is the proverbial hot potato and there is potential all around for fingers to be badly burned. Very badly burned.'

'Are you suggesting that there is pressure to drop the case?' Grayson appeared shocked.

'Absolutely not.' For the first time Warren caught a glimpse of steel. 'We follow this case through to the end. If your suspicions are correct, then we'll nail these bastards, and ACC Naseem feels exactly the same. And if that causes red faces – or worse – then frankly, so what?'

'Then what are you saying?'

'When you handle a hot potato, you need to use extra care. You have to make certain that you follow all the correct procedures to ensure that you don't hurt yourself.'

The metaphor was becoming increasingly tortured, and Warren decided to step in.

'I see what you are saying. Keep the tape recording running and make sure I have my facts straight.'

'That's all I... that's all we ask.'

Grayson took another sip of his coffee. Warren waited, He could tell that there was more to come.

This time, Grayson's voice was even quieter, as if he wanted to avoid being overheard.

'This doesn't go any further than this office.'

'Of course.'

'This case puts ACC Naseem in an especially difficult position. Had he known the direction it was likely to go in, he probably would have passed it over to somebody else. Unfortunately, he's now stuck with it.'

Warren had a feeling where Grayson was going with it. He felt shocked.

'Is it because he's a Muslim?'

'In a nutshell, yes. After that problem with the far-right over the summer, Naseem came under a lot of flak on social media and in the gutter press. I'm ashamed to say that there were even a few in our own ranks who questioned his suitability to oversee such a case.'

Warren remembered it well. Naseem's religion had been used against him in some quarters, with criticisms ranging from insidious questions about how a practising Muslim could be impartial when overseeing an investigation involving Islamophobic organisations such as the British Allegiance Party, to outright accusations of an Islamist conspiracy to destroy those defending British identity.

'Shit.' Warren's shock was fast turning to anger. 'I've not been following the news. Is he in the firing line again?'

'Not yet, but this needs to be handled sensitively. I'm sure you are aware of the child sex-rings recently uncovered in the North of England? All those charged are of Pakistani British Muslim origin. Just like ACC Naseem. The concern is that some are going to claim that Naseem will use this to deflect attention away from the Muslim community back onto white Christians.'

'But that's madness, he'd never do such a thing,' stated Warren.

'It doesn't matter, we both know that sort of conspiracy feeds directly into the belief systems of these people. Facts are irrelevant.

Warren, if this investigation isn't seen to be squeaky clean, the fall-out from this case will go far beyond the Catholic Church and could very well be seized upon by those with scores to settle.'

Warren was shocked by the hypocrisy of the situation and said as much.

'You do realise that I'm a Catholic, don't you?' Now was not the time to mention his brewing crisis of faith. 'And that the exact same allegations could be levelled against me if we don't prove anything?'

'Warren…'

'You can't tell me that nobody has considered that possibility? How long will it be until somebody decides that it might be good PR to remove me from the case?'

'Don't be silly.'

'We can't win either way on this one – try and prove that Bishop Fisher is harbouring paedophile priests and people will claim that Naseem is trying to deflect attention away from abusers in the Muslim community onto white Christian men. But on the other hand, if we can't prove our case, victims' groups are going to claim that the loyal Catholic has managed to protect his beloved church.'

'Warren!' snapped Grayson. 'Take a deep breath and calm down.'

Warren slumped back into his chair, his arms folded.

'You're acting like a teenager.' Grayson took a deep breath of his own. When he spoke again, his tone was softer. 'You're stressed and you're tired. Have you even eaten properly today?'

Warren said nothing.

'I thought not. Go and have a proper lunch, phone your wife and get yourself home at a decent hour tonight.'

Warren nodded numbly. Grayson was probably right. He headed for the door.

Grayson called after him, as he exited the office.

'And no more bloody coffee. You can pass that onto Tony Sutton as well.'

Chapter 70

The man calling himself Peanut could have been any age between twenty and forty; it was impossible to tell. Obviously Peanut wasn't his real name, but he'd threatened to walk out when Warren asked him what he was really called. How much of the man's agitation was fear and how much was due to whatever chemical cocktail he was coming down from, was unclear.

The call had come in to the main switchboard moments after Warren had left Grayson's office, from an unregistered mobile phone. Not only had he refused to give a name, he'd insisted that he had to speak to Warren personally. Warren had arranged to meet him when he was free, later that afternoon.

The number he called from wasn't the same as the number that had reported Lucas Furber's body, but Peanut claimed he hadn't been the one to call in Furber's death. After listening to the two recordings back-to-back repeatedly, the team had been unable to decide if the callers' voices matched or not. Forensic voice analysis would tell them either way, if Warren decided the expense was necessary.

The CCTV Richardson had obtained from Sainsbury's clearly identified Furber as he bought the reduced quiche that constituted his last meal. Unfortunately, it also showed him arriving and leaving alone. Intermittent sightings of him on other surveillance cameras on his way to and from the store, also failed to identify anyone else with him. The man in front of Warren was the only person they knew of that had actually known the victim in any meaningful sense.

'I saw him in December. He was in a bad way.'

'Drugs?' asked Warren. After his recent admonishment from Grayson, he'd taken extra care to ensure that the PACE recorder was running.

'No, well, not really. Booze mostly. A bit of weed or a few pills maybe.'

'Not heroin?'

'No, he'd been off the gear for ages. It's why we stopped seeing each other.'

'How so?'

'I'm a bad influence.' The man smiled, revealing yellow teeth; but the smile didn't reach his eyes. If anything he looked as though he might cry.

'You were close?'

'Yeah.' The word communicated so much that Warren decided to move on.

'Tell me about Lucas.'

The man's face softened slightly.

'He was a good man. He… cared, you know?' The man sniffed. 'I was a mess when I first ended up on the street. I'd decided I needed to get away from things and so I moved to Stevenage. God knows why. I had no idea what to do, or where to go. I needed money and within a week I was doing stuff for blokes that they couldn't get their wives to do for them.

'Lucas got me out of that. He showed me where to get food, how to get help.' He paused. 'We were good together.'

'How long ago was this?'

'About two years. Lucas had been on the street for a year or so longer.'

'When did you and Lucas stop seeing each other?'

'Last summer. We'd been growing apart for ages, ever since we'd moved to Middlesbury in the spring. I thought maybe he was seeing someone else. I dunno, he always denied it. Then he said he wanted to get clean. He'd got a place on a program. One of those ones run by the church.'

'And you didn't join him.'

Peanut said nothing for the next few seconds, suddenly becoming interested in a piece of fluff on his tracksuit bottoms, 'I wasn't ready,' he said eventually.

'Do you know if he was successful?'

'Yeah. That's why I called you.'

'Go on.'

'I saw his picture on the front of the *Reporter* in the Phoenix centre. They said he'd taken a drug overdose. But it didn't sound right.'

'What are you saying, Peanut?'

'I think he might have been murdered. I want you to find out who did it.'

Warren looked at the man carefully. Peanut looked away. The piece of fluff had been replaced by a loose thread that was steadily growing.

Lucas Furber had been a heroin addict for several years by all accounts. Peanut was obviously also a user; he had to know how common it was for recovering addicts to lapse into their old habits. He also said that he hadn't seen Lucas regularly since the summer. If he was to be believed, he had no way to know if Furber had been clean these last few months or not.

'What aren't you telling me, Peanut?'

'Don't know what you mean.' The man's right leg was jigging up and down, the thread forgotten.

'Come on Peanut, Lucas was a former junkie. Is it so hard to believe he couldn't stay clean? What is it that makes you think he was killed deliberately?' Warren paused, and looked the man square in the eyes. 'What are you scared of?'

Peanut suddenly stood up.

'I've got to go. He was killed. Just look into it.'

'Sit down, Peanut.' Warren's tone was quiet but firm. 'We both want to know how and why Lucas died.'

For a long moment the room was silent. Peanut stood stock still; even the twitching had stopped. Eventually he lowered himself back into his seat.

'Why don't I get you a coffee and let you get your thoughts together?'

The man clearly needed something stronger than coffee, but Warren could hardly let him do that in here, and if he let the man out the back he'd probably never see him again. Not for the first time, Warren wished the smoking ban didn't also apply to interview suites; he'd happily tolerate the smell and stinging eyes if it got him what he needed.

When Warren returned, balancing a few packets of biscuits on top of two cups of coffee – he'd ignored Grayson's instruction – Peanut seemed calmer. After practically inhaling a half-dozen custard creams so quickly that Warren wondered when he'd last eaten, he began again.

'It all started back about a year or so ago. In the new year, I think. Lucas was a real news hound. He'd read all the papers in the library and if he found anything interesting he'd use the computers to look up more.' Peanut paused. 'You know people assume that because we're homeless, we're different? That we don't have hobbies or interests. But you have to book time on the computers down the Phoenix centre, and there's always a queue.

'Everyone is on the web or using Facebook. At least half the people I know have smartphones. You don't need an expensive contract if you keep your mobile data turned off and use free Wi-Fi. The library doesn't turn off its routers at night, so if you stand close enough to the window you can still get a signal.'

'What was it Lucas read?'

'An old school friend – I don't know if you'd call him a

boyfriend – killed himself. Chucked himself in front of a train on the London Underground. They reckon he'd been sleeping rough down there. There wasn't much in the paper, just a first name and a photograph apparently, but Lucas became obsessed with finding out more details.

'I couldn't figure out why he was so bothered. It was sad, obviously, but they hadn't seen each other for what? Fifteen years? They hadn't spoken since they left school.'

Peanut took a cautious sip of his coffee, before wincing and replacing it. Warren wasn't surprised; he wished the makers of the coffee dispenser in the waiting room would take into account the fact that powdered milk doesn't cool scalding water as effectively as real milk. His fingers still stung from where he'd slopped it on them on his way back to the interview suite.

'I knew that Lucas had been bullied at school. That it had gone beyond bullying. He went to a Catholic boarding school in the early Nineties. You know what it was like back then; if you were different you were a target.'

Warren nodded his understanding. He'd gone to a Catholic comprehensive school a few years before Furber. He doubted the rampant homophobia – in part encouraged by the school's own interpretation of doctrine – had improved much in the ten years between his own schooling and Furber's. It was no wonder so few of his schoolmates had felt comfortable enough to come out until they went to university, or later.

'Of course the irony was that whilst the priests and the staff were busy preaching how homosexuality was a sin, they were wilfully ignoring it when it took place in front of them. Or they were indulging in it themselves.'

'I see.'

'Yeah. Catholic priests buggering the choir boys. It's become a cliché. How many jokes do you know about it?'

Warren said nothing. At least two punchlines sprang to mind. They suddenly didn't seem so funny.

'They're predators. Pure and simple. I don't think it was because Lucas and his friend were gay – although I suppose it could have fed into their sick fantasies. They just saw an easy target. Lucas' friend's father had died back when he was in primary school. Lucas' mother had passed away too.'

Peanut's voice started to rise. 'It makes you wonder what's fucking wrong with these parents. "Oh, your other parent's died? Well, why don't I still send you away to boarding school, because I'm sure everything will be fine?" Wankers.'

Warren said nothing. Phrased like that, he could see the man's point. He couldn't imagine the pain of being sent away when his own father had died. He'd needed his mother more than ever, and she'd needed him and his brother.

'So what happened?'

'I don't know many details. Lucas only really spoke about it when he was drunk or high, and I wasn't in much of a state to remember everything either.'

'Try your best.'

'Apparently, there was one priest in particular. He didn't arrive until Lucas and his friend were in upper school. The two of them were always in trouble of some sort. I reckon they both blamed God for taking their parents, so a Catholic school was never going to be a great fit. Anyhow, corporal punishment had been banned in state schools, but you could still hit kids in private schools back then. This priest was well-known for putting kids across his knee. Sometimes he did more than that.'

Did this provide a motive for Furber's anger towards priests? Was this enough for him to seek revenge?

'Did either boy report the abuse?'

'Of course not. Who would they report it to? Their parents had dumped them in there. The school was never going to listen to kids like Lucas and his friend. Nobody believed them.'

Warren wondered if Furber or his friend had used the

Survivorsonline forums. He made a note to see if Furber's phone had any details of his internet browsing history.

'Do you know the name of the school or the priest that committed the abuse?'

Peanut shook his head.

'What about the name of his old friend?'

'No idea.'

It wasn't much to go on.

'All I know is that when his friend died, Lucas became obsessed with trying to track down his older brother, to tell him what had happened. The paper said that the police had been unable to track down his friend's next-of-kin, because they didn't have a surname, so he figured he'd have to do it for them. Lucas was convinced that his friend killed himself because of the damage that was done to him.'

Peanut's voice dropped. 'You never get over it.'

Warren was unsure whether he was talking about his friend or himself. What was Peanut's story, he wondered? He doubted it was much happier.

'Why didn't Lucas go to the police, and tell them who he thought it was? They could have found his next-of-kin easily, they have a whole unit dedicated to this sort of investigation.'

'Why do you think?' asked Peanut. It was a fair point, Warren conceded. Lucas and Peanut lived on the outskirts of mainstream society; their dealings with the police were unlikely to have been entirely positive.

'Anyhow, I think he kind of enjoyed the challenge, you know?' Peanut continued. The thing is, people think that just cause he's homeless and a user, he must be stupid, right? But Lucas wasn't. He was smart – fucked up, but smart. He could have done so much more...' He drifted off, and Warren cleared his throat softly.

'Being homeless is boring,' said Peanut suddenly. 'Once you've figured out how to get a meal and score any drugs you need, what else is there to do? It's why we read so much. I reckon Lucas just craved the challenge.' He tapped his forehead. 'He wanted to use his brain. Trying to find his friend's brother's whereabouts gave him something to do.'

'Did he find him?'

'I think so. He spent ages on Facebook in the library, and in the spring he started disappearing off. That's when I thought he might be having an affair, but he kept on denying it. Then suddenly, straight after Easter, he announces that he's moving to Middlesbury and that I can come with him or not. Obviously I did.' Peanut's voice dropped to a mumble. 'He's all I had.'

'Did he say why he wanted to move?'

'Just that he needed a change.'

'Why Middlesbury?'

'Dunno. I'd never even heard of the place. Lucas had a couple of mates who knew the local scene and they put us in touch with people who could help us out. You know, find what we needed.'

'What happened when you came to Middlesbury?'

'We got ourselves sorted and everything was OK for a bit.'

The man went quiet.

'Peanut,' Warren started gently. 'I've not heard anything suspicious yet. Why do you think Lucas was killed? And if he was, who do you think did it?'

Peanut chewed his bottom lip. His left foot had started tapping the floor again.

'Lucas started acting weird after we got to Middlesbury. He kept on making phone calls and disappearing. Sometimes he seemed upset or angry when he came back. Like I said, I thought he was having an affair or something.'

'Go on.'

'One night, probably about a month after we'd moved, I overheard him talking on the phone. It sounded like he was arranging to meet up with someone. The next day he was all hyper. I tried to get him to smoke a bit of weed or something, you know to calm down, but he wouldn't have any. Then he left, said he'd be back "whenever".

'He didn't get back until late, and when he did he was really drunk and angry. It was weird because he'd had a haircut and he was wearing new clothes. He wanted some gear, but I hid it. I was worried that the state he was in he'd do it wrong and end up overdosing. He's done that before.'

'Do you know what he was so upset about?'

'I couldn't get much sense out of him, but he kept on repeating "the bastard's already dead".'

'Do you know who he was talking about?'

'No. I tried to ask him the next day what it was all about, but he wouldn't tell me. In the end I stopped asking about it, because it just ended in a row.'

'Who do you think he went to meet?'

Peanut let out a huff of breath.

'I don't know. I knew most of his mates in Middlesbury because we met them when we first arrived.' He paused. 'The only one I can think of is his friend's brother.'

'Why do you say that?'

'It's the only thing that fits. Everything started to go shitty after his friend's death and when he started to try and find his brother. Then he suddenly ups sticks and moves to Middlesbury. Next thing I know, he's angry all the time. '

'Did you ask him about it?'

'No. I don't know why. It didn't feel healthy, you know? Let the past be the past. I'm not sure what good raking up ancient history would do. Maybe I was just jealous. This guy was probably Lucas' first lover, I guess I was a bit uncomfortable about him hooking up with his brother. I don't know...' His voice trailed off.

'So when was the last time you'd say that you were really close?'

'Dunno. Last June? That's when he started talking about getting clean. It was weird though. I think the course was being run by the church. I heard he'd been seen hanging around with some priest. I thought Lucas would stay well away from that shit.'

'Do you know anything about this priest? Could you describe him?'

Peanut shook his head. 'No, I never met him.'

'But you think it was successful?'

'Yeah, as far as I could tell. He sort of disappeared back in the summer. I heard he'd got a place to stay at Purbury. They're really clear about no drugs. I asked around, but he was staying clear of everyone. It's what they recommend, to stop you getting tempted. I guess it was good for him. Once an addict, always an addict.'

Despite his words, Warren could hear the pain of betrayal in the man's voice.

Warren chose his words next carefully.

'Assuming that Lucas really did take an overdose, where might he get his drugs?'

'Can't say.'

'Come on, Peanut. I'm not interested in busting some little dealer. I just want to know if Lucas bought himself the heroin, or if somebody gave it to him.'

Peanut chewed his lip.

'There's a bloke down by the arches. He'll get it for you. Sometimes he'll give a discount if you do him a favour.'

'Does he have a name?'

'Doesn't matter. He's not seen Lucas since the summer.'

'How do you know that?'

'I asked him before I came here. He'd not read the paper, he didn't know Lucas was dead, so he wasn't worried about being done for selling the gear that killed him.'

Despite Peanut's insistence, Warren couldn't take him at face value. The dealer could have been lying, worried that he was on the hook for manslaughter. Even if he was telling the truth, and Furber hadn't bought it from him, somebody had given that drug to him. If Peanut was right and Furber had been murdered, then

362

Warren needed to know who had bought that drug. This dealer wasn't the only one in Middlesbury, but his team had little to do with that side of policing. He'd have to speak to the drugs unit about it.

Warren made one more attempt to persuade Peanut to tell him who the dealer was or at least give him the names of people who might have known Furber, but he was met with stony silence and crossed arms. Warren decided to change the subject before Peanut decided the interview was over.

'You said you saw him back in December, and he was in a bad way?'

'Yeah. He was at the Phoenix centre, I think he was having counselling there.'

'What was his state of mind?'

'Not good. He was really drunk. He started being dead mouthy and was abusive to the staff. They kicked him out when he started laying into Reverend Billy. Which isn't on, 'cause everyone loves Billy.'

'What was he saying?'

'Stuff about priests all being the same and how he'd burn in hell, which is bollocks, 'cause Billy isn't even a Catholic.'

'Do you know what happened after he got kicked out?'

'I went after him. I'd not seen him for weeks and I wanted to check he was OK.'

'What did he say?'

Peanut looked back down at his tracksuit bottoms.

'He wasn't really making any sense. He kept on saying that they were all the same and that they'd get what they deserved, and that they wouldn't be able to shut him up this time.'

'Who was he talking about?'

'He didn't say, but he'd just been shouting at Reverend Billy, so who do you think?'

Chapter 71

It was 11 p.m. and Warren was exhausted. Several nights in a row of almost no sleep had left him groggy and light-headed. Remembering Grayson's admonishment, he'd hoped to leave work earlier than usual; he still felt that he and Susan hadn't properly dealt with their own disappointment and he was planning on phoning Jane again, perhaps even speaking to Granddad Jack. However, by the time he'd finished up and finally got around to calling Jane, it was past 7 p.m. and Granddad Jack had gone to sleep again.

He and Susan had just finished watching *Newsnight* and his eyes were growing heavy as he lay slumped on the sofa. Nestled against his chest, Susan had already started to nod off. He'd better make a move, he decided, before they both fell asleep and woke up with stiff necks in the early hours.

His phone vibrated. Warren held his breath. A single buzz was probably just a social media notification, although he could have sworn he'd activated 'do not disturb mode' for such trivialities after 9 p.m.

A second vibration.

On the third he swiped 'answer call'.

'Sorry, sir, we thought you'd want to know. Father Frank Madden has gone missing from St Cecil's.'

* * *

Warren arrived at the abbey within ten minutes of the call. This time of night there'd been no traffic and he knew where the speed cameras were.

Tony Sutton greeted him at the rear entrance.

'They discovered his room was empty around 10 p.m. Gabriel Baines has been doing a sort of informal headcount each night before he goes home. Father Madden was last seen at about seven after finishing dinner. He prefers to go to his room and read before he goes to sleep.

'Baines knocked on his door at ten, because the light was on. When no one answered, he pushed the door open and saw Madden's bed was still made. He asked around if anyone had seen him. Nobody had. He found this on the dressing table. Unfortunately, he picked it up, so his fingerprints are already on it.'

Warren didn't need to see the photograph on Sutton's phone to know what the note said.

'Forgive me Father, for I have sinned.'

'What about the officers standing outside the main doors?'

'Nothing. They swear blind that nobody has been in or out of the building whilst they stood there.'

'Could he have climbed out a window?'

'Doubtful, he's the wrong side of 70 and has a dodgy hip.'

The main hall was ablaze with light. Bishop Fisher stood next to Gabriel Baines, wearing a dressing gown. Baines was in a thick jacket holding a torch, his hair damp from the rain.

'Rodney Shaw is on his way. He'll help organise a search of the grounds,' said Fisher.

Warren wasn't sure how wise that was; the last thing he wanted was Rodney Shaw trampling around, hiding clues and creating a plausible reason for any trace evidence that may point towards him.

'That won't be necessary. We have specialist teams for this sort of thing,' said Sutton, beating Warren to the punch.

'Bishop Fisher, may I have a private word?' asked Warren.

The elderly clergyman followed Warren into his office.

'Is there anything that I need to know about Father Madden? Anything that wouldn't be public knowledge?'

Bishop Fisher paused.

'Nothing I can talk to you about.'

Warren bit back a four-letter retort; it wouldn't be professional, and besides swearing at a bishop seemed wrong. However, his voice was an angry hiss as he bent closer to the elderly priest.

'Just remember, Your Grace, you could have told me who the killer's next target was. We could have protected him.' Warren glared at him. 'Be under no illusion – if Father Madden turns up dead, this is on you.'

Bishop Fisher met Warren's stare, unblinking.

'The seal of the confessional goes both ways, DCI Jones. Those asking for forgiveness know that when they partake in the sacrament.'

Chapter 72

By 2 a.m., a thorough search of the house had been made. The residents were all in the main dining room, huddled in small groups, answering questions posed by Warren's team. Even Fathers Kendrick and Ramsden were there, having insisted that they be brought downstairs so that they could be with their brother priests. Father Boyce, clad in his pyjamas and dressing gown, fussed over them, ensuring that they were comfortable and not over-tired. The three sisters, somehow already dressed in their grey habits and wimples, ensured that nobody ran out of tea.

So far though, nobody knew where Father Madden had vanished to. Those who had spoken to him over the past few days had been adamant that whilst he was as worried and upset as everyone else in the small community, he otherwise seemed to be his usual self.

Outside in the main grounds, teams were searching, their torches flashing, as they progressed outwards from the house.

'How the hell can an elderly priest in need of a hip replacement go missing?' asked Sutton for the umpteenth time.

None of the pairs of officers standing watch at either of the two entrances, or the fire exit, had seen anyone leaving the house since before 6 p.m.; long before Father Madden had disappeared.

The only ground floor windows not visible to the teams were locked or permanently fastened for security reasons, and there was no way Father Madden had shinned down a drainpipe.

The rain had finally stopped and Warren and Sutton were standing outside, hoping the cold air might revive them when even caffeine was failing. The scrunch of gravel heralded the arrival of a small van.

'Looks as though the search dogs have arrived,' noted Sutton.

The two men led the dog and its handler upstairs to Madden's room.

'We'll let him have a good sniff of the clothes in the laundry basket and then see if he can track him,' said the handler. 'I have to warn you though, this is Father Madden's room so it'll be full of scent. He might get confused.'

'Well, do what you can. If he can't pick up his scent from inside the house we'll try outside.'

Corbett was a highly excitable springer spaniel. After a good sniff of Madden's discarded underclothes, he started racing around the room, eagerly exploring. Warren tried not to wince. Everyone in the room was wearing paper suits, and Corbett was wearing disposable booties, but he knew that they were running the risk of compromising the crime scene before the CSIs had even started – however, it couldn't be helped. Whilst there was even a slight chance that Father Madden was still alive, finding him took precedence.

Eventually, Corbett headed for the open door. Out in the corridor, he pressed his nose against the floor and trotted determinedly away from the stairwell, in the direction of the sash window at the far end of the hallway.

'Where's he going?' muttered Warren. 'There's nothing up there, the window is locked and we're on the first floor. There's no way Father Madden could climb out of there.'

Nevertheless, Corbett was on a mission. A metre or so from the window, he stopped, turned to his left and stared at the wall.

'Is he confused?' asked Sutton.

'I don't think so,' said the handler.

The wall in front of the dog was panelled oak.

Corbett whined and gave a small bark.

Warren stepped forward. He tapped the wood experimentally, listening to the hollow thunk. Moving a pace to his left, he tapped again. Another hollow thunk. Another pace. This time the noise was less hollow.

'Get Rachel Pymm on the line,' Warren ordered, 'and ask her about any priest holes.'

Chapter 73

'Did you not think it might be helpful for us to know that the house has secret passageways running through it?' asked Warren. He was aware that his voice was unprofessionally harsh, but he was beyond caring. He'd been awake for over twenty hours, after weeks of similarly punishing routine and had lost track of the volume of coffee he'd drunk to stave off exhaustion.

For his part, Gabriel Baines looked embarrassed.

'They were part of the original eighteenth-century structure, built by Howard Langton himself to protect his family, and other Catholics, in the event that there was another crackdown.

'When we decided to convert the house into a retirement home the ones that we knew about were all boarded up because they aren't safe anymore and they're full of rats and other vermin. Some of our residents in the past have been a bit... confused at times, and we didn't want any accidents.'

Warren, Sutton, Baines and Bishop Fisher were in the bishop's office, along with the head of the search team. Rachel Pymm had just arrived after a blue-light escort via the CID office. Her pyjamas were visible under her long over-coat, and her hair was sticking up at odd angles. Pymm had been sound asleep when Warren's call went through. Her husband had beaten her to her handset and had been furious that she had been disturbed.

'She needs her sleep, for Christ's sake, she's absolutely exhausted. What sort of a manger lets an employee with her medical condition work those sort of hours…' That was the point at which Pymm had finally wrestled the phone away from her husband. She'd clearly placed her hand over the mouth piece, but he could hear her angrily hissing something about 'not needing her husband to fight her battles for her'.

Warren felt wretched, but he knew that'd he'd had no choice. Rachel Pymm had found the plans during her research, and probably knew more about them than anyone else alive, other than the killer.

'Most of the priest holes were little more than hollow spaces, where a priest or other fugitive could hide out until the danger had passed,' she said, as he helped her spread out photocopied sheets from Vernon Coombs' boxes of research. Warren was familiar with the idea of priest holes, having visited several Warwickshire-based former Catholic homes such as Baddesley Clinton with his grandparents as a child.

'However, this particular compartment was an escape route. A vertical shaft that runs alongside the main chimney to help disguise it within the house's original dimensions. There was an exit on each floor, hidden behind wooden panelling. It ends below the house's basement and then runs underground to escape the house.'

'Where does it emerge?'

'Down by the old cloisters,' she replied.

'We found an old entrance years ago, but we bricked it up.' Baines sounded desperate.

'What's the betting it isn't anymore? Get a team down there, batons drawn. If the killer is still in the tunnel we don't want him escaping.'

The wait for confirmation that the tunnel exit was covered by officers was barely two minutes, but seemed far longer. Warren

371

was well aware that every second that passed was another second that Father Madden was potentially in danger, but the elderly priest had been missing for over five hours now. The chances were that he was already dead.

Warren raised the radio to his lips.

'Everyone in position?'

Quiet affirmatives rang in from the team by the tunnel exit, as well as teams stationed at the hidden entrance on each floor.

'Execute.'

At Warren's command the forced entry specialist next to him rammed a crowbar between the wooden slats. Warren cringed as the ancient panelling splintered, but there was no other choice; there was no telling if the original, exquisitely engineered mechanism still worked and they needed to preserve the element of surprise.

The panels swung out effortlessly.

The sound of repeated blows echoed from the floors above and below.

'The other entrances must still be blocked up,' said Sutton as he shone his torch into the dark space beyond.

'Well, that wasn't put there by Howard Langton,' remarked Warren as the light reflected off an aluminium ladder.

Sutton leaned into the shaft, looking down.

'Shit, we've found him.'

* * *

The rope had been tied around a support beam and was over a storey in length. Easily enough to snap Father Madden's neck.

An inspection of the entrance down by the old cloisters revealed it had been unblocked. That made it easier for the body recovery team to reach the dangling priest. Even then, somebody had to climb up the ladder to help ease him down to the officers. It had also made it easier for the killer to escape. The rope had been carefully cut either side of the knot; it looked suspiciously similar to a pile of coiled ropes that Warren remembered seeing in photos of the tool shed.

'There's no way that was suicide,' said Sutton. 'Madden was far too frail to hang off a ladder whilst hooking up a noose, then close that hidden panel and step off.'

'I think our killer is beyond trying to make it look like a real suicide,' said Warren. 'He knows that we know it's a murder. What's the betting that within those boxes of research there's a report of someone been found with a noose around their neck and a suicide note pinned to the abbey gates?'

'Shit. You know Rachel is going blame herself for this, don't you? She and her team have been ploughing through those old diaries looking for any hints of who the next target might be.'

'I'll speak to her, there's no way she could have foreseen this, and besides without her we'd have been blindly clambering into a dark hole, with no idea who or what awaited us.' He shuddered. 'Anyway, there was nothing on the Survivorsonline site to give us a clue who might be next, so knowing the probable method would have been little use.'

'I know one person who probably knew,' said Sutton darkly. 'I've a mind to go down there and arrest that arrogant bastard.'

'For what?'

'For knowing exactly who in this rotten place is a paedophile and therefore on the killer's list.'

'And charge him with what? Don't you think I've thought about this? I've even spoken to DSI Grayson about it.'

Sutton snorted. 'Oh, please. You know Grayson will never stick his neck out over this. He has three years to go and he wants one more promotion because he's still on the final salary pension scheme.'

'He won't stick his neck out, because the CPS will never let us charge. Arresting a revered Catholic bishop and demanding he breaks his oath? Christ, Tony, use your common sense. It'd be a career-ending move for everyone involved, right up to and including the Chief Constable.'

'Then maybe I'll just go down there and lock us both in his office until he tells us what he knows.' Sutton was breathing heavily, the anger radiating off him.

'Now you're just being silly.' Warren shook his head. 'Go home Tony. Get some sleep.'

Thursday 19th March

Chapter 74

Five hours of intermittent sleep was not enough. Nonetheless, Warren was back in at midday. Grayson had led the 8 a.m. briefing in Warren and Sutton's absence.

As Tony Sutton had predicted, Rachel Pymm had taken her failure to predict the latest killing personally and Warren's first job was to reassure her.

'Rachel, I've seen what you are dealing with. Photocopies of handwritten diaries in old-fashioned English, covered in Vernon Coombs' illegible notes.'

'It's all there though,' said Pymm. 'Father Nolan and Father Daugherty's deaths were just as described in the diaries.' She pushed across a pack of sheets. 'Now Father Madden's death is also here. Vernon Coombs spotted the link immediately.'

'Vernon Coombs spotted the link between Fathers Nolan and Daugherty and the historic killings after the deaths had taken place, he didn't predict them, nor did he predict the death of Father Madden,' said Warren firmly. 'On top of that, Simon Scrope confessed to both of those killings in his deathbed confession. He didn't survive long enough to name his other victims or describe how he killed them.'

Pymm didn't look satisfied. Warren continued.

'Without your research last night, I'd have been sending officers down a ladder into a darkened shaft, with no idea what was at the bottom. For all we knew, the killer could have been standing at the bottom with a knife, or a can of petrol. If nothing else, you saved us hours of waiting for a tactical response team to make the shaft secure, so we could get that poor man down and start collecting evidence.

'Vernon Coombs made studying the abbey his life's work. He didn't anticipate the deaths. I can't expect you to do in a few days what he couldn't do in years.'

Pymm let out a blast of air between her pursed lips. When she spoke, her voice was shaky.

'Then why am I doing this? If the best my team and I can do is help us find the victims after they've already been killed, then what are we contributing to this investigation? You'd have found them eventually. We just can't decipher his research fast enough.'

Warren waited before he said anything, allowing her to compose herself. He could see that she wasn't listening to him.

'What you are doing is vital work, we need your team's findings.'

'I just don't feel like a police officer anymore.' Her eyes were shining. 'Before I got ill, I loved being out there, chasing leads, interviewing suspects...' She broke off, her voice catching. 'When Mags and I interviewed Rodney Shaw, I suddenly realised how much I missed it. Damn it, I was *good* at my job, and now...' She gestured towards her crutches. 'I feel like an IT technician.' She sniffed.

Warren looked at her with concern. In the months since the detective sergeant had been assigned to Middlesbury, he had come to rely on her judgement and expertise. As the unit's 'officer in the case', she was the person in charge of keeping track of all the information flowing into the investigation and driving the HOLMES2 database. It was a job that had been performed in part by Gary Hastings, and before him by DS Pete Kent, and Pymm was proving to be at least their equal. In all that time, she'd never complained once. He knew that it was stress and fatigue that was making her voice her frustrations, but maybe he should have spotted the signs sooner. Had he even asked her how she felt about her place on the team, or had he just taken her for granted?

It was clear that he'd been pushing her too hard. He'd belatedly assigned a small team to assist her with processing the diaries, but should she even be involved to the extent she was? Doubtless she found it fascinating – he knew from speaking to her that she was an amateur history buff, and a long-term Middlesbury resident – but was it too much for her?

From the moment Pymm had been moved to the unit, she had brought a sense of fun and humour to a department that was still coming to terms with the loss of Gary Hastings. Her merciless teasing of fellow newcomer Moray Ruskin was matched by her willingness to give up her own time to teach him and anyone else tips and tricks for using the force's computer system and trawling the wider internet more efficiently.

She wasn't afraid to nag Warren and Sutton about their caffeine intake and how important it was to have a healthy diet, but always insisted her children bake two batches of anything they were trying out, bringing in the 'test run' to share with her colleagues.

But the pace of the last few days was taking its toll on her. Her eyes had dark smudges beneath them, and he had noticed that she seemed to be moving more slowly; most tellingly, she hadn't played a prank on Ruskin for weeks. Her husband had been right to castigate him for phoning her in the early hours of the morning.

'Rachel, you of all people know investigations don't work like that. A case like this generates thousands of leads, some of which are more important than others, many of which lead nowhere. But we have to investigate them all. What you are doing is an essential part of this investigation. Even if you don't discover that magic clue that solves the mystery, when the case comes to court, everything you've done has helped build that case.'

Pymm nodded, but she still didn't look convinced.

Warren steeled himself for what he knew was going to be an awkward conversation; but as her superior officer, he had to broach the subject.

'Rachel, I've noticed that you've been working a lot of overtime lately...'

'Don't even go there!' she snapped.

'I have to,' said Warren firmly. 'The well-being of my officers is an essential part of my job, and I have to make sure that you are all rested and taking care of yourselves.'

Pymm glared at the desktop, before finally her shoulders slumped.

'No, you're right, I am tired. We all are. Even Duracell Bunny Ruskin, is feeling it. You and Tony were up all night.' She motioned toward his coffee cup. 'I know that you are running on caffeine and adrenaline as well, because this case is so important...'

'And so are you,' said Warren as gently as he could. 'The last thing we need is for you to overdo it and go off sick.'

'I know my own limits,' insisted Pymm. Warren wasn't entirely sure he believed her, but what could he do? Pymm was stubborn. Probably even more stubborn than Tony Sutton. But then she had to be.

Warren was no expert on multiple sclerosis, although he'd made it his business to find out more about it since Pymm had joined his team. From what he knew from her personnel file and what information Occupational Health and Pymm herself had shared with him, Pymm had lived with the condition for several years. She had the relapsing-remitting form of the disease, meaning that she enjoyed long periods of relative remission, interrupted by unpredictable relapses, that could leave her unable to work for days or weeks. What caused the relapses was unclear, but Pymm had herself identified prolonged periods of stress as a potential trigger.

This was what worried Warren the most. But he knew there

was little point arguing with her. The tenacity that had kept her on the front-line of policing for years after her diagnosis, was the same obstinacy that meant she wouldn't let anyone dictate to her what she should be doing, her husband included, if that morning's phone call was anything to go by. Warren had learnt that it was best to trust her judgement.

Before her diagnosis, she had been a detective sergeant, working out of Welwyn. Although not yet in need of a wheelchair on a daily basis, over the past few years her mobility had steadily deteriorated to the point where a desk-based role was the best position for her. Keen to remain at the heart of investigations, she had undertaken additional training over several years to earn the necessary accreditations and develop the appropriate skills to become an 'officer in the case'.

When a vacancy had come up in Middlesbury, she had applied immediately. Not only was it more convenient for her, given that she lived locally, she liked working in small teams. Warren had been impressed with her from the moment she'd arrived at interview, and he'd been glad that John Grayson had agreed. Yet it was clear from what she had said that she still missed her old job. And from what he'd seen on the video of her interview of Rodney Shaw, she was good at it. When the case was all over, he vowed to have a proper heart-to-heart with her, and ask her what *she* wanted to do.

He found it hard to imagine the team without her now. He just hoped she didn't overdo it.

Chapter 75

'Lucas Furber was known to be obsessed with priests, Catholic priests in particular. A former friend of his claims, that he had been abused as a child along with another boy, name unknown. This boy had an older brother that Lucas Furber was reportedly trying to contact after reading that his friend had committed suicide on the London Underground. I want to know who this person was, who his brother is, and what school he went to.'

Warren had stopped by Ruskin's desk as he circled the office, catching up. Only a handful of hours had elapsed since he'd crawled home for a short sleep, yet it was as if he had been away for days. The HOLMES2 computer system was making links and generating leads for the ever-growing team to action at an ever-increasing pace, and he felt as though he was walking the wrong way on a conveyor belt.

Pymm had been right, everyone was struggling with the pace; even the seemingly indefatigable probationer looked tired. Nevertheless, the Scotsman practically jumped to attention.

'There are over hundred suicides on the London Underground each year, with a spike around the Christmas and New Year period.'

'Well, we know that Lucas Furber was 35 years old so that means he went to secondary school between about 1991 and

1998 if he stayed on to sixth form,' said Warren. 'Do we know what school he went to? They probably still have records of who attended which you could cross-reference with the records from the London Underground.'

'No, his first appearance on the PNC was several years after he left school.'

'OK, then you'll need to whittle down the suicides. We know he was male, so that gets rid of half the cases.'

'A bit less unfortunately, most suicides are male.'

Warren acknowledged the correction.

'Next, look at ages. Furber was 35. We don't know if his friend was the same age, so you'll need to play it safe and add five years either side, in case they were in different years.'

'Males aged thirty to forty. That hardly whittles it down, they're probably the biggest risk group for suicide.'

Warren clapped him on shoulder. 'Don't forget about the source of the information. He could have been confused about the year the accident happened. You know what it's like when the New Year rolls around and you keep on forgetting to write the new date.'

Ruskin groaned. 'A year either side?'

'I'd make it two.'

Chapter 76

Warren, Sutton, Deacon Baines and Bishop Fisher were in the bishop's office along with Deputy CSM Meera Gupta. A badly creased plan of the abbey grounds was spread across the bishop's desk.

'The architects drew this up when they were converting the house.' Baines pointed at the plan. Under instruction from Warren, he was careful not to touch it, just in case the killer had used that actual document. 'As you can see, some of the escape tunnels and the priest holes are marked.'

Warren compared the plans to the photocopied sheets that Rachel Pymm had discovered amongst Vernon Coombs' notes. 'The shaft that Father Madden was found in is on the plan, but the tunnel running through to the exit down by the old cloisters isn't.'

Baines looked apologetic. 'A full survey of the house and grounds would have been prohibitively expensive; we just blocked up the most obvious ones to make the house safe. It's possible that there are other tunnels that we don't know about.'

A team of CSIs had spent the past few hours searching the tunnels for evidence that they had been used to covertly access the house during the previous murders. So far they had found no indication that the killer had used them either to enter the home or smuggle

Fathers Nolan or Daugherty out. But did the killer know of routes that weren't on the plan? Again, Warren thought of Rodney Shaw. The man had been involved in the conversion of the house and been in charge of maintenance for years; if anyone knew about secret tunnels it would be him. Or, for that matter, anyone who had seen the ancient diaries and papers stored in the archives could also have stumbled across tunnels that weren't marked on the architects' plan. Could the killer have been helping Vernon Coombs do his research?

'Could people in the wider community have known about these tunnels?'

Baines pursed his lips in thought.

'The priest holes and escape tunnels weren't a secret. The local Middlesbury Historical Society and the Friends of Middlesbury Abbey have had tours of the house and the abbey grounds, I wouldn't be surprised if some of them requested a photocopy of the architects' plan. Obviously, English Heritage have a copy; I don't know if it's easily available via their website, but I'm sure you could contact them for one.' He gestured at the photocopied sheets on the table. 'As to this material... I don't know. We've always been quite open about letting researchers come and see the archives, as long as they were careful.'

'Do you keep a list of who requested access?'

'No, sorry.'

Warren suppressed a sigh; it had been a long shot.

They'd contact English Heritage to ask if anyone had requested a copy of the architects' plan recently, and they'd fingerprint the folder that the plan was kept in, but he didn't hold out much hope.

* * *

After leaving the retirement home, Warren drove straight over to the morgue. As he waited for Professor Jordan to come and meet him, he called Moray Ruskin to see how he was progressing.

'I have a list of twenty-eight possible identities for Lucas Furber's friend,' said Ruskin. 'Pretty much all of them committed suicide by jumping in front of a train. I kept in the three suicides by other means in case Peanut heard "suicide on the Underground" and just made assumptions,' said Ruskin.

'Good work. What do you propose doing next?' asked Warren.

'I was thinking of contacting the next of kin to see if they can tell us what school they went to. Then contacting their school and asking if they ever had either Lucas Furber or this suicide victim on their pupil roll.'

'Good work, Moray. I'll get DSI Grayson to authorise assistance from Welwyn to speed things up.'

He put his phone away as Jordan approached. He was already in surgical scrubs.

'We really must stop meeting like this, Warren.' The attempt at humour fell flat.

Warren agreed; he'd been to more autopsies linked to this case than he'd been to during his previous three years at Middlesbury combined. He still didn't like the smell. After swapping his street clothes for protective attire, he joined the American-born pathologist.

'First of all, general health of the subject.' Jordan dictated into his microphone.

Warren had asked for the fastest possible turnaround in this instance. Jordan had been willing to oblige, but pointed out that the quickest way to get results would be for him to relay them directly to Warren as he performed his dissection.

Warren had tried to hide his reluctance as he agreed.

'I've already weighed the deceased's major organs and performed a gross examination. The subject is 178 centimetres in height, and seventy-two kilograms in weight, with musculature indicative of a sedentary life-style. Skeletal X-rays show signs of arthritis and significant wear on the ball of the left femur, consistent with the need for a hip replacement

'Brain is of average weight and appearance, and his lungs

are clean and apparently healthy. Heart is of expected size with moderate plaque formation within the coronary arteries although not enough to have contributed to death. The liver presents signs of the early stages of alcoholic cirrhosis.'

'He was known to be a bit of a drinker,' said Warren.

'More than a bit, I'd say. There was a fair amount of whiskey in his stomach.'

Warren recalled that Sutton had reported that Madden was in the habit of retiring early and reading. He wondered if that was a cover for his drinking.

'What about cause of death?'

'Strangulation.'

'Not hangman's fracture? The drop was long enough.'

'No. And he didn't drop.'

'What do you mean?'

Ryan pointed towards Madden's throat.

'Look at the colour of these marks. You can see that these abrasions can only have been made if the heart was still pumping blood. The rubbing is consistent with a rough, hemp rope, of the type found around his neck. I've also found these.' Warren leant closer. Within the rubbed, angry looking flesh, Warren saw tiny cuts, with traces of dried blood.

Jordan rolled back the eyelids, pointing out the pinprick haemorrhages on the whites of the eyeball.

'Petechiae, indicating strangulation.'

'What's your interpretation, Ryan?'

'I think that he had a bladed instrument, such as a knife or scalpel, held against his throat, perhaps to make him more compliant. The blade was sharp enough to break the skin, hence the cuts. He then had a noose placed around his neck, and he was hoisted up, dying slowly through strangulation.'

'And he was definitely killed where he was found?'

'I can't see any evidence from the patterns of livor mortis to suggest that he was moved after death.'

'What about drugs?'

'His stomach contained a substantial amount of alcohol, but I found no pill fragments or other evidence of ingested drugs. Obviously, we'll need a blood toxicology report to be certain.'

Given recent events, it came as no surprise.

Another murder.

Friday 20th March

Chapter 77

They say that a murder investigation is more of a marathon than a sprint, but Warren had always thought that was an over-simplification. It was true in the sense that even if you arrested the culprit at the scene of the crime – literally with blood on their hands – there was still a long slog to the finishing line in the dock of the crown court. But unlike a marathon, the pace in a murder investigation varied continuously. There were no pace-setters holding his team back to prevent them running out of energy before the finish line and no cheering crowds helping them push on when the end seemed a million miles away. And aside from the odd CSI, nobody was dressed as a Teletubby.

At 8 a.m., three weeks to the day that Father Cormac Nolan had been drugged then set alight, the pace was closer to a sprint than a jog. There were now three confirmed killings at the abbey, as well as the suspicious death of Lucas Furber. The whiteboard, and Rachel Pymm's hi-tech equivalent, HOLMES2, were filled with different threads; hundreds of data points linked the four separate killings and the sophisticated computer system was generating hundreds of 'actions' for officers to deal with.

Beyond the walls of Middlesbury CID's briefing room, the number of officers working on the investigation was increasing day by day, hour by hour. It was one of the few times that Warren didn't resent his DSI's absence. He knew that DSI Grayson's continual presence at headquarters was smoothing the requests for more resources that Warren and his team were continually making, as well as deflecting, reducing and absorbing the heat and scrutiny the murders were generating.

The latest press conference to formally announce the death of Father Madden and update the public on the progress in the other killings wasn't scheduled until later that morning, and even Grayson wasn't looking forward to it. There had been no disguising the heightened police presence at the abbey the previous day and the official response that there had been 'a suspicious death' in the abbey had done nothing to quell the rumours and speculation. The slaying of retired priests – not to mention the apparent attempts to hide their true nature by dressing them up as suicides – had captured the imagination of the public and the investigation was front page news, not only nationally, but internationally, with wall-to-wall coverage online and in the broadcast media. The press office had taken the unusual step of bringing more staff in to deal with record numbers of queries; additional officers had also been deployed to keep reporters and other nosey parkers out of the abbey grounds.

Immediately after the press conference, Grayson was travelling to London for a meeting with senior church officials, top brass from both Hertfordshire Constabulary and the Home Office and, rumour had it, the Home Secretary herself. Good luck to him, thought Warren. Hopefully, the team would have some more progress for him to share with them.

'Where are we in tracking down the person who copied the keys to the chapel and the undercroft?' asked Warren.

'We know approximately what time the killer went to the locksmith and what time he picked up his keys. Unfortunately, the taxi drivers cannot recall anything about the fare, and it was paid in cash.' Mags Richardson took a swig from her water bottle.

'However, both times the fare was picked up and dropped at Stonehill Mews on the west side of town. I'm liaising with traffic to see if there are any other cameras out that way that may have picked up the suspects' car.'

'Good, keep at it.'

'Rachel, how are your team getting on with Coombs' notes?'

'I've been looking through them to see if I can find who helped him compile his work. I've not found any direct acknowledgements, but I did find a sort of to-do list.'

'What does it say?'

'Mostly lots of guff about things he needs to find out, but there was this one entry…' She pushed a photocopy across the desk and pointed to an entry scrawled in Coombs' familiar, slanted scrawl. 'Buy Fr GB a pint to say thanks.'

'Fr GB?' asked Ruskin.

'Gabriel Baines?' suggested Sutton.

'Great find, Rachel, he's already on our list. If nothing else, he may be able to tell us who else worked with Coombs.'

'Moray, what have you got?'

'Two things. First of all, I've got a reply from one of Lucas Furber's Facebook friends, and you'll never guess where he went to school.' Moray Ruskin was flushed with excitement. He didn't wait for Warren or anyone else to guess. 'The Venerable Thomas Tichborne School for Boys.'

'That's the school that Father Wilfred Dodd was "retired" from when it closed down,' said Sutton.

'Which explains why Lucas Furber was so upset. He told Peanut that "the bastard's already dead". Wilfred Dodd died of leukaemia back in 2012,' said Warren. 'Excellent work, Moray. Do you have the pupil rolls for Thomas Tichborne?'

'It closed down, so I'm awaiting an email from the Department for Education. Maybe they can point us in the right direction.'

'What else have you got?'

'I've been liaising with the social media team as they sift through the Survivorsonline website. They've found a reference to Father Madden, but there's no way they could have found it before his death by just searching using the keywords we had at that time. Father Madden was known to work as a school chaplain at Blessèd Mary Primary School. Doing a search for the name of the school returned a single exchange.' Ruskin picked up his iPad and started to read.

'In April 2013, somebody posted a thread saying, "there was a right dodgy priest at my old primary school, Blessed Mary. He used to get drunk and make you sit on his knee and read him Bible stories. Don't know if he ever did anything else but it was creepy as fuck. I was too young to work out what was going on then, but I know now he had a hard-on all the time. He did it for donkey's years. They shipped him off to some place out of harm's way in the end."'

'Bugger. There are none of our search terms there at all,' said Warren. 'Have we got the complete records for the residents of Saint Cecil's from the diocese yet?'

'I believe it is one of the things DSI Grayson is going to bring up in his meeting this afternoon,' said Pymm.

'Get the social media team to use their past places of work as keywords for their search.'

'Any luck with that warrant to release the website's server logs and archives?' asked Pymm. 'It'll make things a lot easier for IT if they can run the data through their own search engines instead of relying on the website's own crappy algorithms.'

'Not to mention how useful it will be if they can attach IP addresses to some of those usernames,' said Sutton.

'We've got the warrant, but they haven't been able to serve it, since the service provider is based in Bulgaria,' said Ruskin.

'Not a surprise,' grunted Sutton.

'I imagine there's nothing on the PNC?' asked Warren.

'No, and I've a negative from local forces in the areas where he worked. It looks as though as far as the police were concerned, Madden was flying under the radar.'

'Assuming he was guilty of the allegations,' cautioned Warren. 'Let's not forget that Father Daugherty was falsely accused, and Father Madden wasn't actually named directly on the site. It might not even have been him, there's no date given as to when the alleged offences took place.'

'Should we visit the school and find out if anyone knew anything?' asked Sutton.

Warren thought for a moment. It was the obvious next step. If nothing else, they owed it to Father Madden to find out if he really was targeted for his alleged past actions, or an entirely innocent victim. They might even find a suspect.

However, after their argument the previous day, he was reluctant to send Tony Sutton before they had a chance to talk. The man was tired and grumpy; Warren wanted someone with a bit more tact.

'Good idea. Hutch, fancy a day out?'

'I'll fetch my Thermos from the car.'

'Whilst Hutch is visiting Blessed Mary Primary School, I want Tony to supervise a team looking for overlap between these three victims and the late Father Dodd. So far, we know that all four priests had spells as school chaplains within the Herts and Essex diocese, and all of them were "retired" by Bishop Fisher, who may or may not have been aware of their behaviour through confession. Our killer is likely using Survivorsonline, but are there other connections?'

If Sutton perceived Warren asking Hutchinson to go and visit the school, rather than him, as a slight, he gave no sign of it.

'Did the men's lives previously overlap before this?' continued Warren. 'I'm going to look into authorising warrants to demand pupil rolls and staff records for all of the schools and institutions involved. Let's see if any individuals crop up more than once.

'I'm also going to speak to DSI Grayson about getting the Sexual Exploitation Unit involved. We need any of their intelligence that isn't on the wider HOLMES system or the PNC. The nightmare scenario is that there's some sort of paedophile ring operating here.'

With the meeting finished, everyone scurried off to their assigned jobs. Sutton sidled up alongside David Hutchinson.

'They're slippery buggers, Hutch. Don't let them wriggle out of giving you the information you want.'

'Noted, Tony.'

Warren looked at Sutton's back as he left and suppressed a sigh. They really needed that talk.

Chapter 78

Forensics from Father Madden's murder were coming in. Headquarters at Welwyn had sent additional CSI teams to supplement those already working at the abbey and in the retirement home.

Rachel Pymm had taken a break from supervising the team reading through Vernon Coomb's photocopied notes to enter the data into the computer as it flowed in. Already, the rope used to hang him had been identified as of the same brand as two other coils of rope found in the abbey's tool shed, although there was no way to determine if that was significant or a coincidence.

'Luckily for you, though not so lucky for those of us working down there, the escape tunnel is partly flooded.' Gupta's voice came through clearly over the briefing room speakerphone.

'That's left us with some clear footprints leading to and from the entrance to the priest hole and Father Madden's room. Unfortunately, the impressions don't match any of the prints we already have on file from this case. Size ten men's work boots.'

'Well, we still have both pairs of Rodney Shaw's work boots in evidence, so if it was him, he's wearing a third pair,' said Sutton.

'There is more though,' the CSI continued. 'These mysterious boot prints match impressions around the outside entrance to the escape tunnel, suggesting that the killer may have entered the house through the unblocked tunnel entrance.'

'Which makes sense,' agreed Warren.

'The problem is that we can't find any prints leading away from the tunnel entrance.'

'It was raining that night, could the marks have been washed away?' asked Sutton.

'Quite possibly. But there are other inconsistencies.'

'Go on.'

'In the corridor outside Father Madden's room, there is a mess of footprints, suggesting the killer walked between the priest hole and his room several times. There is also mud on the rungs of the ladder, and some small spots of blood, which fits with the narrative that the killer entered the escape tunnel, climbed the ladder, then entered Father Madden's room. The killer then led Madden, probably at knifepoint, back to the priest hole and made him climb down the ladder. There are black cotton fibres on the ladder, matching the black cotton shirt that Father Madden was wearing. The only fingerprints that we have found on the ladder are the deceased's.'

'Could Father Madden have actually climbed down that ladder? He was waiting for a new hip,' asked Sutton.

'I asked Professor Jordan, and he said that it would have been very painful and slow going, but if he was in fear for his life, then yes, it was probably possible.'

'You said that the killer walked between Father Madden's room and the priest hole several times,' said Warren. 'This scenario only needs two trips there. Do we know if the suicide note was written in Father Madden's room and left behind before he was taken down the ladder, or if it was written down in the escape tunnel? That would account for at least one more trip.'

'There might be trace evidence on the suicide note that can answer that question, but don't get your hopes up, Forensic Document Analysis are still trying to match Father Madden's handwriting samples to the note. There is another potential suggestion, but Andy and I can't decide what we think. It does fit with the lack of footprints at the tunnel exit.' Gupta sounded a bit unsure.

'Go ahead, I'm all ears.'

'One set of footprints looks as though it might be heading down the corridor, away from Father Madden's room, in the opposite direction to the priest hole. It's unclear, and the print is badly smeared. There is also only one pair of prints.'

Warren tried to visualise it in his mind's eye, but struggled.

'What's your interpretation?'

'The killer returned from the priest hole and then started to walk down the corridor. The footprints end because the killer took the boots off.'

Warren saw the implication immediately.

'Which suggests that the killer didn't exit by the tunnel, but headed back into the house.'

'Jesus, were they still in the house when we arrived?' finished Sutton.

Chapter 79

Primary schools had certainly changed since Detective Sergeant David Hutchinson had attended one. Or his kids had, for that matter. Signing in at the reception desk, he caught glimpses of brightly-coloured corridors through the reinforced glass partition that separated the warm, loving environment of Blessed Mary, from the dangers of the outside world. The faint sound of children singing drifted to his ears. He placed the laminated visitor's badge around his neck.

'Sorry to keep you, officer, Mr Morris will see you in his office. I'll get the duty students to take you down there.'

On cue, an earnest looking boy and girl, about 10 years old, appeared. The green lanyard for his badge signalled that he had undergone enhanced DBS checks as a police officer, and could therefore be trusted to walk to the head's office, escorted by a child. A sad reflection of the times, Hutchinson mused, although if today's tighter precautions had existed a few years ago, they might not be in the current mess.

The hallways seemed a lot smaller than he recalled, but the echoing squeak of his rubber-soled shoes took him right back; the smell from the kitchens was a lot more pleasant than he remembered.

Eventually they arrived at Morris' office. The two children politely wished him well and headed back to reception. Hutchinson wondered if the well-scrubbed youngsters were typical of the school's pupils or if they were selected especially for the role. Thinking back to his own school days, he doubted he would have been top of the list when choosing who visitors should first meet.

Linford Morris was a trim-looking man with a neat beard, flecked with grey.

'I see you also worship the Toons,' noted Hutchinson, nodding towards a Newcastle United flag that was at least as large as the image of the Virgin Mary beside it.

'It's part of my penance, for my past sins. When we converted to an Academy last year, I did suggest renaming ourselves St James' Park Academy, but some philistine said that people would get confused with the London Underground station.'

'The apostrophe's in the wrong place,' said Hutchinson.

'Well what can I help you with DS Hutchinson? I doubt you've come here to commiserate over our team's poor performance.'

'Father Frank Madden.'

Morris' eyes narrowed.

'Yes, he was our school chaplain for a number of years, until he retired, back in 2011, if I recall. What about him?'

'It's not yet public knowledge, however he has passed away.'

Morris paled.

'He wasn't… you know…?'

'I'm not at liberty to discuss the specifics as yet, but the death is suspicious.'

'Good Lord.'

'I wonder if you might have any thoughts about Father Madden's death?'

Hutchinson watched the man carefully.

Morris picked up a pen on his desk and inspected it, before replacing it in exactly the same spot. His words were similarly precise.

'Father Madden was highly regarded and much-loved by the many staff and children that have passed through our school in the twenty-odd years that he was school chaplain.'

'I see. Do you know why Father Madden retired? He was still relatively young.'

'I believe that he was suffering from some mental health issues.'

'Can you elaborate any more on those issues?'

'I'm afraid not, I wasn't a party to those discussions.' He paused. 'Could his death have anything to do with his mental health problems?'

Was that a note of hope in his tone? Although it was now common knowledge that Fathers Nolan and Daugherty had been murdered, rather than committing suicide, it was possible that Morris wasn't aware of that development. As yet, nothing had been released to the press about the link to child abuse, but doubtless speculation was rife on social media. If Morris was aware of any unreported allegations about Father Madden, he might be worried that they could be a trigger for murder. It was small wonder he was hoping for a suicide due to unrelated mental health issues.

'I'm afraid that I can't comment on the specifics of the case yet,' said Hutchinson.

He chose his next words carefully.

'Were you aware of any allegations of inappropriate behaviour by Father Madden.'

Morris spread his hands, an unconscious attempt to give the appearance of openness. Hutchinson wasn't fooled.

'There were no allegations of inappropriate behaviour from any of our children, or their parents towards Father Madden.'

'That wasn't exactly what I asked, Mr Morris.'

Hutchinson settled back in his chair and waited. He could see that Morris was conflicted. On the one hand, he had the reputation of his school to consider. But on the other hand, he was clearly uncomfortable about lying to protect that.

'As I said, there were never any allegations made to me, or

the governing body, by students, past or present, or their parents about Father Madden's behaviour.'

'But?'

'It was well known that Father Madden liked a drink. And that on occasion he may have been under the influence of alcohol in school. Now and then, his words might be a bit slurred, and a couple of times he nodded off in assembly – although to be fair, when you've sat through year two singing "Oh Little Town of Bethlehem" every Christmas for the past twenty-odd years...' The man smiled weakly. Hutchinson remained impassive.

'Anyway, one of our staff felt that Father Madden was a little too familiar with some of the children. He would sometimes sit them on his knee when they were reading to him. He came to me and expressed his concern.'

'What did you do, Mr Morris?'

Morris paused.

'You see, what you have to realise was that nobody ever complained and nobody ever saw him touch a child. I mean it was probably completely innocent. Father Madden had been a priest for decades. That sort of behaviour was perfectly normal back when he started.'

'So what did you do?'

'I had a quiet word with him. Explained that times had changed, and that he needed to be more careful – to protect himself, if nothing else.'

'What was his response?'

'He was very embarrassed, obviously.'

'And was that the end of the matter?'

Morris sighed.

'Unfortunately, no. A few weeks later, a different member of staff also came to see me. He said that Father Madden had clearly been the worse for wear during a practice for the year six confirmation mass. One of the little boys was not a very confident reader and was very nervous. Father Madden suggested that he

401

went and practised his reading with him on his own. When the teacher went to fetch him a little later, he was sitting on Father Madden's knee.

'I get the impression that the two teachers may have spoken about it, and one may have encouraged the other to come and see me, but I don't think that matters.' Morris picked up the pen again, and carried on scrutinising it as he continued speaking.

'Sometimes, you just know. My two colleagues are very experienced teachers, and neither of them had any grudge against Father Madden. I went to the head of governors and we spoke at length.

'Neither teacher had witnessed Father Madden actually touch a child inappropriately, nor had we had any complaints. In our opinion, there were no grounds to involve the police.'

Hutchinson forced himself to remain quiet.

'In the end, we decided to ask the diocese for advice. I had specifically told Father Madden not to be so tactile, so he had deliberately ignored my instructions. Furthermore, it was clear that he needed help with his drinking. Bishop Fisher himself spoke to Father Madden and within a couple of weeks, he announced his retirement.'

Chapter 80

Warren had had enough of Tony Sutton's negativity towards the church. Sutton had been snide and down-right dismissive from the moment he met Bishop Fisher. Warren had no worries at all that these feelings were in anyway impairing Tony Sutton's ability to do his job; the man was far too experienced for that to happen. However, it didn't look professional, especially in front of junior officers. His comments to David Hutchinson at morning briefing were not in themselves a cause for concern, but Warren's discussion with Susan earlier that week before was still on his mind.

Warren could understand a dismissive attitude towards a religious institution if the man was an atheist. Perhaps even if he was of a different faith, although in Warren's experience truly religious people tended to be generally tolerant of others' differing beliefs. Yet Sutton was a religious man who went to church each Sunday. Warren knew that Sutton wasn't a Catholic, but why the attitude? As far as Warren knew, his friend's background was squarely English – there were no hints of Irish or Scottish ancestry that might have left a sectarian outlook. What was the issue?

As his direct line manager, Warren could just have him in the office for a chat. He could even put him on a warning, but

Warren already felt bruised over their previous encounter over his supposed treatment of Moray Ruskin. Warren wasn't sure that his protective attitude towards the probationary constable was unduly influenced by Gary's death, but it had taken a lot of backbone for Sutton to stand up to him the way he did, and Warren felt he owed the man the same.

Warren looked at his watch. It was getting on for lunchtime. He'd seen Sutton place his insulated lunch box on his desk when he'd come in that morning, but he knew it wouldn't take much to persuade him to ditch the healthy sandwiches his wife had been forcing him to eat and join Warren for something more substantial.

That decided, Warren slipped his jacket on and headed towards Sutton's cubicle.

'What can I do for you, boss?'

Sutton was busy at his computer, working his way through an email inbox that looked almost as full as Warren's.

'Fancy a working lunch, Tony?'

'Sounds good, I need to do something a bit different.' Sutton grabbed his lunchbox.

'My treat.'

'Now you're talking,' said Sutton, placing his sandwiches back on his desk.

The two men headed towards the lift.

A fine drizzle had started and the two men had to jog towards Warren's car.

Sutton was out of breath, but it didn't stop him commenting on Warren's choice of radio station as soon as he started the engine.

'Seriously, Chief? Absolute 80s? You're 41. Have you still got all those dodgy compilation CDs? What were they called, "Guilty Pleasures"?'

'Stop fiddling with that glove box, or you're walking in the rain,' ordered Warren.

'The offer still stands for me to educate your ear. Just say the word and the next time you and Susan come around, Marie and I will help the pair of you.'

'Tony, you celebrated your forty-seventh birthday a month ago and yet you still listen to the chart show. I bet even Moray has grown out of Radio One. Does Josh know that his old man is so "down with the yoof"? What do his university mates think of him having such a cool dad?'

'With all due respect, sir – piss off.'

Warren laughed. It felt good to be away from the office. And Tony was right, it was about time the four of them got together for a meal. He made a mental note to arrange a date as soon as the pace of their current case slowed.

Indicating left, he pulled into the car park of the Albion. A chain pub, it still had a good menu. Even on a Friday lunchtime, it was quiet and the two men were able to find a secluded table where they wouldn't be disturbed.

'Well, if I'm going to break my diet, I may as well do it properly,' announced Sutton as he ordered the gourmet burger and chips, with onion rings. Warren ordered the same, along with two halves of lager.

The two men made small talk until their drinks arrived. Sutton's son Josh was preparing for his final university exams and thinking about going into teaching. Warren offered to ask Susan if she could arrange a bit of work-shadowing.

After raising his glass in a silent toast, Sutton took a mouthful, wiped his mouth with the back of his hand and replaced his drink on the table.

'So, why are we here? What couldn't you discuss back at the station?'

Sutton was the sort of man that appreciated the direct approach, so Warren decided not to prevaricate.

'What do you have against Bishop Fisher and the Catholic Church in general?'

Sutton took another mouthful of beer.

'I don't know what you mean.'

'Why have you been so snide about Bishop Fisher's reluctance to discuss what has been said to him in confession?'

'You know why. I don't agree with the notion that religious beliefs put a person above the law.'

'How do you mean?'

'I don't think that a person should be able to commit a crime, go to confession, and be absolved of all wrong doing.'

'So you don't believe in confession and the forgiveness of sins?'

'No, I believe in that completely. I believe that God forgives the truly repentant, but I don't accept that such a confession should then spare the guilty from repercussions on Earth. And even if I did accept that, why is it only open to members of that particular religion? Why should members of a particular faith be shielded from their actions? Isn't the law the same for all?'

'But they aren't shielded from their actions. They are still responsible for them in a court of law.'

'I'm not just talking about the sinner, I'm talking about the priest that hears the confession. I fundamentally disagree with the idea that a priest can withhold information that others would have to disclose. Even legal privilege or medical confidentiality doesn't go that far. If a lawyer or a doctor hears about a crime, or a planned crime, they have to disclose. If a pupil comes to Susan in confidence and tells her about abuse – either to them or someone else – Susan is required by law to pass that information on. This so-called "seal of the confessional" is morally wrong when it seeks to circumvent those protections.'

Sutton was voicing many of the arguments that Warren had himself considered, some of which he had even put to Fisher. But Sutton's vehemence seemed out of proportion. They were police officers; they spent half of their working lives trying to persuade people to give up secrets that they would rather not. Why was he so angered by this situation?

'The seal of the confessional is surely there to encourage the

406

penitent to confess fully, to face up to what they have done,' said Warren. 'If they thought that the person hearing their confession was going to tell everyone what they had just heard, then they wouldn't tell them everything. Isn't part of the reason for people confessing their sins that because facing up to our failings is the first step to overcoming them?' Warren was playing Devil's Advocate to a degree, but he felt he needed to probe deeper to understand his friend's anger.

'Yes, that I agree with.' Sutton took another sip of his drink. When he started talking again, his voice was quieter, more reflective.

'You know my history. I started going to church again after my divorce from Angela. One of the first things I did was sit down with the vicar and confess everything. I told him about the affair that destroyed our marriage. I told him about my failings before then as a husband, and as a father, and I told him about the things I still did that I was ashamed of.

'The longer I spoke to him, the more I found myself revealing. I was uncovering things that I'd kept hidden even from myself. Things that I needed to address before I could move on and be a better dad to Josh and a better person to his mother. And later, a better husband to Marie.'

'But could you have done that if you thought the vicar would tell other people what you had just told him?' asked Warren.

Sutton thought about it before he answered.

'Perhaps not. But the point is that nothing I told him was illegal. I was confessing to being an arsehole, not a bloody child molester. Priests should not be given immunity from legally obtained warrants. If a magistrate has deemed our line of enquiry legitimate, then we should be able to insist that a priest answers questions in the same way that anyone else does.'

'But nobody is compelled to answer our questions. Suspects always have the right to remain silent,' Warren pointed out.

'Which the jury is allowed to interpret as they see fit. Besides which, it goes back to what I said before about being compelled to disclose knowledge of a crime. If a priest knows of a crime – especially one such as child abuse – then they must report it to the authorities. Failure to do so should result in prosecution, the same as with any other person in a position of trust. End of.'

Warren's reply was interrupted by the arrival of their food.

'What makes this a "gourmet burger"?' asked Sutton, after the server had left.

Warren recognised the attempt to change the topic and decided to park the discussion for the time being.

'I think it's the wooden stick holding it together,' he suggested, as he set about dismantling the construction. He'd given up asking for burgers without garnish years ago; it was fifty-fifty at best that they'd pay any attention to his instruction. He'd found through long experience that if he then complained, it simply meant that he ended up sitting without any food for ten minutes, watching everyone else eat, as his meal disappeared back into the kitchen, only for the same burger to return with the lettuce and tomato removed, and most of the mayonnaise scraped off. He may as well do that himself; at least his food would still be hot by the time he ate it. Besides which, Susan liked salad, and he usually passed it over.

'Help yourself to my lettuce, Tony. I've seen how much you enjoy those healthy lunches Marie has been making for you.'

It was hard to be entirely sure what Sutton mumbled through his mouthful of burger, but it sounded suspiciously like 'bugger off'.

* * *

With lunch over, the two men ordered coffee. To Warren's surprise, Sutton ordered decaffeinated.

'Marie's been nagging me to cut down for ages, I thought I'd give it a go now and again. See if it stops the palpitations and acid indigestion.'

408

'You should probably get that looked at,' said Warren, ordering a cup himself. It couldn't hurt, he supposed.

'Nah, I've always had it; eating and sleeping at odd times and too much caffeine.'

'Well, Rachel Pymm will be delighted,' said Warren.

Sutton scowled. 'If you say a word to her, the track list for DCI Warren Jones' "Guilty Pleasures" will be emailed to the whole team.'

Warren laughed, before falling quiet again. As they'd eaten, Warren had mulled over what his friend had said. On the surface, it rang true. Sutton was one of the most fair-minded people that Warren knew. It was well within character for him to be affronted by the apparent double-standard that allowed a person hearing confession to abrogate their legal and moral responsibility to report crimes of which they were aware. Even worse was the implication that a penitent could make a full and frank confession of the most heinous of crimes, safe in the knowledge that their confessor would take that knowledge to their own grave.

Like Sutton, Warren believed that whilst absolution could be granted in the eyes of God, it did not absolve the sinner of any Earthly punishment. When he judged the mood was right, he said as much.

By now, Sutton was more relaxed. The fire had gone; but Warren wasn't convinced that he had got to the bottom of the other man's anger. Eventually, he said so.

Sutton sat back and let out a huff of air. For a moment, Warren thought the man was going to walk out. But eventually his shoulders slumped.

'Hell, if I can't tell you...'

He paused.

'You know that I'm a born-again, right?'

'Yes, of course.'

'And that I attend St Peter's, the Anglican Church on Parson's Lane.'

'Yes.'

'Well, I wasn't always. Anglican I mean.'

'What do you mean?'

'I was born a Catholic.'

'Oh. I had no idea.'

'Well you wouldn't, unless you look right back in my personnel file and see that I attended Cardinal Manning Roman Catholic comprehensive.'

'I can't say I've ever looked.' Warren could see that the other man was clearly wrestling with something deeply personal.

'When I was there… things… happened to some of the kids.'

'Oh, Christ, you weren't…'

'No, thank God. My old man was a copper, remember. He and his mates would have been right round and beaten nine shades of shit out of them, then made sure that there was no evidence they were even there. But I heard of things happening to kids that I knew. One of them was a bit more forthright than some of the others and he openly claimed that he'd been touched inappropriately by one of his English teachers, Mr Benson.

'To be honest, we never thought Benson liked boys, because he creeped the girls out so much, but anyway, this lad wasn't having any of it. He went right to the headmaster, a monk by the name of Brother Carmichael, and told him what had happened.'

'Then what?'

'I never found out exactly what happened in that office, but all I know is that we never saw the kid again.'

'He disappeared?' Warren was shocked.

Sutton laughed mirthlessly. 'Nothing that dramatic. He was expelled. Two days later, the headmaster gave an assembly on how lying was one of the deadly sins and how bearing false witness could ruin the lives of good men and women. He never mentioned the kid by name of course, but we all knew who he meant. And all the way through it, I remember this look of smug satisfaction on the face of that bastard English teacher. He'd gotten away with it. At the end of the assembly, as we filed out the hall, I looked back and saw Benson being patted on the back. One of the maths teachers even gave him a hug. It was as if he was the victim.

'So there you go, lesson learnt. They look after their own.'

Sutton drained his coffee in one gulp, before continuing, a look of grim satisfaction on his face.

'Of course, the fucker couldn't keep himself out of trouble. Ten years later, he was jailed for molesting his own nephew. He did it from when the kid was six until he turned fourteen and finally told his mum. The bastard even called Brother Carmichael as a character witness, for all the good it did him. Nothing was ever said about the allegations from school – even if anyone did bring them up, I imagine they'd be classed as hearsay and ruled inadmissible – but at least justice of a sort was done.'

'And that was why you left the church?'

'Yeah, pretty much. I stopped going the moment I left school. Later, when I realised something was missing from my life, I couldn't bring myself to go back to the Catholic Church, so I joined the Church of England. It's pretty much the same, to be honest, but with different hymns and some of the vicars wear frocks outside church as well as when they are at the pulpit.'

Warren smiled at the man's attempt at humour.

'But you must realise that the seal of the confessional holds true in other religious faiths, not just Catholicism? And that the Church of England has its own dirty secrets.'

'Yeah. Doesn't mean I have to like it though.'

A thought suddenly struck Warren.

'Tony, what was the name of that kid you went to school with?'

Sutton smiled.

'I'm ahead of you there. He died about eight years ago from throat cancer. And before you ask, Brother Carmichael died in

1990 and Mr Benson has been pushing up the daisies since 1996. I cross-referenced the residents of the retirement home with priests that worked at my old school, and there were no hits.'

'Oh well, worth a try. It would have been a hell of a coincidence, don't you think?'

Chapter 81

By late evening, the suspect column on the whiteboard had a new name.

'Deacon Gabriel Baines. Bishop Fisher's right-hand man, and the self-described business manager for the retirement home.' Rachel Pymm gesticulated with a laser pointer as she spoke.

'We started looking at him seriously, when it became obvious that many of the reasons why Rodney Shaw is our prime suspect could also be applied to Baines.'

She took a sip of water.

'Baines was born in 1956. After a degree in business from Durham university, he took up a position at Merkitt's Bakery a family-owned company, eventually being promoted to the board. Along the way, he married Erica, the daughter – and heir – of the company's founder.

'In addition to his work on the board, Gabriel Baines became increasingly involved in his local church. Obviously, as a married man, he couldn't become a Catholic priest, so he became a deacon, and was ordained in 1997.

'Because of his experience in business, including seeing Merkitt's through a rather rocky patch during the Nineties' recession, he volunteered his services to help sort out the finances of his local parish. It was then that he first met Bishop Fisher.'

'When was that?' asked Sutton.

'Probably about 1999 or 2000.'

'Before the opening of the retirement home then?'

'Yes. That didn't open until 2004, and it was by working with Baines that Fisher was able to put together a financially sound proposal to both the diocese and English Heritage.'

'So Baines has been a part of the home since the very beginning,' stated Warren.

'In which case, it's quite plausible that he knows all about Fisher's little secret, and probably knows which of the residents have a murky past,' said Hutchinson. He'd already filled the team in on the details he'd uncovered about Father Madden.

'OK, I get that, but why now? And why the parallels with the original sixteenth-century murders?' asked Sutton.

'As to why now, it could have been a long time in the planning,' said Pymm, 'or perhaps he only found out the identity of those priests relatively recently. In terms of parallels with the original murders, don't forget I found a suggestion in the notes left behind by Vernon Coombs that he was one of the people that helped him research the abbey's past. Whatever he found, it was enough for Coombs to make a note that he needed to buy him a pint to say thanks.'

'It's still a bit circumstantial,' said Sutton.

'I agree, but he may have form in this area,' said Warren. 'Rachel, do you want to continue?'

'In 2003, his father-in-law, the owner of Merkitt's Bakery, died. His wife had passed away some years previously, which meant that the company went to his only child, Baines' wife.'

'Are we suggesting that Baines killed his father-in-law to get his company?' Sutton.

'No. The old man died after his third heart attack in as many years. He was a chain-smoker, overweight and rather too fond

414

of a drink. There was nothing suspicious about his death at all. However, his daughter was grief-stricken and less than a year later, she did die suspiciously.'

'How?' asked Hutchinson.

'An overdose of prescribed sleeping pills, washed down with whiskey. Baines came home late after midnight mass. He said his wife was already asleep in bed. It wasn't until he tried to wake her Christmas morning that he realised she was dead.'

A ripple went around the room.

'Pills and booze. Sounds familiar,' said Sutton.

'What did the coroner say?' asked Hutchinson.

'Inconclusive. There was insufficient evidence to rule whether she deliberately took an overdose or did so by accident. Mrs Baines was known to be having trouble sleeping, and had been depressed since the death of her father, who she was very close to. That Christmas would have been the first one without him.

'On top of that, her marriage to Gabriel Baines was known to be strained, in part due to her excessive drinking. There was some tittle tattle that he may have been growing a little too close to one of his parishioners, but that was never confirmed.

'Rumour has it that he had been trying to get her to attend marriage counselling, but she was reluctant to speak to their priest. Despite her husband's position within the church, she wasn't known to be especially religious, and she had openly scoffed at the idea of marriage counselling from an avowed celibate.'

'What happened to the company?' asked Sutton.

'They had no children, and Mrs Baines herself was an only child, so Gabriel Baines inherited the lot. Six months later, he sold the whole company to their biggest rivals, and pocketed about one-point-two million in cash.'

Sutton let out a whistle.

'So let's go through this,' said Warren. 'Gabriel Baines has worked with Bishop Fisher since the early days of the retirement home's founding. Somehow, he finds out about the past of some

415

of the residents. Either Fisher told him, or he found out another way. Then what?'

'At some point, he helps Coombs in his research and realises the irony that five hundred years ago, the abbey suffered from, and covered up, the same sort of abuse that the modern church is still wrestling with,' said Sutton.

'And so he decides to even the score? Fulfil some sort of karmic cycle?' suggested Hutchinson. 'It sounds a bit far-fetched.'

'This whole case is crazy,' said Sutton.

'If he really did kill his wife to gain access to her company, does that sound like the sort of person who would kill child molesters?' said Hutchinson, still looking sceptical. 'He's hardly standing atop the moral high ground.'

'Maybe he feels guilty about what he did, and this is how he wants to atone for his sins?' suggested Ruskin.

'Moray has a point,' said Sutton. 'In prison, child molesters are housed separately for their own protection. Even hardened murderers see themselves as a class above them and attack them to reinforce the distinction. Perhaps Baines sees himself in a similar light?'

'Well, that's a motive of sorts. We'll no doubt find it's a lot more complicated when we actually interview him,' said Warren. 'What about the means and opportunity to kill the three priests?'

'He has full access to the whole site, especially the vestry,' said Pymm. 'He could easily have got access to the keys. By all accounts, he spends pretty much every waking hour on site, even though he bought a very nice cottage with the profits from selling the company.'

'Again, that's pretty circumstantial. Besides which, his wife killed herself on Christmas day. The church and St Cecil's could be the only support mechanism he has,' suggested Hutchinson.

'Maybe so, but alongside Rodney Shaw, Baines has complete access to the place, and knows that at least some tunnels weren't marked on the architects' plan. His fingerprints, shoeprints and

DNA are probably everywhere, which is going to make forensics a challenge.'

'Speaking of Rodney Shaw, where does he fit into the story?' interjected Sutton.

'The two of them must have known each other from the start. Maybe they both knew about the home's secrets and decided to do something about it?' suggested Pymm.

'That might explain why Baines was so reluctant to report the missing money. If he knew that Shaw was stealing money to fund his gambling habit, the last thing he'd do is call the police in, for fear of what else we might uncover. Maybe he was worried that Shaw might crack and tell us what they were planning,' said Ruskin.

The room was silent as everyone present digested that thought.

'I'm not sure I buy that,' said Sutton. 'How about if Baines tried to frame Shaw?'

'Go on,' said Warren.

'Well, he had the opportunity. He's effectively Shaw's line manager, he directs him day to day. He could easily make certain that Shaw was where he needed him to be, leaving behind evidence where we could find it, like his work boots and wax jacket. He probably knows about Shaw's marital issues, so he'd know that he's living alone, without an alibi. He might even have known about Shaw's little card games.'

'He's in charge of cashing up and handling the money, so he could have arranged for some to go missing and reappear in that biscuit tin,' added Ruskin.

'And Nolan's fingerprints?' asked Warren.

'Easy enough. Just place the tin on top of the tools that Father Nolan needed to use; he picks it up and moves it to one side, job done,' said Sutton.

'What are his movements for the two nights of the murders?' asked Warren.

There was a pause.

'Right, track them,' ordered Warren. 'We know he was called on his mobile phone the night of the fire. Was he on site? Was he at home? Does he have an alibi?'

Richardson tapped notes into her iPad.

'So what do we do? Do we bring him in for questioning?' asked Sutton.

Warren thought about it for a few moments.

'Not just yet. Let's see if we can find a smoking gun before we tip him off. Find out more about his whereabouts on the nights in question. He also does outreach work with the homeless, does he have any connection to Lucas Furber? We've assumed that Furber's reaction to Baines when he turned up was to do with his dog collar; maybe it was more personal? Maybe he already knew Baines somehow?'

The meeting over, they all rose. Warren had a lot to think over. He looked at the clock on the briefing room wall. Relatively speaking, it was still fairly early on a Friday night. He decided to check his emails, make sure that nobody needed anything else, and finish up. Susan was still feeling down from their disappointing news earlier that week and he felt guilty for neglecting her. It was all too easy to get sucked into a case and forget everything else going on in his life, and even though Susan had plenty of her own work to keep her busy, he hated the thought of her sitting at home alone in front of the TV.

He probably shouldn't be eating a takeaway after his pub lunch earlier in the day, but he decided 'to hell with it'. He'd surprise Susan with her favourite curry. Maybe even another box of chocolates.

He sent her a quick text.

Don't worry about dinner; I'll sort something for us on the way home.
Wxx

418

Seconds later, Mags Richardson called his name.

'Sir, I just got this email. I think you need to see it.'

She waved her tablet computer.

Warren jogged over to her desk, her excitement contagious.

'We've got a hit on the ANPR cameras on the A506 on the outskirts of Copperston, on the days that the killer visited the locksmith.'

'Is it definitely our killer?'

'The timing's right. The car's seen about twenty minutes before and twenty minutes after the taxi pick-ups and drop-offs, which fits easily with him parking up and phoning for a cab.'

'Brilliant work. Do we have a name yet?'

'We do. And you aren't going to believe it.'

'Who?'

'Gabriel Baines.'

Heading back to the briefing room, Warren took a moment to compose another text.

Sorry. Change of plan. Don't wait up.

Wxx

Saturday 21st March

Chapter 82

Dawn was still several hours away when Warren and Sutton met the forced entry team in the quiet cul-de-sac where Gabriel Baines' house was located.

'We'll serve the search warrant at the retirement home after we've raided Baines' house. There's no point going in mob-handed and hauling everyone out of bed unnecessarily, they're going to be pissed off as it is. There's no chance of him getting past the officers standing guard and destroying evidence.' Warren was on the phone to Grayson as he stood outside Baines' home. In his pocket he had an arrest warrant, as well as a search warrant for Baines' house and car. An additional set of warrants authorised searches of Baines' office at the retirement home and other areas within the home that he might have access to, including Bishop Fisher's chambers.

The ink from the local magistrate was barely dry.

The team had worked pretty much through the night. After Mags Richardson's revelation that Gabriel Baines' car had been logged by ANPR cameras as he picked up the copied keys from the locksmith in Copperston, Warren and DSI Grayson had visited the home of the duty magistrate to request a warrant shortly after midnight.

The granting of warrants was never a rubber-stamping, but the two officers had really had to work for this one.

'You want another warrant to search a retirement home for priests, including, if necessary, the office of Bishop Emeritus Nicholas Fisher? You also want a warrant to search the house, car and other linked property for this Deacon Baines?'

'Yes, ma'am.'

Together, Warren and Grayson had laid out the grounds for the request. The magistrate had listened, before finally scrawling her signature on the bottom of the sheets.

It was the early hours of Saturday morning when the two men drove back to CID, the parting words of the court official echoing in their ears: 'I hope for your sake you find what you're looking for, because the shit's really going to hit the fan otherwise.'

She was probably right.

'They've done a walk past and his car isn't on the drive,' relayed Warren.

'It sounds like he's done a runner, but don't take any chances. I'll get a bulletin out on his car's licence plate. Keep me posted,' ordered Grayson.

* * *

'The curtains are closed, and there's no sign of movement, or his car.'

Like Warren, Tony Sutton was wearing a stab vest. The forced-entry team looked as though they were about to storm an embassy. The three-person CSI team, that were going in after entry had been secured, were busy checking the equipment in the back of their vans and sharing a Thermos of coffee. Even at this time of year, they weren't going to put on their restrictive and sweaty paper suits and other protective gear until necessary.

Although it appeared that Baines had disappeared, Sutton was taking no chances. There were basically three probable scenarios and the team had to be prepared for any of them.

'Scenario one: Deacon Baines has done a runner and we're going into an empty house. He's shown a significant degree of ingenuity, so be aware of any potential booby traps. Electricity to the property will be switched off as we make entry, and the gas disconnected, although we can't do anything about any residual in the pipes.

'Scenario two: Deacon Baines is still in the property, potentially in the process of destroying evidence. For that reason, we will be making a forced entry, without notice, so we can secure the property before he destroys anything else.

'Scenario three: Baines is still in the property and he decides to make a run for it. The property is detached and has a rear exit to the garden, but the garden itself has no rear access, only gated side access. As we effect entry through the front, two teams will also enter the rear via the side gates.

'Otherwise, let's hope it's scenario four: Baines is tucked up in bed with his teddy bear and his car is having its MOT.'

* * *

The precautions taken by the forced-entry team proved unnecessary in the end, with entry to Baines' property textbook smooth. The uPVC double-glazed front door yielded to the miniature battering ram on the first attempt, and within seconds, the shouts of 'Police', were replaced with calls of 'living room clear' and 'kitchen clear', followed moments later by similar shouts from upstairs.

The house was empty, with no sign of Baines.

Entering the cottage, Warren wondered how much change from the one point two million pounds in profit Baines had made selling his wife's family company remained, after he'd bought such a beautiful house in the most expensive part of town. For a single man with no children or close family, the property seemed excessively large.

'I thought widowed deacons were supposed to remain celibate,' remarked Sutton, as he eyed up the king-size bed in the master bedroom.

'Perhaps it was the one from his old house?' said Warren. He was tired, and despite having supposedly cleared the air with Sutton the day before, he was not in the mood for his sniping.

'You mean the one his wife died in? How romantic.'

Warren's reply was cut off by a call from downstairs.

'Sirs, in the kitchen. You need to see this.'

Warren and Sutton moved as quickly as they dared without slipping; the plastic booties had rubber soles – embossed with 'police' to make their footprints distinct – but the stairs were polished, wood laminate.

The white-suited CSI wore gloves as he held up the piece of paper.

Handwritten.

Seven words.

'Forgive me Father, for I have sinned.'

Chapter 83

'According to neighbours, Gabriel Baines' car arrived back at his house yesterday evening, at about 7 p.m. From what residents at the retirement home remember, this would fit in with the time he left.'

It was 8 a.m. and Warren was briefing the incoming day shift. DSI John Grayson was sitting in on the meeting. Unusually, his tie was loose and his jowels shadowed by the previous day's stubble. Even more unusually, his phone was face down on the desk and he was studiously ignoring it. Warren could hardly blame him. The search warrant for the retirement home had been executed at 7 a.m. and Bishop Fisher was not impressed. Doubtless, his displeasure would be expressed directly to the chief constable, who would no doubt want to pass it on to Grayson.

'Baines' cottage is on a secluded street. His property and the others adjacent to it have very tall fences and hedges. Consequently, whilst the rear of his car can be clearly seen by his neighbours, nobody has actually clapped eyes on him.

'The neighbour across the road works in a night club, and arrived home shortly before 3 a.m. The car wasn't in the driveway at that time.

'Anything on ANPR?' asked Ruskin. As usual, the young constable was fresh and eager.

'Mags has got traffic processing it as a priority.'

'So what are we going with?' asked Grayson.

'Well, the first possibility we have to consider, is that Baines has been taken by the killer. We've sent the suicide note to document analysis as a priority job.' Warren studiously ignored Grayson's scowl. The costs for this case were mounting exponentially. The high-profile nature of the case meant that within reason, they had a blank cheque – but Warren knew that Grayson would still be asked to justify their expenditure at some point in the future.

'If that's so, where is he?' asked Grayson.

'We don't know, but the three priests' deaths largely re-enacted deaths from Coombs' abbey history. Rachel and her team have been going through all of Coombs' photocopies to look for any other suspicious deaths from that period, however it's taking time, even with all the extra bodies helping out. She's found the deathbed confession made by Simon Scrope, but it doesn't tell us any more than what Coombs had already told us. He was apparently very ill when it was made and although he alludes to killing more people, he doesn't say how.'

'So how would our killer even have known about those deaths?' asked Sutton.

'Obviously we can't be sure that he does. However, Coombs, and possibly Baines, photocopied a load of contemporaneous diaries from the monks living at the abbey at the time. Coombs made notes cross-referencing those diary entries that appear to correlate with the events described in the confession, although the diaries describe the deaths as suicides rather than murders of course.'

'So if Scrope did kill more than he originally confessed to, those deaths may be described in the diaries?' said Grayson.

'Yeah. It's hard going though. Howard Langton, who first tried to write a history of the abbey, paid to have the monks' diaries translated from the original sixteenth-century English and medi-eval Latin into more modern English but it was still the eighteenth century and largely handwritten.'

'Christ, it's like a cross between *Time Team* and *Who Do You Think You Are*,' said Sutton. 'If ACC Naseem ever finishes that memoir he's rumoured to be working on, this has got to be worth at least a chapter.'

After the laughter had died down, Grayson asked the obvious question.

'If Deacon Baines wrote that note, what does he need forgiveness for?'

* * *

It was mid-morning, and both Warren and Sutton had been on the go since the early morning raid on Baines' home. Warren had snatched a couple of hours sleep between getting the warrants signed and executing them, and Sutton hadn't done much better, but neither man felt able to go home until they had some indication of what might have happened to Gabriel Baines. Was he the person responsible for killing Fathers Nolan and Daugherty, or was he the killer's next victim?

If he had written the suicide note, was it a precursor to him killing himself, and bringing his role in the string of murders to an end, or were they going to find his body, posed in a manner similar to those ancient killings?

'Is that note asking for forgiveness for the killings, or is it asking for forgiveness for other sins?' asked Sutton.

'Such as killing his wife?' suggested Warren.

'Perhaps. Although if that's the case, it doesn't answer the question about whether he made the confession of his own free will, or he was coerced into doing so,' said Sutton.

'Something that's bugged me all along is why the confession is incomplete,' said Warren, '"Forgive me Father, for I have sinned". That's just the opening line. Where's the rest of the confession?'

'Well, judging by the repeated attempts and the sloppy

427

handwriting, Father Nolan was so pissed he could barely hold a pen. Maybe that was as much as he could manage?' mused Sutton.

'True.'

'And in the case of Father Daugherty, it seems that he didn't commit the sin in the first place. Perhaps he flat-out refused to write the confession, and that's why the killer had to write it himself?'

The men's conversation was interrupted by the click from the boiling kettle.

Warren shovelled a heaped spoonful of coffee into both mugs. Even if they'd had a jar, decaf was not an option.

At this time of day, the queue in the franchised coffee shop that had replaced the old canteen was longer than either man could be bothered to face, so they had opted to use the communal coffee facilities.

This made little difference to Warren, who typically refused to use the franchise as his own protest against the creeping privatisation of public services. He also objected to the price; almost three pounds for a coffee. Even allowing for the inordinate amount of time it took the 'baristas' to prepare each cup, Warren just couldn't see how that cost could be justified when fifty pence a cup should easily cover the cost of instant coffee, tea bags and milk, with a little left over for some supermarket own-brand custard or bourbon creams. That assumed of course that everyone paid what they owed.

'There is another possibility, maybe Baines was a kiddy-fiddler himself?' said Sutton.

'Perhaps, but from what we know about him, he's never worked in a school or with young people, and obviously as a deacon he wouldn't be hearing confession. We'll keep on looking, maybe he helped coach a football team or took kids camping,' replied Warren. 'We should also look and see if he has, or had, access to nieces and nephews, or friends' kids.'

'The other alternative is that he didn't do something directly. Maybe he was a facilitator?' suggested Sutton.

'How do you mean?' asked Warren as he took a quick sniff of the milk from the fridge. 'I think we're better off having it black.'

Sutton pulled over the sugar, and started spooning it in.

'He and Fisher have been as thick as thieves for fifteen years. He helped set up the retirement home – could he have known Fisher's ulterior motive?'

'You mean keeping these men safely away from the rest of society? Why don't you just tip it in?' asked Warren, as Sutton added his fourth spoonful.

Sutton ignored him.

'If he did know, then that implies that Fisher told him about what he heard in confession – which makes a mockery of that self-righteous crap about the seal of confession being absolute.'

Warren wasn't in the mood to argue about that again.

'Well, it's speculation until we find Gabriel Baines and question him.'

'You think we still might find him alive?' Sutton looked sceptical.

'I hope so, I think he could be the key to this whole thing.'

He glanced at his watch.

'The early results from the search of his house should be in soon.'

'Then I'll see you upstairs,' said Sutton as he headed towards the door.

'Haven't you forgotten something?' asked Warren, shaking the honesty jar.

'Sorry, I left my wallet upstairs.'

Warren sighed and chucked a pound coin into the container, to join the rest of the money contributed solely by him. Four bloody years he'd been trying to convince his colleagues to put their fifty-pence pieces in the jam jar. He had yet to succeed.

'Oh the cheeky sods...' He swore as he looked inside. Yesterday there had been twelve pounds worth of coins in the jar – every single one of them with his fingerprints on. There was still twelve pounds in there, but somebody had replaced most of them with a ten-pound note. His colleagues seemed to have selective blindness for the jar when it came to paying for their coffee, but as soon as they needed change for the vending machine...

In the distance, Warren could hear Sutton's laughter echoing down the corridor.

Chapter 84

'Early forensics are in,' said Warren, heading towards the main briefing room.

Deputy CSM Meera Gupta had called at midday to update the team. Warren had placed her on hold as he assembled everyone then transferred her to speakerphone.

'Alternative light sources identified blood on the kitchen work top, and some small spots on the wall. It's been cleaned up and there are traces around the downstairs toilet bowl. Best guess, the blood was cleaned up with kitchen towel and flushed away. We've found smears along the laminated floor in the hallway leading to the front door and down the driveway, with some on the handle. Again, cleaned up. With your authorisation, we can fast-track the DNA.'

'Do it. How much blood was there?'

'Not enough to declare it a murder, but it looks suspicious.'

'Off the record, what's your interpretation?'

'Purely speculation, but I could imagine someone with a dripping wound being dragged towards the front door and down the driveway.'

* * *

431

'We've seized all of Baines' footwear to check the tread patterns and for traces of petrol. For what it's worth, he shares the same foot size as Rodney Shaw. We've also taken samples for DNA processing, and we've sent his laptop to Welwyn.' Gupta looked weary behind her facemask.

It was midday and Warren was wearing a paper suit standing on plastic boarding in Gabriel Baines' hallway

'Aside from the unidentified blood, are there any indications whether he left of his own free will or was taken?' Tony Sutton was similarly attired. Neither man was ready to go to bed, although Warren was going to insist on it as soon as they finished at the scene.

'Difficult to say at this stage. His bathroom seems fully stocked, but he could have had a toilet bag. Unfortunately, unless you can find someone that spent a lot of time with him, there's no way to know if there is anything missing from his wardrobe.'

'Had his bed been slept in?'

'Again, no way to tell. It was made, but that could have been from the previous day. We've taken the sheets to see if there's DNA from anybody else.'

'That would certainly raise a few questions,' noted Sutton.

'Boss, we've got a result back on those prints.' The CSI passed over an iPad to Gupta.

'We found some clear latents on the door handle,' she explained. 'I photographed them and sent them off as a rush job against the prints we already had on file for this case. Looks as though we've had some hits.'

She scrolled through the results.

'Most of them were too smeared to be any use, but we have five positives. Three match Deacon Baines. The other two are from Rodney Shaw.'

Sleep could wait.

Chapter 85

It was the third time that Warren had found himself travelling to Rodney Shaw's house to arrest him. His solicitor was going to be furious, and unless they charged him, Warren knew that he was likely to be facing a wrongful arrest lawsuit.

However, there was no choice. If Shaw was involved in the disappearance of Gabriel Baines, they had to arrest him immediately, both for the sake of Baines and to stop him destroying evidence.

'Shaw's car is outside his house, I can't see any sign of Baines' vehicle.' Tony Sutton was talking into a radio as he and Warren performed a quick drive-by of Shaw's house. The atmosphere in the car was tense; Sutton hadn't even teased Warren when the car radio had burst into life with Tears for Fears' 'Everybody Wants to Rule the World' as he started the engine.

'What do you reckon the chances are that he's here waiting to be arrested?' muttered Sutton.

Warren didn't answer.

* * *

Early afternoon, and there was an air of crisis in the main briefing room. Two men were missing, and it was unclear if either or both of the men were killers or victims. Yet another forensics team had been dispatched to process Shaw's home. His neighbours weren't even attempting to hide their curiosity now, and both Sky and BBC News had reporters standing as close to as they could to the scene, speculating furiously about the third search of Shaw's home in as many weeks.

'Here's what we know so far,' said Warren. 'Deacon Baines was missing from his house when we raided, a "Forgive me Father" note was on his kitchen table and there are blood stains leading out of the house. Rodney Shaw's fingerprints are on the door jamb. Baines' car is missing.'

'Rodney Shaw is also missing. He too has a "Forgive me Father" note on his dresser, with signs of a struggle. His car is present in the driveway. What has happened here, folks?'

'Rodney Shaw has kidnapped Baines from his own home,' said Sutton immediately. 'He either killed him, or subdued him by force, and used Baine's car to take him away.'

'Why use Baines' car?' asked Hutchinson. 'And how did he get to Baines' house? They live on opposite sides of town.'

'He wanted to cast suspicion on Baines. He could have driven to Baines' house, kidnapped him and put him in his own car. He could even have borrowed Baines' car to pick up those copied keys. Then hidden that car somewhere else and...' Sutton stopped as he realised how convoluted it was starting to get. Ruskin picked up the narrative.

'They worked together for years, they were probably friends. Baines might have just picked Shaw up on his way home from work and driven him back to his own place. That might also explain why Baines let him borrow his car; "my cars being serviced, mate. You couldn't let me borrow yours to do some chores?"'

'Of course, we could have it the wrong way around,' said Hutchinson.

'You mean Baines could be the one to have kidnapped Shaw?'

'Why not? Twenty-four hours ago we were ready to pin it all

on him. All of the above scenarios still work if Baines kidnapped Shaw. We haven't had the forensics back on the blood yet, so we don't know who it belongs to.'

'Then we need to know the movement of Baines and Shaw's cars,' said Warren. 'If Baines killed Shaw, then he would have presumably needed to pop back to Shaw's house to plant the "Forgive me Father" note. There's no way he could have done that without passing at least one traffic camera. Do we have any ANPR data yet, Mags?'

She held up her iPad. 'They're working on it, top priority. You'll know when I know.'

'What about tracking their mobile phones?' asked Ruskin.

'The warrant's being processed. Again, you'll know when I know.'

'There is a third possibility,' said Ruskin. 'They could have been working together.'

There was a pause whilst Ruskin's statement sunk in.

Sutton went first.

'So what's with the "Forgive me Father" notes, then?'

'A way of muddying the waters whilst they escape?' suggested Ruskin.

'Perhaps it's a joint suicide note? They've done what needed to be done, now they're going to kill themselves?' said Hutchinson.

'If they were going to escape,' said Warren, 'they probably need funds. I imagine Deacon Baines is a wealthy man, given the money that he inherited from his late wife. Get DSI Grayson to authorise a warrant for the release of Baines and Shaw's financial records.'

Richardson nodded, tapping the request into her iPad.

'The signs of a struggle can be faked easily enough,' said Ruskin. 'The forensics report didn't indicate life-threatening volumes of blood at the scene. Either of them could have taken one for the team and cut themselves.'

The table fell silent as the team digested the ideas presented; Warren was conscious of the passing of time. Whilst they sat here waiting for more information, potentially at least one person was in mortal danger. The problem was, they just didn't know who or where that person might be, or the nature of the threat. Regardless, they needed to be ready to move the moment more information came in.

'In all of these scenarios, what is the motive?' asked Warren.

'Both men have been involved in the retirement home since before it was even built. Could either or both of them known the secrets of the residents?' said Sutton. 'Perhaps a bit of vigilante justice?'

'They could even have been victims themselves. Rodney Shaw became addicted to heroin as a young man. You only need to look at Lucas Furber to realise that drug use can be a coping mechanism for a traumatic childhood,' suggested Hutchinson.

'And that scribbled note in Vernon Coombs' notes, reminding him to "buy Father GB a pint" suggests that Gabriel Baines at least helped with his research and would have been familiar with the stories from the abbey's past,' said Richardson.

'For that matter, Rodney Shaw could also have attended the talk that Vernon Coombs gave, last summer,' said Ruskin.

'So where does Lucas Furber fit into all of this?' asked Sutton.

'Well, we know from his friend that he was abused as a kid, probably by a priest at his boarding school. He could have hooked up with Baines and Shaw after their confrontation,' said Ruskin.

'Wasn't Furber supposedly in contact with the brother of his old school friend who killed himself because of the abuse they suffered?' asked Richardson.

'So the story goes,' said Ruskin.

'Could this brother be either Shaw or Baines?' asked Hutchinson.

'Unfortunately, no. Neither of them have – or rather had – a brother, as far as I can tell and according to their employment files, neither of them went to a boarding school,' said Ruskin.

'If they were working with Furber though, why would they kill him?' asked Sutton.

'Assuming that they were the source of the doctored heroin, maybe they were worried that Furber would give the game away? His behaviour was increasingly erratic during that time,' suggested Warren.

'And presumably Rodney Shaw knows about heroin overdoses,' said Ruskin.

'Didn't Furber get clean over the summer? We know that Rodney Shaw is involved in outreach work with young people, trying to steer them away from drug use and crime. Is he involved in drug rehabilitation?' asked Hutchinson.

'We can find out,' said Sutton.

'But that means that Shaw would have known Furber when he broke in to the grounds back in January. Why would he have called the police? Surely the last thing he'd want is Furber sitting in custody, potentially telling anyone who'd listen about their intentions?' said Hutchinson.

'Do we know who called the police that night, and when?' asked Ruskin. 'If Bethany Rice phoned Gabriel Baines directly, he could have called the police before he even realised it was Furber,' asked Ruskin.

'Check the interview transcript and find out,' ordered Warren.

'You know, whilst we have been talking about the motives of Shaw and Baines, we haven't looked at who else definitely knew about the secrets of those priests,' said Pymm.

'Bishop Fisher,' said Warren.

'I suppose he could be faking his frailty, but he's well into his eighties,' said Ruskin dubiously.

'I doubt he was physically involved.' Rachel Pymm smiled. 'Sometimes us weaker people just need somebody big and strong, and not very clever, to carry out our dastardly plan. Isn't that right, Moray?'

'She's bullying me again,' complained Moray as the team chuckled.

Warren let the moment of levity pass, before returning to the subject in hand.

'He's certainly in a strong position to manipulate events,' said Warren, 'but why now? Some of these priests have lived there for years.'

'He's getting old,' pointed out Sutton. 'If he has created this community specifically so he can keep an eye on these men, then maybe he's worried about what will happen when he's no longer there.'

'Which suggests that Survivorsonline is just a coincidence,' said Ruskin. 'Obviously, he wouldn't need to use that site, he'd already know who was guilty from the confessions that he heard.'

'Then why target Father Daugherty? Surely, if he was innocent, he wouldn't have anything to confess?' said Richardson.

'Unless he didn't believe him,' said Hutchinson.

Warren rubbed his face.

'This is getting too complex. We need to start ruling out some of these theories.'

He looked at his watch. 'OK, folks. We've got plenty to be getting on with. Mags, let us know when the ANPR and mobile phone data arrives. Moray, where are you with identifying Lucas Furber's friend and his brother?'

'Welwyn have ruled out most of the suicides on the Underground. There are three names left, all homeless, none with a verifiable surname. I'm waiting for the Department for Education to run those first names through the pupil rolls at Lucas Furber's old school, Thomas Tichborne, for the years that they were likely to have attended the school. Some poor civil servant is giving up their Saturday as we speak,' said Ruskin, 'but assuming the names are real, they shouldn't create too many hits. I can't imagine there were that many people called Keith, even as far back as the Eighties.'

'Keith Chegwin,' said Pymm, immediately.

'Who?'

'Probably a bit before your time,' she conceded.

'Keith Floyd,' said Sutton.

'Nope.'

'Keith Harris,' said Hutchinson.

'Was he a footballer?'

'Keith Richards,' said Pymm.

'Now him I have heard of, he was the drummer with The Who,' said Moray.

'Tell me you're not serious,' groaned Sutton.

'OK, leaving aside Moray's woeful knowledge of pre-millennial pop culture, let's move on. Rachel, any more insights from Vernon Coombs' research?' interrupted Warren.

'We're into the last part of the last box, two more collections of diaries to go. We're getting quicker, you get used to the eighteenth-century English, although last night I dreamt I was in a BBC costume drama.'

'Any more suicides or suspicious deaths?

'Plenty of deaths, some more gruesome than others, no apparent suicides as yet.'

The door to the briefing room opened, and a civilian support worker popped her head around the door.

'Urgent phone call, from the Social Media Intelligence Unit, DCI Jones. Do you want it transferred to here or your office?'

'I'll take it in my office.'

The handset started ringing, the moment he entered his office.

'I've sent you an email with links to a channel that popped up on YouTube a few minutes ago. Its metadata is full of tags that our system flagged. We're trying to track down the owner of the page, but no luck yet. It's not pretty, sir.'

Chapter 86

The videos were horrific; even more so projected onto the large, wall-mounted screen in the main briefing room.

'The recording must be the second half of the confession. The "Forgive me Father", note was just the first bit,' said Ruskin. He looked pale and shaken and had not even made a joke when Rachel Pymm had slipped a comforting arm around his shoulder.

'Forgive me Father, for I have sinned.' Father Cormac Nolan's voice was slurred and his head lolled forward. The camera had been identified as a Samsung Galaxy mobile phone, but the user had turned off the location data, so there was no more useful information in the uploaded file.

The seat that the elderly priest was slumped upon was easily identified as the wooden kneeler that his burnt corpse would later be found beside. His mouth moved, but there was no sound for several seconds, until it suddenly returned.

'I think the killer has muted the soundtrack so we can't hear his voice prompting Father Nolan,' said Warren.

The priest's voice was getting weaker, his eyes now closed. He was barely hanging onto consciousness as he gave a rambling account of weekends away with the choir and the things he made the boys do. Twice more the sound dropped out, as someone off-camera helped him.

Finally, the confession came to a halt, the drugs and alcohol finally overwhelming him. The screen cut to black for a few seconds, before returning. Nolan was slumped in the same position as before, his eyes closed, his mouth open. But now his hair was wet, his jacket damp, his trousers soaked. The camera had been moved back a couple of metres. The discarded petrol can was just visible in the edge of the shot.

It was the second time Warren had seen the video, but he still found it hard to watch. Out of the corner of his eye, he saw Moray Ruskin steeling himself. Everyone could guess what was coming next.

The scrape of the match came from behind the camera, before the flame arced toward the helpless priest. The burning match fell short of the man in the chair, but it didn't matter. Everyone watching the screen in the briefing room flinched; Warren could almost feel the flash of heat as the petrol fumes ignited with a whoosh.

Tony Sutton's muttered curses were drowned out by the sudden screams from the newly awakened Father Nolan. The man flapped his arms uselessly, as if unable to decide where to beat himself first. Lurching to his feet, the flaming apparition remained standing for a few more seconds before collapsing back onto the kneeler, which toppled over. Mercifully the video then ended.

* * *

The second video, this time of Father Madden, was similarly graphic. Shot again on mobile phone, the elderly priest was hoisted slowly by the neck, the person pulling the rope maddeningly out of shot.

'The camera is so steady, it's almost certainly on some sort of tripod,' said Warren.

'So it could all have been done by a single person,' stated Sutton.

As before, the sound cut out for extended periods, whilst someone off camera presumably prompted Father Madden to make his confession. The priest's voice became increasingly strangulated and his breathing became more and more ragged, as he told of how he liked young children. Even in the dimness of the escape tunnel the camera phone's powerful flash picked up the slow darkening of Madden's face. His final words before his eyes closed one last time sounded like a plea for forgiveness.

'Christ, no matter what those men did, nobody deserves that,' said Hutchinson.

Warren agreed. He'd seen some horrendous sights as a police officer, but this one would be part of his dreams for a long time.

'No video with Father Daugherty,' noted Sutton.

'Maybe he died before he confessed?' said Ruskin.

'That would explain why the killer had to write the 'Forgive me Father' note himself,' said Richardson.

'Perhaps,' said Warren. 'However, neither of the videos showed the men writing their notes themselves.'

'Presumably the killer would have been in shot if they had been filmed writing it,' said Sutton. 'Father Nolan was so far gone he probably needed help just sitting up and Father Madden probably needed assistance as well, you can see how terrified he is.'

'It's also possible that Father Daugherty had nothing to say. If those allegations were false, what would he have to confess?' said Richardson.

'That poor, poor, man,' said Rachel Pymm quietly.

442

Chapter 87

'Baines' car has been found.' The call had come straight through to Rachel Pymm's number, which Tony Sutton had rerouted to his own desk, to minimise distractions as she and her team ploughed through the final diaries, desperately looking for more clues to how and where the next killings might take place. The horrifying YouTube videos had left the team feeling shocked; they still didn't know if Shaw or Baines were innocent or guilty, and the thought that there might be yet more victims had raised the sense of urgency still further.

'It's empty, abandoned on the edge of town, doors open. A member of the public called it in, assuming it had been dumped by joy riders,' he continued.

'They were probably hoping joy riders would steal it and get rid of the evidence for them,' said Warren.

'Forensics are doing a search on site before they take it into the garage for a more thorough screening.'

'Let's hope they're quick about it.'

* * *

It was almost two hours later when Rachel Pymm called Warren over to her desk. She looked exhausted.

'Rachel, why don't you go home. You're no good to us, if you make yourself ill.'

She smiled her thanks but called his attention to the photocopied bundle in front of her.

'This diary dates back to a year before the attack on Matthias Scrope. It details the death of the abbey's apprentice blacksmith.'

'What does that have to do with Simon Scrope's killings?'

'The apprentice died during an especially harsh winter. They think he covered up the windows in his workshop against the cold. When he hadn't been seen for a while, someone went to find him and they found the shed full of smoke and the young man dead on the floor. His face was said to be flushed bright red, as though he was angry.'

'Carbon monoxide poisoning,' said Warren.

'Yes. Suicide by charcoal burning became something of a thing a few years ago, especially in Hong Kong, but I'm sure that experienced blacksmiths of the day probably knew enough to avoid suffocation when working with charcoal.'

'But the blacksmith died before Mattias Scrope was abused.'

Pymm flicked through the pile.

'This is a later entry, from a different diary about six months after we believe that Matthias Scrope was attacked. The author states that Brothers Patrick and Eustace had been found in "mysterious circumstance" in the Blacksmith's workshop, their faces flushed red.'

'No mention of a suicide note pinned to the abbey gates?'

'Not this time, but I am beginning to get the feeling that by this point, the first thing Abbot Godwine or one of the other senior priests did as soon as there was a suspicious death, was go and check the abbey gates before anyone could read whatever was pinned there.'

'The church covering its arse over child abuse allegations is hardly unprecedented,' noted Sutton, darkly.

'That's too big a coincidence,' said Warren. 'We need to know where Shaw and Baines are, and if they are safe.'

444

He forced himself to walk back to his office, leaving his team to do their jobs without him hovering over them. Sometimes it was just a waiting game.

* * *

The wait wasn't as long as Warren feared.

'They've opened the boot on Baines' car.' Tony Sutton had answered Rachel Pymm's desk phone again. 'They've found a tyre iron with blood and hair on the end of it. No fingerprints.'

'Get it tested, priority job. If we know who brained who, we can finish writing this story,' ordered Warren.

'Harrison also says the boot is covered in a fine black powder. They'll need to test it in the lab, but Andy Harrison reckons it's charcoal residue.'

'Shit. I suppose it's too much to hope it's from a barbecue,' said Warren.

'No such luck, Andy reckons that the way it's covering everything suggests that it's probably fresh, not left over from the summer.'

It was too much of a fluke; charcoal residue turning up in the boot of the Baines' car, and Rachel Pymm finding evidence of a possible murder by carbon monoxide poisoning.

Warren glanced at his watch again. It was early evening and the two men had been unaccounted for for at least sixteen hours. Weariness, worry and caffeine were combining to make him feel nauseous, but he had a feeling that the night wasn't over yet. He headed back to the coffee urn.

Chapter 88

'The preliminary results are back on the blood stains at Baines' house.'

Warren placed the second mug of coffee he was carrying down on Sutton's desk.

'Bloody hell, that was fast.'

'No DNA yet, but it turns out there are at least two different blood groups represented, both with Y chromosomes,' reported Sutton.

'Multiple male victims.' Warren thought for a moment. 'Get onto Andy Harrison. Ask him to test the blood on the tyre iron to see if it comes from one or two victims. Do we know Baines and Shaw's blood groups? That'll tide us over until we get the DNA back.'

'I'll see if I can gain access to their medical records, although if Shaw used to be an intravenous drug user, he won't have been donating blood, so they might not know it,' cautioned Sutton.

'Do your best.'

Warren took a mouthful of coffee, wincing as he scalded his tongue.

'So let's think this through logically. If there is one blood type on the tyre iron, but two in the house that suggests that both the person who was hit with the tyre iron and his attacker bled at the scene.'

'Blood spatter analysis should let us determine the sequence of events,' said Sutton.

'It'll take time with mixed samples,' cautioned Warren. 'They'll have to identify the owner of each spot. It could take days.'

'We don't have days,' said Sutton, in frustration, rubbing his eyes.

'If there are two different bloods on the tyre iron, and two in the house that leads to multiple possibilities.' Warren held out a fist and uncurled one finger.

'First, the same scenario as before, it's just that the attacker also bled onto the tyre iron.'

He uncurled another finger.

'Second, that the whole scene was staged. There's not enough blood at the scene to automatically assume that the wounds were fatal, especially if the blood is divided between two people.'

'For that matter, the scene could still have been staged if only one person was hit with the tyre iron, just to muddy the waters,' said Sutton. 'Of course, there's another possibility.'

'There could be a third person and both Shaw and Baines are victims,' completed Warren

* * *

'We've got the location data for Baines and Shaw's mobile phones,' said Sutton, his hand over the telephone receiver. 'It's coming through on email now.'

It had been an hour since the last forensics report about Baines' car and Warren was glad he wasn't a smoker; he'd have filled an ashtray by now, he was so stressed.

'Have we got a real-time position?'

'Yes, but they haven't moved from their current location since 1.40 a.m.'

'Where?'

'The abbey grounds.'

'That sort of matches the ANPR data for the Baines' and Shaw's cars,' called out Richardson, tapping away at her own computer.

Warren strode over to her desk.

'What do you mean "sort of"?'

'Shaw's car hasn't moved since Friday night, but Baines' car was pinged on an ANPR camera at 1.30 a.m., heading towards the abbey. There are no cameras around there, so we don't see the car again until 2.28 a.m., now travelling away from the direction of the abbey. It then continues out of the town centre along the Cambridge road. The last ANPR record is on the outskirts of town at 2.34 a.m. That would have been the last camera to pick it up before it was abandoned.'

'So Baines and Shaw – or at least their mobile phones – were dropped off at, or near, the abbey at 1.40 a.m.?'

'Yes, sir.'

'Then that's where we need to be. Tony, start organising a team to search the abbey grounds. We'll join them in—' he glanced at his watch '—fifteen minutes. We've no idea what to expect, so I want paramedics standing by. Give them a heads-up that they may be dealing with one or more casualties suffering from carbon monoxide poisoning. I doubt we'll get an armed response unit there within an hour, so I want everyone in stab vests with incapacitant spray and batons.'

'We still aren't sure what's happening here,' said Grayson, who'd appeared unannounced by Warren's elbow. Richardson gave a start and Warren felt a childish satisfaction that he wasn't the only one the DSI managed to sneak up on.

'Has either Baines or Shaw killed the other and left them on site with both mobiles, or is there a third party involved, who's dumped the bodies and driven off in Baines' car?' asked Grayson.

'That would explain the multiple blood types found in Baines' house,' said Warren. 'Mags, do we have the ANPR movements from earlier in the weekend?'

She scrolled down the document.

'We have hits on Baines' car travelling towards Rodney Shaw's house at 8 p.m. Friday evening. Then it's picked up again, eleven minutes later, travelling away. There are two more hits consistent with him driving directly to his house.'

'So what does that mean? He picked up Rodney Shaw and took him to his house?' asked Grayson.

'Could be. Does he drive back to Shaw's house?' asked Warren

Richardson scrolled further.

'No, the car doesn't appear to leave Baines' house again until it sets out for the abbey at half past one, and it doesn't travel back in that direction after it leaves the abbey.'

'So the "Forgive me Father" note was placed in Shaw's flat during that brief window of time,' said Grayson. 'Does that mean that Baines attacked Shaw at home, trashing the place and leaving the note behind, before taking him back to his own house?'

'Not necessarily,' said Warren. 'He could still have attacked Shaw at his own home, then travelled by different means back to Shaw's house to stage the incident.'

'For that matter,' said Richardson, 'Shaw could have trashed his own house, leaving the note, before being picked up by Baines.'

'Meaning he could have attacked Baines, or the two men could have been working together,' said Grayson. 'What worries me most is that their movements are unaccounted for for almost an hour between the car arriving at the abbey and leaving again.'

'We'd better make certain that everyone else is accounted for,' said Richardson. 'We don't want any surprises. Should we evacuate the site, move the residents somewhere safe?'

Warren turned to Grayson. That was definitely a decision above his paygrade.

Grayson thought for a moment.

'Not just yet. Let's get the site locked down and everyone in the same place in the first instance, but I'll look into a contingency plan.'

'Of course, if there is a third person involved that has killed both Baines and Shaw or is working with them,' Warren pointed out, 'then all bets are off.'

* * *

Warren and Sutton had hitched a lift in a patrol car. This time of evening on a Saturday, the worst of the post-shopping rush hour was over, nevertheless blues and twos cleared what little traffic there was out of the way and they raced towards the abbey far quicker than they could have managed otherwise.

'The cell-tower coverage just isn't precise enough to pinpoint them any more accurately,' groused Sutton as the car swung into the abbey car park. A uniformed constable already had the visitor gate open.

'They could be in the grounds or in the house,' continued Sutton, 'or even in some damn hidey hole that doesn't appear in the plans that English Heritage have on file and that Rachel and her team haven't stumbled across yet.'

'We need to do a complete search, but we have no idea who the killer's next target is,' said Warren.

The sergeant in charge of the maintaining the crime scene greeted them as they arrived. Warren made a mental note to ask later how someone had accessed the site without being spotted.

'We're gathering all of the residents and staff on site in the main dining hall. They were about to have their evening meal anyway, so it shouldn't be a problem.'

'Good, I want a team searching the house from top to bottom. We're looking for Gabriel Baines and Rodney Shaw as suspects or victims, but I want to know about anyone else that's missing.'

He paused for a moment. 'On second thoughts, I need to speak to Bishop Fisher. Escort him to his office and keep an eye on him until I'm ready. No visitors and don't let him near his computer, I don't want any evidence disappearing.'

* * *

With the search of the house underway, Warren turned his attention to the abbey grounds. Two minibuses of additional officers had arrived from Welwyn, fully kitted for a search of the grounds, including stab vests, batons and incapacitant spray. Nobody was taking any chances, with two ambulances parked further down the road. Warren prayed they wouldn't be needed.

Mags Richardson had also just arrived, wearing a stab vest and carrying her baton, with photocopies of everything that Rachel Pymm and her team had found so far.

'The ANPR cameras indicate that Baines' car was in the vicinity of the abbey for over forty-five minutes. They could have been doing literally anything in that time,' Warren said.

'Let's start with the outbuildings first,' said Sutton. He had laid a map of the abbey grounds on the bonnet of the car. 'Presumably, if the killer is planning to suffocate his victims, then he needs an enclosed space, or somewhere that can be easily made airtight.'

'The chapel and the undercroft would fit the bill, but both of them are still sealed as crime scenes, so we should be able to easily see if they have been tampered with,' said Richardson. Her finger traced towards the walled gardens. 'Then there's the greenhouse, and the tool shed, again both of which should still be sealed.'

'What about the apiary?' asked Sutton. 'Do they seal them to stop the bees getting out?'

'I have absolutely no idea,' confessed Warren. Richardson signalled her ignorance also.

'Well, we'd better make sure that we have protective equipment before we go poking around in there,' said Sutton. 'Health and Safety will do their nut if someone gets stung to death by a gang of pissed-off bees.'

'That just leaves the visitor centre and the toilet blocks. All the other buildings are little more than ruins,' finished Warren.

As the sergeant supervising the additional officers started issuing orders, Warren turned to Sutton and Richardson.

'We're completely in the dark here. We've no idea if either Baines or Shaw is the killer. We don't know if the killer has another target or if he's finished, and we don't even know that the victim or killer are on site; Baines' car was abandoned miles away.'

'I know, but what else can we do, Warren? At least if we can secure the abbey site we can be sure that the priests are safe,' said Sutton. 'Besides which, the killer seems determined to follow some sort of plan and every victim so far has been murdered within the abbey grounds, just like the original killings.'

'And each of the killings has taken place where the original killings happened,' said Warren. 'Father Nolan and Matthias Scrope's father both burned to death in the chapel undercroft. Father Daugherty and Brother Benedict were found face down in the river. Brother Isaac supposedly hung himself in the infirmary, which no longer exists, but Father Madden was killed within the retirement home, which partly overlaps the ruins of the old infirmary.'

'By that logic, the next killings should take place in the black-smith's workshop,' said Richardson.

'Which is no longer standing,' said Warren. 'Nor are the ruins on the map.'

'So where was it?' asked Sutton.

The three officers stared at the map. They all saw it at the same time.

'Where better to have the blacksmith than next to the horses he was shoeing?' asked Warren.

Sutton stabbed a finger at the area marked 'stable block'.

'The old blocks are just ruins now, but there's a sign pointing towards an interactive attraction for children up that way. What's the betting it's a recreation of a sixteenth-century blacksmith's workshop?'

* * *

Warren, Sutton and the two uniformed officers were within fifty metres of the wooden hut when they smelt the burning. The smoke wasn't that of wood smoke. Neither, mercifully was it the burnt pork smell of human flesh.

'Charcoal,' muttered Sutton.

Warren nodded his agreement, it reminded him of the smell of a barbecue, just before the meat was placed on the grill.

The two officers' deduction had been correct; signposts on the pathway had invited visitors, in particular children, to see a 'recreation of a blacksmith at work'.

'The door's been blocked up,' observed the officer to Warren's left. She was right, the hut's wooden door didn't quite reach the ground and it looked as though a blanket had been forced into the gap.

If they were correct, then whoever had been trapped in the hut may have been slowly suffocating since the previous night. Warren braced himself for what they were about to find.

* * *

The paramedics that had accompanied the team to the abbey had been told to stand down; there was nothing they could do for either of the men inside the blacksmith's hut.

'Until Professor Jordan performs a full autopsy, I'm going to suggest that the cause of death was asphyxiation, specifically by carbon monoxide poisoning.' The on-call doctor had arrived in record time, and been in the hut for only a couple of minutes. It hadn't taken a great leap of logic for him to deduce what had happened, after seeing the smouldering piles of charcoal briquettes, and the carefully blocked up window and doors.

Warren nodded. He'd seen the flushed skin, and a cursory check of the carotid pulse had been all that was necessary for him to decide it was a murder scene and exit quickly into the fresh air, already feeling light-headed.

'What about the head wounds?'

'Obviously that's Professor Jordan's call, but there's a lot of fresh blood around the lesions and some on the floor, suggesting that bleeding occurred for a significant amount of time after the wounds were inflicted. Professor Jordan will have to look for smoke particles in the airways and run blood tests, but I've seen victims of carbon monoxide poisoning before, and it's indicative.'

'Any idea what the weapon might have been?'

The doctor pursed his lips. 'Now you're asking me to go out on a limb.'

'Gut feeling, off the record.'

'A blunt object, probably fairly narrow.'

'Would a tyre iron do the job?'

'Off the record? It'd do the job quite nicely.'

Even after a short period of time in the hut, Warren's eyes were stinging. Tony Sutton gave a gravelly cough. Richardson flapped her jacket ineffectually. 'This'll have to go straight into the wash,' she grumbled.

'So what do we do now?' asked Sutton.

'Well, at the very least, we know there's a third person involved,' said Warren. 'Baines and Shaw didn't wallop their own heads with a tyre iron and suffocate themselves.'

'But who? Those two were our strongest suspects. And where is the killer now? Baines' car was abandoned more than sixteen hours ago.'

Sutton looked as exhausted as Warren felt. Neither man had enjoyed more than a couple of hours' sleep since the previous morning, and they had been working long hours for the past three weeks. Richardson didn't look much better. The adrenaline comedown coupled with the lack of sleep made the thought of starting all over again daunting in the extreme. Warren was suddenly glad that they had commandeered a police car to get them to the abbey; he doubted he was safe to drive himself home, now that it was all over.

He pulled his mobile phone out of his pocket. Grayson had

heard the weariness in Warren's voice as he'd reported their discovery, and promised to send over a DI from Welwyn to take over managing the crime scene until the morning.

The phone vibrated in his hand. Warren recognised the main switchboard number from CID that all external calls were routed through. He answered it, expecting to hear Grayson's voice. He prayed that his replacement wasn't going to be unduly delayed, he could almost hear his bed whispering in his ear.

'Sir, it's Moray.' A somewhat unnecessary introduction, given the man's booming Scottish voice. Warren pressed speaker phone, so that Sutton and Richardson could also hear.

'The pupil roll's in from Thomas Tichborne and I was right – almost nobody called their kid "Keith", even back then.' Ruskin was excited, and Warren contemplated turning the speaker off, they hardly needed it. 'Just one pupil has that first name. A Keith Boyce.'

'Why does that surname sound familiar?' asked Sutton.

'Did he have a brother?' asked Warren.

'Yes, an older brother, attended five years earlier. Angus Boyce.'

Despite his fatigue, Warren recognised the name immediately, 'Christ, I'm an idiot. I knew that something was off about that note on Vernon Coombs' photocopy. "Buy a pint for Father GB." Gabriel Baines was a deacon, he wouldn't be called "Father". Father Angus Boyce though...'

'Angus, commonly abbreviated to Gus,' filled in Sutton.

'Father Angus Boyce is in charge of the care of Fathers Kendrick and Ramsden,' said Warren.

'What's the betting that at least one of them is on morphine for pain relief?' asked Richardson.

'It also explains why there were black cotton threads on the bridge when Father Daugherty was found. His coat was buttoned up, he couldn't have transferred fibres from his shirt to the wall. But if his killer was a priest—'

'He was probably wearing exactly the same clothes as his victims,' finished Sutton.

'We don't want him anywhere near that home,' said Warren. 'Tony, call ahead to the officers guarding the house. Tell them to be on the lookout just in case he comes back.' He returned to the phone call, 'Moray, get Grayson to put out a bulletin for the arrest of Father Angus Boyce, we should have his photograph on file.'

'Will do, sir,' responded Ruskin. In the background, Warren could hear a commotion. Ruskin came back on the line. 'Sir, Rachel Pymm needs to speak to you urgently. She's found something. I'll transfer you to her line.'

'Sir, I've been looking through the last of those files.' Rachel Pymm's voice sounded panicky over the phone speaker. 'I made a mistake, Abbot Godwine was also a target of Simon Scrope.'

'I thought you said he was still alive when he abandoned the abbey in 1539?'

'He was, and Simon Scrope remained behind and went into hiding in the town, but Scrope made his attempt years earlier.'

'What did he do?'

'I can't be sure exactly, but two of the monks' diaries report that Abbot Godwine took gravely ill towards the end of 1522, just a few weeks after the killing of the final monks involved in the abuse. The symptoms that they describe match poisoning. The same diaries later note that Abbot Godwine employed tasters for his food from then on.'

'Shit. If that's true, then Boyce might try to kill Bishop Fisher as some sort of finale,' said Sutton. 'Completing the job that Scrope failed at five hundred years ago would have some sort of symmetry to it.'

'We're still at the abbey,' said Warren as the three officers started to run towards the house.

'Where's Bishop Fisher?' Sutton asked the officers guarding the main doorway.

'I think he's in his office.'

Another officer emerged, a clipboard in his hand. 'Sir, Father Angus Boyce is on site, and is unaccounted for. He arrived by bicycle at 7 a.m. this morning, and several people reported seeing him during the day, including Fathers Kendrick and Ramsden. Nobody has seen him since about 6 p.m. None of the officers on the main door have seen him leave the house.'

'He must still be here,' said Sutton. 'When did he leave yesterday?'

The officer flicked back through his log.

'He left with Deacon Baines, in Deacon Baines' car, at five-thirty Friday evening.'

'Shit, the timing works. They must have met up with Rodney Shaw; there would have been plenty of time that evening for Boyce to kill them both,' said Warren.

'I bet he even nicked Shaw's bike,' said Sutton darkly.

'The whereabouts of Sister Clara are also unknown,' continued the officer. 'She didn't appear in the dining room when everyone was summoned.'

'Hold on, could Sister Clara be helping Boyce?' asked Sutton.

'Why do you say that?' asked Warren.

Sutton started to count the points off on his fingers.

'She always seems to be involved. She reported Father Nolan's room hadn't been slept in and she and the other sisters have full access to the house as cleaners and carers. They're practically invisible; I'll bet they know as much about this place as Baines or Shaw did. Also, the Friends of Middlesbury Abbey said that at least one of the sisters was in attendance at the talk Vernon Coombs gave.'

'Hutch said that it was one of the sisters that mentioned this supposed argument between Father Nolan and Rodney Shaw that nobody seems to have actually witnessed,' said Richardson. 'What's the betting that Sister Clara was the one to start that particular rumour?'

'She also helped look after Fathers Kendrick and Ramsden; she'd have full access to their morphine,' said Sutton. 'And remember that nice double-bed at Baines' house? How likely is it that we find traces of her DNA on the bedsheets? Assuming Baines was celibate since his wife died, seducing him might not have been too difficult. I just wonder what her motive is and why she teamed up with Boyce?'

Warren frowned slightly. 'Well, we can worry about that later. What concerns me now is that she has access to the kitchen, we need to track her down.'

He turned to the officer with the clipboard.

'Come with us,' Warren ordered him, 'and keep your baton handy.'

They entered the bishop's office without knocking.

The elderly clergyman sat behind his desk, eyes closed, his hands clasped.

He looked up as the officers burst in.

Next to him there was a bowl of soup, a glass of water and some crusty bread.

'Have you eaten anything, Your Grace?' asked Warren urgently.

'No, I was giving thanks first,' he said. 'What is this all about?'

Warren let out the breath that he had been holding.

'Constable, radio for a CSI to come and take the food as evidence. Don't handle it yourself just in case, we don't know what Boyce or Sister Clara may have put in it.'

'You think they might have poisoned my food?' Bishop Fisher had turned pale. 'I overheard the officers at the door talking. Do you really think that Father Boyce is responsible for the murders?'

'We believe so, Your Grace. I'm assuming that you didn't make the soup yourself?'

'No, of course not. The sisters made a batch of it, Sister Clara gave it to the officer on the door as I was waiting for you.'

'Shit, we could be looking at multiple poisonings,' said Sutton.

'And everyone else is in the dining room, where we put them for safekeeping,' said Warren.

'We'd better go to the kitchen and secure the soup before somebody decides to bring it out,' said Sutton.

By now, two more uniformed officers had arrived at the office door.

Warren pointed at one at random, 'You and Sergeant Richardson look after Bishop Fisher. You've seen photos of Father Boyce and Sister Clara – do not let them approach, use force if necessary.'

He turned to the uniformed officer beside him and squinted at his name badge.

'Constable Patel, come with us.'

Warren, Sutton and Patel made their way rapidly to the dining room. To their relief, the priests were milling around, but there was no sign of the tainted food.

'Sealed bottled water only, no food or other drinks until I clear it,' Warren instructed the bemused officers guarding the elderly priests.

The rear exit from the dining room led into a short corridor, its lights extinguished. To the right, another door led back into the main reception. To the left, the kitchen doors, with their glass windows, provided the only illumination, a sickly green from the emergency exit sign.

Warren tiptoed down the corridor, towards the kitchen, before peering carefully through the doors. The weak light reflected off a large soup tureen sitting on a wheeled cart.

'I can see the soup, but I can't see any sign of Sister Clara or Father Boyce,' he whispered.

'Why are the lights off?' muttered Sutton.

'Keep that baton handy,' Warren ordered Patel quietly, as he gently pushed the door open and stepped in.

The kitchen was cool, the ovens turned off. On closer inspection, Warren could see an electrical cable leading from the tureen to a socket on the wall. An orange light turned to red as the thermostat switched the heating coils back on.

Warren's eyes were slowly adjusting to the dark. The door to what appeared to be a walk-in pantry was slightly ajar, a dark lump stopping it from closing. It was a foot.

'I think we've found Sister Clara,' muttered Warren quietly.

On Warren's signal Patel moved towards the body.

As the constable leant forward, the pantry door suddenly crashed open, knocking him over. A shadowy form followed through, arm swinging. Patel gave a grunt of surprise as the wooden rolling pin caught him full in the face.

Boyce leapt over the prone man and headed straight for the door. Warren and Sutton braced themselves to stop him, but the disgraced priest grabbed the cart and thrust it violently towards them. The trolley travelled barely a metre, before reaching the end of its cable. The sudden jerk was enough to tip the tureen over and the two officers had to throw themselves backwards to avoid the tide of scalding hot soup.

Patel was staggering back to his feet, his nose clearly broken.

'Stay with Sister Clara,' ordered Warren as he and Sutton took off after Boyce.

Bursting back out into the corridor, the two men caught a glimpse of their target as he slammed through the doors at the far end of the corridor. Warren and Sutton followed him seconds later.

The two officers standing by Bishop Fisher's office door were reaching for their batons as Warren and Sutton followed Boyce into the reception area. Boyce's shoes squeaked as he turned on the polished wooden floor and headed up the ornate stairway.

'Mags, follow us,' ordered Warren as he and Sutton followed the fleeing priest up the stairs.

The first flight of stairs was carpeted, and led onto the first floor balcony. By the time the three police officers made it onto the balcony, Boyce had already exited into the corridor beyond.

Following him, they entered the wood-lined hallway. One of the priest holes smashed open during the frantic search for Father Madden still gaped open, like a yawning mouth full of stained, brown teeth.

Boyce ignored the hole, heading for the stairwell at the opposite end. Unlike the opulent flight of stairs leading down to the reception, these were purely functional and Boyce's shoes made loud, echoing booms as he pounded up them. Warren and Sutton gasped for breath as they followed him. Richardson overtook them, her marathon training giving her an extra-burst of speed. Emerging onto the second floor, Warren managed to suck in enough air to shout after the running man.

'Give it up, there's nowhere for you to go. You're on the top floor.'

Boyce ignored him, and continued to the end of the corridor. Reaching the far end, he turned and pulled on a narrow door, before ducking in and slamming it behind him. Warren caught a quick glimpse of a green fire exit sign.

'He must be heading for the roof,' said Warren as they continued to race after him.

Sutton was halfway between Richardson and Warren, and only five paces from the exit when it happened. One moment the DI was sprinting for the end of the corridor, the next it was as if his legs turned to liquid, sending him crashing face first to the floor. Warren managed to dodge his falling friend, before skidding to a halt. Richardson, hearing the thud, turned also.

'Tony?' said Warren.

The only response was a slurred mumble.

'Shit,' he turned to Richardson, who'd sprinted back to join them. 'Call an ambulance.'

Warren dropped to his knees beside Sutton.

The man's eyes were rolling, his jaw had opened, and drool was coming out. Warren grabbed his left hand; it felt limp.

'Tony, can you hear me?'

Nothing.

'Tony, squeeze my hand if you can hear me,' Warren repeated, fighting to keep the panic from his voice, even as he tried to regain his breath.

The man's grip remained limp.

462

Richardson had her fingers under Sutton's chin, probing gently.

'He has a pulse, but it's very fast and erratic.'

Sutton gave a groan.

'Tony. Stick your tongue out for me, mate.'

Sutton's jaw worked, but his tongue flopped around loosely.

Warren grabbed his friend's other hand.

'Give us a squeeze, pal.'

This time the grip was stronger.

Sutton was mumbling again, Warren leaned closer

'…leave…'

'No, I'm here, I'm not going to leave you. I'm not going anywhere.'

Sutton squeezed harder.

'Get… bast…'

'Say again, mate.'

'Leave… get… bastard…'

'Leave you? No, I won't leave you. He's got nowhere to go, he can wait.'

'…jump…'

It took Warren a moment to realise what his friend was telling him.

Almost five hundred years ago, Matthias Scrope had thrown himself from the roof of Middlesbury Abbey. Angus Boyce had just headed up to the roof of the retirement home. There was only one way for this to end.

'Let the bastard jump,' Warren said, his voice harsh. 'I'm not leaving you.'

Sutton squeezed his hand again.

'… duty…'

Richardson's radio crackled.

'Paramedics are on their way up, sir.'

Sutton squeezed his hand again.

Warren bit his lip. If Angus Boyce hadn't jumped yet, it would only be a matter of moments before he did so. Would Warren's presence make any difference? Could he talk the man down?

His duty was clear, he had to try.

Yet his best friend was lying here, in the middle of what appeared to be a stroke. He glanced at Richardson next to him. She'd opened Sutton's collar, preparing him for the paramedics Warren could already hear coming up the stairs.

Warren felt helpless. He'd not been able to do anything for Gary Hastings, it was too sudden, too unexpected. Yet what was he accomplishing here? His First Aid refresher course was fully up-to-date, but Richardson was just as qualified. There was nothing he could do that she couldn't do at least as well.

He looked Sutton directly in the eye before squeezing his hand one last time. He owed him that much at least. Getting back to his knees, he headed towards the stairs.

Chapter 90

'Stay where you are. Don't come any closer.'

Warren froze, the icy wind whistling across the rooftop. The clouds had cleared and the moon, barely half-full, still provided enough illumination for Warren to make out the shape of the person before him.

The house was three stories high and Warren guessed that each floor was about five metres in height. Fifteen metres in total; fifty feet. A fall from that height was likely to be fatal. Even if the fall itself wasn't deadly, the sudden jerk of the rope around the man's neck certainly would be.

'Don't do this,' pleaded Warren.

'Why? Are you going to tell me it'll be all right? Perhaps you'll let me go?'

'You know I can't do that. But I can get you help.'

The shadowy figure stepped up onto the thin parapet that encircled the building's roof. One more step and it was all over.

'I don't need help, I'm beyond that. Besides, I've finished. There'll be no more killing. I've done what I needed to do.'

'What was it you needed to do?' Keeping the conversation going was all Warren had. He was out of options.

'You know the answer. I needed to right those wrongs. I needed to make sure that those who sinned received their punishment.'

Warren bit his lip. He really had no idea what the figure in front of him wanted him to say.

'Tell me about those wrongs. Tell me what needed to be righted.'

'Oh, I think you've figured that out, DCI Jones. You know about this little safe haven that Bishop Fisher has created here. A place where abusers can live out their lives in peace, shielded from the consequences of their actions. They won't even be judged in the afterlife, because Bishop Fisher has forgiven them their sins. He's absolved them of all wrong-doing. They'll never be tried for their crimes on Earth or in Heaven, when really they should have rotted in jail then burned in hell for what they did.'

'And you are the person to fix this are you? You get to be the judge, jury and executioner? Who gave you that role?'

'Who else was there? Nobody believed those children. Nobody was going to seek justice for what happened to them.'

'Murder is a sin. Who is going to absolve you of your sins? If you jump off this roof, you'll escape Earthly punishment but your soul will be damned for eternity.'

'Maybe it should be! Maybe it's what I deserve. Maybe I'm no better than those I've killed.'

'Surely you can't mean that?'

Boyce opened his mouth, but was interrupted by a dull, vibrating noise from Warren's coat pocket.

Warren swore.

'Don't answer that,' ordered Boyce.

'I'll switch it off,' said Warren, lifting the phone carefully from his pocket, manipulating its touch screen, before placing the handset on the black, tarred roofing felt.

'Do you know what the biggest sin is in this place? Bigger even than the crimes of Fathers Nolan, Daugherty and Madden?'

'No, tell me.'

'Collusion. Keeping silent. Bishop Fisher hid behind the seal of the confessional, burying those sins, absolving the sinners of responsibility, protecting them – and his precious church – from the punishment they deserved.'

'But that doesn't justify killing Gabriel Baines or Rodney Shaw. Neither of them could hear confession. Neither of them covered things up.'

'Of course they did. They must have known. They've been at the side of Bishop Fisher since before this place even existed. He must have told them.'

'Why? Why would he tell them? The seal of the confessional is absolute. No matter what those priests admitted to, Bishop Fisher would never have told Deacon Baines or Rodney Shaw.' Warren raised his voice. 'They were innocent. They didn't deserve what happened to them.'

'No, they weren't. Nobody in this place is innocent. Gabriel Baines killed his wife to inherit her fortune and hide his affair, and Rodney Shaw has been in on this since the start.'

'Father Daugherty was innocent. He was falsely accused. That's why he refused to confess. He hadn't done anything wrong.'

'No. That's what they all said. Cormac Nolan denied everything until the drugs took hold. Frank Madden's face turned purple before the bastard confessed. Gerry Daugherty was a coward, he died before he had the guts to confess his sins.'

'Confess what sins? The girl that accused him admits she made the whole thing up. That poor man had a nervous breakdown because of what was done to him. Bishop Fisher took him in because that's what this place is for.'

'No! It's a hiding place for sinners.'

'No, it isn't. We've gone through the records of everyone who has ever stayed here. We've trawled through that damned website with a fine-tooth comb. Apart from Father Daugherty, who was innocent, the only men with any allegations against them were Father Cormac Nolan, Father Frank Madden and Father Wilfred Dodd. And those four are the only men who moved here upon the advice of Bishop Fisher, because of "mental health issues".

I've seen the diocesan records myself. There are over twenty men living here, and everyone else is over 75 or ill, with no one else to care for them. They either applied to move here upon retirement or were recommended to move here by the current bishop.'

'No, they were all guilty.'

'Of what? Tell me what you know and how you know it and I promise we'll investigate. We'll throw everything at it.'

The man said nothing. Warren's eyes had adjusted to the dim moonlight and the faint glow of lights from the windows below. He could see the riot of emotions on the other man's face. He had to keep him talking.

'Tell me about your brother.'

The man stiffened, and for a moment, Warren thought he'd called it wrong and he'd pushed him too far.

'Keith's story remained untold when he was alive. Tell it to me now and I'll make it part of the official record.'

The silence stretched between them. When Boyce finally spoke, his voice was low; his tongue sounding thick in his mouth.

'For years I thought he was a wicked person. He was always getting into trouble, hanging around with the wrong sort of people. Then when he left school, it all got worse. The drugs. The thieving. The homosexuality.'

The man wiped the back of his hand across his face.

'Jesus forgave the sinner. Hate the sin, love the sinner. I really tried. I begged him to come to me for forgiveness, but he refused. I said he could come and stay with me in Rome, thinking that maybe if I could get him away from all those bad influences and help him reconnect with God, then he could be saved.

'But he said the church was full of hypocrites and that he wanted nothing more to do with it. Or with me.'

Boyce sniffed again. '1999 was the last I heard from him. I didn't know any of his friends and Mum passed away shortly after I left for Rome. I didn't know where he lived or how to contact him.'

'How did you find out about him dying?'

'I was in Haiti when I heard, helping out in the field hospitals as a medic. I'd been using Facebook for a couple of years, when I got a friend request from Lucas Furber. I recognised the name and his photo looked familiar, but I couldn't place him. So I accepted the request. He said he was a mate of Keith's.

'I was angry that he'd had the temerity to contact me. He was the one that I blamed for Keith's problems. Whenever Keith was in trouble at school, Lucas was beside him. They were always being caught smoking or drinking or skipping lessons. I'm sure Lucas was the one who introduced Keith to drugs. And I'd heard the rumours. About them.'

'What did you say?'

'Nothing at first. I couldn't decide whether I was ready to forgive him or not. I went and spoke to my advisor and he told me to pray and ask for the Lord's guidance.' He snorted. 'I don't know what else I was expecting him to say, we Catholics aren't the most imaginative. If in doubt, kick the problem upstairs.

'So I did, and in the end I decided to at least ask how my brother was. I supposed I assumed that they were still together. He told me that he hadn't seen Keith since they'd left school. And then he told me about what had happened to him.'

The man gave another loud sniff.

'Of course, I didn't believe it at first. But he sent me links to the story in the newspaper. About how he was believed to be homeless and that he'd jumped the barriers and thrown himself in front of the train. There was no way it was an accident, he stood up in the suicide pit to make certain the train hit him dead on.

'I guess a part of me always knew that something like this would happen. That he was destined to either die on the streets or kill himself. You know, nobody even knew his surname?

'Anyway, Lucas told me he was contacting me because he thought I should know what had happened to them at school. About the things that Father Dodd had done to them. And how no one had believed the two "queer kids".

469

'Lucas told me about my brother, Keith. The real Keith; about the fun side that I never saw because I'd been too busy being the big brother now that Dad was gone. I was the one that everyone expected to make the school proud; off to seminary in Rome. Another Tommy Ticher on his way to the Vatican.

'Keith and I were only at school together for two years and Father Dodd joined the summer I left. He never taught me, and I only met him once. I've often wondered if things might have been different…'

He cleared his throat.

'Lucas told me about Survivorsonline. He wanted to know what had happened to Father Dodd. He said he wanted to look him in the eye and get an apology. He just wanted a confession. 'By this time Thomas Tichborne had closed down. So we asked on the alumni website if anyone had heard anything. Somebody said that he had retired to some home. St Cecil's was the obvious place.

'Lucas tried to go and see him, although he was escorted off the premises before he got as far as the front door. He then persuaded me to apply for a leave of absence to return to England to deal with my brother's affairs.'

'What happened when you got back?'

'I met up with Lucas; he was living rough in Stevenage. Lucas was convinced that he needed to be closer to the home, so he and his boyfriend moved to Middlesbury and we decided to visit.'

His voice took on a brittle, amused edge.

'It's not difficult to gain access to a priest's retirement home when you've got one of these on.' he pointed towards his neck. 'Obviously Lucas wanted to come as well, so I got him cleaned up and told the sister that answered the door that he was Father Dodd's nephew.'

'Then what?'

Boyce's voice grew harsh.

'The bastard was already dead; he died peacefully in his fucking sleep.'

470

Warren wasn't entirely sure that dying from leukaemia could be characterised as 'peaceful', but he decided to press on.

'So what happened next? Why are we here, Gus?'

Boyce was silent. Eventually he sniffed. 'I'm a priest. I've done loads of funerals, but I never thought I'd be the one to… not my little brother.'

Boyce fell silent again; in the moonlight Warren could see the tears shining on his cheeks. When he spoke again, his voice was choked.

'It was so lonely, you know? It was a council funeral, of course. I managed to persuade them to bury him instead of cremating him, but neither Lucas or I had enough money to give him a proper send off. We were the only mourners. Mum and Dad were gone, and we didn't know any of his friends. Everyone I knew was either in Rome or Haiti.'

Boyce said nothing for a long moment. When he finally spoke, his voice trembled with emotion.

'I was going to fly back to Haiti when Lucas called me. He'd been back on Survivorsonline and said he'd found out a bit more about St Cecil's. He said that other priests who'd abused children had ended up there, and that he had their names. He emailed me the link to the pages on the forum.'

'So what did you do?'

'Nothing at first. It had nothing to do with us. Neither of those priests abused Keith or Lucas, or had anything to do with Thomas Tichborne.' He sighed. 'But Lucas wouldn't let it go. He said that no one had believed him and Keith until it was too late. He said that we should at least get them to admit to what they did. Perhaps even get the police involved.'

'So what did you do, Gus?'

He laughed mirthlessly.

'I got a job here. It was dead easy really. I'm a trained medic and they were spending a fortune looking after Fathers Ramsden and Kendrick, because the funding for adult social care is so

471

poor. I lied and said that I wanted to come back to the UK to be near my mum, and it was that simple. Deacon Baines got Bishop Fisher to pull a few strings and there I was; living and working in a retirement home full of bloody paedophiles.'

The story was almost unbelievable, but it fitted everything that Warren and his team had already worked out.

'When did you realise that Bishop Fisher knew about the abuse?'

Boyce was quiet for a long moment, and Warren worried that the conversation was over. Eventually. Boyce started again.

'The idea that Lucas and I had was that once the priests were comfortable with me, I'd get them to open up. So I'd play cards with Cormac sometimes, and talk about the footie with Gerry. But it didn't work out that way.

'I started to convince myself that perhaps I was wrong. Anyone can post stuff on the internet, it doesn't mean it's true. Lucas was angry, he said that I was falling for their charm. That I was being groomed. That I was no better than those who refused to believe the victims of their abuse.

'I was confused and didn't know what to believe. I thought about going to Bishop Fisher and telling him everything. Surely he'd know what to do? But then he came to me. He asked if I would be willing to help out hearing confession for the local parishioners. I said yes, and he started musing about how the sacrament of penance was one of the most privileged parts of a priest's vocation, but also the most burdensome. He said that God forgives all that he hears, but that we as priests must be careful never to judge.

'And that was when I realised. He knew. He'd always known. It was the only explanation that made any sense.'

Warren said nothing, unsure whether to encourage Boyce to continue talking and chance breaking the spell, or to remain silent and risk Boyce killing himself. In the end, his instincts won out. Boyce was telling his story, probably for the first time ever. He wasn't going to do anything until he'd finished.

'I knew that I needed evidence of what Bishop Fisher had done. So I decided to look in his files; his password was the date that he was ordained. I copied the name and history of every priest in that wretched place then searched the internet and Survivorsonline for their names and the schools that they worked at.'

'That's how you found out about Father Madden,' stated Warren.

Boyce nodded.

'Why didn't you just tell the police? There's been a sea change in attitudes towards complaints in recent years. Historic accusations from decades ago are being examined everywhere from the BBC to the NHS, and the Catholic Church is no different.'

Boyce snorted. 'Don't be naïve. The church has been covering up abuse for *centuries.*' He turned on the spot, wobbling slightly as he swept his arm in an arc.

'Look at this place. Five hundred years ago they were brushing abuse under the carpet, buying off people who made a complaint. What makes you think they are any different now?' he turned back to Warren, who cringed as the man's shoes came within millimetres of the edge of the parapet.

'But back then, there was somebody who did his best to right those wrongs.'

'Simon Scrope.'

'Exactly. I went to Vernon Coombs' talk last summer. Father Kendrick wanted to go, so I took him down. And that was when I saw what needed to be done. At the end of the talk, Vernon said that he had only scraped the surface. He hadn't been expecting to find Simon Scrope's confession, but when he did, he realised it was incomplete and he needed help to find the rest of the story from amongst the other monk's diaries. I volunteered immediately.'

Boyce fell silent. When he resumed talking, his voice was quiet, almost wistful, 'Somewhere up on that hill out there, overlooking the abbey in which he was refused burial, are the remains of Matthias Scrope. He suffered in the same way that my own brother did and he had no one to believe him. But he did have someone to avenge him.'

'But Wilfred Dodd was already dead.'

'That didn't matter.' Boyce's voice rose again. 'It may have been too late for Keith and Lucas, but there were men in this house who committed acts against dozens of children. And there were also the men that helped them get away with it.'

The wind whistled across the roof. Warren could think of nothing more to say. There were so many questions he wanted to ask, but he knew that Boyce was now figuratively, as well as literally, at the end of his tether. One wrong word, and the man would jump.

'Tell me DCI Jones. Are you a Catholic?'

'I'm not sure what that has to…'

'Yes or no?'

'Yes.'

'Will you hear my confession?'

'What? How? I'm not a priest.'

It was clear that he wasn't asking because Warren was a police officer.

'It doesn't matter. I just need to tell someone my sins.'

'But I can't give absolution. I *won't* give you absolution'

Boyce laughed mirthlessly.

'Oh, I'm well beyond absolution. I'm not going to ask for forgiveness for what I've done, because I don't feel sorry for killing them.' His voice cracked. 'I just need someone to hear what else I did. What I'm really ashamed of.'

He inched closer to the edge; the heels of his shoes now overhanging the drop.

'Will you hear my sins, DCI Jones?'

'Step back off the wall and we can talk about it.'

'The time for talking is over. I just want you to listen.'

Warren was at his wit's end. The situation had spiralled out of all control.

'OK, Gus, I'm listening,'

'Bishop Fisher, Rodney Shaw, Deacon Baines; I'm as guilty as they are. I deserve the same punishment.'

'Why? What did you do?'

'It's not what I did, it's what I didn't do.'

'No Gus,' shouted Warren. But it was too late.

Boyce's last words as he stepped into the void dripped with self-loathing.

'Keith was my little brother, and I didn't believe him.'

Wednesday 25th March

Chapter 91

'Ah, Warren, take a seat and make yourself comfortable,' Assistant Chief Constable Naseem gestured toward the comfortable-looking visitor's chair. The sting of Warren's grazes meant he'd rather stand, but his aching ankles wanted the weight taken off them. In the end he decided to follow instructions and he lowered himself down.

'How are you feeling?' asked Naseem.

'Not too bad, sir. A few scrapes and strains, but I'll be back to normal soon enough.'

'Well, take all the time you need.'

Naseem was at least the third senior officer to tell him that, but he still wasn't sure if they were saying that because human resources' guidelines suggested that they ought to, or because they truly meant it. He'd decided not to push his luck, and so after an appointment with Occupational Health, he'd self-certified and returned to desk duties.

'How is Tony Sutton?'

'He's making progress, but it's too early to tell.'

Warren had made it to Accident and Emergency in record time after his rooftop confrontation with Boyce. He'd met Marie Sutton in the corridor.

'They're saying it's a mini-stroke caused by an abnormal cardiac rhythm. He's been complaining of palpitations for weeks. Apparently, Marie had been trying to get him to go to the doctor, but you know how stubborn he is. He just blamed it on too much coffee and stress... I should have said something...'

'Don't go there,' warned Naseem. 'He's a grown man. Do they know if, you know...'

'They've broken the clot up. He was speaking when they took him down for an MRI and he managed to squeeze my hand. They've pumped him full of drugs to thin his blood and they're trying to get his heart back in a normal rhythm. But he's out of danger, for now at least.'

A wave of relief had washed over Warren, but the guilt still gnawed at him. He'd let another friend down.

'Coffee?' offered Naseem, 'It's not as good as John Grayson's but it hits the spot.'

Warren gratefully accepted. What Naseem's choice of blend lacked in sophistication, his crockery more than made up for. Say what you like about Grayson's snobbery towards the bean, ultimately he just wanted a mug full of caffeine, and unless he had visitors a rank or more above him, those mugs were large and usually had borderline inappropriate slogans on them. John Grayson was an easy person to buy for in the office secret Santa.

Warren took a grateful sip before placing the cup back on its matching saucer, taking care not to chip the delicate bone china.

He positioned himself a little more carefully, supressing a wince. The grazes along his lower back were healing nicely, although the same couldn't be said for his suit, which had provided scant protection as he'd been dragged along the rooftop by Angus Boyce's dead weight on the end of the rope. It was just as well he'd been wearing modest, dark-coloured underwear.

The slam of his feet into the concrete parapet had left him hobbling, but at least his left shoulder – subject of much abuse over the past few years – had held up.

'A lucky man, that Father Boyce,' said Naseem.

Warren nodded politely, although given what the man would have to live with for the rest of his life, perhaps he would have been better off dead. But that wasn't his call to make, and his actions as he grabbed at the end of the rope around Boyce's neck had been instinctive.

He was never going to stop the man falling of course; Warren wasn't nearly strong enough for that. But his desperate attempt had resulted in him being dragged along the rooftop, and that had saved Boyce. A successful hangman's fracture relied on a sudden jerk. Warren had reduced the force imparted by the jerk so that the intended instantaneous death didn't occur. Susan had tried to explain the physics to him – something about the rate of change of momentum being equal to the force in Newtons – but she'd been rambling, thinking more about the fifty-foot drop that Warren had almost been dragged over.

Death by strangulation would have been Boyce's eventual fate, but he had been cut down before that could happen. Warren wondered if, as he dangled there, the man's thoughts had turned to Frank Madden; Boyce had slowly strangled the elderly priest over the course of almost an hour, as he elicited his supposed confession. Perhaps he'd ask him someday.

'Obviously I've read the report, seen those horrible YouTube videos and heard the recording made on DC Ruskin's mobile phone of your rooftop exchange – quick thinking by both of you by the way – but I wanted to hear what else he had to say for himself.'

Naseem drained his cup and placed it carefully in front of him. It was an open secret that ACC Naseem was already writing his memoirs: a frank account of the most interesting cases that he'd come across in his years in the police – to be published after retirement, obviously. Warren suspected that more than one of his own cases would feature in the book.

He didn't really mind. A former colleague of his was carving out a very enjoyable second career as an after-dinner speaker. He said it was a toss-up between the Women's Institute and the Crime Writers' Association as to which was the more bloodthirsty audience.

'The bruising to his throat has subsided enough for him to talk now and he wants to make a full confession – to the police, this time, not a priest. He's been assessed by the mental health team and he's basically mad, but not mad enough to avoid trial.'

'Well, that's something, I suppose.'

'He's essentially confirmed everything that he told me on the rooftop, under caution this time, and he's been largely open about everything else. He still feels no shame about killing Fathers Nolan and Madden and says that if he could go back in time, he would also kill Father Dodd for what he did to his brother. I think he's on the fence about Father Daugherty. I'm not sure he really believes he was the victim of false allegations, although a psychiatrist I spoke to says that might be a protective response. It will have taken a lot of mental contortions for him to justify to himself what he did; admitting that he killed a man based on unfounded hearsay destroys that whole justification. Either way, he was prepared to kill everyone in that house; the soup in the tureen was full of half the chemicals in the garden shed. Mind you, it would have tasted so foul it's questionable how many people would have taken more than a mouthful. If I had to guess, I'd say that we forced his hand. Rachel Pymm and her team have found some more suspicious deaths in the diaries, so I wonder if he might have been planning more murders, before killing Bishop Fisher as a final spectacular.'

'So, what about Baines and Shaw? How were they involved?'

Unbidden, images from the video found on Boyce's phone sprang to mind. They say that carbon monoxide poisoning is a relatively painless way to die: the victim becomes drowsy, before passing out. However, the raw terror in both men's faces, and their pleading voices as it became apparent what was going to happen to them, would haunt Warren for a long time. It was especially heart-breaking knowing that like Father Gerry Daugherty, neither man could fulfil Boyce's demands for a full confession; they had nothing to confess to.

'Bishop Fisher assures me that neither man was aware of the confessions that he had heard. Boyce simply refuses to believe him, even though his belief that Bishop Fisher is morally culpable because of his refusal to break the seal of the confessional directly contradicts his assertion that Fisher must have told Baines and Shaw about their sins.'

'Did he always intend to frame them?'

'This is where it gets a bit murky. I'm not sure if Boyce truly remembers what exactly happened and when. I think it's fair to say that he felt casting suspicion on Shaw and then Baines was a perfectly legitimate way of causing confusion so that he could carry out the killings undisturbed. He hinted on the rooftop that he believed that Gabriel Baines had killed his wife all those years ago, to cover up his affair and inherit her wealth, although the original investigation was inconclusive. That probably added to the justification he felt in using him. But it's still unclear how much of it was planned in advance and how much was a response to events as they unfolded. We know that some of the seeds of confusion were sown very early on. He borrowed Baines' car to pick up the keys to the chapel, and we are now reasonably sure that we can trace the false rumours about an argument between Father Nolan and Rodney Shaw back to Boyce.

'He was very friendly with the two men, which seemed natural. Almost everyone in that home, except for Baines and Shaw, was elderly and ill. It made sense that Boyce, who was only forty, would gravitate towards these two. The three of them would often go for a drink and Deacon Baines was something of an amateur chef, so they regularly went around his for a meal; Boyce would even stay over sometimes when he wasn't doing the night shift looking after Fathers Kendrick and Ramsden. When the deaths started, the three of them became even closer.'

'Keep your friends close, and your enemies closer,' quoted Naseem.

'From Boyce's perspective, yes. Because of his relative youth and energy, Bishop Fisher came to rely on him more and more; he pretty much had the run of the place just like Shaw and Baines.'

'Easy enough for him to skim off the money from the safe to frame Shaw then,' said Naseem.

'Yes, he just engaged Baines in conversation as he was placing the takings in the vestry safe one evening, and memorised the code. And he knew that Shaw kept his wax jacket and spare work boots hanging up in the greenhouse, so he could easily place Shaw forensically at the scene of Father Daugherty's murder.'

'And all the while he was listening to his friends' woes and nodding sympathetically, I'll bet,' stated Naseem. 'If nothing else, he was a cold bastard.'

'I suppose he was, in a way.' Warren paused. 'And unfortunately, he made it too easy for us to suspect Shaw, and then Baines. I wish we'd connected the dots sooner, and then we could have saved them both.'

Ever since Boyce had been revealed as the killer, Warren had been plagued by guilt. Had he and the team been blinded to other possible suspects by becoming obsessed with Shaw? Had they twisted the evidence to fit their preferred narrative, rather than changed their theory to fit the evidence? He had a lot of soul-searching to do.

'Well, there are lessons to be learnt from every investigation. I'm sure that this one is no different.' It was hardly a ringing endorsement, but then the man sitting opposite him was as much a politician as a police officer, Warren reminded himself.

'What about Sister Clara?' asked Naseem.

'Wrong place, wrong time. They worked closely together caring for the priests and Boyce used her as a smoke screen. There's

482

no evidence that she was in anyway involved with helping him. She suffered a nasty concussion when he ambushed her in the kitchen; hopefully she'll make a full recovery.'

'What about Lucas Furber? Why did Boyce kill him?' asked Naseem.

'That's where he clams up. Again, the psychiatrist reckons that acknowledging Furber's death might be what undermines his whole mental justification. We don't know if Furber was aware or involved in the planning of the killings, or if all he wanted was a confession, but it looks as though he had a significant change of heart around about Christmas. By then, I think Boyce had convinced himself that he was on a divine mission and that nothing could be allowed to derail it.'

'And Boyce killed him by doctoring his drugs?'

'We believe so. We've shown Boyce's photograph to a few of Furber's acquaintances, and they reckon that Boyce may well have been the priest that helped Lucas get clean from the heroin. Whether he did that because he wanted to help his brother's old friend, or whether he just wanted a wingman who wasn't an unpredictable junkie is unclear.

'Boyce's main duties in the house involved overseeing the care of Father Silas Kendrick and Father Lionel Ramsden. Father Ramsden has a morphine pump. An audit of the ampoules has found one missing. We haven't worked out precisely where Boyce got the heroin from, but we have found traces of it along the window ledge, above the radiator in his room.

'Exactly how he persuaded Furber to take the doctored heroin I don't think we'll ever know, but Lucas was in such a fragile state mentally that leaving a wrap of heroin and some needles next to him – especially when he was so drunk – was probably only going to have one outcome.'

'Again, he was a cold bastard.'

'I think so. He's tried to justify everything as a result of him doing God's work, ensuring that those who are guilty haven't

483

escaped justice on Earth. I suspect that even though he's been judged fit to stand trial, his legal team will probably try an insanity plea.'

'Trying to recreate five hundred year old deaths to kill modern day abusers identified purely by allegations on the internet will probably go a long way to support that particular defence,' Naseem mused. 'Still, even if he is found not guilty by reason of insanity, he'll be spending plenty of time locked away.'

'Has there been any word about the wider impact of the case?' asked Warren.

'Everything uncovered in your investigations has been passed on to the relevant abuse enquiries. The press, of course, are free to say what they like about the deceased and we are hoping that the publicity surrounding the case might encourage some of their other victims to come forward and make statements.'

'And what about the... legal... implications?' asked Warren. He knew he was asking questions above his paygrade but he felt he deserved an answer.

Naseem steepled his fingers. He chose his words carefully.

'The Crown Prosecution Service believes that there is insufficient evidence that Bishop Fisher disregarded the allegations of child abuse for there to be any realistic prospect of a conviction, and that to pursue the matter any further would not be in the public interest.'

Naseem looked over to the framed scripture discreetly hung on the wall to the left of his desk. Warren didn't speak or read Arabic, but amongst the gold-lettered text he recognised the sweeping letters that spelt out *Allah*.

'In the meantime, we will have to hope for justice from elsewhere.'

Warren wasn't surprised, but he was still disappointed. He'd done a lot of soul-searching over the past few days and he had eventually come to the same conclusions as Tony Sutton. That morally, the seal of the confessional should not be absolute in

484

such cases. However, the reading that he'd done on the subject had soon shown that centuries of canon law disagreed with that assessment.

Unfortunately, none of his research had eased his spiritual malaise. Until recently, Warren had taken his Catholicism for granted, yet he found himself sympathising with his friend, Sutton, who had sought a means to fulfil his spiritual needs outside of the church. He found himself asking why he still identified as a Catholic. Was it just a spiritual inertia? His family were Catholic, he'd been brought up as a Catholic, and he'd always regarded himself as a Catholic, even as he'd picked and chosen which parts of the creed he should follow. Yet could he remain part of an institution that structured itself in such a way that protecting itself from outside scrutiny lead to the hiding of such evil acts becoming more important than preventing them, or bringing the perpetrators to justice? What was more important? The doctrine of canon law, or the laws of human society, applicable to everyone, not just believers?

With a change in the law unlikely any time soon, Warren realised that knowing the answer in his own heart would have to be enough.

Epilogue

The bright sunlight tried its best to banish the chill in the air, but Warren could still see faint wisps of his breath as they climbed the small hill over-looking the abbey below. Over the past few days, the swelling of his ankles had subsided, and he felt only a few twinges. Beside him he heard the cackle of Rachel Pymm's laughter as she said something to Moray Ruskin, whose arm she was holding for support on the soft grass.

Slightly ahead of them, Mags Richardson and David Hutchinson were consulting a hand-drawn map.

'From the description we have, it should be somewhere in this area,' said Richardson.

'It's a shame there's no way of knowing for sure,' said Hutchinson.

'In that case, let's choose that spot,' said Pymm, pointing at an ancient oak tree, from which the abbey and the town below were clearly visible. 'Moray, go and give that tree a hug. If not even your arms can reach all the way around then we know it was probably growing here back in the sixteenth century.'

'You'll be getting yourself back to the car if you aren't careful.' Pymm sniggered and gave him a squeeze.

Warren looked around him. Most of the team were there; only

Tony Sutton and John Grayson were absent. The latter was down in Welwyn Garden City, meeting yet again with senior brass. The former was hoping to be discharged from hospital soon, although it remained to be seen when – or if – he returned to work.

Granddad Jack was in a similar limbo. Warren had spent a few days of his leave visiting him in the hospital. The old man continued to make a steady recovery, but he had yet to leave his bed for more than a couple of hours at a time. A place in a residential respite centre had been found for him, but the hospital was reluctant to discharge him just yet. Warren had lain awake for the past few days worrying about him, and the future.

In more poignant news, Karen Hardwick had given birth two days before. Warren was hoping to go and see the child that Gary Hasting never got to meet. Warren still felt like a fraud every time he visited her, even though Hardwick had made it clear that she didn't blame him for Gary's death. He hoped that she'd return to the unit after her maternity leave finished, although he could hardly blame her if she decided not to.

Nevertheless, the birth of their child had put Warren and Susan's own plight in perspective. Over the past few days, the couple had spent a lot of time talking, breaking down the wall that had been starting to grow between them. Susan had even attended one of the counselling sessions that Warren had finally got around to booking. Gary Hastings had been denied the chance to be a father, and for some reason, Warren felt that to give up on his own chance, because of a bump in the road, would be an insult to his friend's memory. Susan agreed with him and they had decided to press on with their own efforts to start a family.

Warren opened the carrier bag he'd carried up from the road.

'I'm not sure what words, if any are appropriate,' he confessed.

'Perhaps just a moment of silence?' suggested Pymm.

Warren nodded his agreement. Taking the mallet from the bag he elicited Mags Richardson's help, whilst David Hutchinson unwrapped the flowers.

When they'd finished, he stepped back and joined his friends and colleagues. The simple ceremony had been Rachel Pymm's idea and everyone had agreed immediately. It gave a sense of completion after a case that had really gotten under everyone's skin. Justice of a sort had come to those hurt in the past few decades, but they were only the most recent victims of a wickedness that had been going on for centuries. It was a small gesture, but it felt right to finally honour the memory of someone forgotten for so long.

The wooden cross was small, but its brass plaque had enough space for its simple message.

'RIP Matthias Scrope 1510 – 1522.'

The End

Acknowledgements

This book is a work of fiction, but the story within is inspired by real-life. However, it is important to make it clear that whilst the ongoing ructions within the Catholic Church are all-too real, the details in this book are entirely made up.

To the best of my knowledge, the Granadians are a fictional order and I have done my best to ensure that they bear no resemblance to any real-life Holy Orders, either current or historic. Similarly, there is no Diocese of Hertfordshire and Essex, and the priests, schools and other characters are entirely fictional. Any resemblance or similarity to real persons or institutions is purely a coincidence.

Writing a book is always a team effort, and I have many to thank for their assistance. First of all, the team at HQ Digital and Harper Collins have been as wonderful as ever, in particular my editor Clio Cornish, Nia and the digital team, the talented graphic artists that produce my beautiful covers and the proofreaders and others that turn a Word document full of mistakes and errors into a fully-functioning book. A special shout-out also goes to Malk Williams, who so brilliantly brings Warren to life in the audiobooks. I really enjoy our chats, and I hope to work with you more in the future.

As with all of my books, there is a lot of detail that, if left to my own devices, I could get horribly wrong! So big thanks to Charlotte for her pharmaceutical knowledge (if they ever read our Facebook Messenger conversations, I will have a lot of awkward questions to answer!). As always, my two favourite lawyers, Caroline and Dan have helped me with their expert knowledge of PACE and the limits of search warrants. Special thanks goes to

Richard, my medical advisor. Thanks so much for your openness and honesty mate, I hope you are happy with what I've written.

As always, Hertford Writers' Circle have been generous with their feedback, particularly on that difficult opening section. The Crime Writers' Association continue to provide friendship and advice, and I'm very proud to be part of such an organisation.

The book that you see before you differs dramatically from the book that I first typed 'The End' on, so many months ago. So many thanks again to my Beta-readers, Dad and my beloved Cheryl, who again provide inspiration and critical feedback in equal measure.

Finally, I want to say thank you to you, the reader. Feedback and reviews are always appreciated, but just knowing that so many strangers have given up their time to read my work makes it all worthwhile.

So until next time,

All the best,
Paul.

Dear reader,

Thank you for taking the time to read *Forgive Me Father*. For those who have spent time in the world of Warren Jones and his team before, a heart-felt welcome back and I hope this latest adventure meets your expectations! For those new to the series, thank you for your willingness to try a different author.

This story covers distressing and controversial ground, and I make no apology for that. Whilst the characters, the settings, the organisations and the stories told within are fictional, they are inspired by events that we now know were, and are, too common.

In this book, we see Warren and the team still coming to terms with the events in *The Common Enemy*. We also properly meet some newer characters, and I hope that you enjoy reading about them as much as I have enjoyed writing about them.

Best wishes,
Paul Gitsham

You can follow me on Twitter @dcijoneswriter or Instagram @paulgitsham

Visit my facebook page: www.facebook.com/dcijones or my website www.paulgitsham.com

Or email me on dcijones@outlook.com

Dear Reader,

Thank you so much for taking the time to read this book – we hope you enjoyed it! If you did, we'd be so appreciative if you left a review.

Here at HQ Digital we are dedicated to publishing fiction that will keep you turning the pages into the early hours. We publish a variety of genres, from heartwarming romance, to thrilling crime and sweeping historical fiction.

To find out more about our books, enter competitions and discover exclusive content, please join our community of readers by following us at:

🐦 *@HQDigitalUK*

�� *facebook.com/HQDigitalUK*

Are you a budding writer? We're also looking for authors to join the HQ Digital family!
Please submit your manuscript to:

HQDigital@harpercollins.co.uk.

Hope to hear from you soon!

Turn the page for a sneak peek at *At First Glance*, the next in the DCI Warren Jones series...

Prologue

The car sits still, the engine idling. When the vehicle rolled off the production plant in Bavaria, more than ten years earlier, its makers had prided themselves on their precision engineering; its finely tuned engine producing barely a whisper.

Extra-wide stainless-steel exhaust tips had put an end to that, giving the diesel engine a throaty grumble that belied the fact that the car was the least powerful model in its range. The new M3 badge, added by the driver after he'd bought the crash-damaged car for a song in an online auction, reinforced the lie. There was no point wearing a fake Rolex to impress the foot soldiers if your choice of motor gave you away.

He pressed the throttle and the engine gave a louder growl, amplified as it bounced off the concrete walls and metal doors of the lock-up garages, adding its own discordant note to the bass beat pumped out by the top-of-the-line speakers he'd had installed.

He told everyone that he kept the engine running so he could make a quick getaway if the police showed up. In reality, he did it because he could. A few months ago, some old bird came out to have a go. She knew why he was there, as did her idiot son – he could see the terror in his eyes as he hung back, his balls too small to back up his Mum – but she didn't say anything about his business.

"If you're going to sit here all night switch the engine off and turn down the radio. It's keeping the kiddies awake and polluting the atmosphere."

She had guts, he'd give her that. But he couldn't let that sort of disrespect go unchallenged. This was his territory. His turf.

He'd been tempted to flash the gun he kept under the seat. An ancient revolver he'd bought fully loaded down the pub, with half a dozen spare bullets, he only had two rounds left after he'd spent an afternoon out in the sticks trying to knock bottles off an old oil drum. Ten shots later, the drum had two new holes, and the bottles were untouched. He'd returned to the pub that night to buy some more ammunition and found out why the weapon had been so cheap. He'd been angry, but not angry enough to demand his money back for a gun that used obsolete bullets; getting into an argument with a gun dealer when all you had to back you up was an almost empty piece that you could barely aim was the very definition of stupid.

In the end, he'd told her to mind her own, and carried on revving the engine. She looked as though she was going to make something of it, but her son pulled her away.

He'd won the battle, but he spent the rest of the evening with one eye on the rear-view mirror, ready to floor it if the silly bitch called the police.

That had been months ago. She hadn't called the police then and she hadn't called them since. To be honest, he'd be surprised if she was still around; he was no doctor, but the yellow sagging skin, the hollow eyes, and the sloppily tied headscarf that accentuated her lack of hair, rather than concealed it, told him all he needed to know.

He revved the engine again; this was his territory. He called the shots around here.

He looked at the dashboard clock. Where were they? Sunset was after nine this time of year, but they should have been here by now.

He wasn't worried; even if they had been lifted and the police turned up, the gear was safe. He kept it in a hollowed-out compartment accessible only by a secret panel hidden in the glovebox. The *bloke who'd installed it reckoned it would easily fool the local plods in Middlesbury. On the downside, if the car was ever in a head-on collision, the front passenger was screwed; wraps of heroin and bundles of twenties were no substitute for an airbag. He'd thought it best not to mention that to his girlfriend.*

He saw a flash of movement in the rear-view mirror. An individual in a hoodie, head down, face concealed by the peak of a baseball cap, shuffled into sight.

Finally. Where had they been? Their customers would be crawling up the wall by now. Not that he gave a shit about some junkie's cravings, but he wasn't the only game in town and even heroin addicts had minimum service expectations.

He released the door lock as the figure drew alongside the car.

This was his territory.

He ran it.

Nobody was going to mess with him on his own turf.

Were they?

Chapter 1

The blood covering the interior of the BMW 3 series was already partly clotted by the time DCI Warren Jones arrived at the scene. Early June and it had been dark for less than two hours by 11 p.m. The hastily erected arc lamps threw confusing shadows against the white screens that shielded the scene, interspersed with the blue, strobing effect of the half-dozen police cars sealing the immediate area around the lock-up garages where the car had been found.

"Any idea who the victim is yet?"

Detective Sergeant David Hutchinson flicked the page over in his notepad, his paper suit rustling.

"The car is registered to a Kyle Hicks, known to his associates as 'Kicks'. He's on the computer for a range of drugs offences. I sent a photo back to Rachel Pymm and she says it matches his mugshot."

Warren leant through the open drivers-side window; the smell of blood mingled nauseatingly with the man's post-mortem bowel movement. The Christmas tree shaped air freshener hanging from the rear-view mirror didn't stand a chance.

"Looks like a single swipe, right through the carotids. It must have been a very sharp blade."

The man's head was arched back, his glassy eyes wide with terror, his mouth agape in a silent scream. The man's right hand was still pressed ineffectually against his ruined throat, but the crimson stains on his left hand and sleeve suggested that he'd tried to stem the bleeding with both hands. The sheer volume of blood coating the windscreen, dashboard and steering wheel attested to the futility of the gesture.

Warren stood up straight, he'd seen Crime Scene Manager Andy Harrison approaching.

"Any indication of how long ago it happened?"

"Coagulation of the blood was well underway by the time the first responders arrived, so I'd say it happened at least fifteen minutes before then."

"That's consistent with the time given by the person who found the body. He called 999 at 21:55 hours," confirmed Hutchinson.

"Any witnesses?"

"None so far. Most of the rubber-neckers turned up to see what all the fuss was about."

"What's the status of the cordon?"

"An inner exclusion zone around the lock-ups, roadblocks on all surrounding streets, with Stop and Search in force. The Brownnose Brothers are supervising, but the streets are a maze," Hutchinson scowled. "If the killer didn't hang about he's probably long gone."

"Can't be helped, Hutch. Get Mags Richardson to start collecting CCTV; I want to know who was in the area. Get Jorge and Shaun to organise a house-to-house, let's see if we can loosen some tongues," Warren refrained from calling the two new sergeants, Martinez and Grimshaw, by their less than flattering moniker, however apt it may be. He was the boss, after all.

"If the victim's a dealer and this is his patch, then the locals may know something. Get Rachel to set up an incident desk and start entering everything into HOLMES."

"If it's drugs, we'd probably better let Serious and Organised Crime know sooner, rather than later, you know what SOC are like" said Hutchinson.

Warren sighed, "You're right. Is DSI Grayson back on duty?"

Hutchinson smirked slightly, "I believe he was seen going back into the office dressed for the theatre and looking pretty pissed off."

"Then I shall let the Superintendent inform our colleagues in Welwyn. Who knows, we might even get a couple of hours to do some detective work before SOC come and steal all the limelight."

* * *

Lenny Seacole was a well-built, shaven headed man of indeterminate age. He'd already spoken to the first officers on scene after he'd reported the murder, but Warren wanted to speak to him personally, now that the adrenaline had worn off and before his memory started to cloud. However, Warren was beginning to wonder just how much of an adrenaline jolt the discovery had given the man. He'd been entirely unfazed by the CSI's request to surrender his shoes for analysis; he'd declined the offer of a cup of tea.

"I come down here most nights. It's a straight walk to the park."

Seacole held a rather sorry looking tennis ball. Dressed in black jeans and a plain black T-shirt, the blue plastic bags tucked into his trouser belt, and the forensic booties covering his massive feet, provided the only splash of colour. Despite the rapidly cooling night air, his lack of jacket didn't seem to bother him, with no trace of goose bumps on his tattooed forearms.

"Was the car parked up when you went to the park?"

"No. He doesn't usually turn up until a bit later."

"So he's a regular?"

"Most nights," Seacole smiled humourlessly, "he's like an ice cream van, although he does as much business in winter as he does in summer."

"What time did you set out?"

"Five past the end of EastEnders."

That placed an early limit on the time of death of after 8:30 if Warren's memory of evening TV schedules served him correctly.

"How long were you in the park for?"

"A bit more than an hour – he needs a lot of exercise."

Warren didn't doubt it. Even for a Rottweiler, Sinbad was a big dog. He suspected that the lifespan of the tennis balls was measured in days rather than weeks.

"And do you usually walk back this way?"

"Like I said, it's a straight walk."

"And the dealers didn't bother you?"

Seacole looked meaningfully over at Sinbad.

"I see your point."

"When did you realise something was wrong?"

"It was Sinbad that spotted it. He started pulling at the lead, which he doesn't usually. He dragged me over and that was when I spotted the state of the windscreen. I figured that he must have been shot in the head or something to spray that much blood about. Anyway, I had a looksee and saw he'd been slashed. It was obvious he was dead, so I called you guys and backed away."

* * *

An hour had passed since Warren had arrived on scene, and everything was running to plan. Teams of uniform officers coordinated by Detective Sergeants Jorge Martinez and Shaun Grimshaw had already interviewed most of the onlookers and started canvassing the houses in the streets surrounding the lock-ups, but it was dark, and nobody had so far admitted to seeing anything.

Andy Harrison's team of CSIs had started working their way outwards from the car, looking for the murder weapon and other evidence. The duty coroner was due in the next hour to do a preliminary examination of the body before it and the car were removed. And best of all, nobody from SOC had turned up to ruin the party.

"There were no direct witnesses to the attack, but a number of neighbours confirmed what Lenny Seacole told us about that area being used by dealers," said DS Jorge Martinez. A skinny man in his mid-thirties, it was the first murder the officer had been involved in since he had been assigned to Middlesbury CID, and he was keen to please. Very keen.

"A couple of old biddies confirmed that a car corresponding to Kyle Hicks' BMW would regularly park up, engine running and sit with the windows down and music playing. One of them gave a description of the driver that matches Hicks," Grimshaw took up the story. He too had also been recently assigned to Middlesbury, alongside his friend, and now rival, Martinez. He too was eager to please. If there was to be a new opening for a Detective Inspector position on Warren's team both men were embarrassingly desperate to fill the role, hence the pair's unflattering moniker. Warren had spent the afternoon going over both officers' paperwork, checking everything was in order before they started the process.

He really missed Tony Sutton.

"Good work. What about his dealers?"

Martinez took over again, "People were reluctant to talk but some reckon there were one, sometimes two of them. Young, probably no more than twenty. They usually wore hoodies and baseball caps and were white. That's all we've got. I doubt their buyers would be willing to give us anything more concrete and I get the impression that everybody else in the area turns a blind eye."

"To be honest," continued Grimshaw, "the general grumblings were that something like this was inevitable. They reckon they stopped reporting the dealing months ago as we never seemed to do anything about it and they didn't want any trouble."

It was a depressingly familiar tale. Cutbacks to the numbers of foot patrols and community-based police officers had eroded what little faith the residents of estates such as this had in the police. Kyle Hicks and his ilk largely enjoyed free reign.

Before Warren could reply CSM Harrison called out,
"Sir, you need to see this."

The CSI was standing past the end of a passageway between two of the lock-up garages next to a white-suited female technician. Another colleague was holding a portable lamp. Three yellow, numbered flags had been placed at roughly equal distances leading through the narrow gap.

"Blood spots. Leading through here and up that garden path," the technician directed the light obligingly.

Warren felt his breath catch in his throat.

"Stop what you are doing. Retrace your steps and make sure everyone is safe and accounted for.

"The killer might still be here."

If you enjoyed *Forgive Me Father*, why not try another twisty crime novel from HQ Digital?

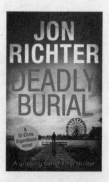

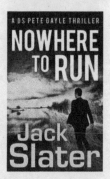

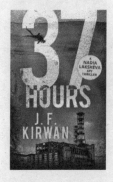